HAPPY MEALS

ALSO BY EATON KRONE

LightSide Novels

A Life Spectacular

HAPPY MEALS

A LightSide Novel
The Euwel: Book 1

Eaton Krone

*In memory of my father.
The bravest man I've ever known.*

*And to all the other brave people
living with Parkinson's disease.*

CHAPTER 1

It was an age-old battle. A battle of man versus nature – a battle nature was about to win. He could feel it.

His face flushed and contorted as a bead of sweat ran down his temple and skirted his jaw. The latter clenched tight to hold back the groan threatening to erupt from deep within, but his body had reached its limits. He only had enough left in him for one final push, and as he gave it everything he had, the groan broke free from its ivory prison; a primal ode to the pain, suffering, and hopelessness faced by so many of his fellow humans.

Ploop.

He looked down.

Really?

All that effort, and his only reward was … *ploop!*

Lieutenant Reginald Kleft couldn't remember having had bricks for dinner the night before, but seeing as that's what was trying to come out, he must have remembered wrong.

Leaning back, Reg rested his head against the wall for a short spell – not the magical kind, of course. It was more the kind you'd find online to download and listen to repeatedly because the previous ten times clearly hadn't worked. The kind where whales croon in the background, or whatever you call the sound that whales make when they're feeling hungry, amorous or irked.

Relax, Reg chanted to himself in the most soothing inner voice he could muster. *That's all you need to do. Close your eyes ...*

... he closed his eyes ...

... take a deep breath ...

... he took a deep breath ...

... and relaaax.

It was working; nothing earth-shattering, but he *did* feel better.

Yes, that's it, he continued, keeping the momentum going. *Just clear your mind ... breathe ... rela—*

A knock at the door dispelled the spell.

The two-thousand-year-old Unyun Trade Federation runs its Militorate like a business, and keeping hundreds of billions of people safe doesn't come cheap. And since elbow-room is expensive, the Unyun Militorate's ship-construction stations are the opposite of luxury-mattress factories, and so is their slogan: Your comfort is *not* our priority. But some are worse off than others, and seeing as Patrol Scouts are perched on the bottom rung of the Militorate's priority ladder, their ships are generally *the* most unluxurious Militor vessels in the fleet, especially in respect of decently sized sanitary facilities.

Which is why it felt as though the knock had been knocked right against Reg's skull. "What *is it?*" he said, trying to sound annoyed. This might have worked if he'd had more breath left in him, but he didn't.

"I know you wanted some ... private time," said a muffled voice from the other side of the door, "but there's something you need to see."

The lieutenant wiped the dark, damp strand of red hair from his forehead along with a mist of perspiration. Drawing another deep breath, he exhaled slowly, trying to vent some of the irritation – among other things – that had been building up inside him for some time. It didn't work.

"Just give me a bloody minute!"

Performing the wiping ritual with a few not-so-muted curses, Reg got up and glowered into the toilet bowl, where a small round ball now lay hidden under cover of a sanitary wad. With some additional choice words, he cleaned his hands with another wad and flushed the cursed bundle from view.

Exiting the facilities, Reg paused to adjust his tight, grey uniform; not because it was necessary, but because it felt like the appropriate thing to do in the circum-stances.[*] Reaching the pilot's chair, he eased himself into it, fearing that hard contact would cause his innards to explode. He avoided looking at his Ronian co-pilot, who fortunately did the same by fiddling with controls that didn't need to be fiddled with at that exact moment.

"Uh, everything okay?" Ensign Spence Jensis asked in a way that said he needed to say something but didn't particularly want to.

"I'm fine," Reg muttered, and proceeded with his own fiddling while forcing his face to stay calm. As the ensign's superior, he had to keep up appearances on the outside, no matter how … pressing things got inside.

"You *really* should see a Medicor, Reg."

---

[*] Clinical studies on the constructed planet of Unyun have determined that clothes-adjustment is as effective in lower-ing levels of embarrassment as head-scratching is in raising levels of intellect, so those currently scratching their head(s) over these findings are advised to stop doing so immediately.

The lack of decorum in being addressed by name instead of rank was nothing new. Reg and Spence were friends, and usually called each other by name when they were alone or off duty; a welcome break from the formalities of Militorate life.

The lieutenant snorted. "Medicors; you *know* how full of crap those a-holes can be."

"And, yes, Spence," he added, holding up a pre-emptive finger, "I see the irony in that. But I've struggled with this for years, and it's not going to change. I'm done being poked, prodded, and swallowing whatever new meds those whitecoats deem fit to jam down my throat."

"But it's getting worse, Reg. You cannot go on like this. When's the last time you had a decent … purge?"

"I said I'm fine, *Ensign!*" Reg snapped, signalling an end to the informalities and the topic under discussion.

"Yes, *sir*," Spence said, picking up on the signal.

He was one of the few people who knew of Reg's digestive issues. It was difficult not to, having shared quarters at the Academy and aboard several Militor vessels. Some things are impossible to hide, no matter how hard you try.

However, while he was used to Reg's moods – which were about as consistent as a bag of trail mix – Spence didn't have to like it, and he wasn't afraid to show that this was still the case.

To avoid the sulky look painting the ensign's pale face, Reg fixed his eyes on a monitor without paying it much attention. The scrawny, rusty-haired, rusty-eyed Ronian next to him was, by all accounts, too timid to be in the Militorate, and likely would have dropped out of the Academy if Reg hadn't pushed him as much as he had.

But with his human friend's help, Spence had scraped through, and now stood out among his peers like a drop of water in a glass of water. Reg, however, had faith that his friend could achieve so much more in his career than merely blending in. To boost Spence's CV, Reg had taken the ensign under his wing on his first assignment as a Patrol Scout; to mould the Ronian into something more. Something … better.

They'd been patrolling the area around a Dumb Planet for weeks now, with nothing much to show other than Reg's ration-packed colon. Even scrubbing toilets[*] on a Caynin-crewed Academy training vessel would have been more exciting than this!

However, Reg knew you had to start somewhere, and although his family had produced a long line of accomplished individuals in service of the Unyun Militorate, he wanted to make a name for *himself*.

In stark contrast, Spence just wanted to belong … somewhere, even if it was only in a small Scout ship patrolling a small patch of space. Unlike Reg, the Ronian was content with flying about aimlessly.

Reg sighed. "I take it you didn't interrupt my private time to give me unsolicited advice?"

---

[*] "Toilet" is a fairly loose term among the dog-like Caynins, especially the younger ones, as it often includes everything from carpets to lawns, sidewalks, and just about any other available surface on which undigested … leftovers can be discarded, including ship decks. Fortunately, the Militorate had long ago come up with an ingenious solution, where all Caynin recruits are to be followed by an officer with a rolled-up newspaper until they've learnt how to use the dedicated facilities. It's also why most Militor Caynins had stopped reading newspapers long ago.

"No … sir," Spence said. "I picked up a flagged vessel on the sensors and plotted a course to intercept. I didn't think you'd mind."

"Are you kidding?" Reg beamed, glad for the break in routine. "Of course I don't mind! Good work, Ensign. Uh, what are we looking at?"

Spence's face picked up somewhat. "Let's just say it's something you've been waiting for since the day we boarded this bucket. See for yourself."

Scanning the monitors properly this time, Reg whistled. "You know what this means, right?"

"I do," Spence said, "but shouldn't we call it in first?"

"No," Reg said, grinning. "This one's mine."

CHAPTER 2

With plenty time left before her shuttle rendezvoused with the *Jolly Dodger*, Captain Phealix raised the temperature of her specially installed hot tub.

Normally, cat-like Faylins don't enjoy any body of water reaching higher than their toes, but Phealix never saw herself as a "normal" Faylin, and her love for water cemented this fact. Taking a sip of wine, she rested her head on the tub's rim while the bubbles massaged her light-blue skin.

This is more like it, she thought. No more squabbling with those knobheads at the Annual Pirate Colloquium. Every year, the same problems. Every year, the same arguments. It was such a mission to get them to agree on … well, *anything!*

At least this year the crews had agreed on serving rum instead of beer with dessert at the Last Supper; the main gala dinner that marked the end of the Colloquium. Other than that, nothing much had been achieved except for a few more ships pledging to adhere to *The Code*; a new set of rules that had already brought a semblance of … civility to the pirating community – even if the semblance was more of a second cousin once removed.

Still, *The Code* had been accepted at the previous Colloquium, for which Phealix was grateful. And while pirates moved slower towards change than bunnies could leopard-crawl over a Velcro mat, at least they were moving in the right direction.

Taking another sip, Phealix placed her wineglass on the hot tub's rim and rested her head to the side. She was about to drift off when the shuttle shuddered, and an alarm started blaring as if it had something important to say. She hoped, for the crew's sake, it *was* important, because they knew better than to disturb her during *me-time* unless there was a bona fide emergency.

Before she could get up, a violent jerk sent a wave of water splashing onto the floor, while her wine toppled into the tub. Watching the bubbles turn red, her face turned a darker shade of blue. If Franki had steered them into another asteroid belt, she was going to lose her—

As if summoned, Franki's voice echoed over the comm system of the small, private bathroom. "Er, sorry to disturb you, Captain, but we're … uh, under attack."

"Under attack?" Phealix said as she shot to her feet. "By whom?"

"I'm not sure, sir, but at this rate, we won't last long."

"Well, try to hold them off. I'm coming."

Stepping from the tub, Phealix's perfectly sculptured Faylin body glistened with water, which dripped from the darker-blue, bushy tip of her tail and the colour-matched ponytail draping down her back. She cast her upward-slanted blue-green eyes at the leather catsuit hanging on the wall. No time. With a scowl, she grabbed and donned her white bathrobe instead. As an afterthought, she snatched her black boots off the floor before rushing out.

When the bathroom door *swished* closed behind her, Phealix's crew eyed her awkwardly. Vahltans preferred walking around naked whenever they were alone or among their own, but with their wingless pterodactyl-like features, other species generally preferred Vahltans covering themselves completely; their elongated heads included.

Phealix was a bit more understanding, but although the Faylin gave her crew some leeway in style, she insisted they wear black leather as a uniform. Which the Vahltans often questioned – not out loud around the captain, of course – because what was the point of covering leather with even more leather? Why not just keep things … natural?

On the flip side, barring a few exceptions, Vahltans didn't much care about the appearance of other species, so seeing anyone in a bathrobe shouldn't have bothered them in the least. But, judging by their frozen looks, seeing their usually well-dressed and -groomed captain in a robe was somewhat unsettling.

As the *Jolly Dodger's* First Mate, Franki felt obliged to recover first, and his throat-clearing suggested the others stopped staring too. This they did by finding alternative things to stare at while the captain plonked down in the chair next to Franki.

"Sitrep?" she said, shoving her slim feet into her boots before clasping them.

"As I said, Captain," the First Mate reported, "I don't know who it is, but they've knocked out our main engines without so much as hailing us first. Whoever they are, they seem fharking de—"

"Franki," Phealix warned. Despite their predicament, she wasn't prepared to let the crew run wild in the expletive department.

"Uh, yes, sir, sorry, sir. They seem, er … *quite* determined to bring us down."

"Bring us down, where?"

"There," Franki replied, pointing at the mostly green planet rapidly growing larger in the window. "It's marked as a Dumb Planet, but we have no choice. If we don't set down soon, we're toast."

Phealix's heart sank into her newly donned boots, and she tugged the robe tightly around her. She didn't have to run an in-depth check to know what planet it was, because there was only one Dumb Planet on their plotted course. They might be toast regardless.

"Well, see if you can get a message out to the *Dodger* before it's too late," she said while securing her seat's safety straps with an outer calm she wasn't feeling. "And try keeping us in one piece, Franki."

When the Vahltan nodded, Phealix shouted over her shoulder, "You'd better buckle up, boys, it's gonna be a rough one!"

She just hoped the shuttle's emergency thrusters would be enough to give them a chance. Then her hope transformed into an idea.

"You know what, Franki?" she said, reaching for a switch on the console between them. "Seeing as our new friends are so eager to meet us, it will only be proper to give them a nice welcoming present, wouldn't you agree?"

Despite furiously concentrating on avoiding death, Franki's leathery beak managed a grin.

"Why not, Captain?" he said.

"Why not, indeed," Phealix said as she flipped the switch, pushed a button and sat back, bracing herself for entry.

CHAPTER 3

Hitting anything from this range had been a tough ask, even for a marksman such as Reg, so when the main engines of the shuttle ahead went dark, his face lit up. Whether it was skill or just plain luck, a hit was a hit, and he kept firing until he landed another one, just for good measure.

"Good shooting," Ensign Jensis said.

"Thanks," Reg said, readying himself for his third hit in actual combat as he lined up the shuttle once more.

"Wait," Spence said, "I really think we should call it in, now. They're not going anywhere."

"And we need to make sure it stays that way; even if it's *permanently*."

"That's not protocol," Spence cautioned.

"Screw protocols," Reg grated. "Once we get these bastards, no one will give a hoot whether we played nice. Sometimes you have to improvise to get yourself noticed in life; to get *ahead* in life. After this, I can promise you we'll be able to choose where we want to be stationed – no questions asked."

Ensign Jensis shook his head. "You know, this is why you got stuck patrolling a Dumb Planet in the first place. You could *already* have been stationed anywhere if you'd just learn to follow orders."

"Orders," Reg scoffed. "Do you see anyone around giving orders? No, because we're Scouts. We have to take the initiative when a situation calls for it."

"Maybe, but that doesn't give us the right to break the rules of engagement; you *cannot* fire upon a vessel without proper warning, much less destroy it!"

"Screw warnings too," Reg said and pointed at the shuttle. "You know who's probably on that thing, right? If we don't stop them now, they might slip away before backup arrives. Then *we'll* be the ones responsible for letting one of the most wanted criminals in the Charted Universe escape."

"But—"

"No buts! We're going after them, and that's that! If it will make you feel better, I'll take full responsibility for whatever happens, okay?"

"Okay, fine, but—"

"I said, *no buts!*"

"I know, b— just look at the screen, will you?"

Reg did so, not sure what he was looking for. "What am I looking for?" he asked, and checked again to see if his eyes and brain weren't miscommunicating. He still couldn't see anything.

"There," Spence said, pointing at several barely noticeable blotches on the screen between the Scout ship and the shuttle.

"What's that?" Reg said as his brain and eyes tried to re-establish communication.

"Not sure, but they do look familiar ... oh, no!"

"Mines!" Reg yelled simultaneously as he, too, recognised the objects for what they were. He frantically grabbed the flight stick to pull away, but it was too late.

As the nearest mine detonated, both the human and the Ronian failed to be jerked from their seats as the ship failed to jerk from the unseen, unfelt explosion that knocked the power out. In the dark, the only sound Reg could hear above his own heavy breathing was Spence patting himself to check whether he was still intact.

Satisfied that all his body parts were still present and connected, the ensign said, "What just happened?"

"Must've been EMPMs," Reg replied shakily, blindly punching at everything on the dead consoles and monitors in the faint hope that something had survived the surge. His efforts bore as much fruit as a burnt bush on a desert dune.

Electromagnetic pulse mines were hard to detect and highly effective at knocking out the electronics of unprotected vessels such as Scout ships, which were designed more for speed and manoeuvrability than attack and defence.

Fumbling at his breast pocket, Reg removed a small emergency glow stick and bent it. As the chemicals mixed inside the stick, its green light bounced off Spence's panicked face.

"What do we do?" the ensign said, his eyes bigger than their natural state, which was already big, even by Ronian standards.

"No need to panic," Reg said, trying to hold back the panic in his own voice. "The escape pod is insulated against EMPs. We'll just use its comms to call for aid."

"I think we'll need more than the pod's comms," Spence said.

"Why?"

"Because the last time I checked, we were following *that* ship towards *that* planet," Spence said, pointing out the window.

"So?"

"We had engines then."

"Of course we had en—" Reg started, before his brain finally discovered the follow-up message in its junk-mail folder. "We're on a collision course, aren't we?"

They both stared at the shuttle ahead, which began glowing red as it entered the planet's atmosphere without the aid of its main engines. Without *any* engines, their own ship was doomed.

"Get inside the pod!" Reg ordered as he unclasped his straps and ushered Spence towards the back.

"What about extra provisions … and weapons?"

"No time!" Reg yelled, punching a panel and shoving his friend through the hatch as it slid open. "Get in!"

Strapping himself into his seat next to Spence, Reg punched instructions into the flight panel, and as soon as the hatch sealed shut, the egg-shaped pod jettisoned from the bottom of the ship. Satisfied they were clear, Reg accessed the comms panel to send out a distress signal.

"Sure, *now* you want to call it in," said Spence drily as he tugged at his straps to check if they were secure.

Ignoring the ensign, Reg sent the message and sat back. As the pod started shaking from its tussle with the planet's atmosphere, he closed his eyes and gripped his safety straps until his knuckles turned white. He could only hope the message reached Command before it was too late. In all likelihood, it was.

CHAPTER 4

Lying on his back amid the tall grass, Isilimo gazed up at the starry sky, which was a tad less starry because the moons were out to resume their perpetual waltz – their soft-blue light masking all but the brightest specks dotting the blackness above.

While Isilimo wasn't alone, he *was* the only one awake, as the other three Ja'naman tribesmen had fallen asleep earlier.

Of course, they weren't supposed to be sleeping. They were *supposed* to be patrolling the village borders for signs of danger. But the local Le'us roaming the area had just fed the day before and, judging by the large carcass of the Kuhdoo they'd left behind, they would remain fed for a few days longer. And although the Night Aahps started hunting after sunset, they mostly stuck to the jungle on the other side of the mountain, making them the Teahupo'o tribe's problem. Just as the Le'us, who preferred the open plains, were the Ja'nama tribe's problem.

Isilimo, or Issy, as his friend called him, was a proud Ja'naman – just not a very popular one, which is why he could count his friends on one finger. Given, "friend" probably overstated his relationship with Mamella, but she was the person who tolerated him more than the others, and was therefore the closest thing Issy had to a buddy.

Mamella was also pretty, but as Issy wasn't blessed in the looks department (having been told so many times by everyone except Mamella), he knew his boundaries. Besides, Issy didn't want to risk their friendship, as Mamella was the only one who made village life bearable. Without her, he might have packed up and left long ago in search of adventure, just like his great-grandfather had done before Issy was born.

No one ever spoke much of Khulu, but from the bits and pieces Issy had managed to drag from his parents, his ancestor had been both a dreamer and a wanderer; just like Issy ... except for the *wanderer* part. Even though his heart yearned for it, there was no way Issy's mind would permit him to set foot outside the tribe's borders. Yet, he could still daydream about it, which is why he now used his free time to do just that.

Staring at the stars, Issy imagined the celestial dots above as other villages floating in the sky, with other villagers staring back, imagining the same thing. His parents dismissed his ideas of drifting villages as childhood fantasies, and cautioned him that blaspheming against their ancestors and the gods would land him in trouble. Village Priestesses were always looking for the next sacrifice, they warned, and if Issy didn't want to be next, he'd better keep his childish dreams to himself.

So that's precisely what Issy had done for years, and generally kept a low profile, which was a feat on its own among the short villagers. And even though his bubbling levels of excitement occasionally blew off the lid of self-constraint, everyone dismissed his stories as just that – stories. Needless to say, "Oddball" Issy had become used to rolling eyes, just as he'd become used to the growing number of unflattering nicknames.

As the "villages" hung silently above, Issy wondered if some of their denizens had the same problems as him – outcast because they thought differently. He was sure they did, just as he was sure there *were* other villages up there. The sacrificial gifts had to come from *somewhere*, descending from the sky in their fiery cages. *Why not* from a village?

As though his thoughts had been heard, processed and approved by the gods, Issy spotted two streaks of bright fire flashing by overhead. Shooting to his feet, he saw the first streak slowing down somewhat before disappearing from view behind the Fire Mountain, while the other shot past until it vanished beyond the horizon. Issy was on the verge of waking his companions, when he noticed yet another light hurtling towards his patrol, before it slowed and descended behind a nearby hill.

While Issy had seen several lights like the first two, he'd only heard about the latter. It meant something special was about to happen; something he didn't enjoy. But he had a duty to perform, and perform it he would, whether he liked it or not. It was *tradition*.

With a sigh, Issy woke his three groggy companions from their unsuccessful beauty sleep and informed them of what he'd seen. They appeared keener to revisit slumberland than to act on the fantasies of "Dreamer Boy". But when Issy grabbed his spear and ran towards the hill behind which the last light had vanished, they had no choice but to get up and follow. If something happened to Issy, questions would be asked, and they weren't creative enough to come up with a plausible excuse.

Issy had bargained on this, and grinned as their foot-falls followed him up the hill. However, the higher the small group ascended, the more his grin faded. The Ja'naman couldn't shake the feeling that things were about to change. And not necessarily for the better.

CHAPTER 5

"Captain?"

Can't a girl get some sleep?

"Captain."

Really? What was *so* important that couldn't wait till morning?

"Captain!"

"What?" Phealix murmured her intended yell.

"Captain," repeated the fuzzy figure above her. "Thank goodness. We thought we'd lost you too."

"What … what do you mean *too?*" Phealix asked as she tried to sit up, but the figure's hand held her down.

"Franki?" she said when the figure de-fuzzed enough to recognise. "What the heck are you doing?"

"Keeping you still, sir," the Vahltan First Mate said as soothingly as any Vahltan could manage, which wasn't soothing at all. "Your head took quite a knock."

Phealix tried to get her ducks in a row or, at the very least, a fuzzy clump moving in roughly the same direction.

"What are you talki—" she began, but when the ducks slipped into the pond of full consciousness, they displaced the lingering traces of memory loss.

As the recollection of recent events flooded her mind, Phealix carefully yet firmly removed Franki's hand from her shoulder and sat up. "I'm okay," she said in answer to the Vahltan's worried look. "The others?"

"Stanni and Kati didn't make it," Franki reported as the worry on his face deepened. And while it was indeed worry, it was more the pragmatic kind that dealt with the loss of manpower rather than the emotional loss of shipmates.

Phealix said nothing, though. It was just one of those Vahltan things.* She glanced at the two coat-covered bodies lying nearby before shifting her attention to the shuttle, or rather what was left of it. Wedged halfway up between two tall, sturdy trees, the back section of the vessel was still ablaze. She hoped the flames wouldn't spread, although the damp jungle didn't seem likely to facilitate a wildfire. Her eyes followed the trench of pushed-up dirt and foliage that terminated at the smouldering remains of the forward section.

"Injuries?" she asked in a business-like tone, despite her growing sense of trepidation.

"Only a few scrapes, bruises, and a severed finger," Franki reported.

"Trigger finger?"

"No, sir."

"Good, because we'll need every trigger finger we have."

---

* As with cleanliness, Vahltans aren't big on friendship. In fact, the original Vahltan term for "friend" roughly translates as "one who owes me", which is why Vahltan bankers are blessed with more friends than they'd care to admit. Not that they'd admit to anything, but that's more a problem with bankers in general, Vahltan or not.

Franki's face said something his mouth didn't want to say.

"What's wrong?" Phealix asked, knowing the bad-news face all too well.

"We, uh, managed to put out most of the flames, sir, but the fire … well, it destroyed the weapons."

As per Colloquium rules, pirates were not allowed entry to the event while armed, which is why the crew's weapons had been locked away in a secret compartment on the shuttle, away from the prying eyes (and crowbars) of other pirates.[*]

"This is all I could retrieve," Franki continued, handing over a stunner gun.

"Well, it's better than nothing," Phealix said, keeping her face straight as she accepted the stunner. "Comms?"

"Fried," Franki said reluctantly, as bad news wasn't something any crew member wanted to report to a captain, especially if you were a member of a pirate crew.

His shoulders slumped. "I'm sorry, Captain," he said, staring at the wreckage. "I just couldn't hold her."

Phealix rose gingerly, touching her side. A bruised rib, maybe, but nothing more. Or so she hoped.

"I'm just glad we weren't *all* burnt to a crisp, Franki," she said, straightening with a wince. "You did well."

Franki perked up a bit. "Thank you, sir. But, um, what do we do now?"

"See what else you can salvage from the shuttle. Then ready the men – we need to leave."

Franki looked hesitant. "Wouldn't it be better to stay with the ship … for when help arrives?"

------

[*] If there's one thing you can trust as a pirate, it's that you can't trust a pirate.

"That's *if* help arrives, Franki. Besides, even if the *Dodger* received the signal, it might take a while to find us. We can't wait around till then."

"I'm sure we'll find something to eat before then, Captain."

"The problem isn't *us* finding something to eat, Franki."

The Vahltan frowned. "Sir?"

"You don't know what planet this is, do you?"

Franki's frozen frown suggested he didn't.

With a sigh, Captain Phealix told him, soon after which the group departed with a sense of urgency, leaving behind the two bodies. To anyone else, this might have seemed improper, but to the Vahltans it was more proper to stay alive, and burying the dead wasn't the best way of achieving this goal with the limited time they had at their disposal.

Phealix paused for one final glance at the wreckage. She was going to miss her hot tub. With another sigh, she joined her eight remaining crew members as they got swallowed by the dark jungle, which resumed its business the way jungles normally do.

CHAPTER 6

"So, now what?"

"We wait," Reg said.

This wasn't the answer Ensign Jensis had expected, but Reg didn't care. He needed time to think, but Spence wasn't making it easy.

The ensign gasped in mock surprise. "You mean to tell me you're *not* going to storm out there, blasting away at everything that moves?"

Reg glanced at the empty holster strapped to his leg. "I, er … I don't have a flasher on me at the moment," he said.

"What do you mean *at the moment?*"

"Well, once you give me yours, I'll have one."

"Mine?! Where's *yours?*"

"I left it in the ship's bathroom."

"Why in Zolt's name would you do that?" Spence exclaimed.

"Hey, remember whom you're talking to," Reg warned.

"Oh, I'm sorry," Spence said, bringing his right fist to his left shoulder in a Militor salute. "Why in Zolt's name would you do that, *sir?*"

Reg glared at him. "Watch yourself, *Ensign*."

"Why? Going to lose your cool like you lost your gun?"

Reg was about to do just that when he thought the better of it. As per proper Militor chain of command, there were better ways to deal with those of lower rank than arguing with them. One of the first things officers were taught was that blame drained downwards.

"Well," he said, "it wouldn't have happened if you hadn't rushed me from the bathroom the way you did."

"But you said—"

"Weapon, Ensign Jensis," Reg interjected, holding out his hand, palm-up.

Spence glared at it as if it was a baby's diaper – not the empty kind. "You *cannot* be serious!"

"I said *weapon*, Ensign," Reg repeated, flicking up the fingers of the expectant hand to indicate where the weapon should go and when this should occur.

Spence glared at the hand for another second before he removed the flasher from its holster and handed it over with an expected measure of grumbling.

Taking the sidearm, Reg checked its battery clip before securing the weapon in his leg holster.

"Thank you, Ensign," he said with an officer's grin.[*]

As Spence clearly wasn't in the mood for talking, both Scouts sat staring at the pod's monitor in silence for the next minute. The external camera atop the egg-shaped pod had automatically switched to night-mode to compensate for the darkness outside, but didn't show much beyond rolling grasslands.

---

[*] Although similar to other grins, there's nothing much you can do about this one unless, of course, you genuinely enjoy the food they serve in the brig.

Tired of waiting, Reg reached for a small control stick and panned the camera anticlockwise towards the north, revealing the rocky slope of a mountain not far from their position. He continued panning until the camera once more encountered grassland. But just before the camera reached its original position, Reg panned it back.

Was that movement he'd just spotted?

Twisting the stick, he zoomed in.

Nothing.

Not really wanting to talk to Spence but also not wanting to second-guess his first guess without a second opinion, Reg glanced at his glum friend.

"Uh, did you also see someth—" he started, but was interrupted by a loud *clang*, causing him to release the control stick with instinctive startlement.

Spence, too, sat bolt upright, exchanging his look of resentment for one of alarm. "What was that?" he said.

"I don't know," Reg said.

He reached for the control stick once more, but snatched his hand back as another *clang* rang out, upon which the monitor went blank. Just before the visuals had cut out, he was sure he'd seen an object flying towards the camera. And as he was quite familiar with rocks, he was quite sure it had been a rock.

Spence was on the verge of saying something, when another *clang* reverberated through the pod's small interior, followed by another, and another, and another. The continuous noise was enough to drive Reg to the brink of madness and, judging by Spence's face, framed by his hands covering his pointy ears, the ensign had already crossed that brink.

Reg reached for the emergency hatch-release lever, held in position by a safety seal.

"What are you doing?" Spence yelled, not only to be heard above the noise but also to convey the fact that he wasn't on board with whatever Reg was about to do.

"Going outside," Reg yelled matter-of-factly in sharp contrast to the look in his eyes.

"Are you insane? We don't know what's out there!"

"Well, we cannot wait for whatever's out there to trap us in here!"

Spence looked ready to argue, but an increase in the frequency of the clanging changed his mind.

"Fine!" the ensign yielded, pulling his combat knife from the sheath in his waistband. He eyed it glumly, and his glum deepened as Reg removed his newly acquired flasher gun from its holster. "I hope you haven't lost your aim since the Academy."

"Of course not," Reg said.

"And I hope you know that, whatever's out there, it's *not* a training drone," Spence aimed the resentful stab at his superior.

"Yes, I know!" Reg replied as the stab hit home.

Reg wasn't sure what waited for them beyond the hatch, but on a Dumb Planet like this, he was confident he had the upper hand – especially considering the hand held a gun. However, as he broke the seal on the hatch-release lever, his confidence downgraded itself to mild hopefulness, and further downgrading felt imminent. But he was *not* about to lose face by backtracking now, and pushed aside all residual doubts to pull the lever.

As the escape pod's hatch slid open, the clanging stopped. For some reason, the ensuing silence felt even more menacing than the preceding noise. But Reg stepped out nonetheless.

He no longer had a choice.

• • •

Reg's first step onto the soil of a Dumb Planet should have been a momentous occasion but, lifting his leg from the puddle of water he'd just stepped in, he had to use the moment to shake some mud off his combat boot. The fact that he'd polished his boots to perfection only a few hours earlier did nothing to mitigate his irritation.

"Fhark," he said under his breath.

"What's wrong?" Spence whispered nervously from inside the escape pod.

"Nothing," Reg lied. "Get out here."

As the final sparks of life flew from the limp-hanging camera atop the pod, Reg glanced at the rocks strewn around the pod. Taking a few steps forward, he kept his weapon trained on nothing, as this was all he could see.

After another splash accompanied by a curse behind him, Reg smirked. He could've warned Spence of the puddle, but despite their situation, or maybe because of it, he needed something to smirk at.

"Thanks for the warni—" the ensign began.

"Shh!" Reg said, wiping the smirk from his face to scan the shadowy landscape for the source of the rustle he'd just heard. Something was moving in the tall grass.

As his eyes adjusted to the low light outside the pod, he couldn't make out much except for the oval silhouette of a plant leaf steadily growing in size. He flicked on the flasher gun's small mounted flashlight to shed more light on things.

The plant leaf suddenly stopped growing, partly because it wasn't a leaf, but mainly because the startled, grass-skirted man behind the leaf-shaped shield had stopped advancing and hefted the crude spear in his other hand. He was even more startled when an equally startled Reg squeezed off a green flasher energy ball that shattered the top of the shield.

Regaining his composure, Reg levelled the gun at the man clutching at his face, which was now porcupined by shards of wood pushing out blood between his fingers. Reg was about to issue the appropriate warning after the fact, when three more short, round, bare-chested men leapt from the tall grass, brandishing spears and shouting warnings of their own.

Coming from three sides, the men were spread too far apart, and as he alternated his aim between them, Reg knew he wouldn't be able to take out all the approaching threats before being skewered by one of their pointy weapons. He also knew Spence wouldn't have more luck, not only because the ensign just had a knife, but also because close-quarters combat wasn't exactly his strong suit – nor any form of combat, for that matter. Spence felt more at home monitoring things from afar, and the men closing in on them *certainly* wasn't far enough.

After swift calculations of death versus surrender yielded unfavourable results, Reg held up his flasher and reluctantly dropped it with the sound guns usually make when they hit wet mud. He stepped back next to Spence, who must have come to the same statistical conclusion as Reg, as he tossed his knife next to the gun without any sign of reluctance.

"You, lie down!" one of the men ordered with a downward wave of his spear. Like the others, bronze skin covered his rounded body as well as his round, bald head, which housed equally round facial features that sternly suggested the captives did as they were told. So that's what Reg and Spence did. Reg only glanced up once, and didn't do so again, seeing as the natives only wore grass skirts that failed to hide certain body parts when viewed from a low angle.

Yanking Reg and Spence to their feet, two of the men bound the Scouts' wrists with crude yet effective ropes. Two more ropes were noosed around their necks; loose enough not to choke but tight enough to discourage any thoughts of escape or resistance.

The man with bits of wood still stuck in his face stepped towards Reg with a growl, but one of the other men, who Reg presumed was the leader, held him back.

"No, Gobatsha," the leader said. "You no hurt them. We go to village. Priestess decide what we do with them."

He turned back to the bound scouts. "We go now. You stay quiet. You no make trouble, or I let Gobatsha decide what we do with you. You hear?"

Reg glanced at Gobatsha's pained yet eager face as he picked up the other end of the rope tied around Reg's neck, daring the Scout to try his luck. Reg merely nodded at the leader, who gave the signal for the group to move out, tugging their hapless prisoners behind them.

CHAPTER 7

It was the same boulder. Phealix was sure of it now.

"Captain, isn't that the same rock from before?" Demi ventured from behind. For a Vahltan, she was a good soul. Not necessarily the brightest, but a good soul nonetheless. And she was handy in a skirmish, which was the main reason Phealix had recruited her.

"Yes, *Demi*, it's the same rock," Phealix grated at the reminder of her shortcomings. Faylins used to be better at this kind of thing! Millennia ago, you could leave a Faylin almost anywhere and they'd be able to find their way through just about any alien environment to reach their destination. They'd been masters at it! Sure, they were still better than most in terms of general navigation, but somewhere along the line they'd lost some of their magic; their … edge. And Phealix hadn't realised how blunt that edge had become until now.

She glared at the boulder they'd passed three times already. She knew they'd passed it three times because it wasn't difficult to recognise the heart-shaped, moss-covered boulder nestled between the roots of a massive, moss-covered tree. Most of the jungle's surfaces, including the soil, were covered by moss, either fully or partially, causing everything to look the same – well, *more* the same than without the moss. If it hadn't been for the odd-shaped rock, they might have followed in their own footsteps for days without knowing it.

Realising it wouldn't help getting upset with her crew, Phealix took a deep breath and calmly said, "We're going in circles."

"Oh, we shouldn't be doing that, Captain," Demi said with cheery sincerity.

Franki must have noticed the captain's expression darkening.

"Sir," he said, nodding at the boulder-hugging tree, "might I suggest we send *someone* up there? You know, to get a better look at where we are."

Despite knowing what her First Mate was trying to do, Phealix also knew he was right.

"Very well," she said, turning to Demi with a look that didn't need verbal accompaniment.

While failing to notice the mood behind the look, Demi had enough intelligence in her arsenal to translate the unspoken order.

"I'd be more than happy to, Captain!" she saluted, before setting off.

"You know the men don't like her very much, Captain," Franki stated. "Not *me*, though," he quickly added as Phealix's eyebrow lifted. "*I* have no problem with her. I'm just saying what the men are saying. They find her too … peppy."

"Well," Phealix said, watching the climbing Vahltan disappear from view among the branches, "I suggest you tell *the men* that, should anything … untoward happen to her, we'll see how peppy *they* feel floating out the airlock. Understood?"

Franki swallowed hard. "Er, yes, sir. Of course, sir."

Trusting the message would indeed be delivered and understood, Phealix waited for Demi's return, which didn't take too long.

"And?" the captain said. "Anything?"

It took a moment for Demi to catch her breath. "Yes … sir," she panted. "I saw … a glow … fire, I think … about three … or four hundred metres … that way."

Phealix glanced in the direction Demi pointed and patted the Vahltan on the shoulder. "Good job, Demi," she said, and turned to Franki. "Well, you heard her. Let's go."

"But we don't even know what's out there, Captain," Franki protested.

"It beats walking around chasing our tails all night, Franki," Phealix said. "Besides, there's only one way to find out what's out there, and that's by going there. So gather the men, but keep it quiet."

Not waiting for an answer, she started walking in the direction Demi had indicated. Taking the stunner from her bathrobe's pocket, she hoped she looked more confident than she felt, because this jungle was getting on her nerves.

• • •

"Who are they?" Franki whispered, peering through the brush.

Phealix didn't answer immediately. Fortunately, with no lack of foliage to hide behind, she and her crew could spy on the men around the fire without being noticed. If indeed they were *men*. She'd heard stories about this planet – none of them good – but had never seen what the locals looked like, so anything was possible. However, with their loincloths and flattish chests, it was safe to presume they were of the male persuasion.[*] Completely hairless, the roundish natives were about half her size in height and twice her size in width, with dark-bonze skin as well as round eyes and ears. It was as if someone had taken an image of a hairless human and squashed it vertically. But despite their lack in height, whatever they were hiding under the loincloths didn't lack in size. Phealix made a conscious decision to block that area from her mind.

Although she couldn't make out what they said, the strange men were obviously engaged in a storytelling session, with one jumping around and waving his arms like a monkey, while the others sat around the fire, laughing at his antics.

"Captain?" Franki probed again.

"Locals," Phealix finally replied, keeping her voice low. "We'd better follow them."

"They look a bit … primitive, sir," Franki said. "Wherever they're going, I don't think it'll help us much."

"Well, I'm sure you'll agree we're all too hungry and thirsty to worry about anything else at this stage. So unless you have rations stashed somewhere, we need to find something to eat."

---

[*] Such data isn't always the most reliable way to establish gender among species, making said presumptions less safe than one might think. For instance, despite their potbellies and ample breasts, it's not a good idea to ask a Kahoian man when his baby's due. They can't get pregnant, and they don't appreciate being emasculated by people who haven't bothered reading their *Basic Biology for Beginners* handbooks in primary school.

Franki's stomach growled in agreement, earning him the universal "Are you serious?" glare from his crewmates.

Shaking her head, Phealix checked to see if the men by the fire had heard anything. Thankfully, *they* hadn't, but the unseen man who'd been quietly patrolling the campsite perimeter *had*, and reached behind the leaf to yank out a surprised, seemingly female creature in her odd, mud-white clothing.

"Come, come!" he shouted over his shoulder, bringing an abrupt end to the merriment around the fire. Grabbing their spears, the men sprinted towards the voice at a pace that belied their stocky build.

Recovering from her initial shock, Phealix knuckle-punched her subduer in the throat, forcing the man to release her robe, and then aimed her stunner gun at the frontrunner of the charging men.

The *tshoop* accompanying the white ball of light that hit the man wasn't loud, but when he dropped and slid to a halt face-first by Phealix's boots, his companions also skidded to a halt, but on their feet. Raising their spears, they alternated nervous glances between the shot man on the ground and the punched man clutching at his throat, gasping for air. They appeared uncertain as to their next course of action, but by the way they brandished their spears, they were inclined to stick the pointy ends of the weapons into the blue creature facing them. However, they soon faced more targets as eight tall leathery creatures, bearing sticks and rocks, stormed from the foliage to defend the female.

One of the locals gave two short, sharp whistles and stepped forward.

"You put down," he said, eyeing the pirates' makeshift weapons as well as the stunner pointed at his chest.

Phealix didn't budge.

"You put down!" the man repeated.

Phealix shook her head resolutely, but when even more spear-wielding men burst from the greenery to surround her party, her resolution took a substantial dip.

"You *now* put down?" the man tried again, looking hopeful. He didn't seem eager to end up like his compatriot on the ground.

With the pirates now outnumbered, and with no real weapons at their disposal, Phealix knew that – even if they were lucky – she and her crew wouldn't be able to take out half of the locals before getting speared in the gut. Teeth clenched, she dropped the stunner, followed a moment later by the sound of rocks and sticks hitting the mossy soil behind her.

"What now, Captain?" Franki grated.

"Just keep calm and do as they say," Phealix said over her shoulder. "That goes for all of you."

She knew this was unlikely, as Vahltans weren't exactly at their calmest when the odds were stacked against them. She just hoped they wouldn't panic and do something stupid. It was a faint hope.

The man who'd given the orders stepped forward and picked up Phealix's stunner, eyeing it with a mixture of fear and intrigue, then held the weapon in the air.

"Look!" he said, turning in place triumphantly. "It ours … Silent Lightning – it ours!"

The others cheered but quieted down again when the man knelt by his companion in the mud.

"Hinga," he said, "your sacrifice bring great power to tribe, and great honour to you. We no forget *Hinga!*"

"Hinga!" echoed a solemn chorus from the others.

Sticking the stunner into his carry pouch, the man walked up to Phealix and bound her wrists with rope, while the others took care of the Vahltans. When all the captives were lined up behind one another, a stout man lifted the limp Hinga and slung him across his broad neck and shoulders.

"Where are you taking us?" Phealix demanded as the leader checked her bonds.

He frowned at her like someone who didn't quite understand what someone else was saying.

"What she say?" he said, looking over at one of his companions, who merely shrugged. With a shrug of his own, the leader ordered the procession forward with a wave of his spear. "We go!"

And with that, they went.

CHAPTER 8

No one from his village, or any other village for that matter, had ever mentioned a Chicken God, so Issy wasn't sure what to make of it.

Such a god *had* to exist, though. Why else would these strangers be sent to the Ja'nama tribe in an egg?

That said, the captives didn't *look* very … chickeny. Maybe the Chicken God created them to look more like Ja'namans than poultry, so as not to frighten the villagers. He shivered at the idea of Ja'naman-sized chicken. Yes, that had to be it! Or maybe not, because the tall beings didn't look like members of the Ja'naman tribe or any other tribe Issy had ever encountered. Aside from their peculiar, grey, thigh-fitting clothing, the two didn't even look alike! Why would a god make things so complicated?

His head started to hurt, so he decided to put the question to bed until it could be woken up and interrogated later.

Gods do what gods do, and it wasn't the place of any Ja'naman to question the will or the actions of the gods. Or so he was taught, growing up.

Despite the conundrum of their appearance, Issy got the feeling the strangers were important. They had to be, because no one would descend from the heavens if they weren't, would they? His head pleaded for him to leave this subject alone, too, so he lay that thought next to the other one for a nap.

But as the party reached the outskirts of the village, Issy knew he needed to figure out how to approach the matter, and fast. If the villagers had their way, the strangers didn't stand a chance. And if Issy's feelings about them were right, they were going to need a chance – even if it was just a slim one.

•••

"In there," Issy said, pointing with his torch.

His fellow patrolman frowned. "But that … chicken coop."

"I know, Impi," Issy said. "But that's where they should go. You'll understand once I explain it to the Priestess."

Impi's face stated that the time of understanding wasn't likely to arrive on his doorstep any time soon. Nonetheless, he ordered the prisoners into the wooden coop, which was done without regard for politeness, before the door was closed. The gaps between the wood slats were big, yet small enough to keep chickens in and predators out. With only a latch and no lock, the coop's door was far from escape-proof, but the spears of the two guards stationed on either side of the entrance served as sufficient incentive for the prisoners to stay put.

Job done, Impi was about to say something, but shook his head and walked away. With his odd views and his use of too many words, the villagers struggled to understand Isilimo, and Impi wasn't about to try doing so now. Village Management could deal with it.[*]

When Impi disappeared behind the nearest round grass-and-mud hut, Issy turned to the guards.

"I need a moment with the prisoners," he said. "Alone."

Judging by the look they gave him, this wasn't going to happen without some encouragement.

"Come on, I'll make it worth your while," Issy said. "Unogada, I'll help you fix that leak in your hut. And Sheba, I'll cover your patrol for one night."

"Two nights," Sheba countered.

"Done!" Issy agreed quickly, as he'd been willing to settle on a month of patrols.

The guards still didn't look convinced but, sharing a shrug, they retreated to a manageable distance. Satisfied that they were out of earshot, Issy approached the side of the coop, where the captives sat huddled in a hushed conversation while trying their best to shoo away some inquisitive, featherless chickens.

---

[*] People might argue that Management, in general, is not as useful as they make themselves out to be. However, many people *won't* argue against one of the few benefits of having Management around – you can shift problems up the chain of command in the out-of-site-out-of-mind kind of way. That's why people in Management get paid the big bucks, and why people not in Management want to be in Management despite their views on Management. Those finding this matter confusing can discuss it with their immediate Manager in the precious five-minute window-period between him returning to the office from his extended lunch break and leaving early to pick the kids up from soccer practice.

"I say we take out those two and make a run for it," he caught the taller one saying.

"I don't think we'll make it, even if—" the shorter one said, but fell silent when he saw Issy approaching.

The taller one turned to see what had distracted his compatriot. "Oh, don't worry," he said, turning back. "He doesn't even know what we're saying. *Dumb Planet*, remember? Now, where were we? Oh, yes, if we—"

"What's a planet?" Issy asked.

The interrupted man's face froze in disbelief.

"Uh, you can … understand us?" he said. "You shouldn't be able to … do that."

"Why not?" Issy said.

"Because … well, it's a Dumb Planet."

"Again, what is a planet? And why is it dumb? The Ja'nama tribe is *not* dumb."

"Um, yeah, of course not, it's just … well, um … you see, a *planet* is what you're on, and it's dumb, because, well, er … no, seriously, how the heck do you know what we're saying?"

Issy shrugged. "I'm not sure. I think it had something to do with the vernaculites I drank."

"Vern— what do *you* know about vernaculites?"*

"Not much, but that's what it said on the box."

---

* For the sake of those who *don't* know, vernaculites are pre-programmed microscopic nanobots that attach themselves to the brain's linguistic area, enabling an individual to interpret verbal and written communication from others, regardless of their heritage. Vernaculites can't always process everything said or read with a hundred percent accuracy but, to be fair, neither can those who naturally speak the same language. Which is why the frown remains *the* most recognisable expression throughout the Charted Universe.

"You just drank something without knowing what it was?" the taller prisoner said.

"What can I say? I was young and curious. In any case, it was strange – I didn't know what the stuff was called until after I drank it. When I saw the box again later on, the strange markings on the side told me it was vernaculites, among other things. What does 'Terms and conditions apply' mean?"

Ignoring the question, the prisoners turned to one another. "Hey, this could help us, Reg," the shorter one said.

"Maybe, Spence, but I wouldn't hold my breath. I still think we should try to … you know, the thing we discussed."

"No," Issy told the one called Reg, "your companion was right. If you try to escape, you *will* be killed."

"So, what, we're just supposed to, what, wait until, what, they kill us the first chance they get?"

"Oh, no," Issy said, "they won't kill you until after the vote on how to prepare you."

"Prepare us for what?"

"For dinner, of course," Issy said. He couldn't comprehend why any god would send people down from the heavens without giving them the basics of how things worked down here.

"You mean getting us cleaned and dressed up before giving us a good meal as the guests of honour?" said the one called Spence.

Issy felt sorry for him with that hopeful look in his eyes. "Well, partly yes … and partly no," he said.

"What do you mean?" Reg said warily.

"Uh, well, you were right about the first part," Issy said. "But you won't like the second part."

Their look of apprehension stated he might be right.

"You see," he continued, feeling a bit embarrassed, "you won't be the ones having the meal because, well, you see, uh ... *you* will be the main course."

Their shock stated he was *definitely* right.

CHAPTER 9

Reg watched the round, grass-skirted figure of the man called Issy disappear into the night.

At first, the Scout couldn't speak, and realised the problem was bigger than he thought when he tried and failed on the second attempt.

Spence helped the lieutenant out of his dilemma. "I was afraid of this," he said, but when Reg's expression demanded more clarity, he added, "The inhabitants of this planet – they aren't exactly known for being ... civilised."

"Well, they're savages," Reg said, "so, no surprises there. This *is* a Dumb Planet, after all."

"You haven't done *any* research on the planet or its denizens, have you?" Spence said.

"No, I only checked the navigational data we needed for our patrol. Why would I check planetary info?"

"For in case you end up in a situation like this," Spence said flatly.

"Well, how was I supposed to know we'd get stuck here?"

"That's your problem, Reg. You *never* plan for the unexpected. You always storm headlong into things without knowing what those things are! It's going to get you killed one day … no, worse, it's going to get *me* killed one day! And, just to make things *even worse*, that day might be today!"

Although Reg wanted to argue, some part of him knew his friend was right, but he shoved the acknowledgement aside along with the chicken that tried to make itself at home in his lap. With its tanned, featherless skin, the bird looked like it had just climbed out of an oven.

"Cannibals, Reg," Spence hissed. "These people are *cannibals!*"

"Oh, I was hoping I'd misunderstood that part," Reg said. "At least that guy, Icky—"

"Issy."

"—said he'd try to help."

"These people are firm in their traditions, Reg. They won't let us go just because someone asks nicely."

"Well, then it's back to my escape plan."

Spence shook his head. "That's the thing. Even if we *do* manage to escape this village, where are we supposed to go? Wahyoo VIII is swarming with tribes who'll jump at the chance to decapitate or eat us … or both. Haven't you heard the stories?"

"You mean *this* is *that* planet?" Reg asked, and shivered when Spence nodded.

When he was little, Reg's parents had told him that children who didn't eat their vegetables were kidnapped in the night and taken to a mythical Dumb Planet filled with cannibals and headhunters. It didn't really scare him at the time, as the scenario gave him enough fodder to daydream of single-handedly fighting off hordes of savages with nothing more than a staff and a self-made slingshot.

However, it turns out the planet *was* real, and Reg now felt the fear that had been absent so long ago. And without so much as his imaginary slingshot at his disposal, they likely wouldn't survive one village, let alone a whole planet.

Dammit, Spence was right … again! They had nowhere to go. And their only hope lay in the hands of a young savage with an above-average vocabulary, which didn't exactly re-ignite Reg's low-burning confidence levels. But at least it was *something*. He just hoped it was enough.

CHAPTER 10

"Chicken God?!"

The villagers jumped at the outburst. Like Issy, they were short and round, and not necessarily in the obese way, apart from a few exceptions. The women, some cradling roundish babies in their arms, wore the same grass skirts as the men, but also wrapped leather around their chests. This had nothing to do with modesty, but more with a growing sense of fashion among tribal women in general. They wanted something to call their own; something special. Of course the men didn't get it, which suited the women just fine.

The Village Priestess was no ordinary woman, though. She didn't follow the new fashion, because the Village Priestess had to wear the Cloak of Bones, as dictated by tradition. While Ongswele was the daughter of the retired Village Chief, it wasn't the only reason for her appointment as Village Priestess. She was one of the few hopefuls who'd figured out how to handle the Great Serpent, and one of even fewer who had survived its Bite of Wisdom.

Ongswele was not a person Issy wanted to rile up, yet riled up she was.

"You no serious, Isilimo!" the Priestess continued, shaking the Staff of Truth, causing the Cloak of Bones to rattle. "You no think *I know* if Chicken God exist?"

"Well, they came from the sky ... in an egg," Issy said hesitantly, glancing towards the other members of his patrol for backup. The men shifted uncomfortably as Ongswele walked up to them. She jabbed the Staff of Truth into the ribs of the man nearest her.

"It true, Sheba?" she demanded. "They come from egg?"

Wincing, the man spoke quickly before the Priestess could have another go, "Yes, Ongswele. It true. It egg. Big egg, but egg."

The other two nodded reluctantly. Ongswele sniffed, turning her attention back to the two strange beings on their knees before her. "Chicken no fly, Isilimo," she said, her smooth, bronze head glistening with sweat. "How egg fall from sky if chicken no fly?"

Perspiration also coated Issy's skin, not only because he was the centre of attention, but also because the fire had again been stacked with too much wood. Of course, the wood-stackers didn't care, as they weren't the ones who had to gather the wood, much to the frustration of the wood-gatherers.[*]

"Maybe the Chicken God has feathers ... you know, like birds," Issy said.

The Priestess forced out a laugh. "Ha! Chicken no bird, Isilimo. If chicken *bird*, it have feathers."

---

[*] Office cleaners feel the same about tea junkies using a fresh mug every time they make a cuppa. If you're one of those people, please spare a thought for the people working so tirelessly to clean up after you every day. And, while you're at it, please remove that overripe banana from your desk. You *know* you're not going to eat it.

"Maybe only the Chicken God has feathers," Issy ventured. "I mean, it *would* make sense for a god to be better than her subjects, wouldn't it?"

"Her?"

"I don't think a rooster Chicken God can lay eggs."

As Issy had intended, the Priestess carefully digested the possibility of having another female god to balance things out a bit. "Maybe," she said at length, "but why they *no look* like chicken?"

Issy tried his personally approved theory. "Maybe the Chicken God didn't want to frighten us with giant chickens, so she sent chickens that look more like us."

"She no do good job," the Priestess muttered, staring at the captives while trying to figure out what to do. When this failed, she turned back to Issy and said, "We ask Great Serpent, no? *He* tell us what we must do."

She held up her left palm, which was riddled with tiny, dotty scars.

Issy wasn't sure what the Great Serpent knew about chickens or their god, but there was no use arguing against holy matters. Especially when Ongswele was in charge of those matters, because for some reason the Great Serpent *always* sided with her.

Ongswele nodded to one of her assistants, who stepped forward, proffering a metal container. To the natives, the box looked like a holy chest filled with power and mystery. To anyone not from Wahyoo VIII, it would've looked like a lunchbox.

The Priestess cast a warning glare at the crowd, who quickly remembered that they'd forgotten to avert their eyes, and then did just that to avoid the Punishment for Peeking. The opening of the Great Serpent's Lair was a closely guarded secret, and anyone caught sneaking a look would be bitten by the Great Serpent, after which they'd die a slow, agonising death. Everyone had seen this happen before with their own eyes, so it wasn't just a myth.[*] Only The Worthy were immune.

However, Issy knew the truth, and he'd been keeping it his own little secret, reckoning it might come in handy one day. Like usual, peeking through his semi-closed eyelids, he watched Ongswele opening the two latches. Reaching in, she dipped her finger in some ointment, which she rubbed on her scarred palm before carefully retrieving the Great Serpent's metallic head. The Great Serpent's body wasn't inside, because it didn't have one.

"You open eyes, now," the Priestess commanded, "and gaze upon Great Serpent!"

Everybody gazed, and despite having seen it several times, they all gasped at the sight of the Great Serpent, as required by the Holy Moment.

"Is that a stapler?" asked Spence from behind Issy.

"Silence!" the Priestess exclaimed.

Issy spun around at the dull thud and groan, just in time to see the guard pulling back the butt of the spear with which he'd punished the prisoner for his unholy interruption. The man called Reg rose with a growl, but

---

[*] Unlike former Priestess Leshano, who'd warned that any Ja'naman eating the fruit from the Tree of ... er, Fruitfulness, would turn to stone. Of course, the apple tree had stood in her backyard, and after getting the distinct feeling she was just being stingy, some kids tested the curse by stealing an apple from the tree. When nothing happened, the rest of the villagers subsequently made sure that there were never any ripe apples left for Leshano to pick herself. Needless to say, she didn't remain Village Priestess for long. Ja'namans might be gullible at times, but they're *not* idiots.

received his own blow to the stomach, and doubled over to join his compatriot in the dust.

The Priestess stepped forward to loom over Spence. "How dare you speak in presence of Great Serpent!" she hissed.

"They just wanted to … share news, Priestess Ongswele," Issy said before things could escalate. He shook his head at Reg, who looked on the verge of escalating things.

The Priestess straightened. "What news?"

Issy addressed the captives. "What did you call the Great Serpent again?"

"A stapler," Spence wheezed with a wary glance at the guard who'd knocked his wind out. "It's a stapler."

Issy turned to the Priestess. "The child of the Chicken God says the Great Serpent is called … a stapler."

The Priestess rubbed her chin, looking intrigued – again, just as Issy had hoped. Naming things was a great honour in general, but naming a holy object … well, that was a divine privilege the gods *only* bestowed on The Worthy.

"Hmm," she mused. "Stapler, you say? It sound very … holy. If they *are* children of a god, they know true name of Great Serpent."

She held up the stapler. "I now know name of Great Serpent. He called … *Great Stapler!*"

"Great Stapler!" the crowd echoed, followed by a deep, collective bow.

"Now," the Priestess continued, "I ask Great Ser— Great *Stapler* about gifts from sky."

Sitting down with her legs crossed, she kept her eyes on the captives. Placing the stapler on the ground, she inserted her left hand palm-up between its head and base.

"Oh, Great Stapler, what you command? We eat?" she said, followed by a dramatic pause, because you cannot be a Priestess without mastering the art of a well-timed dramatic pause. "Or we sacrifice?"

She raised her right hand and, after a slight hesitation, slammed it down on the stapler's head.

"Argh!" she screamed.

The rest of the villagers grimaced. They had never gotten used to the Bite of Wisdom and, judging by her expression, neither had Ongswele.

Whimpering in pain, the Priestess took a deep breath and rose with as much grace as she could muster.

"Great Stapler say ... *we eat!*" she announced with tear-filled eyes.

"We eat!" the crowd echoed cheerfully, as this was the outcome they'd hoped for. Each produced from their carry pouch the obligatory offering of vegetables for the Holy Feast.

However, as per any other feast held by people with mixed tastes and opinions, it didn't take long for the merriment to turn sour.

"No, Seno, you barbeque last time!" a woman protested at the suggestion from the man next to her.

"Yes," another woman backed her, "you men always overcook everything. Always drink and talk too much while meat burn. You no look me like that, Seno. You know it true. Today, women make stew!"

Glancing at the horrified Reg and Spence – aka the main ingredients – Issy ignored the heated discussions flaring up around him as he approached the Priestess. "We cannot do this," he said. "Remember my great-grandfather's warning?"

"Yes," Ongswele said, her eyes still glistening, "and we no more eat our people."

She pointed at the prisoners. "But *they*; they *no* our people." And before Issy could say anything, she added, "*If* Chicken God send them, she send them in egg. We eat egg, so we eat them."

Ongswele's face stated she wasn't going to budge, so Issy had no choice but to change his approach, and leaned in to whisper something in her ear.

The Priestess was speechless for a while, but eventually nodded unhappily and shook the Staff of Truth once again. The crowd gradually quieted down with a mixture of confusion and barely hidden annoyance at the interruption of their dinner plans.

Ongswele held the stapler to her ear for a few seconds before lowering it again. "Great Stapler now say he no more decide fate of Chicken God children," she said, glancing nervously at Issy. "With first light of sun, we go to Fire Mountain. *Tuma* decide what to do."

The villagers didn't look happy. Neither did the two prisoners. However, Issy had at least bought them some time, but having just spent his only currency, he knew he wouldn't be able to buy any more.

CHAPTER 11

Phealix was used to being on her feet, and walked the *Jolly Dodger's* decks as much as possible to encourage exercise among the crew. In fact, the first thing she told recruits was, "If you aren't fit, you aren't fit for the *Dodger*."

However, traversing the flat decks of a ship wasn't the same as hiking across uneven, muddy jungle terrain, and a sudden downpour of rain a few minutes earlier hadn't helped their plight either. They were exhausted. Their captors must have realised this, as they called a halt, much to the relief of the captain and her Vahltans.

Phealix waved over the group's leader, who warily stepped closer. He however stopped as she pointed at his mid-section, most likely thinking she was pointing at the gun protruding from his pouch. To clear things up, the Faylin shook her head and pointed again to the water gourd hanging from his hip cord on the opposite side, and performed a drinking motion with her hand.

Relaxing somewhat, the man carefully removed the gourd and handed it to Phealix while two other men kept their spears ready, just in case the blue cat-like creature tried anything. Accepting the gourd, she stepped back with a slight bow of gratitude and took a seat on the ground a few metres away. Other water gourds were passed among the Vahltans, who promptly emptied the containers, much to the displeasure of the gourds' thirsty owners.

Phealix's throat begged her to empty her own container, but her mind insisted there were more important things to attend to than quenching thirst. Taking a few sips, she looked about to make sure she wasn't being observed before she extracted a small metal vial from her robe and emptied its contents into the gourd.

Thank Zolt Franki had managed to salvage this from the shuttle, she thought.

Flicking the empty vial into a bush, Phealix rose and approached the natives' leader. She pointed to the gourd, and then to him, followed by another drinking motion. The man accepted the container hesitantly, but brought it to lips to finish the last bit of water. Wiping his mouth, he re-attached the empty gourd to his waist.

Noticing the grin on Phealix's face, he frowned. "You strange," he said.

"Don't worry," Phealix said, "it's about to get a whole lot stranger for you, buddy."

Of course, the man didn't understand her, but her face must have said something he didn't like, because he suddenly seemed ready to be … somewhere else.

"Come!" he shouted, waving for his men to haul the prisoners to their feet. "We go, now!"

Satisfied that everyone was ready, the leader set off at a fast pace, regularly glancing over his shoulder at the grin now baked onto the blue female's face.

•••

Many people are of the opinion that a Dumb Planet is a Dumb Planet, and while they're technically correct, some Dumb Planets are, in reality, "dumber" than others. For instance, Wahyoo VIII is much dumber than Earth, which in turn is only slightly dumber than Gloob but considerably dumber than Earth Too.[*]

So, yes, officially, a planet's dumbness has nothing to do with the natural/potential intellect of its inhabitants. Unofficially, the subject is still under debate. For now, however, Dumb Planets are scored on their technological advancements, with bonus points added for advances in space travel. Which is why Earth is still a step behind the Gloobians, who have recently achieved interstellar space travel.

Planets like Wahyoo VIII, however, are right at the top (or bottom, depending on your point of view) of technological dumbness. And even though unauthorised contact with a Dumb Planet is strictly prohibited, the Unyun Federation makes a point of recording and analysing local forms and methods of communication, as you never know when you might need to reach out to someone, dumb or not. But although scientists have studied emancipated individuals of Wahyoo VIII who'd been abducted and sold into slavery, their language is

---

[*] You might be thrilled to hear that Earth Too is also mainly populated by humans – either those who'd been abducted, emancipated and Acclimatised to life in the rest of the Charted Universe, or their descendants. But don't get too excited about the prospect of having a happy reunion one day. Most humans *out there* detest "Earthlings", and they're looking forward to Official First Contact with Earth as much as a Malibu housewife looks forward to sobriety. So, if a human from Earth Too ever asks you where you're from, just say Backwater. It's not a perfect answer, but you'll be better off.

still primitive, which means vernaculites can only interpret the basics of local dialects.

But, as pointed out by scientists – who'd by now given up to pursue more important work, like levelling up their characters in the new online GalactaBattle roleplaying game – the basics are better than nothing.

•••

Phealix only knew the basics of Wahyoo VIII – basically that it wasn't a good idea to be on it. She'd heard the stories of savages; the scattered tribes of cannibals and headhunters forming the bulk of the population.

She wasn't sure if communicating with a native would help, but her list of alternative options had burnt up along with the shuttle. As she could understand what the natives were saying, she just hoped the vernaculites with which she'd spiked the leader's water, would work the other way around on this planet.

The Faylin's thoughts on the matter were interrupted when the party's leader brought the procession to a halt with a raised fist. The other men turned outwards, spears at the ready.

"What's goi—" Franki started, but the leader cut him off by clamping a hand around the Vahltan's beak.

"No speak," the tribesman whispered. "No sound."

Phealix found this strange, as she couldn't hear a thing, until she realised that's what the problem was: she couldn't hear *a thing*. Not an insect. Not a bird. Nothing. Everything had fallen silent, which was, as far as she was concerned, very un-jungly. She scanned their surroundings apprehensively, but couldn't see much other than more of the same trees, vegetation and moss she'd seen up till now.

The silence was finally broken by a guttural sound, which drew every eye towards a nearby bush, whose branches and leaves quivered as something unseen moved behind it.

"Night Aahp," the leader said under his breath and released Franki's beak to grip his spear with both hands.

"What's a Night A—" Demi said, but apparently not enough under her breath, as a huge shadow broke from its cover and charged the group with a deep howl that froze the blood along with everything else.

CHAPTER 12

"Night Aahp!" the leader shrieked when his muscles unfroze to meet the charging beast head-on.

Phealix had never seen a Night Aahp, but she'd once seen a gorilla in a zoo, and this creature made her think of one, only with much larger eyes glowing amber in the scattered moonlight, a much larger mouth baring much more fangs and a much larger body – not just in length with its thick, long tail, but also in height. Even on all fours, its back stood slightly taller than the Faylin.

The creature's size, however, did nothing to impede the speed with which it moved on its muscular arms and legs. It was on the group before the armed natives could manage a handful of steps, and its powerful arm swept the first man aside before he could fully turn.

When the man's body hit the ground a few metres away, it skidded to a halt and rolled over; his lifeless eyes staring at the heavens above. Phealix knew they were lifeless, not just because that's what they looked like, but also because the audible snap of the neck accompanying the blow had announced that this native's time among the living had run out.

The warriors' leader barely had time to duck the next blow directed at his head, but he wasn't so lucky the second time around when the thick extremity swung back, sending him flying into the trunk of a nearby tree.

The bound Vahltan that'd stood behind him had even less luck, as the creature seized him by the arms, raised him up and sank its large fangs into his thin neck. The other Vahltans looked on in horror as Danni's body dropped to the ground next to his head. To escape the same fate as their ex comrade, they stopped looking on and opted for a more prudent course of action by scattering in various directions. Phealix couldn't blame them; Vahltans had keen survival instincts, and her own instincts told her that following her crew *was* the smart thing to do.

She was about to do just that when she saw the beast closing in on the fallen leader lying against the tree, gasping for air. She had no vernaculites left, and couldn't afford to let their best shot at survival be ripped apart. Besides, leaving someone to die – even a "savage" that probably would have served her on a plate for a nice family dinner, or severed her head for whatever reason they severed heads around here – wasn't her soul's default setting.

Spotting the stunner that had dropped to the ground during the man's airborne trip, Phealix dived for it. As the creature lifted the hapless man into the air and opened its jaws for another kill, the Faylin finished her dive with a roll and raised the stunner with bound wrists. Normally, one shot would've been enough to bring a man down, but this was no man. Not one for taking unnecessary risks, she fired three shots that *tshooped* into the creature's back. On the third, the beast stiffened and toppled over along with its prey, who nearly got crushed by the large body slamming into the ground beside him. While Phealix kept the stunner trained on the unmoving hairy hulk, the natives stormed in to make sure the creature remained unmoving, stabbing it with spears until they were sure it wouldn't get another chance at slaughtering them.

Shock and anger welled up inside Phealix over the beast's demise, despite the violence it had inflicted on the group. With her aversion to pointless killing, she never wanted it dead. But she couldn't do or say anything that would compromise her and her crew's own chances of survival, so she kept her face neutral as two men helped their leader to his feet.

The man winced as he touched the back of his head. His eyes struggled to focus, but when they eventually re-established communication with the brain, it told them to shift their attention to the object in the blue creature's hands.

"You give back," the man slurred, pointing at the stunner with a wobbly finger that hadn't yet boarded the focus train.

Glancing at the other natives closing in with blood-stained spearheads pointed at her throat, Phealix dropped the stunner and stepped back, hands raised.

The leader warily picked up the weapon and returned it to his pouch. "Go find others!" he ordered, waving his hand in the direction the Vahltans had fled. One of his men stayed behind while the others set off in pursuit.

When the men disappeared from view, the leader picked up his spear and turned back to Phealix, looking confused. "You save me," he said.

"It's a pleasure," Phealix said and held out her bound hands. "Now, I'd appreciate it if you could return the favour by letting us go."

The man's previous look of confusion paled in comparison to the one replacing it.

"I … hear you," he said, gobsmacked.

"Well, I'm glad your ears work," Phealix said, trying not to sound relieved that the vernaculites had kicked in. Sure, the man might never win a spelling bee, but at least she now had *something*.

"No," the tribesman said, "I *hear* you."

"You mean you *understand* me."

"That what I say."

Phealix had to remind herself of the vernaculites' limitations. "Of course," she said. "I, uh, *hear* you too."

The man's frown deepened as he pointed at the Faylin's face. "I see lips move *this* way, but ears hear *other* way. How it happen?"

Phealix knew this wasn't a conversation she'd be able to finish within her lifetime, so she just eyed him ominously and said, "Magic."

This had the opposite effect to what she'd intended. The man leapt back and raised his spear in alarm.

"Witch!" he hissed, glancing at his comrade.

The latter had been watching the conversation closely without understanding half of it, but that one word struck him like a rock. "Witch?" he hissed back.

"Witch," the leader confirmed.

"What we do, Roro?"

"We go home. Wise One know what to do."

"Who—" Phealix began.

"You no speak!" spat the leader, aka Roro. "You no magic us! Wise One decide fate of witch. Now, sit!"

With no other choice, Phealix sat and waited for the other natives to return with their recaptured prisoners.

"You got all, Tangata?" Roro said, watching the Vahltans being lined up once more.

Tangata nodded and looked at Phealix. "She no run?"

"No, she try to magic me."

"She *witch?*" Tangata gasped.

"She witch," Roro said grimly.

Tangata gave the universal whistle given by every whistling-enabled individual in the universe when they know someone's in trouble other than themselves.[*]

"Wise One hate witch," he said.

Roro looked unsettled, which didn't boost Phealix's positivity levels. "I know, Tangata," he said. "I know."

•••

"So," Phealix said over her shoulder as the procession continued along the footpath cutting through the thick vegetation, "the creature that attacked us; the … Night Aahp? Why would it attack a group like that?"

"I no talk to witch," Roro said, avoiding looking at the Faylin by looking at everything else.

Phealix turned her attention back to the path ahead. "I'm sorry about your man," she said.

"Which one?" Roro snapped. "Man Night Aahp kill, or man *you* kill?"

He touched the stunner on his hip as if it was a hot coal. "You kill Hinga," he growled. "Hinga good man."

Phealix kept quiet for a while as she pondered how to broach the subject without making things worse. "I can bring him back to life, you know?" she said at length, and held back a grin as Roro missed a step behind her. "Your friend; he can live again."

After a long, contemplative pause, Roro said, "You use many words. *Too many* words!"

---

[*] There is no whistle for the latter. No one knows why.

Phealix walked on in silence without pushing the matter, knowing the seed had been planted. It didn't take long for Roro's hopes to water it.

"Hinga breathe air again?" he said, keeping his voice low so the others wouldn't hear.

"Yes," Phealix said. "But I must see to him soon before it's too late. All I need is some water and privacy."

"Water?"

"Yes, I need to … bless some water."

As she glanced back, Roro's face said he didn't know much about witchcraft and therefore didn't know how to argue against its strange rituals.

"Okay," he said after another pause. "But I watch."

"You can watch, as long as you don't stand too close. It will … interfere with the magic."

Roro brought the group to a halt. "We stop!" he said.

"Why?" Tangata asked, perplexed.

"Witch heal Hinga."

"But Roro—"

"She heal Hinga!" Roro repeated resolutely. "No fight me, Tangata."

Tangata didn't look happy, but he didn't voice any further objections.

"Take Hinga round bend," Roro said, pointing ahead, and waited for this to be done. With a glance at the Vahltans, he added, "If anything bad happen, you kill men of witch. You hear?"

"I hear," said Tangata.

"Good," Roro said. Turning to Phealix with a stern expression, he handed her the water gourd he'd refilled earlier. "You no trick us. You trick us, you die."

●●●

Phealix wasn't planning on dying. At least not anytime soon. She didn't fear death as such, but she *did* prefer to go out in style one day. And getting skewered in a jungle by a man who couldn't string a decent sentence together didn't fit into her style guide.

At the bend, a few metres from the tribesman's unconscious body, Phealix turned.

"That's as far as you go, Roro," she said.

The man stopped. "Remember, no tricks," he said.

"No tricks," Phealix promised emptily.

The nervous man watched in silence as the Faylin approached his friend's body.

Keeping her back to Roro, Phealix dropped to her knees by Hinga's side and tried to ignore her own nerves nibbling at her outer calm. Earlier, she had worried that the stunner-shot man would wake up too early and thwart her miraculous "resurrection". Now she was afraid he wouldn't wake up in time.

Except for a few rare cases of fatalities, stunners were an effective way to incapacitate adversaries without killing them. It was a method she and her crew had been using to great effect, because permanently eliminating a source of income wasn't a good business strategy. Incapacitating them today to raid them again tomorrow just made more sense; an idea that was slowly but surely taking root among the pirate fraternity. It was also the first and most important entry in *The Code*: "Thou shalt not kill … unless thou hast no other choice."[*]

However, a stunner wasn't always the most reliable weapon, as the longevity of its effects varied widely among species as well as an individual's size, clothing,

---

[*] It's difficult to explain to some pirates that "no other choice" does *not* include when an unarmed captive lying face-down on the floor startles you with a sneeze.

diet and sleep patterns, among others. Despite his ample girth, Hinga wasn't that big, so the shot that felled him had disrupted all but the most basic bodily functions.

The man's shallow breathing made Phealix nervous. He'd still be out for a while, which posed a problem, as Phealix didn't have a while. Her glance back at the anxious Roro confirmed this. He wouldn't wait forever. This had to happen *now*.

Feeling somewhat silly, Phealix raised the water gourd above her head and started swaying while chanting gibberish, hoping the show would make enough of an impact on the leader. It must have, because she heard the crushing of leaves as Roro stepped closer behind her. Fortunately, he stopped again, either afraid of her warning about negatively affecting the witchcraft, or being negatively affected by it himself. Regardless, he stayed put and watched silently as Phealix's "blessing" ended in a crescendo.

Satisfied her ploy had worked, Phealix brought the gourd back down and bent over Hinga's body. She had performed this trick a few times in the past, and while it usually worked, it wasn't a given. Pinching the man's nose, she poured water into his mouth before clamping it shut. The body's natural response to drowning kicked in, and when the water geysered up between his lips, the rest of Hinga's body followed swiftly as he sat bolt upright. Patting the coughing native on the back, Phealix heard behind her the expected rush of footsteps.

"He alive," Roro breathed, kneeling by his friend. Despite his hopes, he obviously hadn't believed the "magic" would work. "You make Hinga alive!"

Chest heaving, Hinga looked up at him. "I … dead?" he asked.

"You dead," Roro said. "But witch make you alive."

"Witch!" Hinga exclaimed, looking as though he preferred being dead again.

"Yes, but now you alive – it only thing that important. You no worry about witch. We take her to Wise One."

As Roro helped him to his feet, Hinga looked relieved to know that, whatever decision was to be made, *he* wasn't the one who had to make it.

Contrarily, Phealix felt another shot of anxiousness speeding through her nervous system, because *she* knew that, whatever decision was made, the odds were against it going in her favour.

CHAPTER 13

Phealix had – perhaps foolishly – hoped Roro's tribe would turn out to be one of the more … "normal" ones. But as they reached the village, this already slim hope went on an even stricter diet.

A wooden fence, comprising slanted, sharpened poles facing outwards, marked the perimeter of the village. Spaced a foot apart, nearly every pole was adorned by whitish shapes of various shapes and sizes; some looking distinctly – and disturbingly – non-native.

Skulls. Of course they would be skulls, Phealix thought with a grimace. There had to be thousands of them!

Someone close to Phealix had been on Wahyoo VIII and lived to tell the tale – a tale he also told her. Most tribes, by tradition, were cannibals or headhunters, and the once flesh-covered ornaments adorning the fence erased any doubt over the favourite recreational activities of this particular village.[*]

---

[*] SPOILER ALERT: For those wondering if it was headhunting, you're absolutely right. For those who'd been looking forward to figuring it out later, the spoiler *was* preceded by the appropriate warning. Just saying …

The décor didn't end at the fence either. A mishmash of skulls were proudly displayed above the door of each bamboo hut dotting the cleared landscape between the trees. Even the domed structures themselves looked like the tops of heads buried in the soil. And while many of the decorative skulls looked ancient, others seemed disconcertingly fresh.

Phealix shivered at the sight, and then shivered even more when she noticed an open spot where her own skull might soon become a permanent part of village life.

...

The group reached a large, round clearing where a lone three-horned goat sauntered about in search of something to eat amidst the hard-packed, mossy soil. Roro led them to the farthest edge of the clearing, where a flat stone slab rested atop two stone blocks with a myriad of skulls etched into them.

Phealix glanced at the brown-stained slab. She recognised dried blood when she saw it and wished she hadn't seen it. Fortunately, her attention was diverted when the tribesmen forced her and her crew to their knees.

Roro continued on towards a large, upright drum a few metres away. Leaning against it was a large bone; its ends wrapped in leather. Dropping his spear, the tribesman picked up the bone and, using both arms, swung it against the hardened leather of the drumhead.

Phealix and the Vahltans flinched as the instrument's deep boom reverberated through the air. Roro continued to beat the drum with a slow rhythm until the first of the villagers started filing into the clearing, rubbing sleep from their eyes with a mixture of intrigue and annoyance at being roused from their slumber.

Satisfied that all had heard the call, Roro placed the bone back against the drum and waited patiently as more people shuffled into the clearing. When the arrival of villagers finally tapered off, a cacophony of whistles prompted the crowd ahead to step aside, forming a pathway for the procession making its way towards the slab. The group was led by six well-matured men and women using walking staffs to inch their way forward. They however looked like teenagers compared to the man behind them. Carried on a bamboo dais by six burly men, the weathered man sat atop a huge, two-horned skull that had been converted into a chair.

Halting before the prisoners, the carriers groaned as they carefully lowered the dais to the ground. Six other men brought forth six wooden stumps, which they placed three-three on either side of the dais. When all six elderly people took a seat on their allocated stumps, the old man on the skull stomped his staff on the dais to quiet the murmuring crowd. The man's frail, bony arms had lost interest in holding any object heavier than themselves, so he waited patiently for one of the men to retrieve the staff he'd just dropped.

"I no like to wake up from drum, Roro," he said with a crackly voice as the staff was returned to his gnarled hand. "But I see you bring gifts. We no have gifts like these in long time."

However, Phealix wasn't sure how much he could actually see, because if the eyes were the windows to the soul, this man's windows needed a serious polish. Yet, despite their age-induced milkiness, they seemed to have retained their intensity as the man stared at the strange beings kneeling before him. His skin cracked nearly as much as his voice when he lifted his hairless brows to get a better look. "What they are?" he asked.

"*They*, I no know," Roro said, indicating the Vahltans before turning to the Faylin. "But *she* … she *witch*."

A gasp erupted from the crowd; a gasp that also turned into coughs among the eldest elders. When he recovered from his own bout of coughing, the old man leaned forward on his skull, but only slightly, as his bent figure seemed naturally inclined to topple out of the chair without pushing the boundaries.

"How you know she witch?" he said.

Roro took a deep breath.

"In beginning, I *no hear* what she say, oh Wise One," he said, and tapped at his ear. "Then she magic me. *Now*, I hear."

The villagers gasped hesitantly and sporadically, as they obviously weren't convinced of the … magicality of this revelation. Hence the mostly disappointed looks.

"Also," Roro continued quickly when a dubious look crossed the Wise One's face too, "Hinga dead. But witch magic him. Now Hinga *alive*."

To make up for the previous moment, the villagers put some extra effort into their follow-up gasp. *This* was more like it.

The Wise One's eyes narrowed as he looked at Hinga. "It true?"

"It true," Hinga confirmed, shifting uncomfortably under the weight of the attention being shovelled onto him by the staring, murmuring crowd.

The old man leaned back in his chair, or at least as far back as his back allowed, which wasn't very far.

"I *hate* witch," he said, his expression darkening as he glared at Phealix. "You *know* what we do with witch, Roro."

Roro appeared troubled as he glanced at the stone slab. "Yes, oh Wise One."

The Wise One looked at the Elders seated beside him. "What Elders say?"

Still reeling from their first bout of coughing, they merely nodded their vote.

"After sacrifice, witch head come to me," the Wise One said, and swept a glare of disgust across the bound Vahltans. "She make man-bird from mud. Evil creatures no walk among us! First, cut head off man-bird."

Two tribesmen grabbed Franki by the arms and dragged him to the ceremonial altar, upon which he was slammed face down somewhat unceremoniously. The Vahltan attempted to writhe free, but the powerful hands held him firmly in place.

When the rest of the Vahltans' panicked faces turned towards their captain, Phealix glared at Roro.

"Hey, I saved your life!" she hissed. "*And* that of your friend. Are you seriously just going to let them kill us?"

Roro looked like someone who'd expected a specific topic of conversation to come up at some stage but still wasn't quite ready when the topic finally reared its head.[*]

"What witch say?" the Wise One asked.

"Nothing, oh Wise One," Roro said, avoiding eye-contact with the Faylin.

"You *cannot* do this," Phealix pleaded as a short, burly man walked up to the altar, dragging behind him a large, crude blade.

---

[*] Parents know this feeling well, especially when the "Where do babies come from?" conversation pops up for the first time. However, the first discussion isn't nearly as awkward as the follow-up discussion a few years later when the birds-and-the-bees talk simply won't cut it anymore.

Roro kept looking straight ahead. "It tradition," he said. "I can *no* do anything."

"You *have to*," Phealix tried one final time as the man by Franki raised the huge blade above his head with a grunt. "Please!"

Just as the man prepared to bring the blade down, Roro put up a hand. "Wait!" he commanded.

The executioner, aka (officially) the Head Head-collector, aka (to his friends) Big Monna, paused. His uncertain eyes darted between Roro and the Wise One as a bead of sweat ran down his cheek. He was (also officially) the strongest man in the village, but the big, long blade didn't become lighter above his head. Even *his* strength had its limits.

The Wise One sat up semi-straight. "What you doing, Roro?" he said, looking as puzzled as the rest of the crowd, except for the Head Head-collector, who didn't care who did what as long as they did it quickly. The man started to sweat profusely, with streams of perspiration running down his tortured face and shaking arms.

Seeming somewhat uncertain himself, Roro placed his palms together and lowered his head.

"My apologies, oh Wise One, but I think maybe witch not evil. Maybe she … good witch."

"*Good* witch?" the Wise One exclaimed, looking at Roro as if he was a talking Night Aahp with a lisp. "I *no ever* hear of good witch! Why you think she good?"

Roro straightened. "She save Hinga," he said. "Bad witch no do that."

"Maybe witch have evil plan," the Wise One said.

"I no think saving Hinga is evil plan," Roro said, and when the Wise One raised a shaky finger to argue the point, he added, "*And* she save me."

"She save *you*?"

"Yes, oh Wise One."

"How?"

Roro sighed. He seemed reluctant to do what he was about to do, but nonetheless removed the stunner from his pouch and held it aloft for everyone to see.

"What that?" the Wise One said, shifting in his seat.

"It … er … Stick of Silent Lightning," Roro said, adding an ominous tone to the last two words, which had the desired effect. The Elders and the crowd looked upon the sleek weapon with curious fear. The Head Head-collector took the opportunity to lower his blade before it could slip from his hands and sever his foot.

"Witch use stick to kill Night Aahp before Night Aahp kill me," Roro continued, looking at his fellow headhunters, who nodded in confirmation.

"Small stick kill Night Aahp?" the Wise One said dubiously. "No, I no think so. You Head Headhunter, Roro. You clever. But she witch. She trick eyes – make you see what *she* want you see."

Roro, aka the Head Headhunter, had been expecting this reaction. He approached Phealix and hesitantly presented the stunner to her. The guards, however, showed no hesitation in raising their weapons, ready to use them at a moment's notice.

"You show Teahupo'o tribe how stick work," the Head Headhunter said, nodding towards the goat who'd finally found a tuft of grass to graze on. "But you do bad thing to Teahupo'os, Teahupo'os do bad thing to you. You hear?"

Glancing at the spears, Phealix nodded and took the stunner. Getting up, she motioned for the villagers between her and the goat to stand aside, which they did without pause because, silent or not, being struck by lightning did not sound pleasant.

With its third horn pointing up from the middle of its forehead, the goat stared at Phealix sideways while its jaws worked furiously to grind its midnight snack into a pulp. Taking careful aim, the Faylin squeezed the trigger. With a *tshoop*, a white ball of energy struck the goat's rump, upon which it abruptly stiffened and keeled over.

Although only the goat had been shot, each member of the crowd looked as though they themselves had been hit. All stood as stiff as the unmoving goat now lying on its side, its legs pointed outward. The villagers couldn't find the courage to complete their gasp this time round, nor to close their mouths.

Phealix turned back to Roro. "See," she said, handing him the stunner, "I *no do bad thing*."

Roro missed the mocking male gruffness with which Phealix had said that last bit, and as she returned to her spot among the Vahltans, the Head Headhunter turned to the Wise One.

"Witch can no trick *all* Teahupo'o eyes," Roro said, gesturing at the crowd before turning to the Wise One. "And she can *no ever* trick eyes of Elders."

Having overcome his initial shock of witnessing a stick spitting lightning, the Wise One turned to the Elders, who didn't know what to say. Apparently, neither did the Wise One, who took some time to rub his gnarled chin while coming up with the right words to approach this delicate matter.

Finally, with a great deal of effort, the old man rose from his skull-chair. Shooing away the men coming to his aid, he approached the prisoners. The momentum of his hunched-over body carried him forward, but fortunately his staff kept him from keeling over when he stopped in front of Phealix. He leaned over and took a moment to stare into the Faylin's eyes before he eventually managed to semi-straighten himself again. His gaze swept the crowd and settled on the Head Headhunter.

"Maybe you right, Roro," the Wise One said, and spat towards the side, hitting the foot of a hunter who kept his pose professional despite a slight wince. "*Maybe* she good witch. But *we* no decide. At first light, we go to Fire Mountain."

Following his gaze, Phealix looked over her shoulder, where the blue-hued light from the two moons traced the outlines of a nearby cone-shaped mountain that had previously been hidden by treetops. With soft orange light crowning its steamy peak, the mountain looked like a volcano. Mainly because it was one. It certainly wasn't the biggest volcano Phealix had ever seen, but from this angle it was picture-perfect, as if it had been painted by an artist who had the right idea of what a truly majestic volcano should look like; just not what it should look like in proportion to everything else.

When she looked back, Phealix's eyes once more locked with those of the Wise One.

"There," he said coldly, "we let Tuma decide."

CHAPTER 14

"**W**e were here first!" Issy said, crossing his arms.

"But we send Runner to book sacrifice!" Roro protested.

Issy pointed at the older etchings on a rock next to the pathway leading up the volcano.

"That's your booking from last time, Roro," Issy said. "Nothing new has been added."

Roro approached the rock for a closer inspection.

"I no see how it happen," he said, mystified, then glanced at one of the other Teahupo'oan tribesmen, who just shrugged. The Head Headhunter's expression turned into one that hoped, for the Runner's sake, that he was lying dead in a ditch somewhere.[*]

"Well," he said stubbornly, "you also no book."

Issy sighed. "Fine, no one booked. So, what do we do now?"

---

[*] Haurangi *was*, in fact, lying in a ditch, but he wasn't dead. He did however have a broken leg, because he'd ignored the golden rule of Village Runners: Never drink and run; a rule Haurangi's wife was sure to bring up countless times during the remainder of his Running career.

"We, er, sacrifice together?" Roro suggested.

Issy raised a querying eyebrow at his fellow tribesmen, who huddled for a quick deliberation before one of them turned back and nodded unhappily.

"It's settled then," Issy said. "We will sacrifice together."

Walking up to a pool of lime-green liquid within a basin cut into the rock face, Issy picked up one of many wooden bowls on the basin's rim. He dipped it into the pool and passed it on. While other tribesmen took over the distribution process, Issy filled another bowl and proffered it to Reg.

"What the heck is that?" Reg said, eyeing the liquid warily.

"You must drink this," Issy said.

Sniffing the contents, the Scout grimaced. "Are you kidding?" he said. "I'm not putting that filth in my mouth!"

Issy eyed him sternly. "You *must*," he said. "It makes Tuma happy." Nodding towards his fellow tribesmen, he added, "More importantly, it keeps *them* happy."

Among the men was Gobatsha, whose face had stopped bleeding from the shot that had nearly taken off the top of his head along with the top of his shield. Although someone had since removed the shards from his face, his vengeful look seemed likely to stay put for the foreseeable future. The fact that he now aimed the look at Reg while tossing his spear from one hand to the other gave the Scout some fuel for reconsideration.

"If you don't drink it, you will die right here," Issy said, adding another dash of fuel. "Is that what you want?"

Reg looked to where the other tribe's prisoners were also forced to drink the vile-looking contents of the bowls being passed among them. Seeing the Faylin and her Vahltans, his face hardened. No, he didn't want to die, but above that, he had a score to settle, so he'd do whatever needed to be done. He just didn't want to be the first one doing it, so he took the bowl and passed it to Spence.

The ensign's face protested. "Why must *I* go first?"

"Just drink it," Reg ordered.

After a pause, the ensign took the bowl, took a sip, swallowed hard, and doubled over to retch.

"If you don't keep it in, you'll get more until you do," Issy warned. "So I suggest you keep it in."

Taking a deep breath, the Ronian straightened back up. His usually pale face looked even paler, but as he clearly didn't want any more of whatever he'd just had, he kept it in and passed the bowl to Reg.

Taking a sip himself, Reg couldn't blame Spence for his reaction. The vile, bitter liquid clung to every part of his mouth and throat. Coughing, he fought back the urge to vomit as he handed the bowl back to Issy.

When all the prisoners had drunk and retained their share, the tribesmen had some themselves. Although their reactions weren't as severe as those of their captives, their sour looks conveyed their own distaste for the liquid.

Last to drink, Issy returned his bowl to the basin.

"Time to go," the short man said, gesturing for Reg and Spence to fall in behind him as he started leading the procession up the steep path.

Reg suddenly felt what condemned inmates must have felt when they were led to their execution. However, at least those inmates *knew* what was coming. Reg, on the other hand, had no clue, and he couldn't decide whether it was a good thing.

CHAPTER 15

Militorate – Phealix would have recognised those uniforms anywhere.[*] The mystery behind the blind attack on her shuttle had finally been solved. She was going to have a word with those two.

But now was not the time. Now was the time to breathe.

Earlier, she'd thought the trek through the jungle had been unpleasant, but this hike up the volcano's steep, rocky path was beyond nauseating. And the aftertaste of the liquid they'd been forced to drink earlier did nothing to alleviate her feeling of discomfort.

At least the Scouts ahead didn't seem to be faring much better, with the human periodically touching his

---

[*] This is kind of the point of uniforms. Still, if you know any member of the Unyun Militorate's Designer Corps, please tell them their goal has been achieved. Also, please heap some praise on them, because that's the only recognition they'll receive from anyone. No member of the Designer Corps has ever received a medal for their work, which is a bit unfair, seeing as everyone else's medals get pinned to their work.

stomach and the Ronian failing to stop himself from retching now and again.

Her moment of satisfaction was however short-lived when she herself doubled over with an "Uuuuhhh!" that also, regrettably, expelled nothing but air. She shouldn't have watched the Militor pair so closely, especially not the dry-heaving Ronian.[*]

Dry-wiping the foul air from her lips, she decided it best to think about something else, and glanced down at her new attire. The grass skirt irritated her skin, while the leather wrapping covering her mammarian area was *way* too tight.

The Elders had deemed her strange, dirty robe unfit for ceremonial purposes, and had ordered her to be dressed in the local fashion. In general, Phealix had no problem with her body. She was immaculately built, even among Faylins, who were widely known for their athletic physique – excluding, of course, those who had developed a penchant for fast-foods. However, the short skirt didn't cover nearly enough, especially with her tall

---

[*] As with contagious yawning, contagious vomiting/retching (CVR) is a widespread phenomenon. The exact cause of this psychological reaction isn't clear, although the prevailing theory holds that it proactively aids in protecting members within a group against food poisoning. While non-lethal in general, CVR can be harmful, as Norman Lipschitz found out the hard way at a bar in California. Spending the next three months in traction in a local hospital, Norman had ample time to develop a few simple steps to avoid the hazards associated with CVR: 1) Stop feeding your buddy shots you know he can't handle; 2) Avoid looking at your buddy when the inevitable happens; 3) If you *do* look and the inevitable happens to *you*, don't vomit on the boots of one of the locals; and, most importantly, 4) If you choose to ignore steps one to three, it's best not to do so in a Hells Angels bar.

frame. So, yes, she was comfortable with her body, but not with the idea of everyone seeing *everything*. Which is why she'd fashioned some makeshift underwear from the material of her robe, refusing to go anywhere without it … or without her boots.

When the locals had started to object, they'd stopped just as quickly. There are certain expressions that are pretty much the same across most species, and the one on Phealix's face had been one of them. Thus, for the health and safety of the tribe, they hadn't pushed the matter any further. They were happy to keep her crew covered as much as possible, though, which is why they were still fully clothed.

Phealix glanced at the Vahltans with envy, then back at her own garb. She looked ridiculous!

With anger having successfully shoved her nausea aside, Phealix's thoughts turned to the rest of her crew on the *Jolly Dodger*, who should have responded to the shuttle's emergency signal by now.

What in Zolt's name was taking them so long?

She had hoped the little excursion up the mountain would give the *Dodger* enough time to find its stranded crew and swoop in for a rescue. But with each gruelling step, her hope dwindled faster than her energy levels – both of which might soon be depleted.

CHAPTER 16

Rubbing his stomach did nothing to ease the compression building up in Reg's digestive tract. Yet he kept doing it.

Every inch of his torso felt packed to capacity with layer upon layer of solidness, like those Russian dolls one of the officers at the Academy used to collect. Apart from some vague memory that they hailed from Earth, Reg didn't know much about Russians or their dolls. But he hoped that they and the other inhabitants of Earth had similar digestive problems, because the rest of humanity shouldn't be made to suffer alone.

Thankfully, after an hour's hike up the side of the volcano, the muscles in Reg's legs and back were aching enough to split his mind's attention between the two competing bodily issues. Just ahead of the lieutenant, Spence wasn't doing much better, sporting the face of a hyperventilating blowfish.

"How much farther … do we have … to go?" the ensign huffed.

Reg didn't answer, because the top of the mountain was clear for all to see, and answering stupid questions wasn't really his thing.

"Right to the top," Issy volunteered, pointing at the mountaintop.

He had to be used to answering stupid questions by stupid people all the time, Reg thought, glancing from Issy to the other tribesmen leading the way. Which led to another thought.

"You don't speak like the other villagers," Reg said. "Why?"

"I, uh, read," Issy said.

"Well, you're certainly not reading anything *they're* writing," Reg said, nodding towards the other Ja'namans.

"No, the parchments I read aren't from the village."

"Who wrote it then?"

"I don't know," Issy said, his voice perking up at the chance to discuss something he obviously couldn't discuss with his fellow tribesmen. "Several people. But I don't know them. They're not from my village, nor from any other village I know of. All the tribal traders and travellers I've ever met speak roughly the same way the Ja'namans and Teahupo'oans do. The language in the parchments I read is like nothing I've ever seen. And so are the parchments themselves. They're not the same as our leather parchments – the ones with the pictures in them. No, these parchments are called books. Do you know books? Most of my current language skills come from a book called *Basic Language for Basic People*. But novels are my favourite! They contain *words*, not pictures. And these words tell stories, almost like the ones we tell around the fire at night – only better."

"You don't say," Reg said flatly, already regretting opening the sluice gates without knowing how to close them again.

"Oh, yes, you should try it!" Issy continued, not used to sarcasm.[*] "I read one about pirates, planets, spaceships and all kinds of other strange things. It was a bit difficult to follow, but still, I found it fascinating! I tried reading to the villagers, too, but they didn't want any part of it. Except for my friend, Mamella. Sometimes, she asks me to read her stories while the others are sleeping and—"

"Yes, yes, stories are great," Reg interrupted this particular story, which clearly wasn't going to end any time soon without third-party assistance. "If the books aren't from another village, where did they come from?"

"From the Metal Mountain," Issy said.

"What metal mountain?"

Much to the annoyance of the tribesmen behind them, Issy halted. "*That* Metal Mountain," he said, pointing into the distance.

Reg's eyes followed the finger. It wasn't difficult to spot the colossal structure resting half-buried, half-overgrown and half on the border of the jungle and the grassy plain below. A straight, water-filled canal ran behind the structure along a significant stretch of grassland.

Well, that looks promising, Reg thought, then noticed the Faylin also eyeing the structure thoughtfully. Crap, not good!

------

[*] While space travel is a great way to measure a planet's technological development, sarcasm is one of the most accurate barometers of a planet's social development. However, as history has so often proven, it's also a great way to get your planet destroyed by other planets who have no appreciation for this specific social development, especially when said sarcasm is directed at *them*.

But there was nothing Reg could do about it apart from ensuring that he and Spence made it to the so-called Metal Mountain first. He looked at the ensign for confirmation that what he was seeing was indeed what he thought he was seeing. To his relief, Spence nodded.

Yes, even a *crashed* spaceship held more promise than nothing.

CHAPTER 17

By the time they reached the volcano's peak, Reg's ears ached almost as much as the rest of him. While he'd initially wanted to know more about the crashed ship far below, he certainly didn't need to know *everything*.

"I read about a spaceship with something called a *canteen*," Issy continued his barrage of information, "where you can get food any time of the day … *and* night! Isn't that amazing?"

"Yes, amazing," said Spence, whose face radiated a fair amount of strain. "Uh, Issy, do you mind if we take a break?"

Reg couldn't stop himself from grinning, knowing that, like him, Spence's feet weren't the only parts that needed a rest. By now, the Ronian's eardrums must have been on the verge of a meltdown.

"Oh, yes, we might as well," Issy said and whistled the procession to a halt.

This time, no one complained, and even the Teahupo'oan Head Headhunter called Roro looked more than ready to take some weight off his feet. He ordered his prisoners to be seated with those of the Ja'namans.

"We have to wait for the Priestess to arrive in any case," Issy continued. "She had to prepare for the ceremony."

"*And* the Wise One," Roro added.

As she sat down, the Faylin snorted. "*That* might take a while."

To reward the remark, Roro tossed his water gourd to Spence instead of her, then left to check on his men.

While the ensign took a few generous sips, Reg fixed his eyes on the blue Faylin across from him.

"What's wrong, soldier boy?" she asked, and when Reg didn't answer, she added, "Cat got your tongue?"

Reg intensified his glare. "It's *you*, isn't it?"

"Me who?" the Faylin replied, adjusting her grass skirt to cover some not-so-white cloth.

"*Her*," Reg growled.

"I'm sure I don't know whom you're talking about."

"Well, *I* am sure. Your shuttle was flagged on the Militorate's system. So, you're the elusive captain of the *Jolly Dodger*. Not so elusive anymore, are we … *Captain Phealix*?"

The Faylin now matched his glare. "You can count your lucky stars I wasn't on the *Dodger* when our paths crossed, Mr Scout," she grated.

"That's *Lieutenant* to you, you pirate trash," he said, ignoring the astonishment crawling over Issy's face at those last words. "Lieutenant Reginald Kleft. It's a name I want you to remember while you spend the rest of your life looking at the world through bars – if you're lucky."

"Well, *Lieutenant*, firing on a ship without warning isn't exactly in the Militor training manual, now is it? Or don't they teach you soldier boys the rules of engagement at your playschool?"

"With scum like you, there's only *one* rule of engagement that matters," Reg said, flexing his trigger finger. "Besides, you destroyed my ship!"

"You destroyed my hot tub!"

Their glaring match was interrupted from the side when Spence said, "Um, might I suggest we put our previous issues aside to focus on the current one?"

Reg's glare turned to the ensign like a security camera with a worn gear. "You cannot be serious, Spence."

"I'm dead serious, Reg," Spence said. "Let's be realistic for a moment. We're *all* prisoners here and, whatever these locals have planned for us, I'm pretty sure we're screwed. So, it doesn't matter what ships we were on before; we're in the same boat right now. I suggest you guys just accept that fact and reschedule your fharking squabbles for a future date!"

Face flushed, the ensign's chest heaved in its struggle for oxygen, and not just because of their current altitude.

Reg had never seen his friend angry. Highly upset, yes, but not outright angry. He was about to say something, when the pirate captain said, "At least *one* of you has some grey matter between the ears."

Reg felt his own face redden, but his planned retort – which would have been a good one, in his opinion – was thwarted by the Faylin.

"Before you get all hot and bothered again," she said, "your colleague here is right. As much as I hate to say it, we need to work together. That's *if* you'd like to see another sunrise, of course."

The part of Reg that enjoyed sunrises eventually forced out a grunt. "Fine," he said, "but what do you propose? Because the last time I checked – and let me just do so again … nope, nothing's changed – we are unarmed and outnumbered."

"So why don't we level the playing field on both counts?" Captain Phealix said.

"And how do you plan on doing that?"

The captain pointed at the grip of a stunner gun protruding from Roro's carry pouch. Reg cursed himself for not noticing it earlier.

"If you can create a diversion," the Faylin said, "I'll make sure we have a chance to get out of this in one piece."

After a pause, Reg nodded reluctantly. He knew his trust would probably come at a cost, but weighed against the price of one's life, it seemed trust was quite cheap.

CHAPTER 18

Phealix didn't trust the Scouts one bit, *especially* the lieutenant. She'd dealt with many men and women like him before: trigger-happy yahoos with no regard for rules, no respect for others, and no … finesse. Even pirates had more finesse than this ape.

And, no, she thought before she could brand herself a speciesist, I know what I mean.

People like Reg either came from nothing or from everything. And judging by his rank at such a young age, the safer bet would be on the latter. Regardless, given the circumstances, a yahoo might just come in handy.

"What's it like … being a pirate?" the tribesman called Issy interrupted her thoughts.

"How do *you* know about pirates?" Phealix asked, frowning at the Ja'naman's eager face.

"Please don't get him started again," Reg grumbled.

Studying Issy's eager face properly this time, Phealix heeded the warning and opted to use the opportunity to incentivise the little man.

"We don't have time for that now," she said. "I'll tell you everything if we get out of this mess. But that will only be possible if you help us. The question is, *will* you help us?"

The man was quiet for a moment, looking conflicted. "I don't know," he said. "On the one hand, these are my tribesmen, and I've never disobeyed them – well, not like this. *This* feels more like … betrayal. On the other hand, I get the feeling you're important to Tuma."

"Who's this *Tuma* everyone keeps talking about?" Phealix asked.

"The Fire God," Issy said and, after another slight pause, he added, "And, actually … it's Dennis."

"Who's Dennis?"

"Tuma."

"Tuma is Dennis?"

Issy nodded.

Phealix tried to navigate the waters of confusion flooding her head, but ended up paddling in circles. "Why do *they* call him Tuma, then?" she said, nodding towards the other tribesmen.

"They don't … feel Dennis."

"You *feel* Dennis?"

"Yes."

"But you've never actually *seen* Dennis?"

Issy shook his head. "No, but he's *definitely* there, and we enjoy each other's company."

"You spend time together?"

"Oh, yes! I often read to him and tell him stories about the village. I think he likes it."

Noting his self-belief, Phealix didn't have the heart to tell Issy that gods didn't exist; that it was all in his head. Besides, upsetting their only tribal ally wasn't conducive to a successful survival strategy.

"Why would *we* be important to this … Dennis?" she asked instead.

Issy shrugged. "I don't know," he said, "but the closer we get to Dennis, the more I'm sure of it. And if you're important to him, you're important to me. The others won't understand, though. As I said, they don't feel Dennis like I do."

"But why you and not them?"

"I wish I knew. Maybe Dennis is shy. Or maybe I'm – like my mother often says – special. Whatever the reason, no one really believes me. Then again, no one's sure about my connection to the Fire God, either, so they usually don't dismiss me outright. I'll try to talk to them; maybe they'll listen."

"And if they don't?"

"Then you'd better pray for a miracle."

Phealix wasn't religious, preferring not to place her fate in the hands of airy-fairy beings. To her, miracles were just blind luck called by a different name. A glance at Reg confirmed that the Scout felt the same. He nodded at her unspoken statement: if they wanted to get out of this alive, they were on their own. And by the look on his face, Reg planned on staying alive by any means necessary.

Phealix, on the other hand, didn't want Issy or anyone else to get hurt during their escape. But she'd learnt long ago that idealism and reality didn't enjoy frolicking together in the same playpen, and that ideals were generally nothing more than crystal glasses waiting to get knocked off the shelf.

No, someone was going to get hurt.

Someone *always* got hurt.

CHAPTER 19

When the Ja'naman Priestess finally arrived with her freshly polished[*] bony garb, followed by the Teahupo'oan Wise One on his mobile dais, the procession continued towards the lip of the crater.

The men carrying the Wise One's dais nearly dropped it as they lowered the platform to its designated spot, their chests heaving. They looked just as unhappy with him as he did with them – it must have been a bumpy ride. Ongswele grinned as she stepped next to the elderly Teahupo'oan's horned skull-chair without looking at him.

"Is it no time for you to retire, old man?" she asked.

The Wise One's lip curled in disdain. "Is it no time you give back Great Serpent you *borrow?*"

The Priestess didn't answer. Firstly, the Wise One didn't even know it was called the Great *Stapler*. Being so "wise", he could figure this out by himself, because

---

[*] If you're wondering where Ja'namans get the wax to polish stuff, you're better off not knowing, so it's highly recommended you stop wondering and attend to that sudden itch in your ear canal.

she certainly wasn't about to tell him. Secondly, no timeframe had been stipulated in the original Serpent/Stapler loan agreement. And, seeing as she wasn't done with it, she might just keep it a while longer. In fact, Ongswele decided right then and there, she wouldn't be done with the Great Stapler *indefinitely*.[*]

Ignoring the old man's accusatory glare, the Priestess tapped the Staff of Truth until she had everyone's attention, and raised her chin. "Who speak for those we sacrifice?" she said, staring down her nose at the prisoners on their knees in front of the dais.

Issy stepped forward hesitantly. "I do," he said, then pulled himself straight. "And don't you mean those we *might* sacrifice?"

Ongswele raised her chin even further and pushed through the pain that tried to tell her neck to take it easy. Raising one's chin was basic Priestess protocol, but a double-raise was imperative if a situation demanded it.

"Of course," she said. "Tuma know best what we do with Children of Chicken God …"

Noticing the Wise One's mystified glance from the corner of her eye, Ongswele paused to enjoy the moment – just one more thing *she* knew that *he* didn't.

---

[*] Believe it or not, this tradition is practised among the "civilised" peoples of the universe too, although the people working in office environments are more likely to believe it. Those on the receiving end of this abhorrent tradition will state that the Indefinite Borrowing of the Stapler is totally unacceptable, while the defending party will argue that it's completely justified due to the accusing party's Indefinite Borrowing of the Pen. Despite continuous efforts by Management, this issue remains unresolved.

"… and Children of whatever god the Teahupo'o dragged up here," she concluded, looking upon the Vahltans in disgust.

The Teahupo'oans seemed caught between feeling offended by the remark and their uncertainty over how to respond, as the whole Chicken God thing was kind of sprung on them.

"Well," Issy said before things went off-topic, "Den— Tuma doesn't want them to be sacrificed."

For some reason, Roro shifted uncomfortably.

"You *know* tradition, Isilimo," the Priestess countered. "We sacrifice. If Tuma spit out sacrifice, they worthy to take place of honour among tribes. If Tuma no spit out, he happy with meal and bless us."

Issy folded his arms. "Well, Tuma doesn't want another meal," he said. "Besides, we all know that no one has *ever* been spat out, Ongswele."

Both tribes knew of Issy's supposed connection to Tuma, but no one quite believed it. Yet no one dismissed it altogether, either, just in case they were wrong. Ongswele, however, leaned more towards the disbelieving side, and rarely had the time or the patience to put up with Issy's nonsense. Especially when she was tired and hungry – like now. It had been a long day.

"We no break tradition, Isilimo," she grated, folding her arms too. "We sacrifice, we go home."

Obviously not keen on agreeing with the Priestess on anything at the moment, the Wise One nodded nonetheless, and the warriors of both tribes pulled the sacrifices to their feet.

"Ours first," the Priestess said in a tone that stated she wouldn't entertain a debate on the matter.

To her satisfaction, she also didn't get one.

CHAPTER 20

Resisting the arm shoving him towards the crater's lip didn't help, with the face-marred Gobatsha looking more than happy to accompany Reg on his final walk.

"Can't we talk about this?" Reg tried. "I'm sure we can work things out if we just talk."

"No talk," Gobatsha said, adding extra pressure to the spear against Reg's back to assist in melting his stubborn opposition to death. "Only walk."

Shoved onto an overhang jutting out over the crater, Reg stared in horror at the direct drop to the bubbling lava below. Glancing over his shoulder at Captain Phealix, he hoped the Faylin would hold up her end of the bargain. He also hoped the nod she gave him was confirmation of this and not approval of his fate. You never knew with pirates.

When Gobatsha positioned himself for the most satisfying shove of his life, Reg realised the moment for diversion had arrived, because a moment later would be a moment too late. He was somewhat surprised when the diversion didn't come from him, as per the original plan.

With a rumble, the volcano shook, sending Reg and Gobatsha sprawling to the ground. Luckily, they toppled backwards, away from the crater, and as he landed atop Gobatsha, Reg wasted no time in slamming his elbow into the tribesman's face. The accompanying *crunch* had the desired effect, as Gobatsha rolled onto his side, clamping a hand over his broken nose to stop the bleeding. Reg took the opportunity to grab the man's spear, then shot to his feet, ready for the next opponent.

However, Captain Phealix had everything under control. Crouched behind Roro with one arm curled around his neck, she pointed her reclaimed stunner at the tribal warriors advancing on her, spears raised.

The Faylin whispered something in her hostage's ear.

"No come closer," Roro warned, "or witch use Silent Lightning."

Some of the men halted, but not all – mainly those who hadn't yet witnessed what a stunner could do. Captain Phealix rectified this by shooting the man closest to her.

He fell.

The others stopped.

A Ja'naman warrior at the back, however, redirected his efforts at a softer target. Reg didn't notice the man until he unleashed a battle cry, and by the time the lieutenant spun to face his attacker, he knew it was too late

A *tshoop* brought the tribesman's charge to an abrupt end and sent him crashing to the ground. Reg barely had enough time to jump out of the way as the man rolled past towards the lip of the crater, his body coming to rest on the edge with an arm dangling over the side.

Captain Phealix swung the stunner back towards the other tribesmen.

"Anyone else without ears?" she said, swivelling her aim along the line of uncertain warriors.

The men did have ears, and although they couldn't understand what their ears were hearing, their eyes had interpreted enough to know what the blue creature and her Silent Lightning were capable of. Which is why no one moved when Reg joined his co-captives.

"Now what?" he said, taking position next to Captain Phealix and pointing his spear at the wary tribesmen.

"We need a guide," the Faylin replied, glancing at Issy. "Think he'll come?"

"Only one way to find out," Reg said, pointing his spear at the young tribesman for show. "What do you say, Issy? Up for some adventure?"

"Not really," Issy said.

"But what about all those novels you love? Surely they have lots of adventure in them."

"*They* do. *I* don't."

The mountain rumbled again and, after a pause, the tribesman sighed.

"Fine," he said, "I'll come ... but just because Dennis says so."

"Are you sure his name's Dennis and not Simon?" Reg said, grinning.

"What?"

"Never mind," Reg said, grin vanishing. Why did only humans find that amusing? A glance at Spence confirmed this was still the case.

"Where to now?" Captain Phealix said when Issy joined them with a show of reluctance.

"We must go back down the path," the tribesman whispered. "Leave the rest to me."

They started shuffling backwards, keeping their weapons pointed at the natives.

"Where you go with my hunter?" the Wise One croaked from the back.

"And mine," the Priestess added in a tone that didn't sound overly concerned, as this situation could rid her of a constant irritation. Still, she had to ask; it was the tribally thing to do.

Despite what they'd just witnessed, both tribes' warriors took a step forward, but stopped when Captain Phealix pressed the stunner against Roro's head.

The Faylin whispered something in the Tea-hupo'oan's ear.

"She say we go and you no follow!" Roro repeated out loud, then listened for the next instruction. "They free me and Issy when they safe!"

The Priestess seemed somewhat disappointed.

"Seriously, don't even *think* about following us," Reg growled, pressing his spearhead against Issy's neck for effect. This the tribesmen understood without the need for translation, and halted.

"Will they stay put?" Reg asked.

"Not for long," Issy said. "I suggest we run."

Which is why they turned and ran.

CHAPTER 21

Roro surprised Phealix by keeping up the pace instead of trying to slow the group down. In fact, he ran right on the heels of Issy, who led the fleeing party down the pathway. The headhunter obviously knew what was good for him.

It didn't take long before the anticipated shouting erupted from behind, with the Priestess and Wise One barking orders for their warriors to give chase. The old man's barking sounded more like a wordy cough.

The trail leading down the side of the volcano was well-trodden, offering safe passage to all except those in a hurry, which the group quickly discovered after a few slips and slides, forcing them to stop hurrying. Reaching the bottom intact at a slower pace was more prudent than reaching it speedily in a different bodily shape. Besides, as most non-natives were already wheezing harder than the *Dodger's* side-thrusters, speed was no longer a viable option.

About halfway down, they reached a fork, but instead of continuing on the current path leading to the foot of the volcano, Issy went right, taking the one running along the mountainside.

Remembering the fork from their ascent, Phealix halted. "Are you sure?" she panted, eyeing the path not taken. "Isn't *that* the way we came?"

"Yes," Issy said. "And that's why we shouldn't go that way."

"Why not?"

"The tribes will catch up to us if we keep going down; it's exactly where they'll expect us to go. They won't even think about us heading straight on. At least not at first. Believe me, our best chance lies this way."

Phealix wasn't sure of Issy's reasoning, but as she wasn't sure of anything at that stage, she simply had to trust that he knew what he was doing.

"Fine, lead the way," she said, and waited for the last Vahltan stragglers to pass before bringing up the rear.

"Come on, Demi!" she told the Vahltan lumbering ahead of her. "Keep moving!"

However, Phealix knew her crew wouldn't last much longer. Even with their fear of death, there came a time when Vahltans would gladly swap that particular fear for their fear of exercise. Her crew was rapidly nearing this event horizon, hence her relief when the jog ended right after the next bend. The relief was short-lived, though, because it was also where the pathway ended against a sheer cliff, leaving them trapped.

• • •

Stretching from the base of the volcano to about half its height, the cliff looked out of place amid the rest of the slopes flowing downward and outward towards the landscape below. It was as if the flat vertical feature had been chiselled into the mountainside with the biggest chisel imaginable. It seemed … out of place somehow.

But Phealix didn't have time to question her scant knowledge of geology. "Why the heck did you bring us here?" she hissed.

"Shh!" Issy said, pointing back the way they'd come.

The voices of the pursuing tribesmen grew louder before gradually fading again. They must have taken the other path at the fork, just as Issy had predicted.

Satisfied they were safe for the time being but not willing to stake her life on it, Phealix whispered, "As far as escape routes go, you *could* have chosen a better one."

Issy looked baffled. "But Dennis said I should bring you here."

Roro sighed. "Issy right," the Head Headhunter said. "This where *Tuma* say we must come. That why I help you."

"Since when do *you* hear Dennis?" Issy asked with additional bafflement.

Roro pointed towards the top of the volcano. "It first time now … up there."

"But how?"

"It doesn't matter," Reg interjected, slapping the stone to test whether it was indeed what it appeared to be. "Why would this Dennis, or Tuma, or whatever you call him, lead us to this spot? There's *nothing* here!"

"I know," Issy said. "That's why the villagers never come this way … except to bring the Weekly Fruit for Tuma's Eye."[*]

When everyone but Roro exercised the appropriate facial muscles to express their lack of knowledge on this particular event, Issy pointed at the flat cliff next to them, upon which the muscles relaxed.

---

[*] For which the local birds, monkeys and ants are ever so grateful.

"That's also why it didn't make sense when Dennis wanted me to bring you here," Issy continued. "But I'd hoped he knew something I didn't. Seems I was wrong."

Reg snorted. "Clearly," he said, glancing back along the pathway. "We should double back to the split. Maybe we can sneak down without being noticed."

"Even if we do, it won't help," Issy said. "When our people reach the bottom, the trackers will start checking for our trail and send for more men. The whole area will soon be crawling with warriors looking for us, and they *will* find us eventually, whether up here or down there."

"Well, we can't stay here," Reg said, annoyed. "You and your delusions might have just sealed our fate."

"Should I rather have left you to die up there?" Issy said.

"No, but—"

The Scout's reply was cut short by a rumble, followed by a grating sound. Everyone jumped back with a start as a small section of the cliff slid sideways where the path ended, revealing a dark tunnel leading into the mountain.

"What's that?" Franki said.

"It's a tunnel," Issy breathed.

Reg's flat stare blended well with the rest of the stares directed at the tribesman. "Yes, but a tunnel to what?"

Phealix glanced back the way they'd come and weighed their options. The pathway appeared to be clear for now, but if Issy was right, they didn't have much time before the status quo changed its status.

She sighed. "It doesn't matter. I'd rather take my chances with the unknown in there than face certain death out here. Anyone who wants to stay is welcome to do so, but I'm going in."

Hoping the others would share her shaky rationale for doing something that every part of her being was screaming she shouldn't be doing, the Faylin stepped forward to be consumed by the mountain's black interior.

CHAPTER 22

This is a bad idea, Reg thought, eyeing the tunnel; its dark mouth waiting patiently to swallow his sanity along with the rest of him. This is a *really* bad idea.

The Scout didn't mind running headfirst into uncertain situations, as long as *he* was the one in the lead or, more importantly, if he could *see* where he was being led. Darkness terrified Reg. And not the moonlit-night kind of dark – he wasn't *that* bad. But any further drop in illumination caused his mind to reach for the panic button, which is why a night light formed an essential part of his sleep routine. His nyctophobia was also the reason why Reg hated travelling through wormholes, and why he'd never openly admit his fear of the dark, because wormholes formed a big part of Militorate life. Reg couldn't stand even looking at the absolute blackness surrounding him whenever he found himself in a wormhole. If it hadn't been for interior ship lighting, he'd probably claw his eyes out.[*]

------

[*] Medical professionals may deem this a counterproductive measure. And, yes, as many people would know, doctors don't know everything, but they might just have a point here.

Again, Spence *had to* be aware of his fear, but the ensign never said anything. Despite the ensign now giving him an encouraging nod, Reg was petrified as he entered the seemingly endless darkness.

As he inched his way down the sloped tunnel for a few minutes, Reg's hands graduated from mild tremors to uncontrollable shaking. But they were the only tools he had to navigate the sea of blackness engulfing him and, flailing about, they soon encountered something not made of rock. The two round, soft, leathery objects wobbled slightly at the touch of his trembling fingertips. Reg froze in place.

"I'd appreciate it if whoever's doing that would stop doing that," said a voice; a voice Reg recognised yet wished he hadn't.

Please tell me it's *not* what I think it is, Reg thought, as another kind of trepidation joined the Fear Club. Please-please-please-please, *pleeease!*

Something started giving off light, and Reg indeed found himself holding what he shouldn't be holding. Face flushed, he was suddenly glad for the lack of decent light.

"I hope you enjoyed that," Captain Phealix said, removing his trembling hands from her breasts, "because that's the first and – I can assure you – the *last* time it will happen."

Reg's tongue tied itself into creative new shapes to assist his mouth in explaining what had just occurred, because his brain didn't seem interested in coming up with anything useful. "I, er, I'm, uh, sorry, I, um, swear, er, I, um, uh, didn't mean—"

"I found a torch!" Issy interrupted as he approached, shedding more light on things; things that also included the unreadable expression on Spence's face.

"What?" Reg snapped at the ensign. "You *know* I didn't mean to, er …" He decided it best to change the subject by turning his attention to the torch in Issy's hand. "Where did you get that?"

Not knowing what was going on, Issy smiled and said, "I found it on the wall up ahead."

The tribesman stared at the flame with reverence.

"It came on by itself," he said.

"Gimme that!" Reg grated, snatching the torch from Issy's hand.

Ignoring the native, who was alternating his stupefied stare between his now-empty hand and the back of the man who'd made it empty, Reg continued down the tunnel. With embarrassment still plastered all over his face, he didn't want to see Captain Phealix or, more importantly, for her to see him, so he was glad to have the Faylin behind him.

The slow trek down the black-walled tunnel didn't last very long, and the embarrassing incident was soon forgotten as the tunnel opened into an immense void of fiery darkness.

•••

"What *is* this place?" asked the Vahltan Stanli.

"I don't know," Spence breathed.

"Beats me," Reg added, relieved to be free from the confines of the tunnel. He waved the torch around to get a better look at their surroundings, although it wasn't really necessary. The floor was dimly lit by numerous small streams of lava pushing out from the curved walls of the chamber and running along the floor into the darkness. The molten rock gave off enough light to illuminate their immediate vicinity.

A drop of liquid fell from somewhere above onto Issy's forehead. When it didn't burn his face, the tribesman wiped it off with a finger, which he stuck in his mouth.

"Hey," he said, "it tastes like Masepa!"

"Ma-what now?" Reg said without trying to hide his revulsion at someone sticking an unknown substance in their mouth.

"Masepa – the nectar of the Fire God. It's what I gave you before we came up the mountain. We drink it regularly to keep Dennis happy."

"So he's happy when you're not happy?"

"What do you mean?"

"Whatever this Masepa stuff's made of, it tastes like crap!"

"Well, I grew up on it," Issy countered, folding his arms. "It's not *that* bad." Knowing his face wasn't showing its full support for that last statement, he added, "Besides, it's *tradition*, so that's what we do. If you don't like it, it's *your* problem."

Studying the aggrieved tribesman, Reg realised that squabbling with the local populace over local cuisine wasn't the most productive use of their time.

But before he could say anything, Spence said, "This cavern … it seems out of place."

"Yeah," Captain Phealix added, "I wouldn't have thought a cavern of this size could exist under a volcano."

"And what would a *pirate* know about caves?" Reg scoffed.

"I'd say more than a soldier boy."

"Stop calling me that!"

"Why, does it hurt the little boy's feelings?" Phealix said, knuckling a nonexistent tear from her eye.

"Hey!" Spence said. "I know this place is getting on everyone's nerves, but could the two of you *please* get a hold of yourself? Reg, doesn't this place seem, well … out of sorts to you?"

Reg looked about again. The veins of light from the lava only properly illuminated their immediate vicinity, and nothing much beyond that. But if the base and upwards curvature of the dome-like cavern was anything to go by, it was indeed enormous. He couldn't see the roof nor the far side of the cavity. Also, now that he studied the walls more carefully, they didn't appear as rough or jagged as one would expect from a cavern. They weren't exactly smooth, either, but for some reason they didn't appear to have formed naturally.

Despite knowing that Spence might be right, Reg sniffed. "So what are you saying, Spence?" he said, nodding towards Issy and Roro. "That *they* created it?"

"No, of course not. But *someone* did."

"Maybe it was Dennis," Issy volunteered.

"Stop calling him *Dennis!*" Roro barked.

"Geez, can *everyone* just please calm down!" Spence snapped once more. "And that goes for *you* too!" he yelled pre-emptively at the Vahltans, who generally never liked dark spaces, big or small, and appeared ready to point this out for the umpteenth time.

Taking a deep breath, the ensign continued, "Look, whatever this place is, we need to find a way out of here that isn't the way we came in. Agreed?" He waited for the others to nod. "Splendid! Now, I don't know about the rest of you, but I don't want to spend a minute longer here than necessary. So, for Zolt's sake, can we *please* get to it?"

Not waiting for an answer, the ensign took off towards the centre of the cavern.

Reg didn't really want to follow Spence, but he did because, despite its size, it felt as though the cavern was pressing down on him, slowly crushing every inch of his being.

Spence is right, Reg thought as he caught up with the Ronian. The sooner we get out of here, the better.

CHAPTER 23

Reg had to show he was still in charge. So, while Captain Phealix split the Vahltans into two groups to check the perimeter of the cavern for an exit, he took lead of the procession as they trekked deeper into the cavern's interior, following the small streams running along the floor.

Less than a foot wide, the narrow rivulets didn't radiate as much heat as they should, nor did they flow the way they should. In fact, from where it pushed out from the walls, the lava retained its liquid state and flowed in almost perfectly straight canals towards some central point, where a larger orange glow awaited the approaching group. As they neared the glow, it gradually revealed the bottom of a dark, massive shape suspended above an immense pool of bubbling lava.

"What do we have here?" Captain Phealix said, leaning over the edge to have a better look at the basin of molten rock about twenty metres below.

Despite his near-permanent introduction to molten rock earlier on, Reg hazarded a look of his own.

As with the lava rivulets, the air rising from the crater was quite warm but not the pizza-oven kind of heat produced by the lava in the crater atop the volcano.

Stepping back, Reg wiped the sweat from his brow but left the frown where it belonged. "A volcano within a volcano?"

"Seems so," Captain Phealix said, then gazed up at the shape above the lava. "The bigger question is, what is *that?*"

For a while, they stared in quiet puzzlement at the massive cylindrical structure suspended atop two rock columns that rose from the fiery pool, which illuminated the structure along its length. And long it was, easily stretching beyond two hundred metres. Not as well-lit as the bottom, the structure's top towered nearly a hundred metres above the cavern floor, and was only visible thanks to a network of glowing orange veins spread all over the structure's rocky black surface. At its centre, another column rose from the top of the structure, vanishing into the darkness above.

It made Reg think of a burnt log; blackened on the outside yet smouldering inside. This made him think of barbeques, which in turn made him think of the fate he and Spence narrowly evaded in the Ja'naman village, so he stopped thinking about it.

"Someone *must* have built this," Spence said, breaking the silence, "because whatever it is, it *definitely* doesn't look natural."

"No, it doesn't," Captain Phealix said. "It also doesn't *feel* natural."

Reg felt it too. Earlier, he'd thought it was just the gloomy confines of the mountain that had him on edge. But it was more than that. The whole place just felt … wrong.

His mind scolded him for letting his nerves run amok. Pull yourself together! You're a Militor man, for Zolt's sake! If Grandfather saw you now …

Moving his anxiety to the To-Deal-With-Later folder of his mind, Reg set off along the rim of the crater towards the back end of the log-like structure.

"Where are you going?" Spence said.

"To have a closer look. We won't learn anything by standing around all day."

"We don't even know what this thing is!"

"That's why I'm going to have a look."

Spence glanced at Captain Phealix for support, but didn't get any as she rushed to catch up with the human. Reg was used to his friend's hesitance. From their days at the Academy, Spence had been the cautious one, while Reg favoured the act-now-think-later approach. Reg always said their conflicting modus operandi was an essential part of an effective team. Spence always countered that this might have been true if Reg would only listen once in a while.

At the back – or was it the front? – of the cylindrical structure, Reg came across a flat bridge spanning the lava pool below, connecting the lower part of the suspended structure with the cavern floor. Less than two metres in width with no support underneath, the black stone was barely a foot thick, which likely accounted for the nervous grumbling behind Reg when he stepped onto the bridge and jumped up and down to test its structural integrity. When he didn't drop to his death, he turned around to give the thumbs up.

"Is he always such a halfwit?" Captain Phealix asked Spence, loud enough for Reg to hear.

"*Half* would be an improvement," Spence grumbled, also with enough volume to ensure Reg heard.

Without a word, Reg walked by them to shove the torch back into Issy's unexpectant hand, but he cast Spence a glare that said some words would *definitely* be had later on.

I'll show those two what a halfwit is! Reg thought, and then thought that the thought hadn't come out right.

Refraining from sighing at himself, Reg started crossing the bridge with a bravado that swiftly dissipated. Although wide enough to travel across with ease in normal circumstances, the lava pool below began to tug at his mind, mentally shrinking the width of the rocky bridge the farther he went. He had to stop himself from using his arms to balance out the psychological pull of the molten rock below.

After what felt like a lifelong journey, Reg arrived at the opposite end of the bridge, which terminated against the flat circular backside of the cylindrical structure. Up close, it resembled the sawn-off end of a burnt log. Its rough surface consisted of jagged, black blocks that varied in size and, to a lesser degree, depth. Between the blocks ran a network of veins. About an inch in diameter, each vein comprised a thin – nearly invisible – green membrane acting as a tubular conduit for the orange lava flowing within. As with the lava rivulets on the cavern floor and the lava pool below, these veins didn't emit significant heat.

Reg extended his hand warily, ready to pull back at a moment's notice, just in case his initial senses proved unreliable. However, as his fingers brushed one of the veins nestled in the black stone, it didn't singe his skin. Feeling more confident, he flattened his hand over it. While somewhat warm, it was far from searing hot.

Why is it so cool? he wondered. And why is it throbbing like that?

Indeed, the liquid seemed to pulsate, not only through his hands and eardrums but also his entire body and mind.

Why does it feel so strange? he thought.

Why am I feeling happy and not alarmed?

Should I be alarmed that I'm not alarmed?

Should I even care when I'm this happy?

I *am* happy, aren't I?

He paused.

Yes, I think I am.

No, I *definitely* am.

I *am* happy.

"I'm glad *someone's* happy," said a voice from behind.

With a start, Reg snatched back his hand. He couldn't recall having verbalised his thoughts, but apparently he had. Shaking his head, he turned to face Captain Phealix staring back at him, looking irked.

"What the heck is taking you so long?" the Faylin asked, sounding the way she looked.

Reg tried rubbing the dryness from his eyes, which felt like they haven't blinked in years. "What do you mean?"

"We've been standing around for who knows how long for you to … well, do whatever you were doing."

"Don't be ridiculous. I just got here."

"No, she's right," Spence said, joining them with a concerned look. "You've been standing like that for a while."

Reg knew they were exaggerating but didn't want to get into a pointless debate over something so trivial.

"Can we set aside your timekeeping issues and focus on the real problem?" he said instead. "This bridge is going nowhere."

Captain Phealix stepped up to inspect the wall herself. "I guess we're a bit buggered, then."

"Why?"

"My men just finished checking the perimeter. Apart from the tunnel we used to enter this place, there's no other way out. And yes, before you say anything, I know they don't exactly have night-vision[*], but it's pretty hard to miss another exit, even for a Vahltan."

"So, what, you want to go back outside?"

Captain Phealix nodded. "It's better than getting trapped in here," she said. "Issy reckons we *might* still have a chance of slipping down unnoticed before the tribes start searching the volcano itself."

Reg glanced at the tribesman waiting on the other side of the bridge with Roro. "Well, their people had better hope they don't find us," he grated, "because I won't give up without a fi—"

He was cut off by something happening behind him. He knew something was happening because, apart from the surprised eyes of the captain and the ensign now staring past him, he also heard it happening. Turning around, Reg watched the section of wall where he had placed his hand grate inwards and upwards, revealing yet another dark tunnel leading into the loggy structure.

Reg's mind confirmed that it was indeed a tunnel, that it was indeed dark, and that – as with the previous tunnel – he didn't want to enter it either.

Not again, he thought. *Please*, not again!

---

[*] While true, and a bit understated, never call Vahltans out on their shortcomings when a group of them are within earshot. They might be a little night-blind, but there's nothing wrong with their hearing, or their temper.

CHAPTER 24

When the doorway slid open, Issy couldn't stop himself from crossing the bridge, despite the "order" to stay put. Roro followed close behind. He must have realised it wasn't a good idea to be alone with the Vahltans he'd almost sacrificed … twice.

"Another one?" Issy said, peering past Spence at the tunnel leading into the structure.

The ensign yelped, causing a knock-on effect.

"I thought I told you to wait," Reg hissed.

Curiosity piqued, Issy didn't reply as he edged past the others and held up the torch to inspect the opening.

"Where does it go?" he said.

"How the heck should *we* know?" Reg snapped. The human seemed even more on edge than the rest of them. Issy suspected Reg wasn't his tribe's best warrior.

"Hey, I'm just asking," Issy said.

"And I'm just … taking this again, thank you very much!" Reg said, snatching Issy's torch once more.

Unlike earlier, however, Issy's look now radiated agitation instead of surprise. "You know, it won't hurt *asking* once in a while," he yelled after the Scout, who proceeded into the tunnel with grim determination.

Captain Phealix gave Issy an empathetic pat on the shoulder before waving the Vahltans over.

Following the human into the tunnel, Issy still didn't know where the inconsiderate brute had come from, but it sure *wasn't* from the gods, because he couldn't believe that *any* of them could be such assholes.

•••

The trip through the tunnel was short-lived, and so was Issy's indignation at Reg's behaviour, finding himself too astonished to give thought to anything other than the huge cylindrical chamber they'd just entered.

"Well, this is interesting," Captain Phealix said.

Interesting wasn't the word Issy would have used to describe what he saw. Given, he hadn't found the right word yet, but once he did, *interesting* wouldn't be it. Like the exterior, the hollow interior was covered with veins of lava-but-not-quite-lava, but unlike the outer surface, the long, curved inner wall was dotted with countless pustules. Issy had seen (and had) his fair share of pimples, but *this* was like the worst case of acne he'd ever encountered.[*] But that's about where the similarities ended. Varying in size, the pustules scattered all

---

[*] The actual worst case of acne ever recorded was on Earth Too, where Jeremy Kemp spent years suffering from the dreaded condition. With not an inch of his skin left unaffected, Jeremy hadn't been the most popular kid in school, and the permanent scarring did nothing to increase his popularity as an adult, either. Not that Jeremy minded, though, as all the alone-time spent in his parents' basement had turned him into one of the most successful online gamers of all time, raking in millions of creds. So, if Mitch Hardy is reading this: Who's the freak now, you twat?

over the cylindrical surface were too big to be pimples – with most standing almost as tall Issy – and also not the correct colour, as many of them pulsated with a faint, lime-green light. It was as if a swarm of gigantic, lethargic fireflies had managed to get themselves stuck in holes with only the tips of their backsides protruding.

As the group quietly proceeded along the smooth, black stone walkway running the length of the chamber, Issy tried counting the bulbous glowing objects, but seeing as mathematics wasn't exactly big on Wahyoo VIII, he lost interest when he ran out of fingers.

Spence broke the silence. "Do we really have to go deeper?" he said, glancing back at the structure's exit. "This place gives me the creeps."

With a face struggling to hold back its own creeps, Reg said, "What else would you suggest, Spence? We're not exactly swimming in options here. Would you prefer someone making a midnight snack out of your finger, or use your skull as a doorstop?"

"Well, at least we *know* what awaits us out there," Spence mumbled.

Issy felt the same. He too didn't like this place one bit. It felt too – what was that word again? – oh, yes, alien. "Maybe I can talk to the Priestess," he ventured. "Maybe I can convince her to let you go."

"She doesn't strike me as someone who's overly accommodating to strangers," Reg said. "Especially strangers who humiliated her during her favourite pastime. Do you honestly think she'll listen if we go out there and plead our case?"

"No," Issy admitted after a pause, "she won't. But your friend is right – this place does seem a bit … off."

"A *bit*," Captain Phealix said. "Year-old milk is less off than this place."

"How would you know what year-old milk is like?" Reg said. "I'd have thought you liked things … fresh."

"Well, you know we don't *just* raid ships, don't you?"

Reg's face said he didn't.

Phealix sighed. "When you're running out of supplies in the middle of nowhere and you stumble across a derelict ship, you don't just fly by without checking it out."

"Of course *you* would check out the milk first."

"Aw," Captain Phealix crooned, "your first attempt at a Faylin joke. How cute. I *have* heard better, though."

"It must be fascinating," Issy said, trying to end the glaring match between the captain and the lieutenant. "… you know, being a pirate … getting to do stuff like that?"

"It beats being in the Militorate," Phealix said, flashing Reg a smirk before continuing down the walkway.

What's the deal between these two? Issy thought as the human stomped off after the Faylin, clearly wanting to say something but failing to find the words. They're worse than the Ja'namans and the Teahupo'oans during their territorial spats. Realising he might never find out, Issy just sighed as he fell in behind the group.

The walkway didn't end where the chamber ended and continued down yet another tunnel. While it had a much wider diameter than the tunnel through which they'd entered, this passageway wasn't dark – its walls dotted with over ten fingers' worth of glowing pustules. Maybe even twice that![*]

---

[*] With Issy, "twice" could mean anything between two and a hundred billion pustules, but just to keep you in the loop, it was more in the range of two dozen.

"Don't touch anything," Captain Phealix cautioned as she entered the tunnel. Not that anyone needed to be cautioned; they all seemed more than happy to stay away from the pimply lights as the group proceeded in single file towards the light at the end of the short passageway.

Issy waited for everyone to pass him, not because he had good manners – which he did, just in case anyone was wondering – but because the pulsating pustule closest to him suddenly drew his attention. It wasn't the way it looked that pulled him closer, but more the way it *felt*. Sure, he hadn't touched it but, in some strange way, it had touched him. And it felt good. And he wanted more.

Before he could stop himself, Issy raised his hand.

A part of him warned that what he was about to do was *not* the greatest idea he'd ever had. The other part of him didn't really care about its counterpart's opinion on the matter, though. It *wanted* to touch the pustule's round, glowing membrane. It *needed* to. So that's why that part did it, and it was glad that it did it. And, ultimately, so too was the other part.

Why had I been hesitant? he thought. This feels … right, somehow.

Sure, he suddenly felt a little bit weaker too, but at the same time he felt … happy. Admittedly, he was happy most of the time, but this … *this* was more like the place happiness went to for a recharge.

He smiled.

"I distinctly remember saying *not* to touch anything," Captain Phealix hissed, snatching Issy's arm away from the pustule. "Why are all men born without ears?"

The yank back to reality came as a shock, albeit a strangely welcome one. Issy shook his head to rid himself of some stubborn, lingering fuzziness, but as the feeling of happiness faded, it was replaced by revulsion. It felt as though he'd just taken a dip in a Night Aahp's poop pit.[*]

Issy remembered something someone had said, and gave a delayed reply, "I have ears."

"Then start using them," Captain Phealix said as she ushered him through the glowy tunnel.

Glancing back over his shoulder, Issy caught a final glimpse of the pustule he'd touched, but quickly looked ahead again. He rubbed his eyes, because the fuzziness seemed adamant to linger a bit longer and play tricks on his mind, which insisted he'd just seen a shadowy shape pressing against the membrane of the luminous pustule. Shaking his head once more, Issy pushed the illusion from his thoughts as they approached the far end of the passageway.

Unbeknownst to the tribesman, the illusionary shadow remained in place. Had he stayed and inspected it more closely, he would have thought the shape looked familiar. And, had he given it more thought, he would have concluded that the shape looked familiar because it was shaped like a hand.

---

[*] Despite their wild nature, Night Aahps are obsessed with personal hygiene. This includes keeping their caves and immediate surrounds clear of manure by digging pits far away from their abodes. Of course, they don't appreciate others unburdening themselves in their backyard either – something many creatures find out the hard way if they answer the call of nature too close to a Night Aahp's cave. It's usually also the last thing they ever find out.

CHAPTER 25

Exiting the passageway, Phealix and Issy didn't have trouble catching up with the others, because the others were standing still, studying their surroundings with contagious frowns that immediately infected the Faylin and the Ja'naman too.

With a floor diameter of about twenty metres, the round chamber at the front of the structure was not only smaller than the cylindrical chamber they'd just left, but also more puzzling, mainly because of the thick column at its centre. Nearly five metres in diameter, the dark-green, crystal-like column rose from the floor to the domed roof about thirty metres above. Intertwining inch-thick orange and lime-green veins ran up the length of the column and branched out along the roof and walls. Forming a circle around the column were six similarly veined pedestals, each supporting a smooth slab of shiny black stone.

"It's *the temple*," Issy breathed.

"What temple?" Phealix asked.

"My grandfather," Issy said, mouth agape.

"What about him?" Phealix prodded when the rest of the information didn't present itself.

"Grappy ..." Issy continued after another lengthy pause, "he told me about this place, once. He said that Khulu – my great-grandfather – had warned the tribe about a temple in the mountain. No one believed Khulu, including Grappy, because if there *had* been a temple, the tribe would have known about it."

Looking ashamed, Issy sighed. "I, too, didn't believe it. Until now."

"What did he say about it ... about the temple?" Phealix prodded further.

"Nothing much. Only that it was a dangerous place; a place roamed by bad spirits."

Reg snorted. "Yeah, right."

Issy frowned at him. "You don't believe in spirits?"

"Nope," Reg said. "Once your ticket is punched, it gets tossed in the trash."

Issy frowned. "What's a tick—"

"Captain!" Franki called out nervously from one of the pedestals. "Something's happening!"

Phealix rushed over to the First Mate, who stared at his hand atop the slab.

"It's vibrating," the Vahltan said.

"What did you do?" Phealix said.

"Nothing," Franki said, trying his best to look innocent. However, when Phealix's face reflected that this wasn't working, he added, "I swear, Captain, I *barely* touched it."

"Why in Zolt's name would you touch it at all?"

"I don't know. I ... I just felt I ... had to."

Before Phealix could berate the Vahltan for his lack of self-control, the slab started emitting a soft, orange light that caused both of them to jump back. The light intensified and flowed into fiery symbols that silently hovered about half an inch above the slab's surface.

"That's it, *no one* touches *anything* else!" Phealix commanded. "Is that clear?"

In addition to the threat posed by the tribes outside the mountain, the mountain's interior had gradually been heaping pressure on the captain's spirit.[*] It felt as though an avalanche was about to crash down on her.

"Are you alright, Captain?" Franki asked nervously, as he'd never seen the captain having a panic attack.

"We need to go," Phealix said, placing her hands on her knees as she tried to control her breathing.

"Are you serious?" Reg said. "We just got here!"

"Yes, and now it's time to leave!"

"Well, *we're* not going anywhere," Reg said.

The human glanced at Spence for backup, but it was clear from the Ronian's expression that the lieutenant would have to look elsewhere for support. And when the crystal column started emitting a greenish glow, Reg suddenly didn't look too keen on backing himself either.

Taking another deep breath, Phealix straightened and started backing away from the glowing centrepiece.

"As I said," she grated, "*we need to go.*"

Before Reg could reply, a voice interrupted them; a voice Phealix's ears couldn't hear.

"WE HAD SO HOPED YOU WOULD STAY."

---

[*] Like Caynins, Faylins are quite sensitive to the spiritual side of life. Even those who aren't religious per se have a powerful sense for the metaphysical. Many people have tried to call Caynins and Faylins out on this supposed connection, but both species tend to ignore such debates. What they feel is what they feel, and that is that. How others feel about it isn't their problem. The same goes for people's opposing views on licking stuff.

• • •

Having had contact with telepaths all her life, not hearing speech was nothing new to Phealix. But telepaths communicated through one's mind – *this* felt different. It was as though a chorus of voices had just spoken to the very core of the Faylin's existence; corrupt whispers that corroded every part it touched, leaving behind a dark stain that would never completely fade.

When Phealix's ears finally reclaimed their usefulness, she heard dull thuds emanating from the exit, which caused everyone to spin in that direction.

Nearest the passageway, the Vahltan Khalli was the last to turn, and did so slowly, as he didn't particularly want to see what had crept up behind him. Although tall himself, even by Vahltan standards, Khalli wasn't used to looking up at many people. But this was no ordinary person.

Langnians were arguably the tallest humanoids in the Charted Universe, but the Langnian in front of Khalli was no ordinary Langnian. Sure, it was tall and lean, with the same long, thin legs and the same narrow, elongated head of a Langnian, but that's about where the similarities ended, because Langnians didn't have black rock for skin. They didn't have dark-green crystallised joints, nor did they have two holes where their eyes were supposed to be. And even if they'd had such holes, the cavities wouldn't be filled with fiery lava swirling behind a thin layer of transparent green film. Also, Langnians' arms didn't end in green, sharp-edged blades from the elbows downwards. Therefore, having so many things that Langnians didn't have, it was safe to assume this wasn't a Langnian – at least not in the traditional sense.

Whatever the creature was, no one had much time to figure it out as the black figure lunged forward with its sharp, sword-like arms that penetrated Khalli's chest and promptly protruded from his back, their sharp tips dripping with blood.

"YOU WILL DO," the creature *said*, lifting the hapless Vahltan into the air while pulling him closer.

As their eyes locked, Khalli's body began to spasm, and rapidly changed colour from dark brown to light grey as his body tissue started to shrivel and crack before it disintegrated into a pile of ash on the floor.

"MUCH BETTER," the creature said, looking at the ash settling about its feet. *"THANK YOU FOR YOUR SACRIFICE, BROTHER."*

"What the fhark is that?" the Vahltan Jenni exclaimed from the side, raising the rock she'd procured as a weapon earlier.

Phealix didn't have an answer, but whatever was standing in front of them had just killed one of her own, and *that* wasn't something she was prepared to let slide. Grabbing her stunner, she fired off three shots that dissipated upon impact with the creature's torso. It didn't even flinch. So she did the only thing she could think of and kept firing until the stunner's battery clip ran flat.

Beside her, Reg held his spear at the ready.

"Now what?" he grated from the side of his mouth.

Crossing its weaponised forearms again, the creature stepped forward. *"NOW,"* it said, eyes blazing, *"IT'S YOUR TURN."*

CHAPTER 26

With the creature closing in on them, Reg tightened his grip on the spear until his knuckles turned as white as his face.

Before he could use the weapon, though, the panicked Vahltan Jenni hurled her rock at the advancing creature, striking it against the head. Staggering slightly from the impact, the rocky creature recovered and leapt towards the pirate with its crossed blade-arms, which it swiftly uncrossed again to slice through the Vahltan's neck.

Reg had no love for criminals, but even *he* felt queasy as the pirate's head rolled across the floor and came to rest with a soft, wet bump against the base of the crystal column. Distracted, the lieutenant didn't have enough time to stop Issy from grabbing the spear from his numb fingers. The tribesman pulled back the weapon and threw it at the creature's head, where it penetrated the fiery left eye socket.

This time, the creature reeled back with a soundless yet perceived wail that blew through Reg's being like a phantasmal blizzard; unseen shards of fear that froze the lieutenant's body in place. Unmoving, he watched as the creature flailed at the spear's shaft, but its sharp forearms couldn't get a grip on the wood. The left blade changed in shape and colour, turning from hard, dark-green crystal into a flexible film, forming a tentacle-like appendage that – similar to the creature's remaining eye – was filled with lava. The extremity curled around the wood and pulled the spear forward, away from its face. When the dislodged weapon clattered on the floor, the appendage solidified back into a blade.

The creature turned to Issy with a stream of molten rock seeping from its damaged eye. *"YOU SHOULD NOT HAVE DONE THAT,"* it emitted as a liquid trail of orange ran down its cheek and jawline to drip from its chin. The drops promptly transformed into stony pebbles that, in turn, disintegrated into puffs of grey ash as they hit the floor.

Having never faced living lava-filled rock before, Reg wasn't quite sure what to do, but he knew he still needed Issy, and there was no way he'd let this thing get near the tribesman without a fight. Captain Phealix must have thought the same thing, because she closed the gap between her and Reg to form a flimsy wall between Issy and the rocky terror.

"What *are you?*" Reg said, although he didn't really want the creature to "speak", as each perceived word seemed to taint every part of the Scout from the inside out. But, seeing as the situation begged for the question to be asked, he had to oblige.

"THAT IS OF NO IMPORTANCE," the creature said as it advanced on them, its body still glistening with Jenni's blood. *"SOON, I WILL BE YOU, AND YOU WILL BE ME. WE WILL BE ONE. WE WILL ALL BE ONE."*

• • •

Without his spear, Reg braced himself for hand-to-hand combat, but to his surprise the creature halted after a couple of steps. Despite its obvious lack of functional ears, it cocked its head to the side as if hearing something, then looked back at the fleshy beings.

"IT SEEMS THIS IS YOUR LUCKY DAY," it said with a drippy eye. *"WE WILL FINISH THIS LATER."*

The creature spun about and disappeared with surprising speed and surprisingly little noise through the passageway, from which faint shouting and screaming echoed shortly thereafter.

"No, seriously, what the fhark *was* that?" Reg said, staring at the exit like someone who'd just received an unfavourable tax audit.

Captain Phealix, her stunned eyes also fixed on the passageway, merely shook her head.

Reg finally pulled himself together. "Well, whatever it is, we'd better hunt it down and kill it." He glanced at Jenny's head, lying face-up against the pillar, whose now-pulsating green and orange light did nothing to make a severed head look any better. "Before it does the same to us."

"Are you mad?" Spence exclaimed, and gestured at the head, just in case Reg's eyes weren't functioning properly. *"That's* why we *shouldn't* go after it."

Captain Phealix turned her attention from the head to Reg, her face darkening. "Believe me, if anyone wants to make that thing pay, it's me. But I'm not putting even more of my crew's lives at risk without knowing what it is, or how to kill it. My stunner didn't even faze it."

"Well, *he* did some damage," Reg said, throwing a thumb at Issy.

"Not much," the Faylin countered. "And it still kept coming, didn't it? Who knows what it'll take to bring that thing down. And even if we do, how many of us will be left standing?"

Before Reg could answer, more shouting erupted from beyond the passageway.

"That sounded Ja'naman," Issy said.

"And Teahupo'oan," Roro added.

"See," Reg said, "there's fighting going on, and we're not part of it. Come on, Spence!"

Not waiting for a reply, he charged off towards the exit, followed by two edgy tribesmen.

Captain Phealix and Spence glanced at one another, but the ensign sighed and took off after his friend. With a final look back at Jenni's shortened body, the Faylin and the Vahltans trotted up the passageway, where the membranes of the previously glowing pustules had split open, now hanging limply, darkly, empty.

CHAPTER 27

About halfway along the temple's cylindrical, pustule-covered main chamber, the group stopped to check on the lifeless body of a man lying on the walkway. Blood still seeped from the perforated Ja'naman's wounds, mixing with scattered ash that must have belonged to another Ja'naman, judging by the second spear lying nearby.

While Reg and Spence picked up the weapons, Issy knelt by the body, then looked up at Phealix. "Mekoti," he said dolefully. "He and his wife just had their first baby last week … a boy."

"I'm sorry, Issy," Phealix said, squeezing the little man's shoulder. "But we need to go."

While feeling guilty about not giving the tribesman a moment to mourn the loss of his fellow tribe members, the Faylin's growing feeling of angst didn't leave enough room to deal with other emotions right now. Something was happening to the temple, and it wasn't just the light from the pustules intensifying around them – although that certainly was part of it. It felt as though something was stirring; waking up. And she had no intention of being there when this occurred.

By the way the others shifted on their feet, they felt it too – including Issy. With a reluctant nod, he joined the others as they hurried towards the exit. The group encountered two more piles of ash, which they only paused at to claim discarded Ja'naman and Tea-hupo'oan spears, before moving on swiftly as their urge to escape escalated into near panic.

Exiting the short, dark tunnel leading out of the tem-ple, the group halted when they spotted a rocky black figure on the opposite end of the bridge. Although sim-ilar in colour and texture, the creature wasn't the same shape or size as the one they'd faced earlier. Despite the cavern's low light, the dark figure looked Ronian. Whatever it was, it advanced on a Teahupo'oan headhunter, who soon found himself unarmed as his hurled spear glanced off the creature's chest. Roro wanted to rush forward, but Phealix held him back.

"Let me go!" the Teahupo'oan growled.

The Faylin, however, held firm, so Roro could only look on as the creature closed in on his fellow headhunter. One of its forearms became flexible and shot out to wrap itself around the hunter's neck; its tip piercing the back of the man's skull, just below the base. As the Teahupo'oan's body went limp, the crea-ture held him upright. When the Teahupo'oan's legs stiffened, the creature released its grip and turned its stare towards the group by the temple entrance.

Although she knew rock couldn't smirk, Phealix could swear the creature had just done exactly that, be-fore it turned and raced off towards the cavern's exit with a stiff-moving headhunter in tow.

When the figure disappeared from sight, Phealix war-ily crossed the bridge to pick up the dropped spear and turned to face an angry Teahupo'oan.

"Why you no let me help him?" Roro bellowed.

"Because the only thing you would have achieved was to end up as dust beneath my boots."

Roro's now angry-confused look prompted Phealix to point at her boots. "These," she said.

"I no care about … boots!"

"Well, I hope you care that your head's still attached to your body and, for that matter, that you still *have* a body."

"Er," Spence interrupted, "if it's not too much to ask, can we *please* table this for later and get out of here?"

Phealix glanced back at the temple entrance. "You have no argument from my side," she said, ignoring Roro's indignant look at being ignored. At that moment, she didn't care, because: 1) men never seemed to appreciate being saved; and 2) the need to get out of there outweighed showing consideration towards an unappreciative man's feelings.

Fortunately, Roro didn't say anything further as he set off after Reg, who was already heading towards the cavern's exit. The tribesman's face said enough, though.

Phealix shook her head. What is it with men and their perpetual desire to meet a premature demise and then get upset if you don't let them? However, she knew she didn't have time to figure it out. In fact, she realised, she'd *never* have enough time, because if no one could come up with an answer to this mystery over billions of years, there probably wasn't much point in her trying to do so now. Thus, not wanting to waste any more time or energy on a lost cause, she simply gave a generous sigh before leading her Vahltans over the lava-lined floor towards who knows what.

• • •

Seeing as Issy had dropped the torch in the temple, the group yet again had to feel their way up the tunnel leading out of the volcano. This time, however, Phealix stayed away from Reg, as she didn't want to undergo another groping session, accidental or not.

As they exited the mountain, dusk caressed the clouds and the landscape with its soft light. In different circumstances, Phealix would have loved to sit down and enjoy the scenery, but things needed to be done … although she wasn't sure exactly *what* yet.

Parroting her thoughts, Spence said, "So, now what?"

"I don't know," Phealix replied.

"Well, I still say we go find that bastard and put another spear through its eye," Reg ventured, looking as though he'd found renewed strength now that they were back out in the open.

"Could you *please*, for a change, think things through – or even just think, *period?*" Phealix said. "As you might have noticed, there are more than one of them. We don't even know how many. So we can't just go chasing after them without a plan."

Reg scoffed. "And I suppose you have the perfect plan, do you?"

At that moment, Phealix didn't have a plan other than boxing the Scout's ears to wipe that smug look off his face. However, before the urge got too strong, she turned away to look at the landscape below. Taking a deep breath to calm herself, she swept her gaze across the grasslands until it terminated at the border of the jungle.

"Oh," she said, "I forgot about that."

Stepping forward, Reg's puzzled expression verified that he too had forgotten the same thing she'd forgotten. However, his eyes hit the memory's Refresh button when they encountered the crashed ship in the distance.

"Oh, uh, yes," he said, trying and failing to avoid looking sheepish. "That might work."

CHAPTER 28

With the loss of their fellow tribesmen, Issy and Roro understandably looked somewhat down. Understandably, that is, to anyone but Reg, who sort of understood but didn't have the time or the patience to deal with it.

"Hey, perk up, boys," he told the tribesmen on the hike down the volcano. "You're still alive."

This isn't something anyone had to tell the Vahltans who, although looking somewhat agitated at their loss of manpower, seemed okay with the notion of not being dead themselves. The two locals, however, were another story.

"You've never lost a fellow tribesman, have you?" Issy asked.

Thinking quickly, Reg forced his face into sad-mode. "Actually, our training officer, Corporal Beabur, was killed in our first month at the Academy," he said.

"Oh, I'm sorry," Issy said. "How did he die?"

"He broke his neck falling off a treadmill."

"What's a treadmill?"

"Never mind that. The fact of the matter is, *I* pushed through … and so should you."

Reg didn't have to see the faces of Spence and Captain Phealix behind him; he could just feel their scorn burning holes into the back of his skull. They didn't say anything, though. Like him, they must have known that the tribesmen's sulkiness wasn't doing anyone any favours. Reg had nothing personal against the two locals. In fact, he quite liked Issy – for a savage, that is – and the one called Roro mostly kept quiet, which also made him okay in the lieutenant's eyes. But they had a mission, and while he didn't really know what that mission was, lugging along emotional baggage wasn't helping their cause.

Realising the baggage wouldn't get lighter by itself, Reg tried playing in unfamiliar territory.

"Look," he said, placing an awkward hand on Issy's shoulder, "I'm, uh … sorry … about your friends."

This did nothing to console the Ja'naman, and seeing as he couldn't scrape together enough authenticity for any further consolation attempts, Reg changed the subject. "Hey, you're pretty good with a spear."

"Out here, you have to be," Issy said flatly. "If you miss, you die."

"Still, that was one helluva throw back there. How did you know to aim for the eye?"

Issy shrugged. "It just came to me."

As Issy obviously didn't want to talk about the matter any further, Reg pushed the conversation into yet another direction.

"So, um, this Metal Mountain," he said. "What can you tell us about it?"

"Not much," Issy said with a slight rise in enthusiasm as his love for storytelling prepared itself for a grand entrance, much to Reg's relief *and* dismay. "It's been there since I can remember."

"Is that where you got the vernaculites from?"

"Not me, personally. But yes, that's where the tribe found it. The Metal Mountain descended from the heavens long before I was born. The tribes believed it to be one of the gods that had died and fallen to the soil to rest among its loyal subjects. Fearing they might disturb the gravesite, the tribes agreed that the mountain should stay off-limits."

"Yet you disturbed it."

Issy sighed. "Yes. My great-grandfather, Khulu, was a bit more … adventurous than the other villagers. For months he tried to convince the former Priestess to explore the Metal Mountain. He argued that it didn't make sense for a god to die in the first place and, even if it did, it wouldn't choose the soil as its final resting place. It would remain *up there*, in the heavens, where the rest of us travel after death."

Reg wanted to say something, but decided that a debate over the afterlife would serve no purpose.

"So, they listened to him?" he said instead.

"Eventually, yes. Especially after Khulu convinced them that the mountain had been sent as a gift. Ja'namans love gifts, and so too do the Teahupo'oans.[*] Which is fortunate, otherwise we wouldn't have been able to enter the Metal Mountain."

"Why?"

---

[*] Gifting is, in actual fact, a time-honoured tradition among most species. A rare exception was the ancient Randukians, who used to believe that everything belonged to them in any case, so who were others to think they could gift anything to them! After being conquered, however, the Randukians soon discovered the joys of gifting. It's just the wrapping part that still eludes them, so if you're expecting a present from a Randukian, don't expect anything pretty.

"Well, as with the Fire Mountain, the Metal Mountain falls on the border of our territories. So both tribes had to consent to the expedition. That's also why both tribes sent an equal number of men to explore the mountain together."

"Let me guess – if one had gone without the other, it would have started a war."

Issy shared a nod with Roro.

"Fair enough," Reg said. "Did they find anything?"

"Mostly things they didn't know what to do with," Issy said. "But also lots of metal, which we mostly use as tools and weapons. Everything was shared equally among the tribes. My family got the box of vernaculites, which my parents have been using as a cutting board."

"With a ship— um, *mountain* that size, I would have thought they'd … well, take more stuff. More than I'd seen around your village."

"And they would have, if the Metal God hadn't chased them off."

"Metal God?" Spence said, intrigued.

"Yes, on their second day of gift-gathering, the tribesmen were attacked by the Metal God. They all managed to escape, except for my great-grandfather, who'd gone deeper into the mountain than the others."

"He died there?" Captain Phealix asked.

"Everyone thought so, at first, but he returned the next morning … in a manner of speaking."

"What manner would that be?" the Faylin said.

Issy frowned. "I'm not sure. They say he returned without his mind, that he'd become a madman, ranting about an impending doom."

"What impending doom?"

"To this day, no one knows, and seeing as nothing's happened, no one really cares anymore, either. Khulu's persistent warnings about the temple also didn't do his credibility any favours. His son – my grandfather – couldn't understand what a temple in the Fire Mountain – even *if* it existed – had to do with Khulu's experience in the Metal Mountain. So, like the rest of the village, he wrote it off as the ravings of a man separated from his sanity. Not long thereafter, Khulu was gone – simply packed up and left without a word to anyone. Most people were thankful for this ... especially my grandfather."

"Your grandfather was *glad* his father had disappeared?" Captain Phealix said, looking perturbed.

Reg knew that Faylins generally viewed family as the key to a strong, stable civilisation, and that the loss of a family member was even more traumatic for them than for most other species.

Too bad pirates don't feel the same about other people's family, Reg thought. Ain't that right, Captain Phealix?

"Maybe more relieved than glad," Issy continued, his face still bathed in shame. "You see, before the Metal Mountain incident, our family had always enjoyed a prominent standing within the tribe, with a long line of Chiefs and Priestesses. As a matter of fact, my grandfather was set to become the next Chief."

"Until your great-grandfather mucked everything up," Reg volunteered.

Issy shot him a resentful glare, but eventually sighed. "Yes," the Ja'naman said. "And not just for my grandfather; for my parents too. Khulu's legacy has haunted our family since then. My parents had to work hard to restore the family name, but even now it remains shaky."

"Where did he go ... your great-grandfather?"

"I don't know," Issy said. "Neither the tribe nor my family had any answers, nor were they keen on finding any. They'd locked the memory of Khulu away along with any further mention of the Metal Mountain – no one was to ever speak of it again, much less set foot inside it."

"So you know nothing about the Metal Mountain yourself?" Reg said, agitated.

"No, sorry."

"But surely—"

"It's okay, Issy," Captain Phealix interrupted, scowling at the frustrated lieutenant. "You've been most helpful. We'll just have to find out what we can as we go along."

Issy looked pleased to have been of use, while Reg looked the opposite. He had hoped to coax some useful information from the tribesman, but instead of getting much-needed answers, Reg was left with even more questions. But he grudgingly realised that the pirate captain was right – they would have to discover the rest for themselves. He just hoped that whatever they found would work out in their favour because, thus far, things have gone from bad to worse. But he firmly believed things could only get better once they reached the ship.

The problem with belief, however, is that it doesn't always work out the way you believe it should.

CHAPTER 29

Reaching the foot of the volcano, they headed into the jungle. The plains were too open, even at night, which had fallen before the group reached the last quarter of their descent. The final part of the hike had delivered a few nasty scrapes and bruises, especially among the now near-blind Vahltans.

"Captain, the *Dodger* … they should have found us by now," Franki said, tenderly touching his backside, which had doubled as a sled after an earlier misstep.

"I know, Franki," Phealix said. "But I'm sure they'll come."

She, too, had been growing concerned about the *Jolly Dodger's* prolonged absence. Cap had better have a good explanation! Phealix knew her First Hand would have one, though, because he knew what was good for him. The only reason she could think of was that the *Dodger* never received the shuttle's emergency signal. It made more sense than Cap just leaving her here, and it was her primary motivation for reaching the crashed ship, aka the Metal Mountain. If its communication system was still intact, they could use it to contact the *Dodger*. Or maybe Salli could assemble something from whatever had survived the crash. As the *Dodger's* Chief Technician, the Vahltan had exceptional skills with all things electronic and mechanical.

Keeping her voice low so the Scouts wouldn't hear, Phealix said, "Franki, when we get to the ship, see if you and Salli can find something with which to contact the *Dodger*. I'll keep an eye on the Scouts. Got it?"

The Vahltan nodded and dropped back to relay the order to the technician.

Phealix turned her attention back to the uniformed human and Ronian. Something must have gone wrong with their emergency broadcast too, otherwise there would have been a Militor ship hovering overhead by now, Dumb Planet or not. The Militorate wasn't in the habit of leaving men or tech behind for others to exploit.

Although they currently shared the common goal of survival, Phealix still didn't trust the Scouts one bit. They would definitely try to contact their brothers in arms at the first opportunity.

And she didn't want to be around once those brothers arrived.

•••

Soon after they'd left the volcano and entered the jungle, it had become evident that the Vahltans had run out of steam. Admittedly, Phealix hadn't felt too peachy, either, and the hanging faces of the Scouts advertised the fact that their choice of fruit also wasn't peach. Even Roro had to have felt the strain of the day's events, as it hadn't taken much to convince him to search for shelter. Fortunately, it also hadn't taken him long to find a cave where they could spend the night.

Now, rolling over for the umpteenth time to ease the pain in her side, the first rays of morning light skimmed Phealix's eyelids.

Finally, she thought as she opened her eyes and squinted at the sunshine streaming in through the cave's entrance.

The Faylin was truly grateful for the breaking dawn, because she was tired of sleeping. At least, she was tired of trying to sleep on the cold, hard floor of the musty cave. Sitting up, her pained groan turned into a yelp as she stared into a pair of big, round, amber eyes staring back at her.

"What the … ?" she yelled, scrambling away from the orbs, which beat their own hasty retreat along with the shadowy shape housing them.

While the others bolted to their feet, brandishing rocks and spears, Roro ran into the cave with one of the torches he'd made the previous evening. Raising the flame, he approached the figure with caution.

"Night Aahp," the headhunter whispered, causing the pirates to tense up – the memory of Danni being decapitated by one of these beasts still fresh in their memory.

"You no worry," Roro said. "It only baby. Male, I think."

"I thought you checked this place before we came in," Phealix hissed.

Roro shrugged. "Maybe it afraid and find hole to hide in. It not big. Easy to hide in hole."

"Why would it come out now?"

"It probably hungry."

"Where's its mother?" Phealix asked, swallowing hard as she looked about. She, too, hadn't forgotten what one of these things could do to a person.

"We close to where we kill Night Aahp. I think this her baby. That why mother attack big group of men. Protect home. Protect baby."

Phealix stepped up next to Roro to get a better look at the grey creature cowering behind a rock. Even if it had been standing erect on its hind legs, it wouldn't have reached the Faylin's waist – *much* smaller than the one they'd faced before. Being a baby, its large, round eyes looked even bigger in proportion to its head, and its teeth barely broke the surface of its purple gums. It didn't have much hair yet, either, with only a small tuft of wispy grey fur crowning its scalp.

Kneeling before the creature, Phealix carefully placed her spear to the side. "Easy, little guy," she said, keeping her voice soft. "We're not here to hurt you."

When the Night Aahp shrank away in fear, Phealix turned to one of the Vahltans. "Frikki, do you still have that energy bar you've been trying to hide from us?"

Frikki's eyes darted between the scowls seizing control of his crewmates' faces. "I'm sorry, Captain, I, uh, don't know what you're talki—"

"Energy bar, Frikki," Phealix said, keeping her glare fixed on the Vahltan until he pulled the snack from his breast pocket and placed it in her hand.

"Thank you," she said, unwrapping the energy bar. However, when she held it towards the Night Aahp, it recoiled with a hiss.

Giving the bar a nibble to indicate its purpose, Phealix waved it in front of the creature. "See," she coaxed, "it's only food. You must be starving. Come on, little fella … you've got to eat something."

Nostrils flaring, the Night Aahp sniffed at the bar before snatching it from the Faylin's hand and gulping it down without putting much effort into chewing.

"If you're done playing mom, might I suggest we get moving?" Reg said from behind.

Keeping her eyes on the creature staring at her, Phealix said, "We can't just leave it here."

"Well, we cannot take it with us, either."

Phealix knew this, but she detested the human for pointing it out. "Yes," she growled, "I know."

"Then let's go," the Scout said, walking to the mouth of the cave.

Phealix took one last look at the small Night Aahp's large, hopeful eyes. "I'll come back for you, little one. I promise."

Getting up, she tried to ignore the whimpering behind her as she followed the others out the cave. It wasn't easy. She knew she was partly to blame for the death of the baby's mother, and if Phealix herself died, so too would he. She therefore revised her promise to include a Death clause, because life had taught her long ago that there was always something waiting to take that life away. And the waiting room was filling up fast.

CHAPTER 30

The rest of the journey to the so-called Metal Mountain was mostly uneventful, aside from Spence nearly being consumed whole by a carnivorous flower. And aside from Franki nearly being consumed whole by quicksand. And aside from Stanli nearly being consumed whole by a gigantic snake that turned out quite hard to kill. But aside from the daily jungle consumption conventions, it really was a mostly uneventful journey.

As the group trekked along the well-trodden jungle path, Reg glanced at the saliva-covered Stanli. The Vahltan still appeared somewhat unstable from the venom contained in the snake's digestive juices. A part of the Scout was disappointed that the huge reptile hadn't succeeded, as the universe would've had one less scumbag to contend with.

The only reason the other part was glad the Vahltan had survived, was that they needed the numbers. For now. However, as soon as the Militorate arrived, Reg would have them all locked up. And if he had any say, he'd have them locked up with a few of those snakes to keep them company. With their track record of killing those they raided – even Militor vessels, if the right opportunity presented itself – these pirate vermin and the rest of their Zolt-damned kind deserved nothing less than to be exterminated; wiped from existence and excised from the annals of history. Except, *maybe*, for Captain Phealix.

It surprised Reg to find himself hating the Faylin slightly less than he should. And, no, it had nothing to do with her looks! Or did it? He wasn't *that* superficial … was he?[*]

The captain looked troubled, and Reg felt he should say something, so he said, "Why are you, er, wearing a nappy?"

"A *what* now?" the Faylin said.

"A nappy," Reg repeated. "You know, a diaper?"

The Faylin glanced down at her improvised bathrobe-underwear. "It's not a nappy!"

"It sure looks like one."

"Well, it's *not* a nappy, *or* a diaper, or *whatever else* your sick little mind can come up with," Captain Phealix grated. "And I'm wearing *this* to prevent your sick little eyes from feeding your sick little mind with things it doesn't need!"

"My eyes aren't doing *anything!*" Reg countered. "And if you're so worried about it, why did you dress up in a skirt?"

"I didn't dress myself … I … I don't want to talk about it."

Her eyes confirmed this.

---

[*] Most women know the answer to this, and while most men would be flabbergasted at seeing most women nod so vehemently at such a ridiculous notion, most women would say that's because most men are just being idiots. And they'd be right, mostly.

"Hey, I was just trying to make polite conversation," Reg said, holding his hands up placatingly.

"Next time, try harder. Didn't the Militorate teach you any manners?"

"*I* have manners," Spence mumbled from the side.

"Well, maybe you can share some with *him*," Captain Phealix said, shooting the lieutenant a glare that he returned with interest.

Reg snorted. "Yeah, like I should care about anything a rat has to say."

"Ah, I've heard some of your Militor buddies use that term – usually before I stunned them. Is that the best description you lot could come up with?"

"There's a reason why 'pirate' has the word 'rat' in it – because *that's* what you are … *rats*," Reg said, nearly spitting the last word.

"And is there a reason why you're such a moron?"

"Well, at least I'm not a murderous thief."

"I've never murdered anyone!"

"Yeah, right! Like I should believe tha—"

The rest got cut off as Reg bumped into Issy, who'd turned to face the squabbling duo.

"We're almost at the Metal Mountain," he hissed, "and we just might make it there if we don't draw any more unwanted attention. So would you mind keeping it down?"

Captain Phealix looked at him apologetically. "I'm sorry, Issy," she said. "You're right. I'm sure the human and I can shut our yaps for a while. What do you say, *Lieutenant?* Think you can manage that?"

Before Reg could open his mouth, the Faylin turned to resume the trek down the path.

Spence was about to follow suit, but Reg grabbed him by the arm. He held the Ronian back until the rest of the party had moved beyond earshot, then ushered the ensign forward at a slower pace.

"What?" Spence said.

"When we get to the ship, I need you to keep an eye on that lot," Reg said, nodding towards the pirates ahead. "If *any* of them tries to sneak off anywhere, you follow. Got it?"

"That's not a good idea, Reg," Spence said worriedly.

"It's not an idea, Spence, it's our job. If they get their hands on comms, we lose them. Is that what you want?"

"Of course not, Reg. But still, we shouldn't split up unless it's absolutely necessary. Don't you remember basic training?"

"Training … pish!" Reg said with a dismissive wave. "You think any of those know-it-alls have ever been in a situation like *this?* No. Besides, didn't our *training* teach us to improvise in unknown situations?"

"Yes, of course, but the basics remain the sa—"

"Screw the basics, Spence. But if it will make you feel any better, it was *not* a suggestion; it was an order. You still remember how orders work, right? You know, from your *training?*"

"Yes, *sir*," Spence muttered. "Of course, *sir*."

If variety was the spice of life, Spence was the antacid. Change wasn't part of his programming, so Reg felt slightly guilty for being so hard on his friend, but only slightly. They had a job to do, and they *would* do it, training be damned.

CHAPTER 31

Black and brown patches of metal peeked through the treetops as the group approached a sizeable, overgrown mound of earth that cradled the wreck's mutilated bow – soil pushed up when the spaceship had ploughed across the landscape during its final moments.

It had been a hard one, Phealix thought.

Judging by the height of the mound, the length of the crash-trench she'd observed from the volcano, and the mangled, burnt metal she now glimpsed through the canopy of trees, the impact with the ground had indeed been tremendous.

With the damage from the crash, as well as the compromised hull having been exposed to the elements for who knows how long, Phealix just hoped there was still something left intact inside. Something she could use to get her and her crew out of this mess. At this stage, she'd settle for just about anything.

Phealix sent Salli up the mound to check for an entrance. Of course, the paranoid human also sent his lackey along. She avoided looking at Reg as much as he did at her. They both kept their eyes on the ridge of the mound while they waited for the Vahltan and Ronian to return, which, thankfully, didn't take long.

"Captain," Salli reported, "if there's a way in, it's not at the bow … or any part of the fore section."

"Are you sure you checked properly?" Phealix said. "I mean, you weren't gone that long."

"I didn't need long, Captain," the Vahltan replied. "I've seen my share of wrecks, and trust me – we're not getting in from this side. At least not without plenty of time and luck."

Spence nodded at Reg to confirm the assessment, but Phealix didn't need the ensign's confirmation, because Salli truly *was* one of the best technicians the Faylin had ever known. While Phealix kept the *Jolly Dodger's* crew together, Salli held the ship itself together, and had performed countless miracles in saving the *Dodger* from certain destruction. Phealix trusted the Vahltan's technical know-how above that of anyone else, but her assessment posed a problem. They didn't have the luxury of time to go door-hunting, and the current market for luck was a bit volatile.

"So, what do you suggest?" Phealix asked.

"I'd say the stern's our best bet," Salli replied. "The aft sections should have less entry burn damage than the fore sections. At the very least, it should have less fused metal."

"Aft it is, then," Phealix said, and as she began to skirt the mound towards the port side of the ship, she noticed Spence nodding towards Reg. The lieutenant clenched his jaw but said nothing as he grudgingly fell in behind the procession.

He must hate this, Phealix thought, having to follow a pirate.

While somewhat disappointed that the lieutenant couldn't see her grin, she realised it was for the better. No need to wind the Scout up any more than needed. He already wasn't using the limited brainpower allotted to him, so diluting it even further with anger wouldn't help. And *everyone* needed to be at their best, because things were bound to get worse before they got better. That's *if* they got better.

•••

"But it's not right to steal," Issy said, perturbed.

The group had nearly reached the edge of the jungle when they encountered a thick wall of foliage barring their way. While waiting for Roro to clear a path through the dense growth, Issy used the opportunity to ask the questions that had been burning inside him for a while now; mostly questions regarding pirates. He however didn't seem to appreciate the fact that pirates were, in essence, a bunch of armed robbers; a revelation that had clearly scribbled over the romanticised picture created by the book he'd read.

Phealix wanted to explain to him that she did what she did for an important reason, and that – unbeknownst to her crew – she'd also been donating some of their … revenue to numerous charities. However, the crew could *never* know about this, as Vahltans usually weren't big on helping anyone other than themselves. To a Vahltan, charity begins at home, and that's also where it ends.

But before Phealix could come up with an alternative reply, Reg snorted. "See, even savages know stealing is wrong," he said, casting Phealix a challenging look. "Why don't *you?*"

"We're *not* savages!" Issy said, sounding as offended as he looked.

Phealix cocked her head at the lieutenant. "See, even the *locals* know bad manners when they see it. Why don't *you?*"

"At least I don't kill people," Reg retorted.

"Says the man who joined the *Militorate … and* who fired on a shuttle without warning."

"Oh, geez, *that* again! Will you please just get off it? You're a wanted criminal!"

"That doesn't give you the right to destroy us upon sight!"

"I didn't!"

"Not for a lack of trying."

Whether it was because he wanted to stop the bickering, or because his burning curiosity hadn't been doused yet, Issy said, "So this *isn't* a mountain?"

"No, Issy," Phealix said, glad to take a break from the tiresome Scout. By the looks of it, the lieutenant was more than happy to reciprocate; his red face studying his feet in silence.

"And there are more of these flying … *ships* … up there?" Issy asked, gazing up at the islands of sky peeking through the leafy canopy.

"Yes. And many of them are much bigger than this one."

Issy's expression said that, if a rock couldn't stay in the air, neither should anything else; mountains included, or whatever you called them. His mouth didn't say it, because it clearly had trouble finding the words to say it.

Phealix sighed. "Look, Issy, ships get built … by people – just like huts. They're *not* gifts from the gods, just like *we're* not gods."

"I figured as much," Issy said. "I mean, you walk like us, you bleed like us, and you argue even worse than us. Gods wouldn't do that."

"What would they do?"

"The opposite," the tribesman grumbled, looking up as Roro emerged from the path he'd just hacked open.

"We now can go to Ja'nama side of Metal Mountain," the Teahupo'oan said.

"It's not a *mountain*, Roro, it's a *ship*," Issy said, and after one look at the Head Headhunter's face, he added with unsurprising enthusiasm, "I'll explain along the way."

Phealix smiled as the two strolled off, with Issy not afraid of using his arms as visual aid in sharing his newly acquired knowledge with Roro, who clearly didn't know what to do with it. But her smile soon faded.

By law, no member of the Unyun Federation was allowed to provide inhabitants of Dumb Planets with any technology or information unless authorised to do so. And although Phealix, by the very nature of her career choice, wasn't exactly the most devout follower of Federal laws, there were *some* she preferred to obey; the law prohibiting interference with Dumb Planets being one of them.

However, she got the feeling that the future of Wahyoo VIII was about to change drastically, and that she – at least in part – was to blame for this. And there was nothing she could do about it.

CHAPTER 32

As the group cleared the jungle, Reg was glad to get an unobstructed view of the wrecked space-ship. He wasn't glad about what the view revealed, though.

While not as scorched as the fore section, the aft half of the vessel had experienced its fair share of battering and burns. Large panels had been torn or ripped away by the forces of entry and impact, exposing the twisted, decaying substructure underneath.

Although Reg wasn't completely sure about it, the oblong vessel looked similar to a multipurpose transport-freighter he'd seen in one of his grandfather's books on the history of trade in the Unyun Federation. But whatever it was, the lack of visible armaments made it unlikely that the ship was military in origin.

The one thing Reg was certain of, though, was that the vessel had been here for a while. The trees, vines and moss growing out of and over most parts of the hull attested to the fact that the wreck had been around for ages. Judging by the height of some of the trees, which had grown far beyond the holes and tears in the sides of the hull, the wreck had to be hundreds of years old, at the very least.

"Wow, this thing has seen better days," Franki said.

"Yep, but I doubt it remembers those days," Captain Phealix said. "It looks ancient."

Although she tried to hide it, the captain looked concerned, and Reg knew precisely why, because he shared those same concerns. The chances of finding anything useful inside looked slimmer than a Langnian on a hunger strike.

"It's some kind of transport, or maybe a freighter," Spence volunteered, earning him a look from Reg, who'd just been about to share this presumption.

"What?" Spence said, giving Reg a look of knowing he'd done something wrong without knowing what. They'd shared many such looks over the years.

"Nothing," Reg grumbled, and nodded towards a section of the wreck that had sustained the most damage. "But I think we've just found our way in."

•••

About a quarter forward from the stern, the ship's hull had nearly split in two from the bottom upwards, with only the top part hanging on to a thin metal thread, creating a huge opening shaped like an inverted V.

"Stop looking so smug," Captain Phealix told Reg, who eyed the split with a self-satisfied grin. "It's not like you've discovered the Lost Book of Zolt. Besides, *we all* saw it."

Reg's grin vanished as he stomped off towards the opening.

"Where are you going?" Spence asked when he caught up.

Glancing over his shoulder to make sure the pirates were beyond earshot, Reg whispered, "In case you missed it, there's a giant opening in the ship."

"I didn't miss anything," Spence said. "I just think we should come up with a plan before storming in there like … well, *you*."

"Don't worry. I already have a plan."

"Oh, and what would that be?"

"It's simple, really. We go in, we grab whatever we can, and we get out."

"Looking for anything specific?" Captain Phealix said right behind them.

Swallowing his heart back down his throat, Reg glared at the Faylin. "I wish you'd stop sneaking up on people like that," he growled. "Oh, no, what was I thinking? That's what you miscreants do for a living."

"Yep," the Faylin said. "Fortunately, we don't have to try very hard with you Militor types. I guess optometry and audiology aren't covered by the Militorate's medical plan?"[*]

Reg's face reddened, but he forced himself to stay calm. "We're burning daylight here," he said semi-calmly, "so if you don't mind, can we get on with it?"

"What a splendid idea. Please, lead the way."

It didn't surprise Reg that the Faylin was so keen on proceeding. She probably couldn't wait to get her filthy hands on whatever she could find. Little did she know

---

[*] Those now having second thoughts about joining the Militorate shouldn't worry. Not only are optometry and audiology fully covered by *MedPac*, but you can also look forward to a superb dental plan. And the higher your rank, the better the cover, which is why Unyun's Militorate is the only governmental arm where you'll retire with better-looking teeth than the day you signed up.

that Reg had planned ahead. He didn't look at Spence, not only because he knew the ensign would follow his order whether he liked it or not, but also because he knew the Ronian's face would confirm that he did, in fact, *not* like it.

The mound lining the trench didn't stand as tall here as at the bow, but Reg still had to use his hands to climb up the grassy slope. Cresting the mound, he continued until he reached the inner slope of the trench to get a better look.

Filled with rainwater, the trench trailed hundreds of metres in a straight line behind the wreck. Because the bow sat higher from the earth it had pushed up during the crash, the lower, back end of the stern was partially submerged in water, and the gaping tear in the ship's hull created the illusion of a metallic beast drinking from a trough.

Eyeing the water disappearing from view into the shadowy tear, Reg couldn't see much beyond a few metres inside, mainly because the sun's angle favoured the opposite side of the ship. Squinting, he contemplated going around, but that would take longer, and as he was still slightly worked up from his little … debate with the pirate, he wasn't feeling particularly patient. So when he heard the others reaching the top of the mound behind him, Reg carefully started making his way down the inner slope of the mound before anyone could raise any objections. But he clearly wasn't careful enough, as his feet slipped from under him, sending him sliding down the slope and into the water, where his arm got stuck on something.

Unfortunately, this also meant his head was now trapped underwater.

CHAPTER 33

Phealix couldn't stop herself from laughing when the lieutenant splashed into the water. Not that she tried very hard.

If you act like a fool, you become a fool, she thought. Serves him right!

But when the Scout didn't immediately come up again, she knew something was wrong. She was about to move forward when Spence pushed past her.

"Bloody fool!" the ensign grated as he slid down the slope in a quick yet controlled descent on his backside. Reaching the spot where Reg had vanished, the Ronian took a deep breath before submerging himself.

With the Scouts' grey uniforms shrouded by murky water, Phealix couldn't see much, but from the way Spence's back occasionally broke the surface, he was struggling with something. And when the ensign came up for air, he confirmed Phealix's suspicion.

"He's stuck," the Ronian gasped. "I can't get him out!"

"Stay here!" Phealix barked at the others before bounding down the slope with exceptional balance, thanks to her tail. Sliding into the water, she nodded at Spence, who slipped with her below the surface.

Visibility was almost nonexistent, but from what little she could see and feel, Phealix determined that the lieutenant's arm was wedged between a bent plate and a twisted metal rod. She also noticed that the lieutenant wasn't moving anymore.

When she and Spence came up again for air, Phealix grabbed the panicked ensign's shoulder. "The rod," she said. "Pull the rod!"

Spence nodded before they took a deep breath and submerged themselves yet again. Grabbing hold of the rod, they heaved until it gave way an inch or so before snapping back into place. Lungs burning, they were forced to go up for air.

"One more time," Phealix said, breathing hard. "Give it everything you've got!"

With a last gulp of air, the pair went down to grab hold of the rod once more. Feet anchored against the plate, they pulled upwards and kept pulling until the rod finally moved a couple more inches. This time, the gap remained open wide enough for them to dislodge Reg's arm. Hauling the lieutenant's torso out of the water, they left his legs submerged while Spence started performing chest compressions, but the human remained unresponsive.

Just when Phealix thought Reg had indeed seen his last sunrise that morning, the Scout started coughing up water. Spence turned him onto his side to expel the rest of the liquid onto the muddy grass.

When he finally stopped coughing, Reg moaned as he rolled onto his back. "What happened?" he murmured, his eyes swimming about as they tried to find something to focus on.

"You almost drowned," Phealix said. "Your friend here saved your life."

Finally regaining their focus, Reg's eyes locked on to Spence. "Thanks, buddy," he said as the ensign helped him to sit upright.

"I had help," Spence said, shooting Phealix an appreciative glance, hoping that Reg would catch the hint. But after a few uncomfortable seconds, it became clear it was a hopeless hope.

Phealix scowled. *This guy's unbelievable!*

Spence looked at her apologetically. "Thanks for *your help*," he said, darting his eyes between the captain and the lieutenant as he switched to auxiliary hope.

Reg either didn't catch the backup hint, or it was tiny enough to qualify for catch and release.

"Has anyone gone inside yet?" he rasped instead.

Realising that gratitude wasn't on the day's menu, Phealix did what any normal person would do. Rolling her eyes, she threw her hands in the air and clambered back up the mound.[*]

Reaching the top, she addressed the two awaiting tribesmen in a voice that tried its best to hide her frustration. "Issy, Roro, could you please light the torches?"

She looked towards the dark, gaping mouth of the hull-fracture. "I think we're going to need them."

---

[*] Admittedly, people usually don't clamber up mounds after performing this ritual, as it kind of hampers the intended effect. However, should you ever find yourself facing a mound after turning around in a situation like that, it's important to keep the momentum going. Page fifty-two, paragraph four of *How To Enhance Dramatic Effect* is very clear on this point.

CHAPTER 34

Entering the ship, Captain Phealix asked if she could borrow Issy's torch.

So polite, Issy thought, handing her the burning stick with an accompanying smile. Unlike *that* one, his thought added with an accompanying glare at Reg.

Earlier, to the side, Reg had told Issy not to trust the Faylin. He said that *he* was a good guy, and that Captain Phealix was a bad guy. Which Issy didn't understand, as she wasn't a guy and, more importantly, didn't look or act like a bad … guy. Yes, she stole from people, but otherwise she seemed to have honour … and manners.

But Reg … what could he say? Reg was a different story altogether. No manners of any kind whatsoever. Issy had witnessed the pinnacle of Reg's rudeness after Captain Phealix helped save the human from drowning. Among the tribes, if someone saved your life, you grabbed them by the shoulders and thanked them with a bow of the head. *And* you hunted a Kuhdoo for them and their family to feast on. *And* you helped to fix anything that needed fixing in their hut for a year and a day. You should at least do *one* of those things … or, at the *very* least, *something*.

But not Reg. No, not even a word or gesture of gratitude towards the person who'd saved him! Sure, there was something going on between Reg and Captain Phealix; some sort of feud that Issy didn't know of.

Still, he thought, if someone saves your life, it should mean something, even among enemies.

At least Spence seemed well-mannered, but maybe that had something to do with him being a – what was it called again? – oh, yes, a Ronian. However, when it came to decency, the human was worse than those *he* called savages. The nerve of it!

Issy wondered if bad manners was a human trait, because if they were all like Reg, he never wanted to meet another human in his life. He merely sighed, though, as there was nothing he could do about it. All he could do was push ahead.

Yes, he told himself, just get on with it.

"What did you say?" Reg asked.

Issy hadn't realised he'd uttered that last bit out loud.

"Nothing," he said.

"Well, keep it down, will you?"

Issy glared at him, but his annoyance was promptly shoved aside by nervous wonder as he stepped into yet another place that was as alien to him as the stories he'd read.

Although the Metal Mountain itself had been declared a no-go area to the tribes, villagers occasionally returned to scavenge the landscape around it for bits and pieces of metal. Those bits and pieces were however nothing compared to the seemingly endless supply of metal surrounding Issy at present. While most of the material seemed worse for wear, it was more than Issy could ever have imagined.

"How could tribes have built this?" he said.

"The … *tribes* out there are way different from the ones you're used to, Issy," Spence said, "and so are their tools."

"I'd love to meet them, someday."

"Not necessarily," the Ronian replied flatly.

With another glance at Reg, Issy realised Spence might have a point, so he redirected his attention at his surroundings. With hull plates missing, there was enough light available to see parts of the ship's interior. And although he didn't know what they were, nor their purpose, the exposed structure, wiring and tubes felt familiar, almost like the carcass of a Kuhdoo.

However, being inside a carcass wasn't very comforting, as carcasses belonged to the realm of the dead. And being surrounded by death wasn't comforting at all.

CHAPTER 35

The water inside the wreck was shallower than Reg had anticipated, barely touching his waist. The two tribesmen, however, held their spears above their heads as they waded chest-deep through the murky liquid.

They didn't look happy, especially Issy. Reg had caught the Ja'naman glaring at him every so often, and he couldn't figure out why. Admittedly, Reg hadn't been overly friendly with the savages, but he wasn't here to make friends. With that in mind, he shifted his attention back to the task at hand; a task that wasn't made any easier by the lack of light.

Using the torch he'd *commandeered* from Roro (much to the Teahupo'oan's irritation), Reg inspected the torn innards of the wreck as he moved towards the starboard side, but couldn't find any viable access to the fore sections. Thus far, all the corridors and crawlspaces exposed by the tear had either completely collapsed or were barricaded by so much metal and plant life that it would take hours, or even days, to clear away; time they didn't have.

As the group neared the starboard side, the light streaming in revealed yet another obstructed mouth of a corridor. However, the metal barricade and the ramp leading up to it seemed out of place. Unlike the other blocked access points, this metal obstruction didn't appear to have formed because of the crash, but rather constructed from various metal rods and sheets.

Glad to be free of the water, Reg walked up the ramp to have a closer look at what lay beyond the barricade. Fortunately, there were enough gaps in and around the metal to make out an unobstructed corridor running off into the darkness beyond.

Reg shifted his attention back to the barricade.

Is that a hinge on the left? he wondered. Yes, like the barricade, it was also quite crude, but it definitely looked like a hinge.

To confirm his hypothesis, Reg shifted the torch to a small hole cut into the right side of the structure. Peeking through it, he spotted a makeshift latch, which he lifted with his finger. The barricade popped open with a *click*. Backing away, Reg swung it open with surprisingly little effort or noise; only a faint *squeak* like a hoarse mouse.

"Hey, you found a door," Spence said.

"And he knows how to use it," Captain Phealix added. "No wonder they made him an officer."

Gritting his teeth, Reg ignored the sniggers from the Vahltans and stepped through the door. Pausing, he raised the torch to study the passage ahead, but still couldn't see much beyond the light of the flame.

"What are you waiting for?" Captain Phealix said. "Or are you more of a ladies-first type of guy? I'd be happy to lead the way."

"I bet you would," Reg grated as he continued into the disconcerting darkness. He couldn't wait to see the Faylin behind bars. And he'd visit her often, just to see the look on her face each time she saw him; knowing *he* was the one who'd put her away. So let her have her snide remarks. Let her have her fun. Because, soon, her fun would come to an end. He'd make sure of it.

• • •

Reaching a T-junction, Reg didn't hesitate in going right, but not because he knew where he was going – he frankly just didn't want the pirate to come up with a snarky remark about his navigational skills.

It hadn't helped.

"Seriously, I can take the lead," Captain Phealix said.

"Think you can do better?"

"Yes, as a matter of fact, I do," the Faylin said, stopping for some reason.

Reg pivoted. "I suppose raiding ships has honed your vile skills to perfection, hasn't it?"

"Why, yes," Captain Phealix said placidly. "Well, that, and the fact that you just walked past a supply closet without noticing it."

Reg glanced to where she'd just nodded, and camouflaged his humiliation with a shrug. "I saw it," he said. "I just … I wanted to … it didn't seem important. And it *still* doesn't."

"I'd rather have a look in any case. If it's not too inconvenient for our fearless leader, of course."

"Oh, not at all," Reg said, keeping his face straight as he turned to Spence. "Ensign Jensis, would you be so kind as to lend them a hand?"

"Yes, *sir*," Spence said, his glare stating his gratitude for being volunteered.

After prying the rusty door open with his spear, Spence squeezed into the small room with the Vahltan Stanli. Not long thereafter, the ensign emerged with a flat, broad case, which he placed on the floor before opening it carefully. Safely packed inside were ten thin transparent tubes, each about ten centimetres long and attached to a lanyard.

"Glow sticks," Reg mused. "These look like older models."

"Much older," Captain Phealix ventured. "I've only seen one or two in museums, and even *they* had newer designs than these things. If I'm not mistaken, that's unrefined petrodium crystals in there."

"Almost no one uses unrefined petrodium anymore," Spence said, warily eyeing the white tube being removed from the case by Reg. "Too expensive and way too— What are you doing?!"

Ignoring the ensign, Reg bent the tube before shaking it vigorously until the crystals inside started glowing with a bright white light. As it illuminated the ensign's face, Reg felt compelled to ask, "What?"

"I was *trying* to say that people stopped using these things because they're too unstable!"

"Well, nothing happened," Reg said matter-of-factly as he hung the lanyard around his neck. "See?"

The looks on the faces of the others clearly stated that *nothing happening* had only been one of the conceivable outcomes, and that the alternative outcomes they'd conceived had not included *nothing happening*. At least Issy and Roro didn't behave like babies, although it probably had more to do with the fact that they didn't know what was going on.

"What that?" Roro asked Issy from the side.

Issy stepped closer to get a better look at the magical device, which glowed like a star but couldn't be a star because stars couldn't hang around people's necks. Not that he knew of.

"I don't know," he said, mesmerised. "It's like … fire … but *not* fire. Maybe he's a man-witch."

"Like Takata and two boyfriends?" Roro frowned.

"No, not *manwi*— I mean a *man* who is a *witch*."

"Oh, *witch-man*," Roro said as the glitch in dialect was cleared up.[*] "My tribe kill witch-man."

"So does mine," Issy said, looking at Reg in a way the Scout didn't like.

"*No one* is a witch," Captain Phealix interjected. "Again, we're *not* gods, and we're *not* witches. Remember what I told you about *technology?*"

The tribesmen nodded.

"Good," the Faylin continued. "*This* is technology. Just because you cannot explain something, doesn't make it magic. Understand?"

Issy and Roro didn't look convinced, but again they nodded.

---

[*] Even vernaculites have problems with dialects sometimes. For instance, when King Zenz from the Kingdom of Strance on Randuk invited Emperor Zaffblahd over for "a friendly game of chess", it translated as "a friendly duel". Which is why King Zenz was quite surprised when he got shot sixteen times by the Emperor's guards as he tried to open his chess set. Later on, Emperor Zaffblahd himself had been surprised when he'd learnt what King Zenz had *actually* meant. However, as he'd planned on killing Zenz at some stage in any case, the mix-up hadn't fazed Zaffblahd too much. He was, however, a bit miffed that no one wanted to play chess with him anymore.

"Great," Captain Phealix said, handing a tube to each of the tribesmen. "Just bend and shake them."

She waited for this to happen, and for the expected looks of wonder when the sticks started emitting light.

"See, *you're* not witches, and you did it – no magic, just technology," Captain Phealix said as she assisted the tribesmen in hanging the glow sticks around their necks, then turned to Reg. "Now, shall we have a moment of silence?"

"For what?" Reg said.

"For the demise of your last two brain cells."

Reg didn't look happy, because that's how he felt, but the pirate didn't give him a chance to verbalise his feelings.

"Do you even *know* how volatile those things can be?" she said. "Especially considering their age. If you want to blow yourself to bits – and I'm sure I'm speaking for everyone else here – could you please do me a favour and do it somewhere none of us are?"

The expressions on the Vahltans' faces agreed with the captain, which was to be expected, but even Spence gave a firm nod!

Heck, what's wrong with these people?! Reg thought, but said nothing, because he didn't have the numbers to win this battle.

Captain Phealix handed more glow sticks to her crew who, despite nothing happening with the other sticks, activated their own sticks with due caution.

Once everyone had a glowing glow stick hanging around their neck, the Faylin turned to her First Mate.

"Franki," she said, "I'll take Stanli and continue this way with the soldier boys and the locals. You take Demi, Salli and Frikki down the port-side corridor we just passed. See what you can find, but if things go sideways, don't take any chances – get out immediately and meet us outside. Roro, will you go with them, in case they need a guide?"

Roro nodded. "I no know *this* place," he said, looking about uneasily, "but outside I show them. If we go outside and you no there, we go to Fight Rock."

It was Issy's turn to nod, being the only one who knew what Roro was talking about.

"Good," Captain Phealix said. "That's settled then."

Reg didn't argue. Instead, he gave Spence a secretive nod that was met by a non-secretive glare. The ensign shook his head in a last-ditch attempt at convincing his friend to change his mind about splitting up. But Reg countered it with a cold that's-an-order glare that Spence had learnt to both hate and accept.

When Roro and the Vahltans headed back the way they'd come, Captain Phealix pulled her First Mate aside. Reg had to strain his ears, but the Faylin's barely audible words lent credence to something that's been plaguing him too, "Watch your back, Franki. We are not alone."

CHAPTER 36

Leading the scavengers up the portside corridor, Franki hoped they would find something of interest. Something functional. Something that would help get them off this rock. Anything! But apart from some rusted power-turners and a medical kit that, by now, would probably do more harm than good, the search hadn't yielded anything remotely useful or, in many cases, recognisable.

The state of the ship didn't make things easier, either, and not just the wreckage itself. With rust, grime and plant life asserting their dominance over time, most parts of the wreck were inaccessible, even those that hadn't sustained severe damage during the crash. Despite the Vahltans combining their strength with the leverage of spears, the doors and hatches either didn't budge at all, or didn't budge by much. And a peek through the small openings didn't reveal anything promising anyway.

They ended up wasting a lot of time trying to open unopenable openings, but Franki knew they had to push on if they were to have any hope of escaping this "Zolt-damned planet", a term he'd been using with increasing frequency since his unfortunate introduction to … well, this Zolt-damned planet!

A seed of optimism germinated and spread throughout the party as they encountered a wider door, above which a barely visible sign declared the area beyond as *CARGO BAY 4* in Ronian. And with all the other barely visible signs and writing they'd seen being in Ronian, it was a good bet that this had been a Ronian vessel.

Holding up his glow stick for a closer inspection, Franki noticed the door itself wasn't completely sealed, sporting a narrow gap on the right. But with cargo doors usually being either completely open or completely closed, the fact that it was neither gave his newfound hopes a well-deserved boost. The door mechanisms must have ripped loose upon impact, and as long as the damage wasn't *too* severe, they might just get the thing moving.

Knowing that spears weren't going to cut it in the leverage department, especially not with such a sizeable door, Franki turned to the other Vahltans.

"Hey, this door isn't going to open by itself, you know," he said, "so stop standing there and go find something to pry it open."

Of course, Franki didn't go himself, because he didn't want to. Fortunately, he had a knack for delegating undesirable tasks – even more of a knack than other Vahltans – which made him a superb First Mate. If it hadn't been for Cap, Franki would've been the *Jolly Dodger's* First Hand. Not that he really wanted the job, as it involved way too much responsibility and, above all, work. Still, he *could* have been.

As Frikki, Demi and Salli rushed off, Franki turned his attention back to the opening on the right.

"What is 'cargo bay'?" Roro asked behind him.

"It's where people ... keep stuff," the Vahltan said, removing the glow stick from around his neck.

"Like pouch?"

"It's a bit bigger than that," Franki said, and pushed the glow stick through the gap, hoping to see something. He didn't have any luck.

"Like hut?"

Retracting the glow stick, Franki sighed. "Yes, like a hut. A big hut."

"Oh," Roro said. "We have hut like that."

"I seriously doubt it," Franki said. He didn't really want to talk. The grimy ship gave him the creeps, and that was saying a lot for a Vahltan, who generally weren't known for setting the bar very high in matters of cleanliness and neatness – two words that, most Vahltans would agree, took up unnecessary space in a dictionary.[*]

Spotting some webbing nearby, he assumed it belonged to a spider, although he'd hate to encounter the spider that had spun it. Judging by the thickness of the threads, as well as the foot-long empty carcass suspended in the web with its dried-out skin draped neatly over the skeleton beneath, it had to be huge. The size of the spider wasn't the only thing that concerned Franki; he hated spiders of all sorts and sizes, but the bigger ones gave him more to hate visually.

---

[*] Most Vahltans also agree that dictionaries themselves take up too much space, which is the second-biggest reason why most Vahltans don't own a dictionary. The biggest reason is that galphones have auto-"correct", and although – due to subsequent auto-misunderstandings – this function has caused more casualties among Vahltans than bird flu, the majority of them believe it's totally worth it.

The thing that bothered Franki even more than the local wildlife, was the captain. Aside from Vahltan underwear, there wasn't much that creeped the boss out, but he'd seen it happen twice now – once in the temple, and now, here. She was good at hiding her feelings, and apart from Cap, Franki was the only crew member that could pick up on subtle changes in her emotional state. He'd never seen her looking as edgy as now. She even let the human Scout rattle her cage; something she'd never do in normal circumstances.

No, while she'd never admit it, Captain Phealix was afraid. And *that* scared the living crap out of Franki.

•••

The Vahltans returned a short while later with the fruits of their search, but while the women had procured a pair of long, sturdy pipes, the proud smile on Frikki's face was erased when Franki shook his head.

"What?" the muscular Vahltan frowned at the First Mate.

Glancing at the bendy branch in his subordinate's hands, Franki didn't have the heart to rain on his parade. Frikki had a head for fighting, and that's about all his head had space for.

"Nothing, Frikki," Franki said. "Thanks, but I think we're covered. Give us a hand with these, will you?"

"You got it, Boss," Frikki said, his smile returning as he dropped the branch and assisted Demi with her pipe.

With both pipes wedged into the gap, everyone grabbed the ends and started pulling sideways with everything they had. When that wasn't enough, they tried again; this time with *everyone* really putting in everything they had, as everyone thought everyone else would have done so on the first attempt. The second attempt also yielded nothing, but on the third, a loud clink announced that something had snapped, followed by a brief screech of metal as the door slid left a couple of inches.

Panting, Franki shined his light through the gap once more and spotted a tear in the floor. Good, that should provide more leverage, he thought, and directed the far ends of the pipes into the tear. Again, the group heaved, causing the door to grind open wide enough for a man to enter, even one as portly as Roro.

Breathing heavily, Franki stepped through first to survey their surroundings. But despite a few narrow rays of light spilling through the holes and tears in the hull, his poor Vahltan night vision couldn't detect much beyond his immediate vicinity, until he spotted a cracked sign next to the door. Holding up the glow stick, Franki wiped the dust from it. He recognised the faded markings, and although he could have used one earlier, he was relieved to have one now.

"What that?" Roro asked.

Franki sighed the sigh that many parents sigh an hour into the first trip with their kid to the zoo.

"It's a diagram of the ship's interior," he explained.

Roro's face demanded further explanation.

"A map," the Vahltan explained further.

"I like maps," Roro said. The tribesman craned his neck to get a better look at the diagram as Franki removed it from the wall. "I draw map of Teahupo'o land on rock."

"You don't say," Franki said.

"I do. Map show best place to get food. We no hunt or gather food in same place every time, so food last longer."

"Very clever," Franki said flatly as he held his light up to the diagram. "Now, what do we have here?"

After a quick check of the immediate vicinity, Franki ordered everyone to split up to cover more ground. The First Mate didn't like being alone, but due to time constraints, they had no choice. And when the lights from the others' glow sticks turned into tiny bobbing specks as they set off in various directions, the big, dark cargo bay felt even bigger and darker than before. But whether it was because of the last thing the captain had said to him, or because he sensed it himself, Franki indeed felt they weren't alone. And he liked that even less.

CHAPTER 37

For the umpteenth time, Spence swore under his breath as he bumped into yet another unknown obstacle. Luckily, the noise blended in with the occasional cracks and snaps that rang throughout the wreck's ever-failing structure.

Of course, being able to see properly would have aided his need for silence in following the group ahead. But to evade detection, he had to keep his glow stick covered most of the time with a rusty bucket he'd found along the way. With the lack of light and his constant focus on trying to avoid colliding with stuff, he nearly bumped into the group a few times, especially when they had to retrace their steps due to blocked routes. Thankfully, thus far, he remained undetected. He didn't know what would happen if he got caught, and he also didn't want to find out.

Rubbing his shin, Spence bit back the pain as he limped along, but froze shortly thereafter when the group stopped at a large door. Taking cover in a corridor running towards the interior of the ship, the ensign watched from around the corner as Franki inspected the door. The Vahltan gave an order, upon which his mates split up in search of something. Spence tensed up as the muscular one, Frikki, headed in the Scout's direction.

Pressing the bucket hard against his torso, Spence backed farther down the corridor, knowing his cover would be blown the moment Frikki stepped into it. He gave a sigh of relief when the Vahltan continued past, heading straight up the corridor from which the group had come.

Knowing the pirate could return at any moment, Spence held his position and waited, using the spare time for some supplemental under-breath swearing. This time, he aimed the carefully selected words at Reg.

From their first meeting, Spence had known that Reg was as stubborn a person as one could find, and the human's impatience did nothing to up his ranking on the likeability scale. Reg always tried to take shortcuts in advancing himself, mainly – as far as Spence suspected – to earn the respect of his grandfather. And if you combined these traits, you ended up with a bit of a prick bearing officer insignia.[*]

However, where others would have long since given up on Reg, Spence felt sorry for him, and tried to keep Reg in check as far as he could. He always backed the

---

[*] Some would say not all officers are pricks. And that's true. There are plenty of officers out there – good, decent individuals – who enjoy spending quality time with family, taking long walks in the park and making potpourri when they're off-duty. On duty, however, you're required to have at least some measure of prickiness, because the Militorate didn't spend all that money training you to say *pretty please* every time something needs doing. If you have a problem with that, you're welcome to take it up with your immediate superior, who will gladly show you how much of a prick she can be despite her love for kittens.

human whenever he got into trouble with his superiors, and did his best to guide him into making better decisions.

Spence used to convince himself that his efforts had helped to some extent, instilling in him a feeling of accomplishment. But since encountering the pirates, the feeling had all but evaporated. Yes, capturing Captain Phealix might fast-track the lieutenant's career, but Spence had a hunch there was more to the story. For some reason, Reg was beyond control, even more than usual, and the ensign didn't know why. Until now, Reg had never put Spence's life in danger. By splitting them up, however, neither of them had the other's back. And *that* didn't sit right with Spence.

The Ronian decided to confront Reg with his grievances as soon as the opportunity presented itself. And outranking Spence wouldn't save Reg this time – he *was* going to listen.

When Frikki trotted past the corridor a short while later carrying a branch, Spence waited for the group to disappear through the door they'd pried open.

Whether it was because of his nerves or his growing resentment towards Reg, Spence didn't have any spare change left to pay attention. If he *had*, he would have heard a faint scrape behind him. He would have noticed the faint orange glow behind him. He would have known something was behind him.

CHAPTER 38

Although the ship itself was eerie enough to put anyone on edge, Phealix hadn't told Franki that they weren't alone out of mere paranoia.

No, by look and function alone, that first door blocking access to the rest of the ship had been constructed *after* the ship had met its fate. And while it hadn't been built in an aesthetically pleasing fashion, none of the locals had the tools or the know-how to construct a door from metal. From what she'd seen of the tribesmen's technical skills, welding hadn't even begun to scale the probability ladder.

Then there was also the trepidation growing inside Phealix's stomach. Again, the state of the ship might have had something to do with it, but it wasn't *just* that. Similar to her experience in the temple, she felt something gnawing away at her mind, her body, her whole being. She couldn't stop yet another shiver from shooting up her spine, making her fine fur stand on end.

"What's wrong, scaredy-cat?" Reg said. "Afraid of getting lost?"

For once, Phealix was glad for the distraction provided by the obnoxious Scout. She was also glad to catch a glimpse of distress flittering across the human's face. Apparently, she wasn't the only one whose nerves were off-kilter.

"No," she said, "I know exactly where we are."

She again studied the diagram of the ship's interior she'd found earlier on. It was standard operating procedure for pirates to get in and out of a vessel as quickly as possible, and knowing your location was an essential step in making this happen.

"Well, you might know where we are, but you don't know where we're going, do you?" Reg said, holding his glow stick closer to the diagram. "Want me to have a look at that?"

Phealix scoffed. Compared to a Faylin, the human had the spatial awareness of that much-talked-about bull in that ill-fated china shop, especially if it was an elephant bull and the shop was grossly overstocked. Phealix also knew that Reg knew the map only helped so much in the ship's mangled, dilapidated interior, with blocked routes having forced them to backtrack several times already. And if *she* couldn't navigate them through this maze, it was highly unlikely that the Scout would fare much better.

She was about to say as much, but as they rounded the next corner, a gun barrel in the roof farther up the corridor swung in their direction. Instinct kicking in, Phealix dived back into the hallway along with Reg and Stanli, narrowly avoiding the white ball of light streaking their way. Unfortunately, not knowing any better, Issy wasn't so lucky.

•••

When Issy's body stiffened and collapsed, Phealix barely had enough time to pull the short-yet-heavy man to safety before another shot flew by her head to hit the wall behind them.

"Was that a stunner turret?" Reg said.

"I believe so," Phealix said, kneeling at Issy's side. She also *wanted* to believe so because, if not for the nearly imperceptible rise and fall of his chest, the tribesman appeared dead.

Not taking anyone's word for it, Reg peeked around the corner once more and ducked his head back just before another shot hit the wall. "Yep, definitely a stunner turret!"

Ignoring any further attempts by the Scout trying to get himself blasted, Phealix removed the water gourd from Issy's hip and repeated the same drowning trick she'd performed on Roro's friend. Thankfully, immediately after she poured the water down Issy's throat and clamped his mouth and nose shut, the tribesman's eyes flared open and he hunched over to expel the liquid onto the floor.

"What happened?" Issy rasped after his body executed its obligatory coughing and wheezing procedure.

"You got shot," Phealix replied, slapping his back.

"By an arrow?"

"No, by a stunner."

"What is—"

"It's a lightning bolt that doesn't kill you."

"Oh," Issy said, and despite the pain that surely flooded his mind, his curiosity kept its head above water. "Why would there be lightning inside—"

"We don't have time for this," Reg said.

"Just give him a minute!" Phealix growled over her shoulder, then turned her attention back to the tribesman. "How are you feeling?"

"My head hurts … a lot," Issy said, gingerly touching his smooth scalp.

"Don't worry, that's normal," Phealix said. "It should go away soon. Think you can stand?"

Taking another moment to collect himself, Issy rose to his feet, aided by the Faylin, who kept close in case the man's body stopped cooperating again.

Issy must have noticed her concern. "I'm fine, thank you," he said, shaking his head.

Reg turned to the tribesman.

"Fine enough to get up *there?*" he asked, pointing upwards.

Phealix and Issy frowned up at the service duct indicated by the human.

"What are you on about?" Phealix said.

"When I did my quick check earlier—"

"The one that nearly got you shot in the face?"

"—I noticed there's another duct-opening next to the turret."

"We can disable it," Phealix mused after a pause.

"Yes."

"But why Issy? Stanli's good to go."

The Vahltan's face however didn't look good to go crawling through a tight, gloomy space, even with a glow stick.

"Issy is lighter," Reg said. "I mean, you've seen the state of this ship, and I'd bet the ducts are even worse off. No, the less weight, the better."

Phealix looked at Issy's round figure. "I don't think the weight advantage is as big as you think. No offence, Issy."

"None taken," Issy said, seeming unsure of the offence, as Ja'namans were naturally built with a wide girth.

"Well, it's still an advantage," Reg said.

When Phealix shot Issy an uncertain glance, the tribesman said, "Don't worry, I'll be fine. What do you need me to do?"

"You must cut the wires hanging from the turret," Reg said.

Noticing the look on Issy's face, Phealix lightened the load of complexity. "You need to cut the vines of the metal plant hanging from the roof to stop it from spitting lightning at us."

"That's it?"

"That's it."

"I can do that."

"I know you can. Just be careful, okay?"

When Issy nodded, Reg squatted with his back against the wall and cupped his hands, which Issy used to step onto the Scout's shoulders.

As the lieutenant straightened with a groan, Phealix looked up while trying to keep Issy's legs steady, and immediately wished she hadn't – she'd forgotten that underwear hadn't yet made it into Ja'namans' wardrobe, and that their skirts failed to cover certain vital areas from certain angles such as this one. She turned her head to avoid seeing more, but it did nothing to unsee the picture now ingrained in her head.

Why didn't you let Stanli do this? she berated herself for her lack in planning. Stupid!

Reg must have realised what she'd just witnessed, as he gave a satisfied smirk. Unfortunately for him, as he looked up to see Issy disappearing into the duct, he'd done so too soon, because his own face contorted into a grimace. With a smirk of her own, Phealix held up Issy's spear, without looking up this time … just in case. The tribesman grabbed the weapon and started making his way down the duct. Judging by the thuds, grunts, hisses and yelps, the short journey wasn't smooth.

Following a scream and a brief bout of rapid thumps echoing from the duct, Phealix shouted, "Everything okay up there?"

After a pause, Issy wheezed, "Yes … yes, I'm fine."

A few thuds later, Issy yelled, "I can see the vines!"

"Will your spear reach them?" Reg shouted back.

"Yes, I think so!"

"Then start cutting!"

Shortly thereafter, the flashes and claps of electric wires making contact with other electric wires suggested Issy was making progress, before a fading *woooooo* announced the turret's demise.

Not taking any chances, Phealix flashed her spear past the corner to see if Issy's efforts had paid off. When nothing happened, she hazarded a look. The smoke wafting from the turret and flowing along the corridor's ceiling confirmed that the turret had indeed fired its last shot.

As she and Reg stepped into the corridor, a spear waved from the duct-opening next to the turret.

"Uh, a little help here!" Issy shouted.

Avoiding eye contact with the tribesman's dangly bits, Phealix and Reg assisted Issy back to the floor. The man was covered with grime and webbing.

"Any problems?" Phealix asked.

"My hand went through the metal twice, and I had to kill a blackspider," Issy said as he wiped the webbing from his head and goo from his hand. He looked up at the disabled turret. "The plant isn't spitting lightning anymore."

"No, it isn't," Phealix said. "Thanks, Issy."

"No problem," the tribesman said and glanced expectantly at Reg, who hid his gratitude by inspecting the turret.

"This ship still has power," he mused, oblivious to Issy's expectations. "It *shouldn't* have power."

Phealix gave Issy's shoulder an empathetic squeeze, but she herself was too mystified by the ship's functional weaponry to upbraid the Scout for his lack of proper decorum. "If I remember correctly, unrefined petrodium can last quite long," she ventured.

"Yes, *if* it's not activated," Reg said. "But even if the ship's power core had survived the crash, the power in its remaining petrodium should have depleted ages ago."

"Maybe there was still some reserve power left in the turret," Phealix said.

"Maybe," Reg said, but fell silent for a moment as his expression turned into one of alarm. "Or maybe not."

"What do you m—" Phealix started before a flash of light caught the corner of her eye.

Turning in the direction the human was facing, she saw a light flickering on from the ceiling farther up the corridor. The light just before it then also flickered on, revealing a rough shape between the group and the light. When the following light came on shortly after that, the silhouette of the blocky shape grew in height. It extended two appendages, which started flailing about. The shape stepped forward with a *clang*, followed by another *clang* and then another as it steadily moved towards them; its wild, rigid appendages striking the corridor walls on both sides with a deafening noise. Silhouetted by more lights coming to life behind it, the shape kept advancing.

"What's that?" Issy shrieked, his face a mask of fear as he glanced at the others, who'd all pitched up at the masquerade wearing the same face-cover.

"I don't know," Phealix said, backing towards the corridor from which they'd come. "But I think it's time to go."

CHAPTER 39

Spear at the ready, Reg stood his ground, which was a bit confusing, especially for his eyes and ears, which pleaded with him to flee in the opposite direction of the dark, deafening shape advancing on the group. For a second, he thought he was going out of his mind, and the second thereafter, he realised he wasn't the only one who thought so.

"Are you out of your mind?" Captain Phealix shouted above the din. "We have to get out of here!"

Reg kept his ground a second longer before his brain returned from lunch[*] and he, too, slowly retreated to the corridor down which the rest of the party had already fled. With one last glance at the shadow lumbering towards them, he ran after the others. Behind them, the metallic clangour increased in volume, spurring the group on like a whip.

---

[*] Brain-lunches constitute the longest-running trend in the universe. But don't be fooled by its name – a brain-lunch can occur any time of the day, several times per day, or even last a lifetime, depending on the … trendiness of the individual in question.

Reg hated feeling like a coward, but there was a reason why whips worked on cows. Fear. And the noise instilled plenty of it.

•••

Running through the rotting, plant-infested carcass of a crashed ship isn't as easy as it might sound, especially if you don't know where you're going. And if the ship's interior has changed since the time of its construction, maps are pretty much useless.

Reg stared at the dead end before them – a jumble of pipes, roots and vines – then snatched the diagram of the ship's interior from Captain Phealix's hands.

"Where the fhark did you bring us?" he said, ignoring the Faylin's glower.

Using his finger to retrace the last route they'd taken, he tapped on a corridor running off to the right.

"This way," he said.

"No," Captain Phealix countered, "we must go left."

"Says you, who'd gotten us lost *how* many times now? I thought you Faylins had a better sense of direction."

"At least we have *some* sense," Captain Phealix said, looking about anxiously, as the clanging noises now seemed to echo from all directions simultaneously. "You'll lead us straight into that thing!"

Reg didn't know what that thing was, but he wasn't keen on finding out, so he wasn't prepared to stake his life on the instincts of a clueless pirate. Besides, he was sure they'd evade the … thing if they moved quickly enough.

"We'll take the next turn before that happens," he said, trotting back the way they'd come without waiting for a reply. Despite the grunt of frustration behind him, the footfalls that followed came as a relief. He didn't know why, though, as he didn't need *anyone* to keep him safe. Yet relieved he was.

As the group turned right into the corridor they'd left a minute earlier, the clanging grew louder. Rushing to stay ahead of their pursuer, they sprinted to the next intersecting corridor. Just before they rounded the corner, Reg glanced back and spotted lights flickering to life down the corridor they were leaving.

They were running out of time quickly, and they couldn't afford to encounter another dead end. Unfortunately, at the end of the corridor, that's precisely what they encountered.

•••

Reg threw the diagram at the collapsed ceiling barring their way, and howled in frustration as he slammed the bottom of his fist against the wall.

And, as he turned around, red-faced, Captain Phealix's I-told-you-so expression did nothing to lighten his mood.

"Don't even think about saying it!" Reg said, holding up a warning finger.

The Faylin shrugged. "Don't have to," she said, glancing at the barrier before them. "I'd say this speaks for itself."

Reg was about to say something, when the clanging noise intensified. At the intersection, a ceiling light came on, silhouetting the flailing shadow ahead of it. As more lights came on behind it, the shadow kept approaching with a steady *clang ... clang ... clang ... clang ... clang ...*

Cornered, the group planted their feet and readied their spears, although they themselves weren't as ready for what they saw when the last lights finally caught up to reveal their adversary, which halted and lowered its appendages.

Reg couldn't believe his eyes. "You've *got* to be kidding me."

CHAPTER 40

Before them stood a squarish robot, or what might have passed for a robot if only it had a head and wasn't wearing a dirty, ragged apron.

Deprived of expertise in the field of robotics, Issy naturally drew his own conclusions. "The Metal God," he breathed.

"*That's* your Metal God?" Reg said.

"Yes, the one that chased our tribes out of the Metal M— the ship. It *has* to be."

Reg snorted. "I hate to break it to you, but that's no god. It's a robot."

"A ro-what?"

"A ro*bot*," said the robot, who was indeed a robot, albeit a very grimy one. However, aside from its missing head and unroboty cooking apparel, something was amiss; the blocky robot spoke Ja'naman.

"You're from our tribe?" Issy frowned.

"Oh, no, not him," the voice said. "Will you *please* move your fat body out of the way?"

"Fine," another voice said, sounding like nothing Issy had ever heard.

The headless body shuffled out of the way and turned sideways, revealing an old Ja'naman man with two heads – one where it was supposed to be, and another in his hands. The second head was a square block of metal sporting a three-inch-thick cable that ran into the robot's neck-hole, connecting the detached body part to the rest of the robot. The head's only "facial" features were two big, green-glowing eyes, which weren't looking at anything specific at the moment, mainly because the head wasn't pointed at anything specific.

Reg shifted his feet, ready to strike at the first sign of hostility, and Captain Phealix and Stanli looked equally prepared for a fight.

"Would you please put those things down?" said the elderly man, glancing at the spears. "You're making me nervous."

"Not before you tell us who you are," Reg demanded, gripping his spear even tighter.

"Well, why didn't you say so before?"

"Because we didn't have a chance to, before."

"Oh, yes, I guess you didn't. Sorry about that."

There was a long pause.

"So?" Reg prompted.

"So, what?" the old man said.

"Who … are … you?" Reg exclaimed.

"No need to shout, boy. All you had to do was ask."

"I *did!*"

The man chuckled. "Oh, yes, you did, didn't you?"

After another pause, Captain Phealix clearly also had enough. "For goodness' sake, will you tell us already?"

"Oh, um, yes, sorry, dear … er … girl," the man said, squinting at her leather-covered parts for confirmation, and nodded when confirmation was attained. "The name's Khulu. Pleased to meet you."

· · ·

"Khulu?" Captain Phealix asked Issy from the side. "Isn't that your …"

"… great-grandfather?" Issy finished, with residual traces of shock trying their best to fend off the forces of confusion trying to invade his face. "Yes, but that's impossible. He shouldn't … no, he *cannot* be alive."

"Oh, I'm as alive as they get, boy," said the man calling himself Khulu, shifting his squint to Issy. "So, you're the offspring of Utata and Unina?"

Issy gave a slow, uncertain nod.

"I never liked those brats," the man said.

Issy's shock intensified, but not really in the taken-aback kind of way. He couldn't stop the corners of his lips from curling up slightly.

"I see you share my sentiments," the old man said. "Are they still such sticks in the mud?"

Issy nodded, but felt obliged to wipe the faint smile from his face and add, "But they're still my parents, you know?"

"I'm sorry," the old man said.

"Apology accepted."

"No, I mean I'm sorry they're your parents. My deepest sympathies."

At first, Issy wanted to defend his parents. However, he realised that, for once, someone was in *his* corner regarding Utata and Unina, so he allowed his smile to return to its rightful place.

"So this *is* your great-grandfather?" Captain Phealix said.

"He *must* be," Issy said. "No one outside our family knows my parents like the people within our family."

"But isn't he a bit … you know, past his expiry date?" Reg asked.

"Not necessarily," said the blocky head in Khulu's hands, causing Issy to jump, as heads not attached to bodies shouldn't say anything, regardless of shape. And the fact that it said something without a mouth didn't help matters either. Fortunately, its voice, while strangely high-pitched for such a large person-thing, seemed fitting for something with skin made of metal.

"Although, sometimes, I secretly wish he'd just reach that expiry date and be done with it," the suitably metally voice added.

The old man glared at him. "You know, you *could* try keeping it *more* secret instead of voicing it out loud every day. Besides, you should be grateful – who will lug around this heavy, mindless box you call a head if I'm not around?"

"I'd bet the first monkey I find out there in the jungle will do a better job at it."

"Well, it wasn't a monkey who found you after the crash, now was it?"

"You mean you *saw* the crash?" Captain Phealix interrupted.

"Yes," Khulu said.

"That's not possible!" Reg said. "This ship must have come down hundreds of years ago."

"Eight hundred and three years, to be exact," the robot said. "To be more exact, you can add to that another sixty-eight days, four minutes, and twenty-five seconds … twenty-six seconds … twenty-seven seconds … twenty-ei—"

"No species can live that long!" Reg said before the robot continued for another eight hundred and three years. "Especially humanoids."

"I'm with the human on this," Captain Phealix said. "And how can Issy be his great-grandson? He's still in his teens!"

"By Ja'naman standards, yes," the robot said. "But, measured in GST, I'd estimate he's about a hundred years old."

As far as believing looks went, the group suddenly ran out of stock.

CHAPTER 41

Phealix's gape of disbelief alternated between Issy and the robot's head, and finally settled on the tribesman. Studying his face, she tried to calculate the probability of the robot being right, but realised her chances were better of calculating the final digit of pi.[*]

"That's … not possible," she copied Reg's argument, as she was too perplexed to add anything original. "Surely we're talking local time here."

Yes, she thought, that *has* to be it. The days *do* feel a bit shorter here than on most other planets.

---

[*] Mathematicians may (or may not) be happy to hear that this has not been accomplished anywhere in the universe. The consensus still holds that it's impossible. The consensus also holds that Derrick Smith of Earth Too is an imbecile, because he still maintains that the final digit is three. This might have carried more weight if he had a workable mathematical equation to back up his conclusion, which he doesn't, as mathematicians agree that his rationale of "I don't know, it just feels right" doesn't constitute a workable mathematical equation. Needless to say, *Mathematics Today* has recently unsubscribed Derrick from their *Make It Count* newsletter.

"No," the robot replied. "As I said, GST – a hundred years in Galactic Standard Time."

"I'm turning Ten-ten Fingers next month," Issy said excitedly. "Then I'll be ready for the ritual to complete my journey into adulthood."

"What ritual?" Reg asked.

"Don't ask," Issy said less excitedly, glancing down at the area hidden by his skirt; an area Phealix was still trying to forget.

Fortunately, settling for a wince instead, Reg didn't ask, and neither did Phealix – at least not about *that*.

"How is that possible?" she asked the robot instead, steering the conversation back in a less awkward direction. "Like the human said, humanoids *never* get that old. And I haven't seen anything on this planet that should alter this fact."

"Actually, you might have seen it," the robot said, then realised from the Faylin's frown that he should say some more. "The Masepa."

"You mean that vile green stuff we drank?" Reg said, exchanging his wince for a grimace.

"I don't know what you had or what it tastes like," the robot replied, "but it sounds about right."

"This one uses it to make most of my meals," Khulu said, glaring at the robot. "A little more *variation* would be nice, though."

"He … cooks for you – the robot?" Phealix said.

"You can call me Ikkabot," the robot said.

"Ikkabot?" Phealix said.

"Yes, ma'am," said the head in Khulu's hands. "Officially, it's Intelligent Kitchen-keeping Assistant, but I've found *Ikkabot* to be more effective in the successful execution of social interaction. It's also easier to fill out on forms."

"Yeah," Phealix said flatly. "So, you're a cleaner?"

"Oh, no, I'm much more than that. As I said, I cook, too, *and* I repair things around the kitchen. Of course, I had to expand my skills over the years to maintain other parts of the ship."

"So, the front door and the turret – your handiwork?"

"Yes."

"With some help, I might add," Khulu added for those who cared. There were none.

"But how?" Reg said. "Where do you get the power from?"

"There was a substantial amount of petrodium left in storage when the ship came down," the robot replied. "We use it quite sparingly, though, and I've dialled the power core down to minimum levels; just enough to run a few essential systems, like the lights and the turret."

"Why the turret, though?"

"To keep out nosy neighbours," Khulu grated, sweeping a glare along the group.

"You were one too, when you found me," Ikkabot said.

"That was a long time ago, and you'd still be trapped under that pile of rubble if I hadn't come along."

"Well, that doesn't change the facts," Ikkabot said. "Nosy or not, *he* wants to help them."

"*He* who?" Phealix said.

Khulu paused, staring at the robot's head. "Shall we just show them?" he said.

The robot stayed quiet.

"How many times do I have to tell you," Khulu said, "you can't nod without a body!"

"It's a habit, okay!" Ikkabot protested as he stomped off towards the front of the ship, followed by the aged Ja'naman, who shifted the argument over to bad habits.

As the pair walked on with a fair amount of noise, Phealix and the others didn't have much choice but to follow. Behind them, the ceiling lights went off one after the other, and although Phealix had a glow stick, it felt as though the dying lights were boxing her in, and she didn't like it. She didn't like it one bit.

•••

Behind Phealix, some wind escaped the confines of Reg's buttocks. It was a long, sad sound, like a lone panda hugging a whoopee cushion in a sewerage tunnel – which coincidentally, was also what the corridor suddenly smelled like, as confirmed by the look on the faces surrounding the Scout.

Soon thereafter, Reg's stomach started mimicking an approaching storm, and he began walking as though he carried a Fabergé egg between his legs. When they passed a bathroom area, the lieutenant obviously couldn't hold back what he'd been holding back any longer, and ducked in without a care for the state of the facilities.

As the group waited a safe distance from the door, Phealix grew annoyed.

"Did he have to go *now?*" she muttered.

"That would be the Masepa kicking in," Khulu replied, even though the question hadn't been aimed at anyone in particular. "It does wonders for the bowels, you know?"

"So I hear," Phealix said, trying to ignore the grunts coming from the restrooms. It didn't work, so she shifted her attention to something else.

"So, uh, what happened to your head?" she asked the head in Khulu's hands.

"It fell off," the robot replied.

Seconds later, Phealix realised no further explanation was forthcoming, so she asked, "Why don't you just re-attach it? I mean, you built a door and a turret, so you obviously have the equipment."

"It won't work on tenantium. Anything short of re-forging my body will not work becau—"

"Wait," Phealix said, her dumbfounded eyes scanning the robot's exterior, "Are you seriously telling me you're made from … tenantium?"

"Yes," the robot told her seriously.

"Who in the name of Zolt's two dogs could afford *that* – especially in those days?"

"Emperor Klassis II."

Phealix's dumbfounded look found itself extra dumb while she tried to digest the information. "Surely you don't mean the Ronian whose death led to the end of the Ninety-nine-and-a-half-year War?"

"That's exactly whom I mean. He personally de-signed me, you know? There were many who wanted him dead, particularly towards the end, and poisoned food became an increasing problem. So I was the per-fect solution to balance the Emperor's growing need for solitude with his growing need for food and drink. I spent most of my days preparing and carrying snacks and wine after him. I didn't mind, though. I can fit quite a spread on my body."

"I bet you can," Phealix said, eyeing the broad, flat surfaces of the blocky robot's arms and head. Sure, they were fairly dirty, to put it mildly, but still – tenantium!

Stronger and scarcer than most types of diamond, the lightweight metal was the most valuable commodity in the Charted Universe, which likely made Ikkabot one of the most valuable robots in the history of robots. And with a backstory like his, the right collector would spend a fortune to get his hands on the metallic servant.

Phealix didn't need to look at Stanli to see the greedy gleam in the Vahltan's eyes; she simply knew it would be there, so she steered the conversation in yet another direction.

"Why doesn't he just carry his own head?" she asked Khulu.

Glancing at the cable-attached block in his hands, the wrinkly old man said, "At first, I only held it while Ikkabot worked on the ship or prepared my meals. But after a while it kind of became … a thing. I carry it everywhere, now, although it *is* getting a bit heavy."

"It's because you're getting a bit old," the robot said.

"Says the piece of junk more than twice my age."

"At least I don't have wrinkles all over my face."

"At least my face is *above* my shoulders."

"What's going on here?" Reg interrupted, crossing his arms while standing overly straight and presenting an overly straight expression.[*]

The lieutenant's damp face, pale with exertion, turned to Phealix, trying its best to look stern.

"What are you smirking at?" he said, uncrossing his arms to place his hands on his hips.[†]

"Nothing," Phealix said. "Feeling … lighter?"

---

[*] Although used for a variety of reasons, this is the go-to look for anyone who'd just done something embarrassing to convince others that nothing embarrassing had just been done. It's also one of the most unconvincing looks in existence.

[†] When implemented right after the aforementioned action, this follow-up action is also not as effective as the people implementing the action might think. It does make them feel better, though, so at least it's good for something.

Clearly not wanting to talk about it, Reg turned to Khulu. "How much farther?" he asked.

"Almost there," the tribesman replied.

"Great," the Scout said irritably, gesturing for the old man to lead the way. "Let's get on with it then."

As Khulu and the robot unhappily complied with the human's impolite wishes, Phealix and the others fell in behind them. And as they neared the front of the ship, the Faylin started preparing herself for what they would find. She didn't know whom the "he" was they were being taken to, and she didn't worry about it too much. Her primary concern was to determine if the ship's communication systems were still intact, or at least repairable.

However, glancing concernedly at Issy, she *almost* wished they didn't find an operable comms system, because if they did, things were bound to turn ugly.

She just didn't know *how* ugly.

CHAPTER 42

Approaching the bridge access door, Reg took a deep breath, but not because he needed it. For the first time in a long time, he felt good. Aside from not feeling like an overfilled gas canister, his body felt invigorated and, more importantly – like the pirate had so unwelcomely yet accurately pointed out – lighter. But despite his body's insistence that all was well, his mind refused to stop racing.

Walking behind him, Reg felt certain he'd catch a scheming expression on Captain Phealix's face if he glanced back. He could almost hear the cogs turning in her head, trying to figure out how to outsmart him. But if she thought he was going to let her gain the upper hand, she'd better think again. He was ready for anything she could throw at him … which would probably be a spear, but he was prepared for that too.

Taking another breath, Reg stepped through the door. The bridge was more or less what he'd expected; more of an old design but less functional – mainly because nothing appeared to be in a functioning state. The wires pushing out from dislodged panels in the rusty, mostly moss-covered floor, ceiling and walls didn't promote the likelihood of finding usable tech.

Maybe Spence will have better luck finding something … wherever he is, Reg thought. As long as those blasted pirates don't find anything!

However, as Reg couldn't do anything about it now, he shifted his attention to a tree that had pushed up through the floor at the front of the bridge. Over the years, the growing tree had forced its way through the ship's interior and back out the shattered windows, overturning the pilot's chair along with the Ronian pilot who used to sit in it.

Stepping closer, Reg knelt to inspect the grime- and moss-covered skeletal remains, which would have looked like everyday skeletal remains if it weren't for the rusty knife protruding from the top of the skull.

"This one was stabbed," said Captain Phealix a few metres away, hunched by another skeleton lying on the floor along with two others.

"Maybe he was stabbed by the same guy who stabbed this guy," Reg said, rising.

"I don't think so."

"And how would *you* know that, Detector Phea—" Reg said as he approached, before the remains came into full view. "Oh."

He joined the Faylin in staring at the skeleton, whose bony hands still gripped the rusty knife that had pierced its throat.

"Maybe he was trying to extract it," Reg proffered.

"No, the blade went right through; severed the brainstem," she said, and gave the skull a spin. "See?"

As the skull's macabre, hypnotising breakdance ended, Reg fixed the Faylin with a flat stare. "Was that really necessary?"

"No," Captain Phealix replied, "but it makes my point, doesn't it? This guy was most likely dead before he hit the floor."

"So, what, you think he did it to himself?"

"Yes, unless someone thought it funny to pose him like this after the fact."

"Hey, don't look at me," Khulu said in answer to the looks now directed at him. "*I* didn't do it!"

"He's right," Ikkabot said. "The crew were dead long before any of the natives set foot aboard the wreck. But if you still have doubts, maybe it's better if you see for yourself."

•••

"How is this thing still working?" Reg said, frowning at the monitor as it flickered on.

"I fixed it," said Ikkabot's head, now perched atop the vine-covered console next to the monitor, where Khulu had placed it to give his arms a rest.

"You should have fixed your head instead," the old man grumbled, rubbing his muscles.

"Let's not get into that again," Ikkabot said.

"What is it?" Issy said, tapping at the monitor in wonder, then jumped back as video footage suddenly filled the screen. Even when Captain Phealix waived him back with promises that nothing would happen, it took Issy the better part of a minute to return.

"Who are those small people?" the tribesman said, gazing at the screen as if it was a crystal ball housing a rabid dog. "They look like Spence … only tiny."

Reg studied the grainy footage of the bridge, and nodded. "Yes, they're definitely Ronian. But what you see isn't real … well, it was, but not anymore."

He held up a finger to quiet the myriad of questions threatening to spill from the tribesman's lips.

"Let's just say they're like … paintings," he said. "Moving paintings that, well, tell a story of things that happened."

"Moving rock paintings?" Issy said.

"Yes. Now, do you mind keeping quiet so that we can look at the things that happened?"

Issy shrugged, keeping his eyes fixed on the moving rock paintings.

•••

The wide-angle footage showed the Ronian pilot sitting in his seat, doing what pilots do while piloting a ship.

It showed another Ronian walking up behind him, carrying two knives, one of which he raised and brought down to lodge itself in the pilot's skull with a sickening crack and an eruption of blood.

It showed another Ronian rushing the attacker and grabbing his arms from behind.

It showed a Ronian woman, who directed her shocked stare from the pilot's body to the restrained attacker and shouted, "What did you *do?*"

It showed the attacker wrestling himself free and spinning around to stab his subduer in the heart.

It showed the blood-spattered, knife-wielding Ronian advancing on the remaining female crewman, who didn't have enough time to complete her sentence, "I don't understand, why would you—" before she was stabbed repeatedly in the chest.

It showed her lifeless body toppling onto the deck, with the murdering Ronian standing over her, blood dripping from the blade hanging at his side.

It showed the Ronian staring at the knife, unmoving, before he looked up at the camera without remorse. Without any expression at all.

It showed him grasping the knife in both hands, blade pointed upwards, and bringing it up with such a force that its bloody tip protruded from the back of his neck as he crumpled to the floor.

It showed, shortly thereafter, the ship starting to shake violently, the dead bodies bouncing and skidding across the deck as clouds passed by the window.

It showed the clouds vanishing, leaving a panorama of fast-approaching grasslands and trees filling the window before the footage went blank and showed no more.

• • •

"What the heck was that?" Reg breathed, finally breaking the silence that had hung in the air for way too long.

"A mutiny, perhaps?" Captain Phealix said, although she didn't look convinced by her own words.

"If that's how *pirates* mutiny, you're doing it wrong," Reg said.

Captain Phealix shook her head. "Well, I don't have any other explanation."

"You *could* offer a better one. I mean, why would a mutineer just off himself like that after taking control of a ship, *and* then let it crash? It doesn't make sense!"

"No, it doesn't, but I don't see *you* coming up with anything worthwhile."

Reg opened his mouth to say something worthwhile, but realised it might have the opposite effect. "So, who are we here to see?" he asked Khulu instead.

"How should *I* know?" the old man said.

"You brought us here, remember?" Reg growled.

"Did I?"

"Apologies," Ikkabot interjected, "but his mind isn't as sharp as it used to be."

"Says the piece of junk more than twice my age," Khulu said.

"You've used that one before," Ikkabot said drily.

"When?"

"Earlier, when … never mind. Just let them speak to him, would you?"

"About what?"

"I don't know! Just … just get him on speaker!"

"Fine," Khulu said and leaned over to press a button. "There's, uh, someone here to see you."

"I KNOW," a voice boomed, causing everyone but Ikkabot to cringe and cover their ears.

"SORRY," the voice boomed a bit softer. "IS THIS BETTER?"

When Reg's ears recovered enough from their initial shock, he finally removed his hands.

"Yes," he said, looking about, because the PA system (as per normal PA functionality) didn't pinpoint the source of the voice using it. "But who are you? What do you want?"

"I WANT YOU TO LEAVE," the voice said.

Reg placed his hands on his hips. "Is that so?"

"YES."

"And who the heck do you think you are to tell me what I can or cannot do?"

There was a pause that was just long enough to hit the sweet spot between being under- or -overdramatic.

"I," said the voice, "AM … DENNIS."

CHAPTER 43

"Who's Dennis?" Khulu frowned.

Issy couldn't speak, however, as his lower jaw felt too heavy to do anything other than hang around uselessly.

Stanli looked at Issy in a quizzical fashion.[*] "It's not that thing from the temple, is it?" he asked.

"No … and it's not a *thing*," Issy finally managed with a mixture of wonder and confusion. "It's … a *god*."

"Why is a god speaking over the PA system?" Stanli said.

"The what?"

"Wait," Khulu interjected, glaring at his great-grandson. "You went to the temple … in the volcano?"

"Uh, yes," Issy said.

---

[*] It's the standard look among Vahltans, even among those with higher intelligence, which makes it quite difficult to distinguish the more learned ones from their less-well-educated brethren. People are always surprised when they learn there's actually a high number of intelligent Vahltans out there; a surprise shared by an even higher number of Vahltans out there; a surprise that doesn't alleviate *the look*.

"I told you people to stay away from that place!"

"I know, but the tribes wanted to sacrifice them," Issy said, nodding towards the others. "The temple was the only place we could hide."

"Hmm," Khulu mused, "the mountain let you in? That means Tuma favours you."

"Dennis."

"Again, who's Dennis?"

"Tuma is Dennis … well, that's what *I* call him."

"Dennis, eh?" the old man said, rubbing his chin thoughtfully. "I like it."

"THANK YOU, BUT—" Dennis began.

"It's got a nice ring to it," Khulu continued. "Did you come up with it yourself?"

"Yes … well, no," Issy said. "It sort of *came* to me. It felt natural."

"ACTUALLY—"

"Well, now that you mention it, it *does* feel right," Khulu said. "Although, it also doesn't. It's almost like—"

"Never mind that," Captain Phealix interrupted. "What's Dennis doing here? Isn't he supposed to be in the volcano?"

Issy felt stumped by this too. Until now, when Dennis spoke to him, it had always been through feelings. His ears had never played a role in any of the conversations. Hearing an actual *voice* was something new. But something else stumped Issy even more.

"How is it that *you* understand Dennis?" he asked Captain Phealix.

The Faylin shook her head, but stopped as she glanced at Reg's stomach. To Issy, it seemed like a torch went on inside her head.

"What?" the lieutenant said, looking down.

"The Masepa," Captain Phealix replied.

"What about it?" Reg said.

"Khulu said your little … *evacuation* back there might have been from the Masepa kicking in."

"So? The other locals don't hear Dennis either, and they've been drinking the stuff all their lives."

"But *they* don't have vernaculites in their system too … like Issy and Roro."

It was as if Captain Phealix had used her torch to light the one in Reg's head.

"Of course," the human said. "The Masepa and the vernaculites must be working together, somehow, or influencing each other in some way."

"Yes," Khulu said, "that's exactly it."

"How do you know this?" Issy said, feeling slightly dizzy, as there were too many things stumping him at the moment.

"THAT'S NOT IMPORTANT," Dennis said a bit louder to recapture the attention of those who'd lost it. "WHAT *IS* IMPORTANT, IS THAT YOU LEAVE … *NOW!*"

"Well, we just got here," Reg said, folding his arms defiantly. "And I don't see why we should leave just because you say so."

"I SAY SO TO KEEP YOU SAFE FROM *THEM.* YOU *MUST* GO BEFORE THEY ARRIVE."

"Who are *they?*" Reg said.

There was a pause. "THE EUWELS."

"Who the heck are the Euwels?"

"*I AM EUWEL,*" emitted a voice that didn't come through the PA system.

The group swung towards the bridge door, where now stood the tall, dark, rocky creature they'd encountered in the temple. And he wasn't alone.

CHAPTER 44

There was no mistaking it – the tall, thin Langnian-shaped rock-thing definitely was the one from the temple, although its wounded left eye socket wasn't oozing anymore. It was now cluttered with hardened lava that left a thin ridge running down its left cheek like cooled wax down a candle.

"Fhark," Reg breathed, gripping his spear. "Not this guy again."

Under normal circumstances, Phealix would have berated the Scout for swearing, but there were times when the use of strong language was unavoidable.[*] And this was one of those times.

"And he brought friends," she said, eyeing the two rocky creatures on either side of the tall one. Neither of them was the one who'd killed the Teahupo'oan warrior outside the temple, though.

The one on the left looked Stortian in shape but without the curly fur, while the short one on the right looked like a Grey, complete with an oversized belly and head.

-----

[*] People who don't have to drive in city traffic might not understand this, and if you're one of those people, that's just fharking dandy!

Aside from featuring the same rock exterior as the Langnian-shaped creature, they also shared the same green-bladed forearms, as well as the same swirling lava eyes.

"WE HAD A FEELING YOU MIGHT COME HERE," the tall one emitted; the whispery, unspoken words clinging to Phealix's being like malevolent tar.

"How perceptive of you," she said, keeping herself calm while fear pleaded with her to at least do something fearful with her face. "What do you want?"

"IT'S NOT ABOUT WHAT WE WANT. IT'S ABOUT WHAT YOU WANT."

"And what, pray tell, do you suppose we want?"

"TO JOIN US. TO BECOME COMPLETE ... TO BECOME EUWEL."

Strangely, a small part of Phealix wasn't altogether opposed to this, and while it didn't even know the terms of joining, it tugged at her tail, trying to catch her attention. However, she gave her tail a swish to get rid of that part, and forced out a snort.

"You obviously don't know me that well," she grated to mask the quiver in her voice.

"YOU'D BE SURPRISED AT WHAT I KNOW ABOUT YOU," the creature said, turning his look at Reg who, for some reason, loosened his grip on his spear.

"Well, I'm afraid you're mistaken," Phealix said, casting a nervous glance at the lieutenant, who kept staring blank-faced into the creature's half-clumped eye. "Whatever you're after, we'll *never* join you."

"OH, BUT YOU WILL ... YOU ALL WILL," said the Euwel as Reg slowly lowered his spear. *"WE WILL BE STRONG. WE WILL BE ONE."*

•••

Phealix didn't know why Reg's face had gone all placid and his body all slouchy, but she knew it wasn't a good thing, and that she'd have to do something about it, fast. In what she hoped would be a surprise move, she leapt forward to drive her spear into the Euwel's eye, but it turned its stony head at the last moment, causing the spearhead to snap in two.

For a moment, Phealix could only stare in surprise at the spear-tip clattering over the floor, but she had to use the next moment to bring the weapon back up when the Euwel swung its green blade-arm at her head. She groaned as the sharp appendage sliced through the shaft, nicking her left cheek.

Staggering backwards, Phealix touched the small, burning wound, and pulled her hand back to look at the dark blood wetting her fingertips.

The Euwel nodded towards Phealix's companions. *"GET THEM,"* it ordered the shorter Euwels before locking its fiery eyes on the Faylin once more. *"I'VE GOT THIS ONE."*

As the tall creature advanced on her, Phealix dropped the damaged spear and spread her arms, flexing her fingers. Despite their general effectiveness against meaty foes, she knew her sharp, hard nails wouldn't do much against the Euwel's solid exterior. But if the creature thought she'd just roll over and play dead, it was sorely mistaken.

When the Euwel crossed its blades and leapt forward to deliver the killing blow, Phealix braced herself and cried out in defiance. She was however surprised when the cry diverted the creature's trajectory, sending it flying sideways towards the front of the ship. It crashed into a flight console that crumpled as the rocky body slammed into the weakened metal.

Phealix's surprise was nullified as her eyes shot back, just in time to witness Ikkabot directing his next attack to the Stortian-Euwel closing in on him. After clubbing the advancing foe halfway into the rusty bulkhead, the robot grabbed the smaller Grey-Euwel by the arms, stretching them sideways so that it couldn't do any harm. As the Euwel struggled against the robot's hold, Ikkabot unintentionally helped it out of its conundrum by pulling one of the creature's blades out of its elbow socket.

"Oops," the robot said, letting go of the creature's other arm. Phealix stared in shock as the detached blade lost its solidity and oozed through Ikkabot's fingers to the floor, where it formed a small, green puddle.

Free once more, the Grey-Euwel lashed out at the nearest target, which was Stanli, who'd rushed in to finish off the wounded creature. The Euwel, however, thrust its remaining arm into the unsuspecting Vahltan's stomach and pulled the pirate down. As their eyes locked, Stanli's skin started to discolour and shrivel until his body fell to ash on the floor.

"You fharking bastard!" Phealix yelled.

Ignoring her, the Grey-Euwel glanced at the ash by its feet. *"THANK YOU FOR YOUR SACRIFICE, BROTHER,"* it said, and looked at its stumpy elbow, which started sprouting green, oozy veins that rapidly began crystallising to replace the missing body part.

Ikkabot looked at the stunned biologicals. "You'd better go," he said. "We'll hold them off."

"We will?" Khulu exclaimed, the shock of being volunteered for a suicide mission forcing down his arms along with Ikkabot's head.

"*I* will," the robot said. "But it might help if I could *see* what I'm doing."

"Oh, er, yes," Khulu said, lifting Ikkabot's head back up and pointing it towards the console, where the Langnian-Euwel tried to dislodge its stuck arm.

"No need to invite me twice," Reg said, glancing at the Grey-Euwel as the last crystals grew into place, leaving a solid new bladed forearm.

"We can't just leave them!" Issy exclaimed, echoing Phealix's own thoughts.

"You cannot stay," Ikkabot said. "There might be more of them, and if there are, I won't be able to protect all of you."

"He's right," Khulu said. "If you stay, you die."

Not having time to deal with the struggle on Issy's face, Ikkabot turned to Phealix.

"Take the left corridor and stick to it," he said. "Don't worry about stairs and what deck you're on. Just keep following that route. It will take you past the armoury and the ship's core. At the end, go right, then immediately left until you reach the exit."

Phealix nodded, and while she picked up Stanli's spear, Khulu looked at Issy.

"He might be a bit of a knob most of the times," the old man grinned, patting the metal head in his hands, "but sometimes he knows what he's doing. We'll be okay, really. Now, go."

Eyes glistening, Issy shook his head. "We can't."

"We have to, Issy," Phealix said, pausing on her way to the door, eyeing the Langnian-Euwel who had finally freed himself and joined his compatriots to face Ikkabot.

"But—"

"Hey!" Khulu shouted. "Stop being a skirt-shaking veld-rat like your parents! Man up and get these two simpletons to safety!"

After a pause, Issy nodded reluctantly.

"Good, now scoot!" Khulu said, turning back to face the regrouped Euwels.

While Phealix felt sorry for Issy, the growing need to get out of there outweighed all other emotions. And as she herded the tribesman out the door, the last thing she heard behind her was Khulu.

"So," the old man said, "which of you monkeys is first?"

CHAPTER 45

Following the robot's instructions, the fleeing trio encountered no more barricades as they raced down the length of the ship. However, they focused so much on where they were stepping that they nearly ran headlong into someone else.

"Captain!" shouted a voice from up ahead.

"Franki!" Phealix said, fending off a heart attack with a sigh that was camouflaged by her panting.

As the bobbing glow sticks approached, they revealed, much to the Faylin's relief, the faces of Franki, Demi, Salli and Roro. Her relief, however, didn't last long, as she noticed the reunion fell one short.

"Where's Frikki?" she asked.

"I'm sorry, Captain, Frikki … he didn't make it," Franki said as his own look of relief transformed into one of trepidation. "You were right, sir – we're not alone."

"Yes, yes, we know!" Reg interjected. "Now can we *please* get moving?"

Not wanting to hang around either, Phealix ushered Franki down the corridor with the others in tow. "What happened?" she asked the First Mate.

Franki looked about nervously. "We were searching a cargo bay when more of those freaks from the temple attacked us."

"How many?"

"I cannot say for sure, sir, but there were quite a few. We managed to escape the bay, but those buggers were right on our heels. Of course, Frikki turned to fight them."

Phealix shook her head. "That fool never knew when to back down, did he?"

Franki's beak twisted into a grin. "No, sir, he didn't. But if he hadn't stood his ground, the rest of us wouldn't have made it."

The Vahltan glanced over his shoulder. "I take it Stanli didn't make it either."

"No," Phealix said, keeping her voice as neutral as possible. "There were Euwels on the bridge too."

"What are Eu—"

"That's what those things are called, Franki," Phealix barked, unable to stop her anger from rising again. "And no, I don't know what they are, where they're from, or what they want."

With his follow-up questions thwarted, Franki remained silent.

Feeling a bit guilty about snapping at the Vahltan, Phealix said, "Look, we'll figure it out later, but for now, let's just focus on getting out of here."

When the group halted to catch their breath, Franki glanced back nervously as banging noises echoed down the corridor.

"What was that?" Salli asked, seeming a bit nerve-challenged herself.

"I don't know," Phealix said, "but we'd better pick up the pace."

"Actually, Captain, you think we can spare a minute?" Demi asked.

"No, why?" Phealix said, glancing back up the dark corridor.

"Because it might just be worth it," the Vahltan replied, throwing a thumb at the door next to them.

Phealix turned to the door with a frown that disappeared as soon as she noticed the faded sign above it. "Ha, you might be right," she grinned.

"What 'armoury' mean?" Roro asked from behind.

Phealix glanced at the barely visible green light flashing on the grimy panel next to the door. "It means we might just be in luck."

CHAPTER 46

The armoury's weapon racks and shelves exhibited an impressive array of dust and musty air.

"I don't understand," Captain Phealix said, sweeping her look of frustration across the empty spaces. "The door access panel was activated. Why would Ikkabot activate it if there's nothing in here?"

"Are you seriously wondering why a robot with no head would do something that makes no sense?" Reg said drily. He'd been pessimistic about their chances to begin with, which had greatly lowered his expectations and his subsequent level of disappointment.

"Hey, that robot saved your life," Captain Phealix said.

"It's just a robot!"

"Khulu isn't a robot," Issy said dolefully.

"Um, no, of course," Reg said with a touch of guilt.

The old man either had more courage or less brains than Reg had initially thought, but he and Ikkabot *had* been instrumental in helping the rest of them escape from the bridge, and had most likely paid for it with their lives. Even if the robot had somehow managed to survive, Reg doubted the old man had been so fortunate.

He didn't voice his suspicion, though, as they couldn't afford Issy getting bogged down with grief right now.

"But I'm sure he's fine," Reg lied instead, avoiding the daggers of disdain cast at him by Captain Phealix.

"How can you be sure?" Issy said.

"He seemed— seems to be a tough cookie," Reg said.

"What do cookies have to do with it?"

"Don't worry about that. Your great-grandfather has survived this long, so if there's one old man who can make it, it's him."

After a pause, Issy nodded with a glimmer of hope in his eyes, much to the lieutenant's relief.

However, while Reg might have convinced the tribesman of his great-grandfather's chances, Reg had difficulty convincing himself of Spence's fate. He just hoped the ensign had stayed low while the creatures pursued the pirates, giving him time to sneak off the ship. He also hoped Spence could tell him what Demi was carrying in the worn bag slung across her shoulder.

"Captain, I found something," Salli said, interrupting Reg's thoughts as she hooked out a small black case from under the rusty table in the centre of the room. Getting back up, she placed the case on the table.

"Is that what I think it is?" Franki said.

"Only one way to find out," Captain Phealix replied. Unlatching the case, she flipped it open to reveal the item stored within. "Seems it is."

It wasn't a flasher, stunner, or any energy weapon Reg had seen before. But he *had* seen it before.

"A projectile firearm," he breathed. "You don't see many of those around anymore."

Captain Phealix snorted as she removed the sizeable Ronian MR45 seven-shot revolver from its case. "You really should get out more, Lieutenant. Don't look so nervous – I thought the Militorate trained you guys to fire *any* type of weapon."

"They did," Reg said. "But that thing is … ancient."

"Ancient or not, it's better than nothing," Captain Phealix said, opening the cylinder and giving it a spin. Satisfied that it was fully loaded, she snapped it shut again.

"Ever fired one of those?" Reg asked.

"Yes, with my father," the Faylin said, testing the hammer by pulling it back with her thumb. "He collects all sorts of weapons, new and old. So do I."

"No surprises there," Reg said, eyeing the big hand-gun nervously – not because of what it was, but more because *where* it was, i.e. in the hands of an outlaw instead of his own.

Captain Phealix must have noticed his unease. "Don't worry, soldier boy," she said, as she carefully uncocked the weapon again. "Unlike you, I won't shoot you in the back. Besides, you'd probably shoot yourself in the foot with one of these, so I'll rather hold onto it … for both our sakes."

Reg couldn't decide if he felt offended enough by the remark to overcome his jitteriness, but his ego refused to let Captain Phealix know that the other two emotions wanted to visit. So he merely gave a shrug as the pirate wedged the revolver into her skirt.

"Fine by me," he said, eyeing the big grip protruding from the Faylin's grassy apparel. "I don't think it will do much good against the stonies in any case."

"Stonies?" Captain Phealix said flatly.

"You know, the Euwel?"

"Yes, I know what you mean. I just find it fascinating how you Militor types always feel the need to attach nicknames to everything around you."

Before Reg could say anything, a monitor on the wall to his right flickered on. He and Captain Phealix shot each other a frown before they approached the grimy screen, which Reg wiped with his forearm.

"It's still working," Demi said from behind.

"This room was sealed quite well," Salli said, "which must have protected it from the elements all these years. That's the only reason I can think of."

Although the monitor *did* still work, it was very close to retiring, and Reg struggled to see what the grainy, glitchy display was trying to show him. After slapping the side of the screen, the picture quality improved marginally – just enough to make out some essential details, like the location of the camera.

Showing footage of the ship's core room, nothing moved on the screen until a figure walked into frame, moving stiffly towards a control panel near the camera. Despite the low image quality, there was no mistaking the figure and the uniform it wore. It was Spence.

"What's he doing?" Captain Phealix said, watching the ensign fiddling with the panel.

Reg shook his head slowly. "I'm not sure, but it looks as though he is—"

The floor beneath their feet started vibrating lightly.

"—tampering with the power core," Captain Phealix finished. "Why in Zolt's name would he do that?"

Reg didn't give an answer, mainly because he didn't have one, and kept his eyes fixed on the screen in the hopes that one would present itself.

Stepping back, Spence looked up at the camera, as if he knew someone was watching.

As the vibrations intensified, the empty handgun case behind Reg and Captain Phealix rattled sideways until it fell off the table's edge and clattered onto the floor.

"I have to get down there!" Reg said as he pushed past the others and dashed out the door.

"Wait!" Captain Phealix yelled after him, following suit with the rest of the party in tow. "If he's overloaded the core, we need to get off this ship!"

Reg, however, kept himself deaf as he charged down the corridor, where loose boxes rattled slowly down the sloping floor and dislodged wires swung from the ceiling. The far end of a pipe tore loose from its crumbling fittings above Reg, and would have smashed his head in had he not veered sideways at the last moment. As the pipe slammed onto the floor beside him, Reg didn't even pause, and kept going until he reached a corridor running off to the right. The sign above indicated the way to *ENGINEERING*.

"This is madness," Phealix yelled, grabbing him by the arm. "You'll get yourself killed!"

"I'm not leaving him behind," Reg growled, shaking the Faylin off.

Captain Phealix looked him in the eye before turning to Franki.

"Get everyone as far away from the ship as you can," the Faylin said. "We'll find you as soon as we're out."

"But Capt—"

"There's no time for arguing, Franki. Issy knows where to go, so get out of here, *now!*"

The Vahltan seemed to have a few more buts rolling around in his head, but he kept them contained. "You heard the captain," he shouted to the others, "let's go!"

Issy trudged off hesitantly, but after a final glance over his shoulder, he picked up the pace to take the lead. While he didn't know much about spaceships, the tribesman clearly knew they shouldn't be shaking like this.

Reg didn't wait for the group to disappear down the corridor. He'd wasted enough time already, and the wellbeing of anyone other than Spence was irrelevant at the moment. Bounding down a flight of stairs, he continued until he reached an open doorway with a *CORE ROOM* sign above it, and entered without a second thought.

CHAPTER 47

Spear raised, Reg entered the Core Room, but immediately had to shield his eyes against the bright light emanating from the tubular power core that rose from the centre of the round room. At first, he couldn't see a thing, but as his eyes adjusted, he noticed movement off to the side where Spence was loading a transparent petrodium cylinder into a slot in the wall. The ensign locked the container into place with a twist.

"Spence, you're okay," Reg said, taking a step closer, but stopped. Something wasn't right. The ensign didn't even pause or glance in Reg's direction as he turned to pick up yet another cylinder. His movements seemed automated, almost mechanical.

"What are you doing, buddy?" Reg asked.

"I'm fuelling the power core," Spence said with a voice that matched the stiffness of his body. It was slow; a hollow drawl devoid of emotion.

Captain Phealix rushed in, but Reg held up a silencing hand before she could say anything. "Why would you do that?"

"We need power," the ensign drawled, locking the cylinder into place. "More power."

"What's wrong with him?" Captain Phealix said.

Reg held up his finger, because apparently his hand wasn't doing a good job at keeping the Faylin quiet.

The vibrations running through the ship intensified into a mild shaking. Whatever wasn't affixed or tied to something else started shifting around. Reg glanced worriedly at the core, which shone more brightly by the second. Its containment field wasn't built to hold as much energy as it was currently being fed. And the fact that the vessel was nearly a thousand years old didn't help matters either.

"There's more than enough power, Spence," Reg said. "The ship cannot handle all this juice, so if you don't decrease the levels, the core will overload. C'mon, Spence, you *know* this."

The ensign marched over to the control panel and pulled a lever. "I do," he said.

"Then why?"

"Because I have to."

"I don't understand."

Spence turned to Reg and looked at him with glazy eyes. "You will," the ensign said.

As the ship started shaking more vehemently, dislodged fixtures began falling from the ceiling and walls, sending sparks flying from damaged, exposed wires.

Bugger this, Reg thought, taking a step towards the panel.

"WE CANNOT ALLOW YOU TO DO THAT," said an unheard voice.

Reg brought up his spear and spun towards the far side of the room, where a Ronian-shaped Euwel rounded the left side of the power core. As the creature halted, another one rounded the right side of the core before it, too, stopped.

Captain Phealix brought up her revolver and alternated her aim between the rocky newcomers. "What's going on here?" she said.

Instead of answering, Reg looked over at Spence. "Hey, buddy. It's me ... Reg. How about you join us over here so we can get the hell out of this place?"

Spence, however, walked his mechanical walk over to the Ronian-Euwel and turned to face the lieutenant with a blank stare. "I have a better idea. Why don't *you* join *us*?"

"What?"

"If you join us, we will be strong," the ensign said with a voice as distant as his gaze. "We will be one."

Reg's shiver matched the tremors coursing through the ship. He turned to the Euwel next to Spence.

"What did you do to him?" Reg growled.

"WE OPENED HIS EYES," the creature said.

"You brainwashed him!"

"NO, FOR THE FIRST TIME IN HIS LIFE, HE SEES CLEARLY. AND SO WILL YOU."

For a moment, Spence appeared more lucid as he looked at the lieutenant pleadingly. "Help me, Reg. Please ... help ... me."

Reg stepped forward, but Captain Phealix grabbed him by the arm. "What are you doing?" the Scout exclaimed, trying to tear himself loose, but this time the Faylin's firm grip held him in place.

"We have to go," she said, looking up as even more parts of the wreck dropped from above. "If you go to him, it's over for you."

"You don't know that!"

"I do. Look at him and tell me I'm wrong."

Reg watched as Spence's eyes glazed over once more.

"You won't die, Reg," the ensign said. "Just come over here and join us; break the shackles that imprison you. No more chasing the approval of a bitter grandfather. No more cancerous ambition consuming you from the inside. No more rules. You can be free. You can be happy. Truly happy. Don't you want that, Reg? Don't you want to be happy?"

As Reg stared at his friend, the Euwels stared at him; their eyes glowing brighter than before.

I *do* want to be happy, the lieutenant thought. And why shouldn't I be? Spence is right. I *deserve* this, don't I? Why keep this plastic life going? It's cold, hard, empty. I can be stronger. I can be better. And, yes, I *can* be happy.

He tried to step forward, but something held him back, so he tried again with more force until a sting on his face brought him back to reality.

"What the …" he said, staring hazily at Captain Phealix, who seemed ready and more than willing to administer a second slap.

"Are you with me, soldier boy?" the Faylin shouted above the din. "Or do you need another wakeup call?"

"No, but Spence—"

"Spence isn't there anymore!" Captain Phealix said, and waited for Reg's eyes to confirm that Spence was indeed not standing where he'd stood earlier. The ensign was gone.

"Where did he go?" Reg asked, perplexed.

"He went in the opposite direction, and if I hadn't stopped you, you would have followed him like a love-sick puppy."

"We must go after him!"

"No, we need to get the heck out of here while we still can!"

To emphasise this, a beam tore loose from above. Rearing back, they narrowly evaded the giant piece of metal before it slammed through the weakened floor, leaving a hole where they'd stood.

"WE HAD HOPED FOR YOUR COOPERATION," the Euwel on the right said as he and his companion advanced on their targets, *"BUT IT SEEMS WE'VE RUN OUT OF TIME."*

Reg didn't know what the creature was talking about, and Captain Phealix didn't give him the opportunity to find out, as she raised her revolver and fired a shot at the nearest Euwel. The loud bang nearly burst Reg's eardrum, but he held his pose as he watched the slug slam into the Euwel's body. It staggered back from the impact, but recovered almost immediately and looked down at the point of impact. Using the tip of its bladed forearm, the creature dislodged the bullet from its small crater. The flattened piece of lead dropped through the floor grating with a series of clangs.

The Euwel looked back up at Captain Phealix and swept its sharp arm towards the Faylin's neck, but she evaded the blow by falling backwards while squeezing off another round. This time, the bullet ripped through the creature's eye and exploded out the back of its rocky skull with a splash of orange. The Euwel remained standing for a second, and Captain Phealix was about to pull the trigger again when the creature crumpled to its knees and toppled face-down onto the floor.

Reg didn't have time to aid the Faylin, as his own attacker bore down on him. Using his spear, the Scout parried the first blow directed at his head by the Euwel's bladed arm, then ducked the follow-up blow from the other arm and sliced at the nearest target; the creature's kneecap. It surprised Reg when the spearhead didn't shatter as it cut into the green joint, albeit with a measure of resistance. Without proper support, the Euwel toppled sideways and landed next to its unmoving companion. A wail pierced Reg's mind like the whistle of a kettle in a barren canyon, with echoes of pain and anger bouncing through his mind.

Glancing at the green liquid oozing down its wounded leg along with a trickle of fast-cooling lava, the Euwel turned its right blade-arm into a flexible appendage, which it jammed into the gaping hole at the back of its fallen companion's head. The arm started glowing lime-green and, to Reg's consternation, glowing green veins sprouted across the wound and rapidly crystallised to repair the injured body part. By the looks of it, the creature would be back on its feet in no time, which is why Reg didn't give it more time.

"I don't think so," he growled, bringing the spear down atop the Euwel's glowing forearm. Unlike the creature's kneecap, though, the spearhead cut through the appendage like a hot knife through melted butter. After flopping onto the floor, the severed body part glowed for a moment longer before it liquefied into a green ooze that sank through the grating.

Reg was so surprised by his success that he only noticed the Euwel raising its intact arm at the last moment. Bracing himself for the pain about to penetrate his body, it surprised him even more when, instead, the creature's neck exploded. Reg turned to the source of the loud boom behind him, where smoke wafted from the barrel of the gun in Captain Phealix's hand, before turning back to the headless Euwel.

Despite green veins trying to patch things up, orange liquid gushed from the creature's stumpy neck like lava, and pooled like lava. It however didn't cool like lava, transforming from its liquid state into rock and, subsequently, into a cake of ash in mere seconds. The bodies of both Euwels followed suit; their hard, black exteriors swiftly turning grey. And when another violent tremor shook the ship, their humanoid forms crumbled through the grating.

"Can we go now?" Captain Phealix said as she headed for the door before any more unwelcome guests could arrive. "*Pretty* please?"

Gritting his teeth, Reg glanced back at the empty spot where Spence had stood earlier. But when another shudder almost knocked him off his feet, the lieutenant followed the pirate out the door.

As the duo ran up the stairs back to the exit corridor, the ship lost its will to hold on; its structure starting to crack and buckle. A violent tremor sent Reg and the captain sprawling on the floor, which probably ended up saving them from the ceiling panel that came crashing down a couple of metres ahead. Scrambling to their feet, they ducked to evade the sparky live wires now dangling from the roof.

With numerous obstacles littering the way, they couldn't run flat out, but kept ducking and skirting their way forward until they finally reached the exit door. The latch, however, was bent to such an extent that Reg couldn't lift it.

As their spears were likely to snap before the latch did, the pair turned to look for something with which to detach the mechanism. Instead, they saw something that was both infuriating and terrifying, as two pairs of glowing eyes came charging down the dark corridor towards them. The black bodies that housed the eyes were only illuminated intermittently by the flashes of live wires touching one another.

Raising her gun, Captain Phealix was on the verge of firing at the left pair of eyes, but the ship, for once, stepped in by slamming down another ceiling panel atop the approaching creatures.

"Think they're dead?" Reg said, keeping his eyes locked on the spot where the orange eyes had vanished under the heavy load.

"Don't know," Captain Phealix replied as she swung her gun towards the door latch. "But I'm not hanging around to find out."

The gun boomed, but the latch held. It took two more shots before the mechanism finally shattered. As the door popped open, Captain Phealix rushed down the slanted walkway-ramp and dropped into the trench's water, whose surface rippled from the shuddering wreck's energy passing through it.

Reg was about to follow her, when he glanced back up the corridor. An explosion of sparks revealed a green appendage wrapping itself around a nearby pipe as one of the Euwels tried to pull itself free. Spotting an opportunity, Reg looked at the spear in his hand. It practically begged him to use it for its intended purpose. He knew it wasn't the spear speaking to him, but rather his own need for revenge. He didn't care.

However, when he turned to re-enter the corridor, the most violent shudder yet sent him rolling down the walkway and into the water. As he came up, gasping, a loud *bonnng* from above called his attention to the top of the hull, where the last thread keeping the stern attached to the rest of the wreck snapped loose.

"Come on!" Captain Phealix shouted as she grabbed Reg's arm and towed him towards the tear in the hull. It was on the opposite side of where they'd entered the wreck, but it was the closest.

The weight of the angled stern pulled it against the main body of the wreck with a deafening screech. The impact brought chunks of weakened metal raining down around Reg and Captain Phealix as they waded through the water at a speed that was less than desirable. Reaching the side of the trench, they scrambled up the mound, where Reg took a moment to catch his breath; a moment that didn't last long.

"We need to keep moving," Captain Phealix wheezed, pulling at his arm.

"I can't!" Reg wheezed back. The time spent on the Scout ship hadn't done his fitness levels any favours.

"You have to," the Faylin said, nodding towards the ship. "She won't last much longer."

To support her prognosis, the topsoil beneath their feet started bouncing from the increasing vibrations. Taking a deep breath, Reg nodded and plodded on after the captain across the grassland. But as they reached the top of the flat hill nearest the ship, Reg's legs caved under him.

"I ..." he said, dropping to his knees as his lungs gorged themselves on oxygen, "I ... think ... this is ... far ... enough."

Hands on knees, Captain Phealix shook her head weakly and breathed deep to say what she wanted to say.

"Just a little farth—" she began, but was cut off as the ship's hull exploded with a blinding light.

Sending chunks of wreckage flying everywhere, it took less than a second for the ground-clearing shockwave to fling them both backwards into the flattened grass, where Reg's head struck something hard.

Nose bleeding, he just lay there, staring up at the sky, wondering why night-time was falling so rapidly.

He blinked a few times to see if it was just a trick of the light. With each blink, his eyes remained shut a bit longer, until his brain decided they should stay shut while it took a little timeout.

CHAPTER 48

When her eyelids finally pried themselves open, Phealix thought about getting up, but her body wasn't too keen on cooperating. However, as she wasn't sure where she was or what had happened, her curiosity forced her to sit up with a groan and play a game of catch-up with her memory.

As her vacant gaze scanned her surroundings, the first thing she noticed was the burning remains of a spaceship centred in a ring of flattened grass and jungle trees, its flames trying to rekindle the failing light of dusk.

I'm sure I'd been in there recently, she thought. But it had looked different then – more like a spaceship and less like an exploded egg.

Her gaze shifted to a twisted metal beam protruding from the soil next to her foot, as well as a mangled control panel resting at an angle near her head, its singed wires popping out wherever they found a space.

How did *those* get here? Didn't they belong *inside* the ship? No, wait, the ship had exploded. Yes, that would explain why it now looked like it had exploded.

Eyes tracking back to the remains of the ship, she wondered why it had exploded in the first place.

She remembered, and then wished she hadn't. Glancing about anxiously, Phealix waited for orange eyes to converge on her. But nothing happened.

Maybe they were destroyed by the blast, her hopeful side volunteered.

Yes, her logical side affirmed as she stared at the smouldering bulk of the former ship. Nothing could have survived *that*.

However, not one for taking chances, she rose unsteadily, ready to go … somewhere. She wasn't sure where yet, as long as it wasn't where she was at the moment.

Something else tugged at Phealix's memory, though. She couldn't go yet. Someone was supposed to go with her. After a brief search, she spotted a pair of dark-grey boots poking out from the angled grass. She approached hesitantly, fearing the worst, but the boots – toes pointing skywards – were still attached to the grey-clad legs of the Scout, which in turn was still attached to the rest of him.

Well, that's a good sign, Phealix thought as she crouched by Reg's side. She patted the human's cheeks softly, careful not to aggravate possible injuries to his head and neck.

When his eyes finally fluttered open, the lieutenant said, "… and that's why I don't dance." His eyes fluttered some more as they registered a different face from the one he'd been talking to in dreamy land.

"Who … what … wh—"

"There's no time," Phealix interrupted. "Can you get up?"

"I don't want to," Reg replied hazily.

"We *don't* have time for this! We have to go."

"Well, I'm not going anywhere until you tell me what's going on. Also, who are you?"

Phealix clenched her teeth, then took a deep breath to deliver the fastest catch-up of her life. "Fine, you're Lieutenant Reginald Kleft, a dumbass Scout who hates me and just escaped the destruction of a ship that was overrun by black-rock creatures who want to kill us and might still succeed if a *certain someone* doesn't get his butt up and going ... as in *now!*"

As the words flowed from her mouth, it watered the recollection blooming on Reg's face.

"Spence," he said weakly, and his body showed as much strength as his voice as he wonkily forced himself to his feet like a bar patron at 4am.[*]

As he did so, Phealix spotted clotted blood clumping the hair on the back of the human's head, and readied herself to catch him should the need arise.

"Maybe you should rather sit back down," she said.

Ignoring her, Reg staggered towards the obliterated ship, until he stepped on something. Looking down, he nearly toppled over as he crouched to pick up the spear. "Spence, I ... I'm coming," he breathed as he rose unsteadily, and was about to set off again when Phealix grabbed him by the arm.

"Let me go," the lieutenant grated, shaking her off.

"There's nothing you can do," Phealix said softly. "He's gone."

"Thanks to you!" Reg exclaimed, glancing at the burning remains of the ship; a grim bonfire around which the unseen minions of death were likely going to party the night away.

---

[*] This is just a rough estimate. It might be sooner, or later, depending on the time the first round of shooters was served.

His face darkened as he turned to Phealix. "If it weren't for you, Spence would still be alive!"

"You're blaming *me*?"

"Who else?"

"How about the guy who blasted my shuttle out of the sky? You know, the one that sent his friend off to do Zolt knows what … *alone*. The one who cares for one person only: *himself*. I'd say *that guy* may have had a part to play in this!"

The loathing in the lieutenant's eyes transformed into pure hatred as he stepped towards Phealix. Backing away, she nearly tripped over an object behind her. It was the spear she'd dropped when the shockwave sent her flying earlier. Snatching it up, she pointed the weapon at the advancing Scout.

"Don't even think about it," she said, moving backwards to increase the fast-shrinking gap between them.

"Why? It's *all* I've been thinking about since you and your fharking thugs entered my life," Reg growled. "I'd been planning on taking you in, but now I know that was a mistake. I should have just offed you in your sleep. Then Spence would still be alive. How many more people are you Zolt-forsaken pirates going to take from me?"

"What are you talking about?"

"My parents," the lieutenant grated. "You fharking bastards killed my parents!"

His glare grew as cold as the blade of the spear now pointed at Phealix's face.

"I think it's time to settle the score," the human said, and lunged forward with a cry that matched the murder in his eyes.

CHAPTER 49

Captain Phealix brought up her spear just in time to ward off the blow aimed at her throat. As the metal rang out, Reg wasted no time in arching the blade down towards the Faylin's abdomen, but she leapt back, causing the spearhead to cut the air an inch from her belly.

Reg's head felt strange. He'd never had the urge to kill as much as he did at that moment. Yes, he wanted justice for his parents, but he'd always wanted the perpetrators to rot in the worst Federal prison he could find – a place where death would be a welcome relief. The whole killing-thing was something new.

Part of him was terrified by his sudden thirst for blood, but not the other part – the part that was now in charge. The part that relished the thought of piercing the Faylin's flesh with the blade, feeling the metal sink in while her life seeped out. He could already see it in his mind. He could even *feel* her sticky blood running down his forearms; the sweet nectar of revenge.

The macabre vision brought him such joy that it pushed all uncertainty so far back in his mind that his other part couldn't reach it, even if it tried. He felt himself being pushed back, becoming a watcher of his own actions.

Planting her feet, Captain Phealix readied her spear once more. "Listen," she said, "I don't know who your parents were, but I can assure you I didn't kill them."

"It doesn't matter," Reg heard himself saying, his voice rasp with hatred. "Pirates killed them, and *you're* a pirate. You're all the same!"

"No, we're not," Captain Phealix said, holding up a hand placatingly. "Can we *please* just talk about this?"

"No, the time for talking is over! The time has come for you to pay. I'm going to enjoy cutting you open, bitch," Reg spat, feeling both delighted and nauseated by the words spilling from his mouth.

Captain Phealix's eyes hardened. "That's going to be difficult without a head," she said, her tail swishing in anticipation as she renewed the grip on her spear.

"Thanks for the idea," Reg heard himself say, and watched helplessly as he swung the blade at her neck.

This time, however, the Faylin was ready and parried the blow with ease. "Aww," she gibed, "you still remember your skills from kindergarten. How cute!"

Reg tried to push back against the rage that suddenly flooded his mind; a primordial surge of hostility that went beyond anything he'd felt before, threatening to drown every last bit of purity clinging to his being. The surge, however, was too strong, forcing him to hack away at Captain Phealix like a deranged butcher.

He was relieved to see the Faylin keeping her head, literally and figuratively. He was also relieved when, after another wild swing at her, she spun and brought the butt end of her spear down on his head. He was especially relieved when his consciousness slipped off to another venue where neither rage nor hatred had an access pass.

•••

As the darkness within his mind faded, Reg opened his eyes, only to find more darkness waiting beyond the confines of his eyelids. However, this was a darkness he could deal with; the natural kind that reared its head whenever the sun took a nap. Something was off, though.

Why are the stars bouncing around like that? he wondered, because the last time he checked, stars had more of a static quality about them.

He then thought it might have something to do with his head bouncing across an uneven surface along with the rest of his body.

What the heck?

He raised his head to see if his eyes could dispel his confusion, but the only thing they saw was Captain Phealix dragging him by his feet, which were tied together by wires; the same constraining jewellery that adorned his hands.

"What the heck?" he repeated out loud, hoping the captain would shine some light on the situation.

"Quiet," the Faylin hissed without pausing.

"No, seriously," he said, struggling against his bonds, "what the heck?!"

This time, the captain did pause to point her revolver at his head. "*Seriously,* keep it down," she replied, glancing about anxiously.

"What's going on?"

"Quiet!" she repeated under her breath. "They'll find us!"

"Who?"

"Le'us."

"What do you mean Le—"

Clamping a hand over his mouth, the Faylin leaned forward. "We're moving too slow. If I untie your legs, will you be able to walk without running your mouth?"

With his legs up and shoulders on the ground, Reg could only manage a slight nod. Dropping his feet, Captain Phealix untwisted the wires from around his ankles and helped him up.

"Now, move," the Faylin said, prodding him with the barrel of the gun.

Reg obliged, even if it was a bit stiffly, but after only a few metres, a rustle of grass over his right shoulder caught his attention. He jerked his head in that direction and wished he hadn't, as a jolt of pain shot through his neck.

"Ow," he grunted.

"Faster," Phealix said, ignoring his pain. "We must reach the treeline before they close in on us."

Behind them, more rustling sounds prompted the pair to break into an unsteady run across the uneven, moon-lit grassland. Even with the aid of their glow sticks, it was hard to see where to step, but they kept stumbling on as fast as they could. Reg eyed the dark line of jungle trees spread out before them. They didn't have much farther to go. However, the rustling behind them increased as their pursuers gained ground, and also spread to both sides.

"They're flanking us," Reg said, glancing to the side, and tripped over a rock.

"I know," Captain Phealix said, breathing hard as she helped him back up and ushered him forward. After only a few metres, they were forced to stop yet again when the rustling finally surrounded them in a small clearing, where the grass had been grazed low by a herd of whatevers.

"Untie me," Reg demanded, holding up his wrists.

The Faylin eyed him warily. He couldn't blame her.

"We don't have time for this," he said with a note of urgency. "Look, I don't know what happened back there, but I'll behave. I promise."

By the look the Faylin gave him, his promise might just as well have been political.

"Fine," he said, "you don't have to trust me, but from what I've heard about these things, you can either take your chances with me, or you can die going it alone."

"Believe me, I've *seen* what they can do," the captain said with a shiver.

"Then you know I'm right, right?"

After a brief internal argument, Captain Phealix sighed and untied the wires. Handing Reg his spear, she looked him sternly in the eye.

"You pull any more of that crap you did back there," she said, "and I'll finish you off myself, without any help from the local wildlife. Got it?"

Taking the spear, Reg nodded. He brought up the weapon and swivelled towards each rustle closing in on them, which led to plenty of swivelling.

Eventually, a long snout appeared from between the blades of the taller grass bordering the clearing. The snout paused to sniff the air, before the rest of the Le'u's body emerged. The light from the moon and the glow sticks played off the copper-coloured scales of the predator's long, scaly body and its long, scaly tail. As it started circling its prey in a crouch, baring sharp fangs, it moaned, upon which three other Le'us entered the clearing to encircle their prey.

At first, they puffed at one another, unsure of the unfamiliar snacks in their midst. But food was food, so the leader finally ordered them forward with a roar that turned Reg's blood cold.

Saliva dripping from their fangs, the creatures closed in, with the leader picking Reg as its target. Dropping to its haunches, the Le'u prepared to transform the pent-up energy in its muscles into a prey-felling leap, and Reg's own muscles tensed up as he prepared for this to happen.

However, just as the leader was about to lunge, a shot rang out that sent him leaping straight into the air with a yelp. Falling on its side, the beast scrambled back onto its feet with a moan to limp back into the cover of the surrounding grass. Following the loud noise and their leader's retreat, the three remaining Le'us weren't keen on hanging around and quickly followed suit.

When the last scaly tail disappeared into the grass, Reg let out the breath he'd been holding in.

"That was the last bullet," Captain Phealix said, checking the revolver's cylinder before sticking the weapon back into her skirt. "We'd better keep moving."

"Think they'll come back?" Reg asked, scanning the dimly lit landscape for any sign of movement.

He didn't ask the Faylin why she wanted to hold on to an empty weapon, because he suspected it provided her with a feeling of comfort. He would have done the same.

"Not sure. They might keep running, or be peed off enough to regroup and return with a vengeance. Either way, I'd rather not stick around to find out."

Not wanting to find out himself, Reg nodded, and they set off at a quick pace towards the treeline.

Reaching the edge of the grassland, Reg glanced back once more and spotted four pairs of amber eyes watching silently as their dinner vanished into the cover of the dense jungle growth.

CHAPTER 50

Shortly after entering the jungle, Phealix's relief at escaping the Le'us was cut short by the snap of a twig up ahead, followed by the crunch of leaves.

Something was moving towards them.

Stepping in next to her, Reg gripped his spear tightly as he pointed it in the direction of the oncoming sounds.

Earlier, Phealix had considered taking the weapon back from the Scout. However, he seemed to be back to his normal self – which wasn't necessarily a good thing either – so she decided to let him keep it. Especially as she hadn't known what might be lying in wait for them. Now, with the approaching noise, she was semi-sure she had made the right call.

A big leaf ahead started glowing, then fell to the ground as a long spearhead hacked off its stem, revealing a hairless, sweaty head.

"Roro?" Phealix said cautiously. "Is that *you?*"

"It me," the tribesman replied as he emerged from the brush, followed by Issy and the Vahltans.

Although elated to see them, Phealix kept her pose. "Glad to see you can survive on your own *outside* a ship too, Franki," she said flatly.

Franki's beak bent into a grin. "What can I say, Captain? I'm a man of many talents."

"I'll be sure to keep that in mind next time I assign cleaning duties."

As the Vahltan's grin disappeared, Phealix turned her dry eyes to Issy and Roro. "Please tell me there's a place nearby where we can rest."

"Yes, Fight Rock," Roro said, looking a bit knackered himself. "We on our way there when we hear big thunder and find you. It no far. There we eat, we rest."

"You have food there too?" Phealix said, looking forward to giving her empty stomach something to digest other than pollen.

"There food," Roro said, shaking his head, "but you no like it."

•••

Roro wasn't kidding when he'd said Phealix wouldn't like the food. It turned out to be more of the lime-green Masepa, which oozed into a basin at the base of the so-called Fight Rock. Apart from having goop seeping down its side, the rock itself – a mossy boulder standing in the middle of a clearing amid the trees – wasn't the least bit impressive, so describing it would be a waste.

However, according to Roro, the rock had great significance. "Here, we kill each other," the Teahupo'oan Head Headhunter stated in the same way people stated "And *this* is our lounge". He glanced at Issy, who paused in his duty of building a fire to nod solemnly.

"What do you mean?" Phealix said, disturbed by the headhunter's nonchalance.

"We fight, we kill," Roro said, crouching to fill a bowl perched on the basin at the base of the rock.

"Your own people?"

"Sometimes own people, sometimes people of other tribe."

"Why?"

Getting back up, Roro shrugged. "Many reasons. Sometimes man steal chicken from other man. Sometimes steal wife.* They fight. Gods decide who right, who wrong. Man who die – he wrong."

Roro kicked Phealix's level of unease up a notch by holding the bowl towards her.

Eyeing the goo dripping from the bottom of the bowl, the Faylin held up her hands and, despite being famished, said, "No, thank you, I'm, uh, not hungry."

"It no matter," Roro said, waving his hand at the clearing. "This sacred ground. You enter, you drink nectar of gods. You no drink, you dishonour gods – we fight."

Drinking more of the liquid had about as much appeal to Phealix as licking a toilet brush, which probably tasted better. But aside from its effects on her palate, Phealix also had misgivings about the effects the Masepa might have on her body. Sure, it'd proven itself to be a superb laxative and a fountain of youth, but she wasn't sure if it came at a price. And if it did, would she be able to pay?

However, seeing as Roro looked serious and fighting wouldn't benefit anyone, she took the bowl and tipped its contents down her throat. Surprisingly, it didn't taste as bad as the first time around. Still not great, but not *as* bad.

---

* This goes for both sexes, and while some non-Teahupo'oans might find it hard to believe, stealing a chicken is a worse offence. Many non-Teahupo'oans might find this easier to believe than others, though.

Taking back the bowl, Roro kept refilling it until everyone had had their reluctant share. Satisfied, he placed the empty container back on the basin and lumbered over to lie down by the fire.

"Now, we sleep," he said, closing his eyes.

While the others also made themselves comfortable in their preferred sleeping positions, Phealix sat down to take first watch. She was surprised that Reg, too, hadn't passed out yet. He obviously had a lot running through his mind, although it must've run quite slowly, judging by his eyes, which drooped like wet curtains.

They both just sat there, staring at the fire in silence. However, when the others' breathing joined forces in a sleepy symphony, Phealix said, "I'm sorry about your parents. What happened?"

Reg didn't answer.

Deciding not to push too much, Phealix said, "You don't have to talk about it – it's none of my business. I just wanted to say I'm sorry."

After some more silence, Reg finally took a deep breath.

"My mother was a scientist," he said without looking away from the fire. "My father, too, although … well, he was also a bit of everything. He wrote poems and short stories, played music, and loved exploring exotic worlds with my mom. They were a solid team.

"My grandfather didn't like it, though. He was born and raised a Militor man. He enlisted when he turned sixteen and worked his way up the ranks faster than anyone. The Militorate wasn't just in his blood; it was in his bones, so he did *not* appreciate my dad's life choices. Of course, he blamed my mom for it. He and Dad constantly argued over her and Dad's career. Needless to say, we didn't visit my grandfather much."

He shook his head slowly, as though he didn't want to relive the rest of the story. Phealix kept silent, giving the Scout the time to say what he needed to say.

"My parents were on their way to Bolton III to study the effects of battery acid on a local water table," the human continued. "They never made it there."

"Pirates," Phealix ventured after a pause that begged for a nudge to keep the ball rolling.

Reg nodded, locking eyes with her before returning his tired gaze to the flames. "It happened shortly after they exited the local wormhole Orifice. They weren't even off their flight path, nor were they alone. They were right amid the traffic heading towards the planet when they got hit. Their ship wasn't big. It wasn't filled with precious metals, gems, or anything else that would put a target on their back. It was basically a lab."

Phealix frowned. "Strange that they'd attack a ship like that, *especially* in public."

"The public," Reg sneered, his eyes as cold as his voice. "*The public* meant squat. Made no difference. No one stopped to help. Everyone just flew by as fast as they could. Sure, people called it in, but by the time the first Protectors arrived, it was too late – the pirates were already gone and my parents' ship destroyed. There wasn't much left; not even bodies. They didn't even get a decent burial."

A tear rolled down his cheek, but his face remained hard as he continued. "I was only nine. My world was shattered. But my grandfather took me in; gave me a purpose … justice."

"You mean revenge."

"Justice, revenge, call it what you will, but I needed it … no, I *wanted* it; *craved* it. It became an obsession; steered me away from my true passion."

"You never planned on joining the Militorate?"

Reg shook his head. "Heck, no! Before my parents died, I always dreamt of enrolling in a top culinary school on Vegon."

As far as expected answers went, this one wouldn't have made page one of Phealix's list. "You wanted to be a chef?" she said, astonished.

"Crazy, right? But I loved food. Even at my young age, I enjoyed cooking for my parents, and they loved trying whatever new dish I concocted – good or bad."

For a brief moment, the human smiled fondly. "I had their full support … until that day."

"I take it your grandfather didn't share in those dreams?"

"No. And after what happened, neither did I. Instead, I joined a Militor school and enrolled in the Academy as soon as I turned sixteen, just like my grandfather. He made sure I pushed myself as hard as I could. *He* pushed me even harder."

"*That's* why you're already a lieutenant at your age. He helped you."

"Actually, he was quite hard on me. I could have been a captain by now if it hadn't been for him."

"He's been tempering the steel," Phealix ventured.

"I guess so. But he never wanted me to become a Scout. That was *my* choice. It gives me more freedom to do what I need to do."

"To find the pirates that killed your parents?"

"Yes … but also *any* pirates."

"We *really* aren't all the same, you know?"

Reg remained quiet for a while, his brow furrowing as an internal battle finally concluded with a slow shake of the head.

"*You* are … different from what I expected," he said.

"Oh, believe me, there are plenty of pirates out there who are exactly what you'd expect. But I'm working on changing that. Do you know the ship that attacked your parents?"

"Yes, but I could never find any trace of it."

"They probably changed its name and appearance since then. Or it might have been destroyed. Do you have a description?"

Reg relayed what he could from eyewitness accounts, and Phealix nodded. "Tell you what," she said, "if we make it off this planet alive, I'll do whatever I can to help track down your parents' killers."

"You'd turn on your own people?" Reg said, perplexed.

"As I said, we're not all the same. Besides, turning on one another is a very important step in the pirate dance. I'll do my best, I promise."

Looking almost as dubious as tired, Reg lay back, clutching his spear.

"We'll see," he said, closing his eyes.

As she gazed into the fire once more, Phealix didn't know why she had made that promise. Maybe it was to give the Scout something to cling on to. Or perhaps she wanted to convince *herself* that they were going to make it out alive. However, like the Scout, she didn't quite believe herself.

CHAPTER 51

"**S**omething funny?" Captain Phealix said, her face a billboard of irritation.

The group had been discussing the Euwels since daybreak, and haven't come close to an explanation as to what the creatures were or what they wanted. But the Faylin's hypothesis was literally laughable![*]

"Soul-eaters, *really?*" Reg replied, wiping the tears from his eyes. He'd needed a good chuckle, and he certainly got one. "That would mean people have souls. I never pegged you as a religious freak."

Captain Phealix's eyes narrowed. "I thought we were past all this animosity."

"Hey, getting past you being a pirate is one thing. But this whole 'soul' business? It's a load of camelhorseshit from a camelhorse who'd had a swimming pool full of

---

[*] The word *literally* has become (not literally, mind you) like a traffic circle. Few seem to know how to use it correctly, and even fewer seem to care. And, should you point out said incorrect usage, some might even politely suggest you go do something impolite to yourself, but you *literally* don't have to do it.

that Masepa. Only religious nuts believe in that sort of thing!"

"I wasn't talking about religion. Souls, on the other hand—"

"Same thing."

"We believe in souls," said Issy determinedly, backed by an equally determined nod from Roro.

"Do you, now?" Reg said, casting them an amused glance before turning his attention back to the Faylin. "What a surprise, *they* believe in fairy tales. *You*, on the other hand … you I don't get. You're an intelligent woman, yet you believe in all this hogwash."

"Scientific studies proved there's an energy within us that goes beyond mere biology."

"You mean studies by 'learned' religious zealots out to prove a point," Reg said.

"They weren't *all* religious, you twat," Captain Phealix countered. "And most still aren't. I'm not religious either, but I *do* believe in a soul – or a life force, if you like."

"No, I don't like!" Reg spat. And indeed he didn't like it, especially not after what he'd experienced in the temple and when he'd attacked the Faylin. It had indeed felt … out-of-body. But of course that wasn't possible. There was another explanation. There *had* to be.

"No one has a soul, or a life force, or whatever fharking silly pet name you can come up with," he continued, just as furious with his own thoughts as with the Faylin. "You're preaching to the wrong choir here."

"I'm not *preaching* anything. All I'm saying is I feel … something whenever we're around those things. Something more than mere emotions."

"Telepaths – that's all the Euwels are, I'm sure of it," Reg said without looking sure of it. "And … and they're implanting thoughts to … to chip away at our resolve; to scare us. Instilling fear in your enemies is one of the oldest military strategies out there. Even nature uses fear in the battle between predator and prey. It's all a game."

"A game that's killed most of my men … and Spence."

"Spence *isn't* dead!" Reg snapped, his face turning red.

"You blamed me for his death, remember?"

"I know but … he's *not* dead, okay?"

Part of Reg knew that – even if his friend *was* still alive – a reunion wasn't likely to pan out the way Reg wanted. Yet he still had hope; a hope he'd cling to with everything he had for as long as possible.

Captain Phealix must have realised this, because she nodded. "Okay," she said in a level tone. "Look, let's take away belief in souls, life force or whatever else is making your hackles rise. We still need to stop these things."

"Of course we need to stop them," Reg said, and took a deep breath to cool his face along with his state of mind. "The question is: how? You realise we're out-numbered and a tad short on weapons?"

"Sure, we might not have much firepower—"

"*Any* firepower," Reg corrected.

"—but we might have enough *man*power to even the odds a bit," Captain Phealix concluded, glancing at the tribesmen.

"*Them?*" Reg exclaimed. "They know nothing of fighting! They—"

"We know plenty of fighting," Issy interjected.

"This isn't a tribal skirmish over stationery, Issy," Reg said.

"Euwel kill Teahupo'o," Roro said, caring nothing about stationery, as he knew nothing about stationery.

"And Ja'namans," Issy added.

Roro nodded sternly. "Euwel kill brothers – we kill Euwel. Our people, they *will* fight."

Captain Phealix nodded at him. "And so they shall."

"Fine," Reg said, turning to Captain Phealix. "You want to fight? Great! But I'm sure you've come to the same conclusion as me: those blobs in the temple – they could *all* contain a Euwel."

He gave the Faylin an opportunity to nod, and she took it.

"And you've seen how many blobs there were?" he continued.

Another nod confirmed it.

"And I guess you haven't forgotten the part where they can regenerate?"

Reg took Captain Phealix's silent stare ahead as proof that all his points thus far had been made, and that he could now deliver the last one. "Even if *every single* villager from both tribes was armed and able to fight, we still wouldn't stand a chance."

"Well, that's all we have," the Faylin said, removing the revolver from her skirt. "Unless you've got some extra bullets stashed somewhere for this thing."

She tossed the useless weapon to the ground.

"What are bullets?" Issy said.

"Ammunition, Issy," Reg explained, and saw he should explain some more. "Bullets. You put them in guns ..." he added, and pointed at the gun, "... those things."

The gears in the tribesmen's heads seemed to try their best to move, so Reg poured on some oil. "They're like tiny spears – spears that can do a lot of damage."

"Did *you* know about this?" Issy asked Roro.

The Teahupo'oan shook his head, looking at a loss. "I no need … 'bullets' to grind corn."

"What are you talking about?" Reg asked.

Issy, too, appeared at a loss for words as he eyed the revolver, but finally shook his head. "If you really think these … bullets and guns will help," he said, "we have plenty."

This time, it was the turn of the non-locals to be at a loss for words.

•••

Approaching Roro's village, Phealix couldn't stop thinking about primitive people wielding advanced weaponry, whether or not they knew they were doing so.

Although some of their practices were indeed savage, she almost envied the tribes for their simplistic lifestyle. She knew that the presence of the pirates and the Scouts had already cracked the foundations of natives like Issy and Roro, and that the events currently unfurling were likely to have more profound, widespread repercussions than even she could foresee. But having guns in the hands of primitives was unthinkable!

As she stepped over a decaying log lying across the path, Phealix asked Issy, "So you and the Teahupo'oans had guns all along?"

"Yes," the tribesman replied. "I think they were some of the last *gifts* the tribes grabbed from the ship before the Metal Go— before Ikkabot chased them out."

"And you, uh, actually use them?"

"Yes."

"You're fortunate no one got killed yet," Reg said.

"Oh, someone *had* been killed," Issy said. "A few years ago, they found Mothuntsho dead in his hut after a loud clap of thunder. He had a hole through his head. No one could figure out how he died grinding corn. But I guess it makes sense now. A tiny spear – who would have thought?"

"I no like tiny spear," Roro grumbled. "Must see spear. No one afraid of spear if no one see spear."

"Take my word for it, Roro," Phealix said, "they cause more fear than you can imagine."

As Roro's imagination didn't stretch that far, the level of conviction in his expression languished in the shallow end of the pool. He was about to say something, when Issy interrupted by continuing a conversation that Phealix had thought was done and dusted. Apparently it wasn't done and, judging by Issy's face, it had gathered a fair amount of dust during its short break.

"I still think I should go to my village to warn them," the Ja'naman tried once more.

Phealix sighed. "We've been over this, Issy. Firstly, we don't know where the Euwels are or how many of them are crawling around out there. So going off alone is out of the question. Secondly, even *if* you make it to your village – what then? Your tribe cannot fight the Euwels alone."

When Issy eyed his spear, Phealix waylaid his impending argument. "Spears won't be enough, Issy. Look, Roro's village is closer than yours. We'll do what we need to do and be on our way before you know it. We'll be in and out in no time."

"Also," Roro added, "you get lost in jungle. You Ja'nama always get lost in jungle. That why so many Ja'nama skulls in Teahupo'o village."

The Teahupo'oan walked on, ignoring the glare Issy shot at him.

Phealix placed a hand on the Ja'naman's shoulder. "Don't worry, Issy, everything will be okay," she promised, and felt guilty the moment she did so. She *really* had to stop making promises like that. However, this one she couldn't avoid. Aside from the fact that she'd do everything in her power to keep these two safe, *they* still needed to convince the tribes to fight. If they were to have any chance, the locals *had to* fight, and they had to *believe* they could win. She just hoped Roro could persuade the Teahupo'oans to help.

However, as they reached the outskirts of the village, it became evident that help was going to be even harder to come by than Phealix had anticipated. The village was empty; not a Teahupo'oan in sight.

Roro peeked into a nearby hut, but couldn't find anyone. "Where they are?" he said, dashing to the next one, which was also empty. A search of the next few huts yielded the same result.

"Over here!" Reg shouted, crouching beside a hut's entrance.

"What is it?" Phealix asked as she and Roro joined him.

"See for yourself," the human said, getting up and gesturing to a spear, loincloth and bony necklace lying on the ground amid wind-scattered ash.

"No," Roro said, his voice trembling. "Not again."

"Who is it?" Phealix asked.

"This hut of Hinga," the tribesman said, picking up the necklace with a shaky hand. "This I give to Hinga after first hunt." With his other hand, he scooped up some of the ashes. "This … Hinga."

He looked up at Phealix, and she knew what his hopeful eyes were asking. However, unlike before, when Hinga had been stunned, the Faylin didn't have any tricks that would "resurrect" Roro's friend. She shook her head solemnly.

Shoulders sagging, Roro looked at the ash by his feet. "I swear, old friend," he said, "I go hunt Euwel. I take Euwel head." Getting up, he let the ash fall through his fingers and watched as the soft breeze carried it away. "Your hunt over, Hinga. Mine begin."

He gave Phealix a determined look. "I ready."

Phealix nodded. "Then let's get what we came for."

CHAPTER 52

Issy was feeling a bit antsy. While he knew they'd had to get the so-called guns and the bullets that went with them, the search of the Teahupo'oan village had taken up *way* too much time in his eyes. He needed to get to his people, fast, but the heavy bags of weapons and ammunition the party now lugged along had dashed all hopes of a speedy journey. At least they were getting close to his village.

Almost there, he thought.

As they ascended the last hill before the village, Issy glanced over at Captain Phealix, who was checking her gun yet again; something she'd done more than one hand's worth of fingers since leaving Roro's village. She now also carried a bigger gun over her shoulder, which they'd found in a storage hut.

"Can I have one too?" Issy asked, eyeing the smaller gun Captain Phealix had wedged into her skirt.

The Faylin looked at what Issy was looking at. "No!" she said. She seemed shocked for some reason.

"Why not?"

"Because it's safer for you," Captain Phealix replied, and cut off his impending protest by adding, "*And* for the rest of us."

The Ja'naman village came into view as they crested the hill. Captain Phealix brought them to a halt.

"Will they help?" she asked, nodding towards the grassy huts dotting the landscape below.

Issy shrugged. "Don't know," he said, and glanced towards Reg. "They don't like strangers very much ... escaped strangers even less."

"Well, they don't have a choice. They'll just have to listen."

When Issy nodded uncertainly, Captain Phealix led the party down the hill to the village border; a fence of dried-out thorn bushes packed tightly together to keep out predators and other unwelcome visitors.

On their way to the village entrance, Issy halted at a gap in the thorny barrier.

"This isn't supposed to be here," he said, stepping closer to inspect the branches trampled flat against the ground. "There's only one way into the village, and this isn't it."

"It's one now," Reg said, squatting to have a look himself. Transferring his big gun to his other shoulder, he picked up one of the flattened branches and raised it towards Captain Phealix. "I give you two guesses who did this."

"No guesswork needed," the Faylin replied, stepping through the gap.

"Captain," Franki said nervously from behind, "if those things *are* in there, we could be walking into a trap."

"I know, Franki. But whether they're in there or out here, we need more firepower. I seriously doubt that most of the guns we found in Roro's village are still functional, not to mention the ammo. So unless you know of a nearby *Mr Jenkins* that sells those things[*], we need to find more."

Not waiting for a reply, she walked another few steps before she halted once more and turned to Issy. "Is it always this quiet?"

"I've been thinking the same thing," Issy said. "Do you think—"

A chorus of voices towards the centre of the village cut him off.

"Wait!" Captain Phealix hissed as the tribesman dashed off, but Issy wasn't going to stop, and the others had no choice but to follow before losing sight of him. Rounding a final hut, Issy halted at a clearing, where the villagers had gathered for what was obviously a heated debate.

Something was amiss, though.

"There should be more people," Issy breathed, his gaze sweeping over the crowd. "Many more. Where are the others?"

Before anyone could say anything, the person around whom the villagers were congregated, noticed the new-comers.

"You!" Priestess Ongswele spat, pointing.

---

[*] With the growing scourge of dairy addiction among Greys, selling both cheese and weapons in one store has been deemed dangerous and irresponsible. The *Mr Jenkins* chain of stores is therefore now only licensed to sell guns, but not cheese. The *Ms Jankins* chain, on the other hand, may only sell cheese. So there's no one-stop shop for cheese and guns anymore. Needless to say, people who love cheese and guns aren't happy about this. Also, needless to say, people who love cheese and guns aren't happy with Greys either.

Issy and the other Ja'namans turned to see what she was pointing at, which turned out to be a perplexed Teahupo'oan.

"You do this!" Ongswele continued.

Roro's perplexity turned into angst as the nearest guards rushed in to surround the intruders. The villagers stepped aside to let the Priestess pass. She halted a safe distance from the group and pointed the Staff of Truth at Roro with the accompanying rattle of the Cloak of Bones.

"*You* do this!" she repeated.

"What I do?" the Teahupo'oan said.

"You take people," the Priestess spat. "You take Ja'nama people!"

Issy, finding himself outside the circle of prisoners, turned to the Priestess. "Ongswele," he said, "that's not possible."

"I think you dead, Isilimo," Ongswele said, looking unsurprisingly disappointed. "*We all* think you dead. Where you were?"

"With them," Issy said, gesturing at the captured group. "And Roro was with us the whole time too, so he couldn't have done … whatever you think he's done."

"No matter if he with you. He Teahupo'o."

"So?"

"Teahupo'o take Ja'nama people – our people. They take your mother and father too."

Shock passed through Issy's body. Despite his almost nonexistent relationship with Utata and Unina, they were his parents, and that meant something.

"Took them, where?" he asked apprehensively.

Ongswele nodded towards the volcano.

"That no sound right," Roro protested.

"Fakaza wake from sleep," Ongswele said, pointing at a nearby elderly man. "He see Teahupo'o people take Ja'nama people toward volcano."

The old man nodded.

"So, no, Roro, it no *sound* right," the Priestess continued, glaring at the headhunter. "It no *is* right. It no is right for Teahupo'o to take our people!"

"But—" Roro tried.

"You *no* speak, Teahupo'o dung! You *no ever* speak again!"

Ongswele nodded at two warriors, who pulled back their spears at the unspoken command. But Issy pushed past to stand between the weapons and the headhunter.

"You cannot do this, Ongswele!" he shouted, arms spread. "You don't know what's going on!"

"What go on, Isilimo?" the Priestess smirked. "You tell us *story?* We *know* you like stories. Stories from … 'book'. Stories that no true."

"Well, this one is," Issy said, folding his arms.

"We see," the Priestess said, folding her arms too. "Go on, Isilimo. Tell us story."

Although he knew it would probably be a waste of time, Issy recounted everything that had happened since the bungled sacrifice atop the volcano. When he finished, the Priestess looked at him coldly.

"They no steal you from mountain?" she said, her glare momentarily bouncing to the prisoners before snapping back to Issy. "You go because you *want* to go?"

Issy gave a resolute nod.

The Priestess's glare turned into a smile, which at first gave Issy a brief sense of relief until he realised that Ongswele had never smiled at him like that before. It was a smile of victory.

"Because you help them," she said.

"Yes," Issy said with a less resolute nod.

"I see," the Priestess said, her face becoming hard. "Then you *traitor*."

"No!" Issy protested. "Haven't you listened to a word I said? Those things are out there!"

"The … Euwel? They no real. They only story you make up."

"They real," a small, round boy said, stepping out from between the front row of villagers. His parents pushed through to grab him.

"Son, you leave village business to big people, you hear?" the father said, looking at the Priestess apologetically. "Sorry, Ongswele. We take him to hut."

"But Father, I see monster Issy see."

"What he talk about?" Ongswele demanded.

"Nothing," the man said. "He think he see something walk with Teahupo'o when they take his sister. He just scared. Monster no real."

"Black monster … eyes glow," the boy said, stretching his eyes for effect. "It *real*."

"See," Issy said, "they *do* exist."

Ongswele turned to him. "He just boy. You also just boy, Isilimo. But traitor boy, and for that, you die with strangers and Teahupo'o dog."

"Kill all!" she ordered the warriors as she turned to walk away.

Issy tensed as Reg and Captain Phealix raised their weapons at the men closing in on them.

"Stop!" a voice yelled.

Ongswele halted, and so did the warriors.

"They speak the truth," the voice continued. It sounded familiar.

"Khulu!" Issy cried.

"I know," the old man said, shuffling through the wall of villagers to stand beside Issy. "You don't have to remind me."

"Khulu?" Ongswele gaped. "It no possible!"

"If it's not possible, I wouldn't be standing here. So I'd say it's entirely possible."

The murmurs spreading like wildfire among the villagers confirmed that some of them, especially the older ones, recognised Khulu for who he was.

Issy took the moment to whisper to the side, "How did you get out of there?"

"Big robot, remember?" Khulu replied as if that was enough. It wasn't, but while Issy felt obligated to delve a little deeper, he didn't get the chance to do so.

"How you still alive?" the Priestess waylaid him, her expression typical of someone seeing someone they thought were dead.

"That's not important, girl," the old man said, and ignored Ongswele's indignation at his disregard for her position. "What *is* important, is that everything Issy said is true. And if you want our people to survive, *you* had better start believing it too."

"Why I must believe mad old man?" Ongswele said, regaining her composure.

"Oh, you don't have to believe *me*," Khulu said, and waved for someone to join him.

The villagers gasped and backed away in fear from the figure approaching with a series of thuds.

Khulu swept his gaze over the crowd and, with a gleam in his eyes, said, "But maybe you will believe a god."

CHAPTER 53

Ongswele had *not* been having a good week. One long-awaited feast and two executions had slipped through her fingers, and now she faced a ghost from the past and something she only semi-believed in – if only to help control her fellow tribesmen, as had all her predecessors. No one had said you had to believe in something yourself to make others believe in it; *least* of all her predecessors. And no, it wasn't Tuma, but if the entity standing before her was indeed the real thing, she had to rethink a few things.

Ongswele's expression appeared as confused as her thoughts.

"Is that—" she asked one of her advisors, but he wasn't there any longer because he was kneeling on the ground – his forehead pressed against the soil between his hands – in unison with the other villagers.

"The Metal God," the man confirmed from the side of his mouth.

The murmurs of "Metal God" echoing throughout the crowd emphasised that what Ongswele was looking at might in fact be what she thought she was looking at. Or not.

However, not one to take unnecessary chances, the Priestess joined her advisor on the ground in the Holy Position.[*]

"You sure?" she tried, only to get shushed by an old lady next to her.

The Metal God remained quiet while someone whispered something to him. Was it Khulu?

"Yes, yes, I know what to say, you old prune," the Metal God whispered back, although he clearly wasn't used to whispering, as everyone could hear him. Ongswele suspected it was because gods didn't really *have* to whisper – something the god proved a second later.

"MY SUBJECTS!" it boomed.

Screams of terror scattered puffs of dust sideways from every ground-bound face. Somewhere, a crying mother tried to soothe her crying baby.

After more whispering, the Metal God said, "Too much? Sorry."

In a still-loud-yet-bearable voice, he repeated, "My, uh, subjects. You have to believe everything these people say. Also, you have to do everything they say. That, um, is it."

"Thank you, Ikk— Metal God," Khulu said, and turned to address the villagers. "You may rise." When nothing happened, Khulu pulled a young man to his feet. "Come on, up you go ... all of you!"

---

[*] This is by far the longest-running and most widely utilised religious position in existence. If you'd like to know more, the Ginormous Archive of General Guidance by Literally Everyone has billions of illustrations and photos depicting the position, as well as slight variations on it across species and religions. However, before you Gaggle it, please ensure you have the proper search safety filters in place. Especially if you're planning on Gaggling it in public.

Like Ongswele, the rest of the villagers must have expected something more … speechful from a god, which is why they rose to their feet with a fair amount of hesitance.

Added to her disappointment over the lack of godliness from a so-called god, Ongswele felt somewhat taken aback that she'd had to kneel to *anyone* or, for that matter, any*thing*.

The Piestess however forced herself to rise in a dignified manner and adjusted her Cloak of Bones in a way that, she hoped, would also appear dignified. It might have worked if it weren't for the dust now caked around her mouth.

"How *you* know Metal God?" she asked Khulu with a slightly shaky voice that didn't support her composure efforts.

"Oh, we go back a long way," the old man replied.

Did he just stop himself from patting the Metal God on the shoulder?

This drew Ongswele's attention to something that had been bothering her.

"Why he hold head in hands?" she asked.

Khulu stared at her for a moment, and after another moment she realised this was all he was going to do, so she repeated, "I say, why he ho—"

"What?" Khulu said, breaking from his trance. "Oh, yes, the Metal God, er, removed his head – in a very complicated, divine manner that none of you would understand – so that he could, er … see everything."

"Isn't that right, Metal God?" he added with a sideward kick to the Metal God's metal leg.

"Oh, uh, yes," said the Metal God, raising his metal head with a metal hand and swivelling it in all directions for all the villagers to see the green eyes seeing them.

"He kick Metal God!" someone at the back shouted with hesitant anger. "He no respect Metal God!"

An equally hesitant angry chorus erupted softly from a handful of villagers. Ongswele couldn't blame their lack of vigour, as no one – herself included – really knew how to behave around a god you could actually see. But there were certain things a Priestess had to do, and defending a god's honour was one of them.

"You no respect Metal God?" she said, stepping forward half a foot. Yes, there were things Priestesses had to do, but sticking your neck out too far wasn't one of them.

Khulu looked about at the confused-frightened-angry faces staring back at him, waiting for an answer, so he gave them one. "That's, er, how you, um … show respect to the Metal God. Isn't that right, Metal God?"

Following another kick to the leg, the Metal God turned his head to face Khulu. After a pause, he said, "Yes, *Khulu* … that is … correct."

"See?" Khulu said, adding another kick. "Respect!"

Ongswele failed to understand this odd practice, but decided to toss it onto her growing pile of failures for the week. "What you want, Khulu?"

"Do you have bread?"

Ongswele frowned. "Bread?"

"Yes, I haven't had bread in ages, and— ow!"

Rubbing his shin, Khulu glared at the Metal God who'd just respected him back. "I mean," he continued, "we must go to the Fire Mountain."

"No," Ongswele said, straightening her back in defiance. "We decide already: Teahupo'o people take Ja'nama people for sacrifice. So we go to Teahupo'o village. We take Teahupo'o people. *Then* we go to Fire Mountain … sacrifice *them!*"

"As Issy told you, the Teahupo'oan village is empty," the tall, blue female prisoner said. "There's no one there; the Euwels took them all."

"I no ever see Euwel – they no exist!"

"Then let us help you get your people back," said the stranger in the strange grey cloth standing next to the blue female. The guards gripped their spears as the man stepped forward.

Issy quickly translated, and Ongswele motioned for the guards to lower their weapons. They stepped aside, letting the tall man approach, but made sure he saw they were ready in case he ventured too close to the Priestess, so he stopped a safe distance from her.

"Look," the man said, "you don't have to believe the Euwels are real. But your people *were* taken, and we can help get them back from *whoever* took them, even if it turns out to be the Teahupo'oans."

After Issy's translation, Ongswele frowned. "We near sacrifice you. Why you help us?"

"For Issy – I'd like to help him get his parents back," the man said, casting a worried glance at Issy, who himself looked worried as he relayed the message.

Ongswele knew she was about to make the biggest decision of her life. On the one hand, she didn't want to look like a weak leader by giving in to the demands of strangers. On the other hand, *these* strangers did have a god with them; a god willing to aid in the return of her people. She *couldn't* say no.

Ongswele swallowed hard. "Ja'nama tribe accept your help. What we do?"

Through Issy, the man told her, and while it didn't make sense, the fate of her people hung in the balance, so she decided to just listen and let fate run its course.

CHAPTER 54

Not surprisingly, the Ja'namans weren't all that enthusiastic about parting with their "gifts" from the Metal Mountain; gifts that had become family heirlooms over the centuries. Sure, they accepted the fact that the gifts could – in some incomprehensible way – assist in the return of their loved ones, but they didn't have to like it, and they weren't afraid to show it. Nevertheless, a small assortment of weapons and ammo had been scraped together. It wasn't much, but it was better than nothing.

For Reg and Captain Phealix, Issy also brought two "long spears" – swords that had been found in the wreck. The swords' glowering ex-owners could only look on as their "bread slicers" were handed to complete strangers for no good reason.

Despite their age and use, the swords – katanas, if Reg remembered correctly – were in remarkable condition, and he had to suck the blood off his finger after testing the curved blade's smooth, sharp edge. Like Captain Phealix's sword, his needed a good cleaning, but there was no time for that. At least the katanas still had their scabbards, which could be slung across the back. Given, they were a bit worse for wear, but at least they were functional.

Issy had also fetched the container of vernaculites, which were subsequently distributed among as many tribesmen as possible. For this, Reg was extremely grateful, because talking through Issy to a wall of blank-faced villagers was getting a bit tedious. In contrast, the villagers weren't that grateful, as they now had too many people with too many words in their midst.

The Priestess, however, wasn't afraid to test out her newly acquired mastery of foreign languages.

"Why you take pestle?" she asked, eyeing the revolver while Reg loaded it with bullets handed to him by Issy. "And why you put small spears in pestle?"

She glanced at some of the bigger guns and added, "And why you take hammer? Spear better than hammer in battle."

Not wanting to explain everything all over again, Reg was relieved when Issy jumped in.

"Remember Mothuntsho?" the tribesman asked.

"Yes," the Priestess said. "Dead with hole in head."

"That hole was made by one of these," Issy said, holding up a bullet.

"Oh," said the Priestess, who suddenly appeared keen to be somewhere else. "I, uh, go see if men ready."

As the Priestess rushed off with a rattle of bones, Reg said, "Thank you."

Issy didn't answer, staring at the last bullet in his hand with a troubled look. Reg knew why.

"I'm sure your parents are okay, Issy," Reg tried, and after the look cast at him by the tribesman, he relented, "Okay, maybe I'm not *sure*. But they were taken alive, which means something."

"What?"

"That the Euwels need something from them."

"What would such creatures need from my parents? What would they need from *any* of us? We don't have ships, or guns, or anything of value."

Reg had pondered this himself, and had come up with a few theories – none of which he wanted to share with Issy, as none of them would make the tribesman feel any better.

"I don't know," Reg said instead. "But if the Euwel could take a whole village, they could easily have killed a whole village too. But they didn't. They took them alive, which means they have some kind of value."

"For now," Captain Phealix said, walking up from behind. "We don't know when that value will run out, so I suggest we get cracking."

Reg nodded and held out his hand, into which Issy placed the bullet. The Scout looked the tribesman in the eye. "You know what to tell the others?"

"Yes."

"Then get to it so that we can get going," Reg said, and looked on sadly as Issy left to bark orders at the assembled warriors.

"You're *actually* worried about him, aren't you?" Captain Phealix said with an unreadable face.

Not wanting to seem weak, Reg ignored the question. "Are your men ready?"

Captain Phealix glanced at her remaining men, of which there was, technically, only one *man* left, and he seemed quite upset about something.

"They're ready," she said without looking ready.

Feeling slightly unready himself, Reg got up and slotted the last bullet into the revolver's chamber.

"Good," he said, slamming the chamber into place. "Then let's go hunt some stonies."

CHAPTER 55

By the time they reached the pathway leading up the volcano, daylight had long since lost its will to hang on, while Phealix was losing her patience.

"Oh, for Zolt's sake, Franki, stop looking like you have man flu!"[*] she said, shooting a glare at her First Mate.

"But Captain," Franki said with an air of petulance that refused to let go of his voice and face, "why can't *I* have the big gun?"

Phealix glanced at the heavy machine gun Demi was carrying up the slope with increasing difficulty. Franki *loved* big guns, but he apparently hadn't considered how much heavier a heavy machine became the more you lugged it around – especially up a mountainside, as Demi's equally heavy breathing confirmed to everyone except Franki.

------

[*] Man flu is, in fact, a very real and extremely serious condition. So, ladies, please don't make fun of it! Unless, of course, you're among yourselves … *and* you have several bottles of wine lined up … *and* the man in question isn't within earshot. If these conditions have been met, please feel free to make as much fun of it as you like.

"We've been over this," Phealix said, trying to keep herself calm. "Demi's better with heavy weaponry than anyone on the *Dodger*, including you."

"But I'm good too, Captain, and as her *senior* I feel I should—"

"And as *your* senior, Franki, I'm ordering you to let it go. We only have a few working guns and not much ammo. We don't know how many of those things are up there, or how many bullets it will take to bring them all down – *if* we can bring them all down. So every shot counts. That's why Demi is on the heavy gun. And if you don't stop complaining about it right now, there will be hell to pay when we get back on the *Dodger*. Are we clear?"

After a moment's pause, Franki said, "Clear as day, sir."

The Vahltan fell back, either to cover their rear or to hide the fact that his sulkiness hadn't diminished in the slightest. Either way, she was glad not to see his face at the moment. She could never understand how adult Vahltans could be such children at times.[*]

"Problems?" Reg asked.

"Nothing that can't be fixed once I'm back on my ship," Phealix grated. "I think the crew needs some … reorientation. And I'll make sure they know who to thank for it."

Reg glanced back at the disgruntled Vahltan. "He's just scared."

"It doesn't matter. He needs to get his head in the game, because I meant what I said – we cannot afford to waste ammo."

---

[*] To be fair, that could be said of most adults, regardless of species.

"Well, if the temple *is* Euwel-infested, we won't have enough bullets even if all of them hit their mark. In which case, we're screwed. You know that, right?"

Phealix *did* know, but there wasn't anything she could do about it other than hope they were wrong. Because if they were right, they were *definitely* screwed.

•••

Reaching the split in the pathway, Phealix was about to take the route running left towards the volcano's entrance, when she thought she heard something. She held up her hand to bring the procession to a halt.

"What—" Reg started.

"Shh," she replied with a finger over her lips and listened intently.

There it was again. It was faint, but it sounded like …

"Was that a scream?" Reg said, frowning at the volcano's peak, only barely visible in the moonlight.

"I think so," Phealix said.

"Why would they be up there if the temple's down here?"

"Beats me," Phealix said, feeling a bit puzzled herself. "But *someone's* up there, and by the sound of it, they need help."

"What was that?" Issy said, rushing up from behind.

"I don't know, Issy. It might be the Teahupo'oans, or it might be your people."

"Then let's go get them," Issy said.

"We can't," Reg said. "We must get to the temple."

"Why we stop?" the Priestess asked as she joined them with Ikkabot on her heels.

Apron removed, the robot now wore a specially sewn leather harness strapped around his shoulders. On the back, attached to the harness, was a heavily laden bag, while the front sported a square bamboo frame that housed the robot's square head. He also looked a bit strange without Khulu, who'd been told – much to the old man's dissatisfaction – to stay at the village, despite his insistence that his bones still had "plenty of fight" left in them.

"Our people are up there, Ongswele," Issy said.

"Then we get them."

"That's what I said."

Reg shook his head. "We don't even know if it *is* them. *I* say we proceed to the temple. If that's the Euwels' base of operations, then that's where we need to go."

"And," he added, cutting off the impending protest splashed all over Issy's face, "for all we know, your people might have been taken there too."

Roro crouched to inspect the muddy ground.

"He right," the headhunter confirmed, getting up. "People taken *this* way," he said, pointing to the path leading left, "and *that* way," he added, pointing to the path going up. The Priestess gave the Teahupo'oan a look that made him shift his feet. It seemed as though, to her, his contributions were about as welcome as a cactus on a jumping castle.

"Couldn't this be old tracks from earlier?" Phealix asked.

With another nervous glance at Ongswele, Roro shook his head. "It rain last night, and there cloud today. This track no have water in. So it *new* track."

"Why would they split up the villagers?" Reg said.

"I no know," Roro replied. "I know only what track show. And track show villagers go this way *and* that way."

"Then that's what we need to do, too," Phealix said.

"Split up?" Reg said. "That's not a good idea."

"You had no problem breaking the rules back at the wreck," Phealix snapped as her tension levels neared their peak.

"And look what happened!" Reg snapped back with deep-seeded anger that seemed directed more towards himself than the Faylin.

Nonetheless, Phealix felt guilty. "I'm sorry, I didn't mean to bring up Spence."

"It doesn't matter," Reg said. "The fact remains that splitting up will weaken us."

"I agree," Phealix replied, "but at the same time there *are* people up there. We cannot just leave them to their fate."

As if to emphasise her point, another scream echoed down from above.

Reg glanced at Issy's pleading face and gave in with a sigh. "Okay, fine. We split into two equal groups and—"

"No, you're right about the temple," Phealix said. "It remains our priority. I'll take Demi and ten men from the tribe to see what's going on up there. The robot and the rest are going with you."

Reg seemed about to argue, but Phealix was having none of it. Pointing at the big bag on Ikkabot's back, she continued before the human could say anything, "I trust you know what to do with that?"

Reg paused, and nodded as he realised the argument was over. "Don't worry, they'll get what's coming to them."

The captain nodded and turned to her First Mate. "Franki, you and Salli keep this lot safe, understand?"

"But Captain," the Vahltan protested, looking at Reg uncomfortably, "I don't think it's a good idea for us to be left alone with a Milit—"

"Oh, I'm sure the Scout will play nice, Fanki," Phealix said, glancing at Reg. "Won't you, lieutenant?"

Reg nodded and grinned at Franki in a way that didn't up the Vahltan's comfort levels, which suited Phealix just fine, because comfy Vahltans weren't productive Vahltans. A bit of edginess kept them on their toes, and pretty soon they were going to need these Vahltans to perform Swan Lake or whatever that tippy-toe dance was called.

"Good," Phealix said with a supporting grin before turning to Issy. "Will you please ready ten of your men for me?"

"I'll get nine," the tribesman replied, "because I'm coming with you."

"No, you're not. It won't be safe for you up there."

"It won't be safe anywhere."

Phealix glanced at Reg for backup, but all he could offer was a shrug. It seemed that, as far as he was concerned, a ninety-nine-year-old "boy" could make his own decisions … and he'd be right.

"Fine," Phealix said, eyeing the tribesman sternly. "But you stay close to me and do as I say, you hear?"

Issy nodded, then summoned over nine Ja'naman warriors to join them. When all were gathered, Phealix motioned her party up the path.

"You, er, be careful, okay?" Reg said awkwardly.

"Oh, I'll be fine," Phealix said. "You just make sure you don't end up like Ikkabot."

"Without a head on my shoulders?"

"Well, that, or going all … roboty on us."

Reg clearly hadn't forgotten Spence's automated behaviour. He nodded, and so too did Phealix before she turned to join the rest of her party without even a glance back.

•••

When the group's torchlights disappeared from sight shortly thereafter, Reg turned to Roro.

"You ready?" he asked.

"I ready," Roro replied, glancing nervously at the Priestess, who was still looking daggers at him.

Reg turned to her. "I trust you'll behave?"

"Only if you speak truth," she said, not taking her eyes off the Teahupo'oan. "If not, death wait for him … *and* for you."

"Fair enough," Reg said, starting the hike along the path. He didn't need to argue the matter with the Priestess. She would soon see the truth for herself – that death waited for them all.

CHAPTER 56

At the top of the volcano, Phealix signalled her party to a halt. She proceeded in a crouch to take cover behind the nearest boulder, from where she witnessed something she wished she hadn't.

At the overhang where Reg had so nearly been sacrificed – what felt like ages ago – a mix of about two dozen Euwels surrounded a group of about two dozen Teahupo'oan and Ja'naman warriors. The men, in turn, encircled a cluster of terrified Teahupo'oan and Ja'naman villagers, all either elderly or small children.

A scar-faced Ja'naman warrior ignored the desperate pleas from a wrinkled old man, whom he shoved into the crater without blinking an eye. He stared down until the fading scream cut off, then walked over stiffly to grab his next victim. The elderly woman looked at the warrior in horror as he manhandled her towards the lip of the crater.

"Why you do this, Gobatsha?" she exclaimed. "I know you from baby. You *no* like this! You *good* man."

Gobatsha stared at her with a lifeless expression that was only broken by a brief flicker of tortured pain in his eyes. When the moment passed, his eyes hardened again as he pushed the woman in without further hesitation.

"Why would he do that?" Issy whispered when the woman's futile scream faded into nothingness.

Phealix had been so engrossed by the horrific scene that she hadn't noticed the others creeping up from behind.

Recovering from another near heart attack, she rounded on Issy, and was about to scold him when she noticed the look on his face; a look that mirrored her own feelings. She looked back at the villagers, where Gobatsha now yanked the Wise One out from among the captives. The petrified old man tried to brake against the hand ushering him forward, but his frail old legs were too weak to resist. He fell over, but was hauled back to his feet and violently shoved towards his pending demise. Although the Wise One's vision wasn't the greatest, he must have seen what was coming. And it was coming fast.

For the old man to stand any chance, there was only one course of action to take, and it was one that Phealix preferred not to take; it was more the sort of thing Reg was prone to do. But as both time and options were in short supply, it *was* the only action available. With a nod towards Issy and the others, Phealix took a deep breath and rose to her feet while raising the assault rifle. She took careful aim at the first pair of Euwel eyes she could find, and fired.

When the back of the Euwel's head exploded and the creature crumpled to the ground, the other Euwels swivelled in the direction the shot had come from, glaring hot coals at Phealix. The entranced warriors just stood there, staring blankly at whatever it was they were staring at.

One of them, however, wasn't all that entranced any longer. Shaking his head, Gobatsha stared in alarm at the Teahupo'oan Wise One he'd been about to cast into the volcano. He let go of the old man's arm as if it were a viper, and seemed about to say something when another tribesman walked up to finish the job. Gobatsha saw him coming and knocked the man against the side of his head with the back of his spear, sending him toppling to the ground, out cold.

A Ronian-shaped Euwel alternated his fiery gaze between Gobatsha and Phealix's group, before settling on the Faylin. He must have deemed her gun more of a threat than the spears wielded by the locals.

"GET HER," he ordered, upon which the tribal drones marched forward.

"Why aren't the Euwels attacking us themselves?" Demi said.

"They probably know the villagers don't want to kill their own people," Phealix ventured.

"We *don't*," Issy confirmed.

"We might not have a choice, Issy."

"Yes, we do," Issy said, nodding towards his fellow warriors. "Let *us* handle our people."

"Fine," Phealix said, eyeing the advancing Ja'naman and Teahupo'oan drones. "We'll keep the Euwels busy." She glanced at Demi. "Ready to kick some butt?"

The Vahltan cocked the heavy machine gun slung over her shoulder. "I thought you'd never ask, sir."

"Then let's give these stony bastards the send-off they deserve," she said, and squeezed the trigger.

CHAPTER 57

Reg carried less anxiousness into the mountain than the first time he'd entered, if only because he could actually see where he was going this time.

The torches carried by the tribal warriors gave off more than enough light to put his mind at ease, or at least to sedate it to a degree. On top of that, the glow sticks still glowed with no sign of petering out anytime soon, which added to the sedation at first, until it kicked Reg's nerves back into overdrive. He had never worked with unrefined petrodium before, and although the longevity of its power was fascinating, it also scared the living crap out of him, mainly because that power was currently strapped around his neck.

But the petrodium wasn't the only thing that had him on edge. They had come to face the Euwels, and that's the one thing they hadn't faced thus far. Apparently, Reg wasn't alone in his concern.

"I expected more resistance by now," Franki said, looking about nervously.

"Maybe they saw we were armed and made a run for it," Salli ventured with a hopeful air.

"Armed or not, they don't strike me as the sort that would run from the likes of us," Reg said. "Especially if they have the numbers."

"Well, they *did* lose a few numbers back in the wreck," Salli said, refusing to let go of her newfound optimism. "It might have rattled them."

"We got lucky," Reg said as they exited the tunnel and entered the huge cavern housing the temple. "We caught them off guard. I don't think they'll make it easy for us to take out their weak points this time around."

The Vahltans remained silent, but Reg suspected it had less to do with them agreeing with him than the fact that they noticed – like he did – the light in the cavern had drastically increased since their previous visit.

Taking advantage of the extra light, he studied the cavern, and while he still couldn't see its ceiling or the farthest walls, he *could* vaguely make out the temple in the middle, even from this far away. He could also *feel* it, and it felt unpleasantly pleasant. The hazy structure pulsated with an eerie orange light like an eerie beacon – a magnet that slowly pulled Reg towards it with whispered promises of hope, power and bliss, fighting his mind's insistence that moving in the opposite direction would be a better call.

I should go there, he thought. Just leave the rest of these fools behind and go there by myself. No, I won't be by myself. I'll have more brothers and sisters than I could ever imagine. I could again have a family. A big family. A *strong* family.

"What that?" a voice said, breaking his trance.

Realising he'd wandered ahead without realising it, Reg stopped and rubbed his eyes to reboot reality. He glanced back at the source of the voice, which turned out to be Ongswele. The Priestess stared at the temple with a mixture of awe, fear and puzzlement.

"It's the temple," Reg managed, shaking his head to speed up his brain's recovery time.

"I no want to believe," Ongswele breathed, not taking her eyes off the glowing cylindrical structure as the last of her men filed out of the tunnel. "But now, I see. Now, I believe. But where … Euwel?"

Reg's gaze swept over the cavern before returning to the temple. "I'm not sure," he said as his mind finally reunited with normality, "but we'll soon find out."

• • •

Covering the flanks and the rear with spears at the ready, Roro and the Ja'namans approached the temple in two lines behind Reg, Salli and Franki, whose raised rifles were ready to take down anything attacking from the front. For the umpteenth time, Reg glanced back at the three Ja'namans with leather bags slung across their shoulders.

"Remember, stay close," Reg said, also for the umpteenth time, and the looks they returned stated that the umpteenth time was now one time too many.

"We know," grated the one closest to Reg.

Carrying Reg's ammo, Mojaki, like his two companions, couldn't understand why they had to tote around heavy bags of small spears when they had perfectly good *big* spears at their disposal.

Oblivious to the glowers cast at him, Reg stopped at the bridge connecting the cavern floor to the temple, and ordered the men to follow in single file. Taking a deep breath, he started traversing the narrow surface of the bridge. Again, while the walkway was broad enough to walk across comfortably, the molten pool below nearly incentivised him to use his arms for balance, like some of the tribesmen behind him were doing. The pool now swirled like a pot stirred by an unseen ladle, ready for the next ingredient.

Reaching the far side of the bridge, Reg noticed that the pulsating veins on the temple walls indeed glowed much brighter than before. The black surface appeared ready to crack from a power growing within, and he could almost swear he heard a hum pulsating in harmony with the light. At first he thought it was only his imagination, until Roro helped him out.

"It different from before," the Head Headhunter said. "Much light. And sound … like Night Aahp hum."

"Night Aahps hum?" Reg asked.

"I no know, but I think if Night Aahp try to hum, it sound like this."

Reg smiled, and not just because he found Roro's comment amusing. No, more than that, he smiled because he knew he might never be able to do so again. And as he entered the still-open passageway leading into the temple, he broadened the smile, because if this was the last normal thing he ever did, he wanted it to feel good. And it did.

CHAPTER 58

The Ronian-Euwel staggered back as multiple shots from Phealix's assault rifle slammed into its head and torso. However, apart from chipping a few chunks off its rocky exterior, it hadn't sustained any significant damage.

"Captain!" Demi shouted, pointing at the entranced tribesmen closing in on them.

"Move!" Phealix said, and started skirting around the advancing men, who were a bit slow on the uptake as each of them slowly turned in place to follow their targets. Issy and his warriors used the opportunity to knock the hostile tribesmen across the back of the head, rendering them unconscious.

Trusting that the locals had the other locals under control, Phealix wasted no time in unleashing another barrage of fire on the Ronian-Euwel, whom she assumed was the leader of the group. While this volley of bullets didn't bring it down either, a small crack opened in the creature's chest where the previous hits must have weakened its shell.

Demi, having seen this too, didn't need to be told what to do, and concentrated her fire on the Euwel's torso until its chest finally imploded. A stream of molten rock oozed from the hole and ran down the Euwel's belly before dripping to the ground, creating small puffs of cooled ash. Shortly thereafter, the creature followed suit.

Looking up from their fallen comrade, the other Euwels clearly realised that their tribal drones weren't up to the task of stemming the attack, and advanced on the pirates themselves.

Phealix opened fire at the head of the nearest Euwel, which promptly crossed its arms in front of its face to deflect the bullets meant for its eyes. Phealix redirected her fire at the Euwel's vulnerable kneecap, which shattered as two bullets tore through it. The creature sagged onto the damaged joint, but immediately morphed one of its blade-arms into a flexible appendage. It jabbed the arm into the still-smouldering chest cavity of the fallen Ronian-Euwel next to him. Aiming for the now-green-glowing appendage, Phealix pulled the trigger, only to be reminded by a click that the rifle needed reloading.

"Cover me!" she shouted.

"On it, sir," Demi said.

While Phealix retrieved a full clip from her bag, the Vahltan stepped forward to unleash more bursts of fire at the other approaching creatures. Fighting the powerful recoil of the heavy machine gun jumping against her hip, Demi brought down two Euwels, who also dropped to the ground without the full support of their knees.

A third Euwel was less lucky as a bullet snuck past its forearm-shield, penetrating its eye and blowing out the back of its head in a fountain of orange. However, as soon as it toppled onto its face, one of the injured Euwels stuck a glowing appendage into the open wound.

Reloaded, Phealix fired three shots at the creature's face before it could shield its eyes, and watched in satisfaction as the back of its head exploded too. She was about to do the same with the other injured Euwel when her time ran out. Glimpsing movement from the corner of her eye, she rolled to the side as a Langnian-Euwel leapt in at the spot she'd stood and slashed the air where her head had been a moment earlier.

Rising from the roll, she opened fire at the tall creature but couldn't land an effective shot on the moving target, and grimaced as the wasted bullets ricocheted off its torso.

"Captain!" came a frantic yell from the side, where Demi was struggling with a jammed gun as a human-looking Euwel closed in on her. But with the Langnian-Euwel pulling back its blade-arm to shorten Phealix's body, there wasn't much the captain could do.

No, she couldn't accept it! She *wouldn't* accept it. She was *not* prepared to lose another crew member to these things. Not again!

Falling backwards to avoid the blade-arm swinging at her neck, Phealix barely had enough time to remove the revolver from her skirt, but managed to fire a shot that took the neck off Demi's attacker before it could ram its blades into the Vahltan's chest.

Looking up in appreciation from the rocky head rolling past her feet, Demi's eyes suddenly grew large as she stared above her captain, where the Langnian-Euwel stepped onto the Faylin's rifle-holding arm, nearly crushing her wrist. Fighting the pain, Phealix swung the revolver towards the creature. However, the Euwel knocked the gun away with one arm before it jabbed the point of its other arm into Phealix's shoulder. This time, though, she couldn't hold back, and howled in pain.

And while Demi still tried to unjam her weapon, the Euwel raised its other arm to finish the job.

Despite wanting to, Phealix didn't close her eyes. She'd always known this day would come, but did it have to come at such an inconvenient time? She still had so much work to do, and now she wouldn't be able to get to it thanks to a malevolent rock bent on spreading death and destruction for whatever reason. Furious, she refused to look away from the creature about to tear up her life's to-do list. She wasn't going to give it the satisfaction of seeing even a trace of fear on her face, so instead she squeezed out one last glare of defiance.

The Euwel, however, went completely rigid, which was hard to notice on something with an exterior composed of rock.

At first, Phealix couldn't figure out why, until she saw a spear tip protruding from the front of the creature's throat. Behind it, Issy retracted his spear, and as the Euwel collapsed, the tribesman raised his weapon and slashed down with enough force to sever the creature's head from its body.

The tribesman stepped over and extended his hand. "Are you okay?" he asked.

Grabbing Issy's wrist, Phealix rose with a wince as pain shot through her wounded shoulder.

"I've had worse," she said, retrieving her weapons. "Thank you, Issy."

The little man merely nodded before dashing off to stop a Teahupo'oan woman from being thrown into the crater by two of her fellow tribesmen. Phealix didn't have time to see if he succeeded, as more Euwels started advancing on her and Demi. Fortunately, the Vahltan finally managed to unjam her gun and stepped in next to Phealix.

Levelling their weapons at the approaching enemies, they started firing ammunition that Phealix wished – against all odds – would last.

Unfortunately, it didn't.

•••

Click-click-click ... click.

It was the sound she'd expected to hear. It was the sound she'd dreaded to hear. It was the sound flicking Phealix's eardrums, announcing an unwelcome reality.

"I'm out!" Demi confirmed the reality, and used her empty machine gun as a club to knock a Euwel's legs from under it before it could knock the Vahltan's head off her shoulders. Ramming the gun into the creature's eye socket, Demi jumped back to avoid the creature's arms, which flailed about as it wailed in agony.

Not giving them time to enjoy the moment, another Euwel closed in on the duo with an intent that leaned more towards disposing of them than swapping brownie recipes. Protecting its head with crossed arms, the creature wasn't going to give Phealix a chance at another quick kill, so she did the next best thing by shooting its kneecap. The next shot might have finished it off if a sad *click* hadn't announced her rifle's own feeling of emptiness.

The Euwel used the opportunity to flex its forearms and jam them into the skull of its fallen comrade. The dark-green crystal-like substance forming the Euwel's injured knee rapidly started reconstructing itself like fast-forming shards of green ice. Unlike its comrade, this one's downtime wasn't going to last. And as Phealix gazed about, she and Demi weren't the only ones facing skewed odds in the one-sided battle.

All around them, the few tribal warriors still left standing tried their best to fend off the onslaught from their rocky adversaries while keeping the old and the young safe behind them. Not far off, a disoriented Teahupo'oan headhunter, who had just awakened from a trancelike state, looked up in apprehension at the tall Euwel looming over him. Raising its arms, the creature stabbed downwards, then lifted the impaled tribesman into the air before pulling him in. As the creature stared into the eyes of its victim, the Teahupo'oan's body discoloured and cracked before crumbling to the ground in a pile of grey ash, joining the numerous other piles now littering the volcano's rim. A quick estimate revealed that the fleshy side of the battle had lost more than half its men, including those who'd been freed from the Euwels' control.

"We're toast, aren't we?" Demi said.

Removing the revolver from her skirt, Phealix started backing away, prompting the Vahltan to do the same.

"Only if we hang around," the Faylin breathed, and realised the next logical course of action might require a bit more volume.

"Run!" she yelled. "Everybody, *run!*"

Emptying her revolver on the approaching Euwels, she removed the katana sword from her back. Striking at the nearest creature's head, it fended off the blow with a blade-arm. Trying her luck, Phealix thrust the sword at the creature's eye, and when it turned its head, she expected the blade to glance off the Euwel's rocky skin. She was however surprised when the tip penetrated the side of its skull and protruded out the other side, dripping with lava. She was so surprised that she almost forgot to retract the blade, and wrenched it free just before the creature crumpled to the ground.

Phealix was forced to shift her surprise to the back of the queue as another Euwel bore down on her, blade raised above its head. Pivoting, she barely had enough time to swing the katana's blade against the creature's side before it could cleave her from the top down. Again, the ancient weapon exceeded her expectations as it cut into the rock, nearly splitting the creature in two. With lava gushing from the wound, the Euwel's skew-hanging top half threw it off balance, sending it staggering towards the crater, where it tumbled into the fiery lava below.

Phealix stared at the katana, and her curiosity at the back of the queue demanded to know what the holdup was. "What the—" she said, but that's all she had time for, as more Euwels advanced on her.

Despite her newfound faith in the sword, Phealix knew she wouldn't be able to take on all her attackers before she got slashed to bits. She turned to join the others, only to find a wall of Euwels barring their way.

At first, the two groups faced each other in silence, until a human-Euwel stepped forward.

"YOU CANNOT GO," it said. *"YOU HAVE A PURPOSE, AND THAT PURPOSE HAS NOT YET BEEN SERVED."*

"I'll give you a purpose," Demi grated, tightening her grip on the rifle's barrel. Storming forward, the Vahltan unleashed a battle cry that drowned out her captain's own cry of "Demi, no!"

Phealix could only look on as Demi leapt towards the creature with the rifle raised above her head, ready to bring the stock down as hard as she could. The Euwel, however, extended its arms, and Demi's eyes widened in shock as her body impaled itself upon the sharp blades. When the life drained from her eyes, the last thing they reflected was the fiery eyes of the Euwel pulling her in. It didn't take long for the inevitable to happen.

"NOW *YOUR PURPOSE IS SERVED,*" the Euwel said as the Vahltan disintegrated. *"THANK YOU FOR YOUR SACRIFICE, SISTER."*

Phealix couldn't move. Her shocked eyes remained transfixed on the mat of ash that had been one of her favourite crew members only a moment before.

How many more have to die? she thought as a pang of guilt threatened to collapse her stomach from within. How many more will I fail to protect?

The answer came in the form of a cry from the side, where two expressionless Teahupo'oan warriors was dragging Issy towards the crater.

Phealix knew she wouldn't be able to reach him in time, and the look on his face said he knew it too.

CHAPTER 59

The guilt trapped in Captain Phealix's eyes was almost as unbearable for Issy as his grim antici-pation of the fate awaiting him. *Almost.* The thought of being tossed into a pit of fire wasn't exactly the easiest thing to shift aside for anyone else, even if that person was Captain Phealix. This thought also kept fuelling his struggle against the grip of his captors, but no amount of wriggling or braking proved effective as the two Tea-hupo'oans manhandled him towards the crater.

Reaching the edge, the heat from below washed over Issy's face. His eyeballs ached as he watched the lava starting to swirl profusely. The headhunters' muscles tensed as they prepared to fling their victim over the edge, and Issy's muscles tensed as he braced himself for this to be done.

"LET HIM GO," a voice rumbled.

Issy's would-be executioners paused, for which the Ja'naman was bewilderedly grateful.

"Dennis?" he said, looking about in search of the voice, which seemed to come from both everywhere and nowhere. Although he'd always felt Dennis's inten-tions, this was the first time he'd actually felt-*heard* the

Fire God's voice in its natural state without the assistance of a … PA system.

"I SAID, LET HIM GO," the voice of Dennis repeated.

"NO," said a Langnian-Euwel as it approached the crater. *"HE IS OURS."*

The lava below started bubbling vigorously.

"HE IS *NOT* YOURS," Dennis said. "NONE OF THEM ARE."

"BUT WE WANT TO BE STRONG," the Euwel said, almost sounding petulant. *"WE* NEED *TO BE STRONG."*

"NOT AT THE EXPENSE OF *THESE* PEOPLE," Dennis rumbled. "STOP THIS, NOW, OR *I* WILL STOP IT FOR YOU."

The Euwel looked at the lava silently for a moment.

"I DON'T THINK YOU WILL," it said, and turned to the Teahupo'oan warriors.

Issy didn't hear or feel a command for the warriors to push him over the edge, but there must have been one, because that's exactly what they did.

●●●

Issy had always expected to die in some silly way … an infection from an inflamed pimple, maybe, or suffocating to death in his sleep in a cocoon spun by an angry silkworm. But being roasted in the volcano had never been high on his probability ladder. Which, given the tribes' perpetual craving for sacrificial events, might have been a slight miscalculation on his part.

Now, as the push from behind sent him tumbling into oblivion, Issy wondered if closing his eyes would alleviate the terror of plunging to a fiery death. He tried it, and was left somewhat confused. Or, at least, his senses were, because Issy was convinced there was meant to be a greater sensation of wind rushing by his ears. Of flesh burning. Of nothing interrupting his private meeting with gravity.

However, none of these sensations manifested themselves. Hence Issy's confusion. He knew he had to open his eyes to identify the source of his sensory deprivation, but the fear of reality returning to unpause his fall kept his eyelids at bay. However, the fear lasted only a few seconds before curiosity got bored and yanked open the blinds to see what was happening outside.

As his eyelids shot open, Issy established that the lack of falling sensations could be attributed to the fact that he wasn't falling anymore, which in turn could be attributed to the vine suspending him in mid-air. It was a type of vine he had never seen before; a leafless, near-transparent green sleeve filled with swirling lava. He had also never seen a vine that long; from where it was wrapped around Issy's waist, the thicker end of the vine disappeared beneath the surface of the lava pool far below.

The vine raised Issy up and gently placed him back on the crater's rim before retracting into the molten rock below.

"YOU CAN'T DO THAT!" the Langnian-Euwel said. *"WE HAVE WORK TO DO!"*

"NO," Dennis said, "THE SHOP IS CLOSED. I'VE ALLOWED YOU TO GET AWAY WITH TOO MUCH FOR TOO LONG. YOU WILL *NOT* HURT ISSY. IN FACT, YOU WILL NOT HURT HIS PEOPLE, NOR *ANY* OF THE PEOPLE ON THIS PLANET, EVER AGAIN. THEY'RE UNDER MY PROTECTION NOW."

"WE'LL SEE ABOUT THAT," the Euwel said, and turned to charge towards Issy.

In a hasty retreat, Issy tripped and fell onto his back. The Euwel was on him before he could move, and wrapped a flexed forearm around the tribesman's throat, pinning him to the ground.

While Issy didn't have an abundant supply of courage, he had never lacked in physical strength. But as much as he tried, he couldn't wrest the appendage from his neck. In fact, it tightened until Issy felt his head was about to explode, and he could only stare up in horror as the creature pulled back its solid blade-arm to finish the job.

A fiery vine shot up once more from the depths of the crater, and this time it was the Euwel's turn to stare up in horror – or so Issy's tear-filled eyes chose to see it. Hovering above the Euwel's face, the tip of the vine split in two and shot into the eyes of the creature, whose choking appendage slowly uncoiled from Issy's neck.

As the vine began to glow brighter, Issy scrambled away from the Euwel, who started to shake as fine cracks branched out from its head throughout its whole body. The thin fissures exposed the film-contained lava beneath the rocky exterior, which appeared ready to explode – something that indeed occurred a second later when the creature blew apart in a cloud of ash.

For a moment, the other Euwels seemed uncertain as to their next course of action – almost as if they were recalibrating – before rushing forward to attack the vine. They didn't get very far, though, as the mountain shook with a force that sent them sprawling to the ground along with everyone else.

A thick column of lava erupted from the crater behind Issy, and he held his arms up defensively, waiting for the hot liquid to rain on him. But instead of crashing back down again, the enormous column transformed itself into an enormous shape.

Lowering his arms along with his lower jaw, Issy got up and stepped back to stare in awe at the being towering above him. With hips clearing the lip of the crater, there now stood what appeared to be a gigantic Ja'naman composed of lava.

Issy had always suspected Dennis to be majestic, but the Fire God's actual size and appearance left the tribesman at a loss for words. Something about the shape looked a bit odd, though, but seeing as he'd depleted his reserve mental capacity, Issy couldn't give it any more thought.

The Euwels slowly rose to their feet and turned to face the being looming over them.

"DON'T EVEN THINK ABOUT IT," Dennis warned.

However, after a brief moment of thinking about it, the Euwels stormed forward with their arms crossed. And while Issy wasn't their intended target, he *was* caught between them and their intended target. And with no time to get out of the way, the likelihood of him being trampled to death was on the undesirable side of the survival scale.

Just before the first Euwel could reach him, though, another vine shot over Issy's head, followed by another, and another. In quick succession, a slew of vines kept shooting out until each penetrated the eyes of a Euwel, freezing every one of the creatures in place. As their arms went limp, the vines slowly lifted the Euwels into the air.

"I DIDN'T WANT IT TO COME TO THIS," Dennis said, "BUT YOU LEAVE ME NO CHOICE."

The Fire God's body started to burn brighter; a glow that surged through each of his viny appendages to the Euwels suspended at the end. When the glow entered the eyes, each creature's body began to shake and crack, causing light to spill through the web of widening fissures. Then, one by one, the Euwels exploded in rapid succession; each bursting into a cloud of ash that sent fine particles flying everywhere.

With ash settling on his shocked face, Issy turned to look at the equally shocked faces of Captain Phealix and the tribespeople, the youngest of whom seemed more mesmerised than shocked, catching some of the snowing ash with her hand, which she promptly brought to her mouth for a taste. The ex-drone tribal warriors stood about, looking dazed, as if they'd just awoken from a terrible nightmare.

Feeling a bit dazed himself, it took Issy a moment to recover, but when he did, he turned back to Dennis and said, "Uh."

Realising it might not be enough, he added, "Thanks … for saving me," he said, and glanced back at the other ash-covered faces. "For saving all of us."

"IT'S A PLEASURE, ISSY," said Dennis, who must have noticed the change in the tribesman's expression; an expression announcing that a river of questions was about to burst its banks. "I SEE YOU HAVE QUESTIONS."

"Yes."

"BUT YOU DON'T HAVE TIME."

"Huh?"

"YOUR FRIEND DOWN THERE …"

"Reg?"

"YES. I KNOW WHAT HE'S PLANNING TO DO … BUT HE SHOULDN'T DO IT."

"Why not?" Captain Phealix interjected, stepping towards the fiery entity with nervous resolve.

When she didn't get an answer, she repeated, "Why not?"

After another pause, Dennis did what few volcanoes can do, and sighed with a jet of steam.

"BECAUSE HE'S ABOUT TO MAKE THINGS WORSE."

CHAPTER 60

The temple's pustule-covered main chamber was empty and, disconcertingly, so too were most of the pustules. It wasn't as though Reg hadn't expected this, because he had. The disconcerting part was that he'd actually allowed his optimistic side to hope for a pleasant surprise.

Nothing in the temple, however, felt pleasant. Where it had previously manifested an oppressing, almost mausoleum-like ambience, the chamber now radiated life; the type of life that didn't spell anything good for any other life. The pustules that were still intact pulsated with a greenish glow that made the hair on Reg's neck stand on end. Not far to the side stood a former pustule that had burst open like a trampled grape; a grape big enough to house a hippo.

"I'd hate to see what came out of *that*," Franki said with a shiver.

"Let's pray we don't," Reg said.

"I'm not much into praying."

Neither am I, Reg thought, but it might be time to make an exception.

He then did exactly that, although maybe not in the right way, because he didn't quite know what to say, or to whom. So he just sent out a distress call to the universe and trusted that the applicable entity would pick up on the transmission.

His growing feeling of dread wasn't just linked to the oversized pustule or the many empty ones, but also to the fact that he couldn't see any of the vacant pustules' former inhabitants. And *that* worried him almost as much as seeing them.

"Where are they?" Salli said, echoing his thoughts. Her expression reflected the worried look on the faces of the tribesmen filing into the cylindrical chamber, their eyes darting in all directions as their brains tried to comprehend what their eyeballs were telling them.

"Don't know, but we have to keep moving," Reg said as they continued along the walkway down the centre of the chamber. Behind him, each *thud* from Ikkabot's heavy footfalls bounced off the rounded walls with a delay that nearly coincided with the step that followed, creating a whip-like effect that drove the horses of angst in Reg's head into a frenzy.

Falling in next to the Scout, Franki glanced over his shoulder at the bag strapped to the robot's back. "Can't we just set up here?" the Vahltan said, looking hopeful.

"No, we must go to the front. I suspect that's where we'll do the most damage."

Franki didn't look happy with Reg's suspicions, and Reg couldn't really blame him, as he, too, did not relish venturing further into the temple. But they only had one shot at this, and they *had* to make it count.

The explosives they'd found in the Ja'naman village wasn't like anything used by the Unyun Militorate, or any other military Reg knew of. Powder-based, the sticks looked more like those used in the mining industry up until a few centuries ago. And although Reg was no expert in … antique explosives, he knew enough to know that most of the older variants worked on the same principle as most of the modern ones – give them a jolt and they go boom.

At first, the jolt part had presented a problem, because the power in the explosives' original detonator switches had long gone. Fortunately, Issy had inadvertently presented a solution when he returned Reg's flasher gun to him. As the weapon by itself probably wouldn't do much damage against the Euwel in any case, Reg put it to better use by connecting its battery clip to one of the detonators. A test-run demonstrated that the explosive sticks were still functional, or at least some of them. It also demonstrated the fact that a test-run so close to the village might not have been the best idea. It had taken some time to coax the last of the shaken villagers back out of their huts.

Now, entering the passageway at the far side of the chamber, Reg just hoped they had enough functioning explosives to get the job done. Exiting the passageway, he wasn't sure they'd even *get* to the job.

While he'd expected to encounter the Euwels at some stage, their absence had planted a seed of optimism; optimism that promptly shrivelled and died.

At first, Reg didn't know what to say, until instinct helped him out.

"Shit."

•••

The smaller domed chamber at the front of the temple still sported the thick, towering column in the middle, but the intertwined lime-green and orange veins covering it pulsated more intensely than before. And while the head and headless body of the Vahltan pirate Jenni wasn't there anymore, each of the six pedestals surrounding the column were now manned by a Euwel.

The mix of Euwels didn't seem to notice the group's arrival, as each was immersed in manipulating the fiery orange symbols hovering above the black slabs atop the pedestals.

Despite their apparent obliviousness to everything except what they were busy with, Reg didn't want to tempt fate by opening fire and wrenching the creatures from their trance-like state, so he signalled Roro over and whispered in his ear. The Teahupo'oan did the same with five of the Ja'naman tribesmen, who nodded in confirmation before each of them crept up behind one of the Euwels. Roro nodded again, upon which he and the others stabbed upwards into the green necks of the creatures, who collapsed with a silent wail that pierced Reg's consciousness and sent shivers down his spine.

So much for being quiet, he thought, swinging his assault rifle back towards the passageway, ready to blast the first pair of orange eyes emerging from it. His hand periodically flexed on the grip of the weapon as he waited for the onslaught to commence. But the passageway remained empty. Behind him, the tribesmen kept stabbing their spears into the smouldering eye sockets of the Euwels, and by the time Reg turned back, only six piles of ash remained.

Satisfied that the creatures were down for good, the Scout looked at the robot carrying the large bag. "Ikkabot, if you don't mind," he said, gesturing towards the column.

"Of course," said Ikkabot's head from the bamboo frame on his chest.

When the robot stepped up to the spot indicated, four tribesmen held the bag aloft while Reg cut its straps

"Careful now," Reg said as the men lowered the bag, although his words of caution weren't necessary. The locals clearly hadn't forgotten the results of the test-run back at the village, and didn't want to re-experience the results while they were anywhere near the blast zone.

Kneeling by the bag, Reg opened it to double-check the wiring connecting the explosive sticks to the detonator switch. Satisfied, he set the timer to ten minutes; enough time for them to escape the temple, but hopefully not enough time for anyone, or anything, to fiddle with the bomb.

Task completed, Reg got up and backed away slowly.

"Okay," he said, "time to go."

"Well, that was easy," Salli said as they hurried through the passageway.

The statement annoyed Reg to no end, and not just because of its jinxing nature, but also because the Vahltan was right – it *had* been easy. But it *shouldn't* have been. With the number of open pustules in the adjacent chamber, they should have encountered more resistance by now. Much more. Or, at the very least, *some* resistance.

It wasn't as though Reg wished more Euwel upon them but, regrettably, as they exited the passageway and re-entered the temple's main cylindrical chamber, that's precisely what they got.

CHAPTER 61

A horde of Euwels, ranging in shape and size, came streaming in through the temple entrance at the other end of the chamber. Aside from the Ronian, Langnian and human moulds, Reg also spotted rocky Ja'namans, Teahupo'oans, Stortians and several other varieties.

And was that …? Yes, there was no mistaking it – a Caynin-Euwel and a Faylin-Euwel standing side by side. With the two species' open dislike for one another, Captain Phealix would have flipped had she seen this … or maybe not. If she could stomach living among Vahltans, she probably got along with just about any other species, Caynins included.[*]

---

[*] For those who don't know Caynins, they're not so bad. In fact, some (especially Caynins) would argue they're better than Faylins – an argument that really takes off when you put a Caynin and a Faylin in the same room. Just note that, should you be … unwise enough to do so, at least be clever enough to remove yourself from said room and close the door behind you. Maybe locking it will be a good idea, too. And you'll certainly score some bonus IQ points for leaving the building altogether.

"Just had to open your mouth, didn't you?" Reg said. Casting Salli a well-deserved glare, he marched through the line of Ja'naman warriors, who eyed the glowy-eyed rocky creatures in a way that perfectly suited people seeing glowy-eyed rocky creatures for the first time.

"That … Euwel?" the Priestess asked with a quiver in her voice. Initially, she'd stayed at the back of the procession, letting the warriors enter the temple first. However, she now found herself at the forefront of an encounter for which she wasn't completely prepared.

"Yes," Reg said. "I suggest you stay behind me until we get out of here."

"We no stay and fight?"

"There's no time. Remember the big boom back at the village?"

The Priestess nodded.

"Imagine that a hundred times bigger."

Ongswele's face said that, while she wasn't sure how much a hundred was, even two times bigger was two times too big. "But what about people Euwel take?"

Reg had wondered about that himself. "They must have been taken up there," he ventured, pointing up. He just hoped Captain Phealix had things under control.

"But tracks show people come here too."

"I know," Reg said, eyeing the Euwels blocking the way, "but as you can see, your people aren't here. So, no, we won't be staying to fight, but we *will* need to fight our way out of here as quickly as we can before the bomb goes off. There's no time for heroics: just stay alive and keep moving. Roro, will you please make sure everyone gets the message?"

Ignoring the conflicting emotions contorting the Priestess's face, Roro nodded and ran down the line to ensure that everyone got the message.

Ikkabot stepped in next to Reg, who silently faced the Euwels silently facing him.

"Do you know why Emperor Klassis II used tenantium in my construction?" the robot asked.

Reg sniffed. "Tax deductions?"

"No. It was to get him to safety should the palace ever be overrun. Would you like me to clear a path for you?"

Reg glanced at the grimy robot. Captain Phealix had informed him of Ikkabot's past, but the lieutenant wasn't convinced that time was on the robot's side. Sure, the tenantium exterior would still last for who knows how long, but the mechanisms, wiring and circuitry underneath had to be well beyond their warranty periods by now.

Still, Reg didn't have the luxury of being picky, so he nodded. "As clear as you can, whenever you're ready."

Reg realised he should've been more specific. He had hoped for a moment to gather himself, but the moment got lost when Ikkabot stormed off without a second invitation, followed by a wave of howling tribesmen.

•••

When Ikkabot's bulky body rammed into the front line of rocky bodies, Reg quickly changed his mind about the robot's usefulness.

The first Euwels didn't stand a chance as they got bowled over by Ikkabot's momentum, and those behind them didn't fare much better, with the robot's sweeping arms clubbing them sideways. Some, however, ducked the follow-up blows and started stabbing and slashing away at the back of the bulldozing adversary.

Reg opened fire at two of the rocky creatures as they leapt atop the robot, and shattered the one's arm before it could do any damage. However, as the creature slid off without proper anchoring, the other one managed to ram its blade-arm into the hole where Ikkabot's head was supposed to be. It must have struck a wire or mechanism, because the robot's left arm went limp. When the Euwel pulled back its blade to have another go, Reg took it off with a well-aimed shot, and kept firing until a bullet exploded out the back of the creature's skull.

Despite the sudden loss of functionality in his left arm, Ikkabot's right arm continued its batting practice, sending two Euwels flying backwards to crash into three of their rocky compatriots, bringing them down in a heap.

Following in Ikkabot's wake, Reg ignored the five figures struggling to get up, and summoned over one of the bag-carrying Ja'namans. Removing a fresh magazine from the bag, he reloaded his rifle while Franki and Salli kept the downed Euwels down for good with shots through the eyes.

Cocking his weapon, Reg was about to swing it back towards the closest Euwel who, unfortunately, was a tad too close. The creature smacked the rifle to the side just as Reg pulled the trigger, sending the shot flying into one of the pustules, which burst open as the bullet ripped through its outer layer. The tall Langnian-Euwel thrust its other forearm through Reg's left shoulder before the Scout could recover.

With a cry of pain, Reg dropped the rifle and sank to his knees. He tried to reach for his katana, but the Euwel pushed its arm deeper into the wound, causing the Scout to grab at the extremity instead. The blade cut into his hands, but despite the pain and the blood running down his forearms, he held onto it. Hissing through his teeth, he stared up into the creature's fiery eyes … or at least eye and a half. Reg recognised this one from the temple and the shipwreck.

"NOW, WE BECOME YOU," the Euwel said, and leaned forward to gaze into Reg's eyes, *"AND YOU BECOME US. NOW, WE BECOME ONE."*

Following a last glance at his party being overrun by a horde of Euwels, Reg's eyes were forced closed by a searing pain that spread throughout his body. He now knew what the final moments must have felt like for Captain Phealix's Vahltans, and he couldn't wait for it to be over. Thankfully, it didn't take long for his wish to be granted.

CHAPTER 62

Accompanied by a deep rumble, the temple floor shook violently, or so Reg suspected. It was difficult to tell because he'd never been roasted from the inside; a process that, naturally, took up most of his attention at the moment.

He was surprised when the pain suddenly vanished from his body almost as quickly as it had manifested. The ache in his shoulder remained, though; an intense, pulsating burn that made him clench his jaw to the point where his teeth felt ready to shatter. But he welcomed the pain, because he *could* feel it. Which meant he was still alive.

Seeing as the whole death thing hadn't quite panned out, Reg made good use of the extra time allotted to him by opening his eyes, which felt like they'd spent a month soaking up the sun in a desert on Irik. Although his sight was a bit fuzzy, he fuzzily noticed that the quake had jerked everyone off their feet, including the Euwels – among them the one that had skewered him. After a moment of disorientation, all who weren't too injured or dead to do so got back up unsteadily. Unfortunately, this also included the Euwels.

"You alive?" Roro asked, kneeling by Reg's side.

"I … I think so," Reg groaned with a voice that sounded as fuzzy as his vision while Roro assisted him to his feet.

"Thanks," Reg said, wincing as he touched the hole in his shoulder.

Roro didn't reply, as he was too busy frowning at the Euwels.

Reg directed his own look of puzzlement towards the creatures, who just stood there with their arms lowered and heads raised. Even the Euwel that had attacked Reg turned and stepped forward, keeping its fiery eyes fixed on something above; something Reg wasn't seeing. Ikkabot turned about in place for the eyes in his chest-mounted head to figure out what was going on, but he didn't appear to have much luck. So he kept turning about in place, as he currently didn't have much else to do in any case.

"Why they no attack?" Roro echoed Reg's thought.

"I don't know," Reg said, double-checking the empty space above, just in case he had missed something. "But this might be a good time to get our asses out of here."

Roro nodded, and was about to relay the message to the others when he noticed something.

"Wait," he said, rushing to the pustule that had caught the stray bullet from Reg's rifle earlier. The tribesman gasped.

With a wary glance at the motionless Euwels, Reg joined the little man to see what he was gasping at and had to suppress his own shock. Inside the ruptured pustule was a Teahupo'oan woman, curled up on her side in the foetal position, covered in sticky green fluid. At first, she appeared dead, until she suddenly heaved, expelling a generous amount of green liquid to the side.

After the natural yelp and recoil that follows when someone witnesses sudden vomiting by a supposed dead person, Roro approached the pustule once more.

"She alive," he said.

Slinging the woman's arm around his neck, Roro gently helped her to her feet, then swept his gaze over the other intact pustules on either side of the walkway. "That where villagers must be. Maybe they alive too!"

The Priestess nodded. "Go look!" she ordered her warriors, who dashed to the nearest unopened pustules.

Afraid of hurting anyone inside, the men carefully started cutting the pustule membranes with their spears to reveal more bodies curled up inside.

With the rescue effort underway, Reg's eyes darted between the motionless Euwels and the passageway at the front of the temple. He could almost hear the timer counting down. While he knew they didn't have time for a major rescue such as this, he also knew that the tribesmen wouldn't stop until they'd freed *all* their people from their surreal prisons. He couldn't blame them.

Reg wasn't sure how long the Euwels would stay put, but one thing *was* a given: the bomb didn't care who did what. It was going to do its job, regardless. But he had no idea how much time had elapsed since he'd set the timer, or what would happen to the temple's structure once the explosives went off.

With too many clashing variables, Reg walked back to stop the device, but slowed down and stopped as his brain raised some valid points. Firstly, with his luck, the bomb would go off just as he reached it. And, secondly, they might never have another opportunity at dealing the Euwels a blow like this.

Just let it go, he thought. What's done is done, and whatever happens, happens.

He just wished the locals would get a move on so that they could get out of there *before* it happened. To aid in this happening, he turned to shout, "Hurry up, we don't have much ti—" before the shockwave from the blast hit him like a lead-laden truck.

•••

For the second time, Reg found himself on the walkway, this time flat on his stomach with his cheek against the floor. Head spinning and ears ringing, he once again forced his eyes open. Unlike earlier, when his vision had been somewhat fuzzy, it now properly swam. Rolling onto his back didn't help, either; the shapes around him refused to solidify into anything meaningful.

Some of the shapes closing in on Reg looked familiar, though; dark, with fuzzy orange-glowing orbs that appeared to float about freely as they moved past him. However, one of the shapes stopped by the human on the floor while the others passed by. Stepping in next to the shape was another, shorter shape. It didn't look exactly like the others, and Reg recognised it as some of the swimminess faded.

"Spence?" he said.

The ensign said nothing, and just stared down at Reg for a few seconds before continuing towards the passageway, followed by the tall Euwel.

Reg lifted his head once more but couldn't keep it up, and neither could he keep his eyelids open. As his head dropped back onto the cold floor, his mind called for a much-needed break, so he took one.

CHAPTER 63

Reg's mission had been successful. That much was clear the moment Phealix and her tribal party entered the temple. The smoke still hanging thick in the vast chamber smelled of explosives that had done what they were supposed to do, leaving a tang that burned the eyes and nostrils and lingered on the tongue.

The Faylin couldn't see the Scout anywhere amidst the hive of activity, which included tribesmen sitting about, looking dazed, while others were slicing into the membranes of pustules.

At first, it alarmed Phealix that they'd tamper with the zitty objects, but the reason became apparent when the limp body of a Teahupo'oan man was pulled from a pustule near her. The man's skin had taken on a dark-grey tone, and a faint orange glow in his eyes started fading as soon as he was laid down. Several others like him lay about, unmoving, and it was clear they would remain that way. But the other emancipated tribesmen showed clear signs of life, with the majority gasping, coughing and/or shivering to some degree or another. Although a paler shade of bronze, they still retained most of their natural colour. Whatever the pustules had been doing to them hadn't been completed.

"Mother, Father!" Issy yelled, and raced ahead to embrace two shaking Ja'namans sitting next to each other, staring blankly at Issy as if he was just a figment of their imagination.

As they seemed to be okay otherwise, Phealix left Issy to his family reunion and continued her search until she spotted a familiar face off to the side, pulling a Ja'naman woman from a pustule.

"Franki!" she shouted, waving at her First Mate. The Vahltan carefully handed the shaky, goo-covered woman over to another Ja'naman before marching over.

"Captain," he said, wiping his hands on his pants without much success. "Am I glad to see you, sir." He looked about with a frown.

"She didn't make it," Phealix said more coldly than she felt, as any emotion over Demi's demise would be lost on the Vahltan. Judging by his face, it was.

Phealix sighed. "Salli?" she asked apprehensively, and was relieved when Franki's finger pointed to where the Chief Technician assisted a Teahupo'oan man onto the walkway.

"Good," Phealix said. "And the Scout?"

"Over there," Franki replied, shifting his finger to the human's body lying farther down the walkway.

"You just left him there?" Phealix exclaimed.

"I couldn't wake him up," Franki said. "So I figured I could do more for the locals while the human slept it off."

Phealix knew her subordinate had done it more from apathy towards a member of the Militorate than sympathy for the villagers, but she also knew that pointing this out would serve no purpose.

"We need to get these people out of here as quickly as possible," she said instead, eyeing the last of the pustules being opened.

"But Captain, the Euwels left, so shouldn't we rather wait for the people to recover first and—" Franki started, but was cut off by a slight vibration passing through the floor. "What was that?"

"Never mind, Franki. Go find Issy and Roro, and make sure that those strong enough help the weaker ones to safety. Got it?"

Franki didn't look convinced, but when an even stronger, longer-lasting vibration shook their boots, his look swiftly changed its mind.

"Yes, sir," he said before rushing off.

Phealix knelt to check on the lieutenant lying on his back.

Franki was right; although the human's chest rose and fell steadily, he certainly was out cold. She looked around to see if anyone could give her a hand with him, but everyone had their hands full with someone else. Even Ikkabot had tribesmen slung over his shoulders and one of his arms as he *thumped* his way towards the temple's exit.

Phealix knew she would have to awaken the Scout, because there was no way she'd be able to carry him all the way by herself, especially not with her injured shoulder. Only then did she notice a similar wound to hers in the lieutenant's shoulder, but as there was not enough time to examine it properly, she patted the man's cheek.

"Wake up," she said, but another vibration called for a more aggressive approach, and she gave the cheek a few harder pats that some might have called slaps. "Hey, soldier boy, I said *wake up!*"

Reg's eyes finally shot open and fixed themselves on the Faylin with a look of confusion that quickly transformed into one of anxiety.

"Spence," he said, clutching at Phealix's arm.

Geez, Phealix thought, how hard *did* he knock his head? "No," she said, and drew out the next part to facilitate the process of comprehension, "it's … *Cap* … *tain* … *Phea* … *lix*."

"I know that," Reg said in a woozily irritable fashion, and sat up in a matching fashion. Touching the wound in his shoulder, he grimaced. "Spence … he's here."

"I didn't see him," Phealix said, looking into his unfocused eyes. "And neither did you. I think you may have a concussion."

Reg tried to get to his feet, but only managed to do so after two failed attempts and subsequent aid from the Faylin.

"I *did* see him," Reg said. "He went … in there."

Phealix followed the Scout's woozy gaze towards the front of the temple, and then also had to follow the rest of the Scout as he staggered in that direction like a drunken sailor who had ten too many.[*]

"We don't have time for this," she said, catching up without much effort.

Reg either didn't hear her, or he kept himself deaf, just as he obviously kept himself blind, because he didn't even look in her direction when she fell in next to him. However, his senses couldn't ignore the vibration passing through the floor.

"What the heck was that?" he asked, glancing down as he lumbered on.

---

[*] This is, in fact, the go-to walk for *everyone* who's had ten too many. So even if you're not a sailor and you're planning on having ten too many, don't go thinking you'll be safe.

"Like I said, we don't have time for this," Phealix said. "We have to go."

"Well, I'm going, aren't I?

"In the wrong direction," Phealix said, and halted.

"I have to find Spence first," Reg said, entering the passageway without pausing.

Just let him go, Phealix thought as she watched the back of the swaying man disappear into the tunnel leading to the smaller chamber. If he wants to get himself killed so badly, just let him get it over and done with.

However, knowing she wouldn't be able to do that, Phealix grit her teeth as she entered the tunnel. For his sake, the human had better hope he didn't get *her* killed, because if he did and *he* survived, she would haunt him for the rest of his days, whether he believed in spirits or not.

CHAPTER 64

Fittingly, it looked like a bomb had gone off in the temple's smaller front chamber. The pedestals were obliterated, and so too was the column in their midst. Only a dark hole remained where it had stood before, mirroring the dark hole in the ceiling above; a hole now encircled by jagged remnants of dark-green crystal that the blast from below hadn't destroyed. By the looks of it, the column had in fact been hollow, and judging by the green goo dripping from above, it hadn't been empty either.

"It must have been a conduit of some kind," Captain Phealix said, kneeling to drag her index finger through the slimy liquid. She rubbed the finger against her thumb to test the residue's viscosity, and brought it to her nose for a whiff. She frowned.

"It's like that Masepa stuff … but also not," she said, rising to inspect the rest of the chamber.

But Reg didn't pay much attention to Captain Phealix, her theories or, for that matter, anything other than the hole in the floor. The dark cavity called to him; a wordless invitation that pulled him closer in spite of the fear knotting his stomach.

Reaching the edge, Reg's muscles suddenly locked up, compacting the knot in his stomach into a solid ball of terror. Frozen, he could only watch as the darkness within the hole suddenly flooded out, consuming the surrounding light until nothing remained. A burning sensation manifested itself in Reg's shoulder; a searing hot pain that spread throughout his body like wildfire, setting every nerve ablaze and forcing him to his knees.

"What's wrong?" asked Captain Phealix's voice from afar, which was odd, as Reg was certain she'd been nearby only a moment earlier.

She was nowhere to be seen, though. Nothing was, except for the blackness that, like his fear, seemed to solidify, causing the sound of the Faylin's voice to drift away even farther until it dissipated into nothingness, only to be replaced by a new voice.

"Welcome, brother," the hollow voice drawled from nowhere yet everywhere.

In the darkness above the hole, a flame suddenly ignited from nothing and hung in nothing, and as Reg looked up at the burning apparition, his pain melted away. His hate, anger, sadness; *everything* melted away. All that was left was him and the flame.

"Serene, isn't it?" the voice continued, forming into something familiar.

"Spence?" Reg breathed. "I *knew* you were still alive! I … I just *knew* it."

"More alive than ever," the voice of Spence said, followed by the rest of Spence as he emerged from the darkness and stepped up next to the flame, which should have been impossible. There was supposed to be a hole where he stood, wasn't there? The soft light of the flame played over the uniformed ensign, sending ripples of shadow flitting over his face. Spence looked cleaner than Reg remembered from earlier, but that wasn't the biggest thing puzzling him.

"I don't get it," he frowned. "They didn't kill you, and they *certainly* didn't transform you, because you don't look like them. You still look like … you."

"I may still be flesh," Spence drawled, his glazed eyes locking with Reg's, "but I *am* them. They need me this way, and I'll serve them like this. So could you. They need people like us for what's coming."

"What do you mean?" Reg said. "What's coming?"

After another tremor, he shook his head. "You know what, it doesn't matter. The only thing that matters right now is for you to come with me. You don't belong with those bastards, Spence. You belong with me … your friend."

"You were never my friend," Spence said. It was strange. The accusation should have been accompanied by resentment, anger, frustration …. *something*. But it was devoid of emotion, just like the Ronian's eyes as he continued. "You merely kept me around because I was the only person you could lean on. I was the rope that kept you from sinking deeper into your pit of despair. A pit you created for yourself. A pit you tried to drag me into, time and again. And I kept letting you, because I had nowhere else to go; no one else to turn to. But no more. Now, I belong. I finally belong. For the first time in my life, I'm happy."

"I … don't understand."

"That's because your eyes are closed," Spence said, turning his gaze to the hovering fire. "It's time for them to open … to *truly* open."

Reg stared at the flame. "What is it?" he said, mesmerised by the orange light. It emitted no heat, yet it made him feel warm inside.

"It's you," Spence said.

"Me?"

"Yes."

"Am I dead?"

"No."

"So, I'm alive."

"No."

"I don't get it," Reg repeated, and his face agreed.

"In this moment, you are *both*," Spence said, "and you are *neither*."

"So I'm *not* dead ..."

"Yes."

"... and I'm *not* alive ..."

"Yes."

"... yet I *am* dead ..."

"Yes."

"... *and* I'm alive."

"Yes ... in this moment."

Reg's face longed to break away from its prison of confusion, but someone seemed to have thrown away the key. "This moment? And what is *this moment*, exactly?"

"It's the moment where you choose."

"What am I supposed to be choosing?"

Spence's gaze settled back on Reg with eyes that felt both warm and cold at the same time. "Whether you want to live ... or die."

Reg opened his mouth to give the obvious answer, but Spence interrupted him. "You may think the answer is obvious, but it's not. In this moment, life means death, and death means life. You can continue your meaningless existence and die eventually. Or you can join us – your old life will die and your new life will continue ... forever."

"What, join the Euwel? Are you insane?!"

"They will join you just as much as you join them," Spence said calmly, his disembodied voice floating in from all directions. "You will be one. *We* will be one."

His eyes suddenly glowed like red-hot coals as he added, "*WE WILL ALL BE ONE.*"

The intensity of the powerful new voice threw Reg off balance as he reared back from his knees and fell onto his backside. His whole body started to shake.

"Get your ass up, soldier boy!" Spence said. He sounded strange, though; more … girly. At least his eyes had returned to their "normal" glaziness.

"I see we'll have to continue this some other time," Spence said, sounding more like eerie-Spence again, but that was the last thing he said before he retreated and vanished back into the blackness.

"Wait, come back!" Reg cried, reaching out as the flame snuffed out. "Please, Spence … come back."

"Spence isn't here," the girly voice interrupted. "Now, seriously, get your ass up!"

Although he'd thought they were open already, Reg's eyes shot open and found themselves staring into those of Captain Phealix. As she hauled him to his feet, the pain in his shoulder flared up again.

"Will you *please* stop hurting me?" Reg exclaimed when reality flooded back into its normal pond.

But before Captain Phealix could say anything, the vibration from earlier returned, and this time it didn't go away. In fact, it turned into a continuous, pulsating tremor that shook the entire building. Above the hole in the floor, two pieces of crystal tore loose from the jagged remains of the column hanging from the domed roof. The first shattered as it struck the floor, sending shards flying everywhere, while the second disappeared down the hole. It took quite a while for the echo of smashing crystal to reach Reg's ears.

Captain Phealix looked at him. "Think you can stop complaining long enough for us to get out of here?"

Reg wanted to say something but, knowing the Faylin was right, he bit it back and nodded.

"Fantastic," Captain Phealix said, looking about as more pieces of rock started raining down around them, "because if we don't leave now, we never will."

As he followed the Faylin to the passageway, Reg glanced back at the hole one last time.

I *will* get you back, Spence, he vowed. I will make this right. I promise.

CHAPTER 65

When the light from the network of orange veins in the temple's cylindrical main chamber started fading from the top down, its curved walls began crumbling, bringing chunks of stone crashing to the floor, followed by splashes of lava. Whatever had been holding the structure together wasn't doing so any longer.

Despite every step sending a shock through his wound, Reg slogged down the walkway after Captain Phealix as fast as he could. Apparently, it wasn't fast enough, because the Faylin turned around with an air of impatience.

"Listen, *Lieutenant*, if you don't get a move on, we're done for!" she yelled to be heard above an intensifying rumble that seemed to vibrate the air itself. To support her prophecy of doom, a large blob of melted rock splashed onto the floor not too far off; a sight that was both spectacular and terrifying but mostly terrifying.

"I'm trying," Reg hissed through clenched teeth.

"Well, try harder! If this is the way you soldier boys behave every time you get an ouchy, the Militorate has gone softer than I thought."

Reg knew what she was doing and hated the fact that it was working. Clenching his teeth even harder, he doubled his efforts, and while it didn't equate to doubling his speed, they reached the temple's exit faster than they would have.

At first, Reg was relieved to leave behind the deafening din of cracking and crashing stone, but his relief was short-lived, as the noise persisted outside the temple too.

"What's happening to this place?" he said, staring in trepidation at the shower of rock and lava dropping from the cavern's ceiling.

"I'd rather not find out, so if you don't mind ..." Phealix replied as she grabbed Reg by the waist and ushered him onto the bridge.

"What are you doing?" Reg said.

"Just making sure you don't lose your balance and roast that marshmallow head of yours!"

Reg wanted to argue, but as unsteady as he felt, the Faylin had a point. Even with her help, he struggled to stay upright, but managed to inch his way forward without tumbling into the molten pool below. However, just as he stepped off the bridge, a huge tremor sent him sprawling forward, and he hit the cavern floor with a cry of pain that got drowned out by a loud crack behind him. He managed to turn around just in time to witness the nearest end of the bridge disintegrating, which would have been okay if Captain Phealix hadn't still been on it. Sadly, she was.

•••

That look, Reg thought with a shudder. That look of ... *knowing* on her face. I will *never* forget that face.

The face also didn't give him time to forget it, as it rose above the edge a moment later. "Some help, here!" Captain Phealix shouted.

Reg rushed forward to find the Faylin dangling by her fingertips, which clearly didn't have enough strength to hold on much longer.

"I can't hold on much longer!" Captain Phealix confirmed. "Help me up!"

Despite the number of times she'd come to his aid, the old part of Reg refused to let him act.

"Why are you just standing there?" Captain Phealix yelled. "Help me! Please!"

Reg heard her plea, but it was pushed into the distance by the voice of Reg's Old Part, which whispered in his head, *"Let her go. She deserves this."*

"No," Reg replied in his head. *"We owe her our life ... several times over. Besides, she's not as bad as you think."*

"Not as bad as I think!" the Old Part said. *"Are you fharking serious? They killed our parents!"*

"Well, she *wasn't actually the one wh—"*

"Don't get technical with me; you know what I mean!"

"No, I don't. You cannot hold everyone equally accountable for everything bad that's happened in our life. Yes, pirates killed our parents, but I won't allow you to kill her *for that."*

The Old Part felt taken aback. *"I would* never *kill a defenceless woman like this. I was merely suggesting we let gravity and that pool of fire down there take care of things for us."*

"You're an asshole, you know that?!"

"Yes. Hence, so are you, which is why I don't understand what your problem is."

"My problem is you*!"*

"Me?!"

"Yes, you! *You never see the grey – it's always black or white with you. No, correction – it's* always *black! All you see is darkness, while life passes us by."*

"Screw life! We deserve justice!"

"Yes, we do. But not at the expense of everything and everyone else, including me. *I'm tired of being consumed by hate. This stops* now.*"*

"What are you doing?" the Old Part yelled, but Reg muted him and bent over to grab Captain Phealix's wrist just as her injured arm lost its grip.

Reg had to fight hard against the pain and the strain threatening to overwhelm him as he leaned back to haul up the Faylin. However, without the backup of his left arm, he could feel his grip slipping, as well as that of the captain, whose own fight against gravity and pain had drained her strength. Her injured arm instinctively shot up to grab the Scout's right arm for extra support; a movement that jerked Reg off balance and onto his side, knocking the air from his lungs.

"Hold on," he wheezed. "Just … hold on."

However, as Captain Phealix's grip finally slipped from his sweat-coated hand, Reg closed his eyes; he just couldn't watch. The Faylin didn't scream, which Reg thought was quite courageous. Strange, yet courageous. But when he opened his eyes again, the reason behind the lack of screaming became apparent.

Gripping Captain Phealix's wrist were the muscular arms of Issy, whose right ankle was in turn clamped by the metallic hand of Ikkabot. Using his functional arm, the robot raised the inverted pair of biologicals and stepped back to drag them to the safety of the cavern floor, where Captain Phealix lay for a while, panting.

"Thank … you," she managed after accumulating enough oxygen to do so.

"No problem," Issy said, helping the Faylin to her feet. She suspected Ikkabot nodded, but it was difficult to tell with his head strapped to his chest.

Reg himself only had enough energy left to lie where he lay and breathe excessively, so that's what he did. However, when the cavern started shaking more violently and haphazard jets of steam began shooting up from the floor, it was clear that his short period of rest was about to be cut even shorter.

Captain Phealix made it even clearer as she got up and turned to the robot.

"Ikkabot, would you mind?" she said, nodding towards Reg.

"Certainly," Ikkabot replied, and before Reg could say anything other than "Ow, ow, ow!", he found himself slung over the shoulder of the robot, who started walking towards the exit.

Ikkabot ignored Reg's protests, and Issy didn't seem to have much interest in them either, so Reg redirected his indignant glare at Captain Phealix trotting along behind them.

She shrugged. "Hey, it beats dying."

Reg's planned argument was erased as he looked past the Faylin, where an enormous section of cavern roof smashed through the middle of the temple, cracking the support columns at the bottom as well as the column at the top. A vast torrent of lava poured from above and enveloped the temple, whose weakened structure and supports collapsed under the weight and disintegrated into the lava pool below.

Glad they weren't near the sinking building anymore, Reg's indignation at being carried made way for relief, which in turn transformed into angst as he realised the rest of the cavern might soon meet the same fate as the temple. He couldn't stop himself from slapping Ikkabot's back to coax more speed from the robot, but it didn't help, as they proceeded at the same pace; faster than a stroll but slower than a sprint.

As more jets of steam shot up behind them, the group entered the tunnel leading out of the volcano. Nearing the tunnel's exit, the tremors escalated into a full-on quake that pulled down large rocks in their wake, which prompted Issy and Captain Phealix to squeeze out every last drop of adrenaline left in their bodies. With Ikkabot leading the way, they cleared the tunnel mere seconds before it collapsed behind them with a loud rumble, spewing out a cloud of dust.

The Faylin and the Ja'naman sat down hard as their legs buckled under them, and coughed even harder as their lungs tried to filter some useful air from between the dust particles.

We made it, Reg thought, following his own bout of coughing. I can't believe we made it!

His belief, however, didn't last long, as the strange, flat rock face next to them – aka the Eye of Tuma – crumbled, sending enormous slabs and boulders sliding and tumbling down the foot of the volcano.

Ikkabot turned to see what was going on, leaving Reg facing the wrong direction.

"Put me down," the Scout demanded, and when this didn't happen, he repeated, "I said, put me down!"

By the time the robot lowered him, the tremors had subsided. Reg limped closer to get a better view of the newly formed hole in the mountainside. While he couldn't see much through the dust cloaking the area below like a thick fog, his ears picked up what could only be described as a hum. It sounded like a stadium full of people grumbling among themselves over the unexpected defeat suffered by their local rugby team.[*]

The source of the hum revealed itself when a gigantic black shape floated from the gigantic hole. Clearing the confines of the mountain, the shape rose through the dust cloud. Like the temple, its sides featured black cubes of rock, varying in size and depth and lined with veins of orange. But that's where the similarities ended. Where the temple had been cylindrical, this object was shaped like a dark grindstone, complete with a hole in the middle. And it was bigger. *Much* bigger. Its sides towered more than two hundred metres from top to bottom, and its diameter would have taken up most of the floor space of the large cavern within the volcano. Upon closer inspection, the top surface of the object might actually have *been* the cavern floor.

The hum intensified as the circular object continued its rise to above the volcano's peak, where it hovered for a while. The sound then transformed into rapid pulses that rattled Reg's bones along with his eardrums; an effect that clearly didn't affect him alone, as Captain Phealix and Issy also covered their ears. Of course, Ikkabot wasn't affected, so he didn't do it.

As the pulses rose to a crescendo, the object shot upwards faster than the eye could follow, disappearing from view and leaving behind a silence that was only broken by the ringing in Reg's ears.

---

[*] This menacing sound usually strikes fear into the hearts of the visiting team's supporters who, unless quite drunk, know better than to try and mute the sound by shouting "Suck it, losers!" But if you ever want to test this theory for yourself, please ensure you're lubricated with enough alcohol to numb the pain of the pummelling you're about to receive.

"What was that?" shouted Issy, removing his hands from his ears.

"What?" Reg shouted back.

"I said, what was that?"

"Oh," Reg said as his ears reclaimed some of their usefulness. "A ship … I think."

"Yes," Captain Phealix said. Though, like Reg, she seemed to have a hard time believing her own words. "I've never seen one that big move so fast. At least not this close to a planet's surface. Heck, I've never seen a ship of that size so close to a planet's surface, period."

"I have, a couple of times," Reg said. "But, no, they did *not* move like that."

The Faylin glanced back up to where the object had disappeared. She shook her head. "Well, that *was* a ship," she said as she started walking along the path. "And I'd like to know *how* there was a ship below us this whole time without Dennis telling us about it."

"Dennis?" Reg frowned, catching up with her. "What's Dennis got to do with this?"

"That, Lieutenant, is precisely what *I* would like to know."

CHAPTER 66

Following the cave-in below, the lava pool in the crater atop the volcano had shrunk considerably into something volcanologists might have termed a volcanic "splash pool" had they not been volcanologists. It almost looked … lost. But Phealix knew better.

"Come on, we know you're in there!" she shouted at the lava below. Her voice was getting hoarse, and she started feeling silly, as she'd been shouting for some time without any reaction other than the occasional bubble breaking the pool's surface. So it didn't surprise her when her latest attempt was met by more silence. Clearly, she was doing something wrong.

"I don't think Dennis likes being shouted at," Issy ventured. "Do you mind if I …"

"No, please, go ahead," Phealix said with a voice that needed a break before it broke.

Issy leaned over the lip of the crater. "Dennis?" he said loudly but without too much force. "Dennis, these people need to speak with you."

When the silence continued, Issy changed tact. "They're my friends, Dennis. Which makes them *your* friends too. It isn't nice to be rude to friends."

After a pause, a small jet of steam erupted from the centre of the pool like a small sigh.

"FINE," Dennis said. "BUT COULD YOU PLEASE DO ME A FAVOUR?"

"Anything, Dennis."

"WELL, UM, THAT'S KIND OF IT. IT'S … NOT REALLY MY NAME."

Issy's cheeks flushed with embarrassment. "Oh, er, I'm sorry. It's just … I always got the, uh, *Dennis* feel from you."[*]

"I KNOW, AND YOU USED IT SO PASSIONATELY THAT I NEVER HAD THE HEART TO CORRECT YOU. IT'S *DENISE*, ACTUALLY."

Issy's cheeks now flooded with even more embarrassment as he pinpointed exactly what had bothered him about Dennis's appearance earlier – a certain ampleness in the chest area that was easy to miss amid all the lava.

"*And* you're a lady," he said as his face turned a darker shade of bronze. "I … I'm *so* sorry."

---

[*] While this *feel* is commonplace, you should never trust it, as it usually results in moments of extreme awkwardness that could have been avoided if you'd only listened to the backup *feel* telling you that your primary *feel* was wrong. Not only is this important in matters of biology, but also career. For instance, now that you know that potbellied Kahoian men aren't pregnant Kahoian women, the next presumption to rid yourself of is thinking they work in catering. Sure, some do, but it's *not* polite to presume so. Most people have learnt this lesson the hard way, which is why *the weather* has become the leading topic of conversation with Kahoian men when conversations with Kahoian men cannnot be avoided altogether.

"NO NEED FOR APOLOGIES. AT LEAST YOU WEREN'T AS FAR OFF AS THE OTHERS. I MEAN, TUMA … *TUMA!* SERIOUSLY?!"

"Sorry to interrupt," Phealix said. "Denn— *Denise*, there are some things I need you to clear up for us, if you don't mind."

She coughed to expel the frog from her throat.

"OH, ER, YES, JUST GIVE ME A MOMENT."

They waited, not quite sure what they were waiting for, and found out with a fright when the voice said from behind, "IS THIS BETTER?"

It wasn't really, as they got another fright when they turned around to face the lava rising from a crack in the ground. Eye-level with Phealix, at least it wasn't as big as before, and it had retained its well-rounded Ja'naman shape, which made it slightly less intimidating. But only slightly.

Pushing her startlement aside, Phealix was grateful to lower her volume. "Yes, much better, thank you … Denise," she said, clearing her throat once more. "If it's not too forward, can you tell us, uh, what you are?"

"NO."

Phealix paused. "Why not?"

"BECAUSE I DON'T *KNOW* WHAT I AM. I JUST … AM."

"What do you mean? Aren't you a Euwel too?"

"SORT OF."

"Sort of?"

"YES. THEY'RE SORT OF LIKE ME, JUST AS I'M SORT OF LIKE THEM. AND WE'RE BOTH … SORT OF … BY-PRODUCTS."

"By-products? Of what?"

"THE MASEPA."

"The Masepa? What's *that* got to do with it?"

Denise paused. "IT'S A BIT … EMBARRASSING."

"We won't judge, I promise," Phealix said, casting a look towards Reg that stated she was speaking on his behalf too.

After another pause, Denise said, "IT'S … WELL, IN PLAIN TERMS, IT'S … EXCREMENT."

Denise waited for the information to sink in, which happened in a gradual yet assertive manner. Reg was the first to voice his opinion on the revelation by dry-heaving to the side, and Phealix had to fight her own stomach's urge to follow suit.

When the Scout finally recovered, he glared at Issy. "Shit?" he exclaimed. "You've been feeding us *shit?*"

"It's not like *we* knew," Issy protested, his face longing to go back to a time where he still didn't know.

Phealix felt sorry for him, as he'd been drinking the stuff his whole life without knowing its true nature. But now wasn't the time for blame or sympathy.

"Excrement?" Phealix said, swallowing hard while keeping a semi-straight face. "From what?"

"I'VE THOUGHT ABOUT THIS FOR LONG. THE MOSS – THE MOSS IS ALIVE, BUT NOT JUST IN THE FLORAL SENSE. IT'S … SENTIENT."

"Sentient moss?" Reg said flatly, glancing at the moss blanketing most of the surrounding rocks.

"YES. I THINK I'M THE EMBODIMENT OF THE MOSS. IT'S CONNECTED TO THE LAND; ALL THE LIFE, ALL THE ENERGY. THE MOSS FEEDS OFF IT AND, IN TURN, SUSTAINS ME."

"And the Euwel?" Reg asked. "Why aren't they like you? Why are they … the way they are?"

"THEY FEED OFF THE LIFE FORCE OF … OTHER SENTIENT BEINGS."

"You mean *people*," Phealix said.

"YES, THOSE WHO'D BEEN SACRIFICED. I CANNOT DIGEST THEM PROPERLY, WHICH IS WHERE THE MASEPA COMES FROM. OVER TIME, IT MUST HAVE FORMED BUBBLES IN WHICH THE ESSENCE OF THE SACRIFICED GOT TRAPPED, LEADING TO THE CREATION OF THE FIRST EUWEL."

"You mean *all of this* happened because you've been, what, constipated?" Reg said, perplexed.

"HEY, YOU DON'T KNOW WHAT IT'S LIKE."

Reg grumbled something and adjusted his uniform before his expression turned firm again. "Right," he said, "so you're telling us you pooped yourself, and now your little shits are running around killing people?"

"I … WELL, THAT'S A BIT … CRASS. BUT I SUPPOSE YOU'RE RIGHT. THEY NEVER USED TO KILL ANYONE, THOUGH. AT LEAST NOT AT FIRST. THAT ALL CHANGED WHEN THEY CAME BACK."

"Came back?" Phealix said. "From where?"

It was odd to see lava shrug, but that's what Denise did.

"I'M NOT SURE. FOR LONG, WE LIVED TO-GETHER IN HARMONY; CONTENT TO SHARE THE VOLCANO. BUT BECAUSE OF THEIR LINK TO THE LIFE FORCE OF THOSE SACRIFICED, THEY BECAME CURIOUS ABOUT LIFE OUT THERE. AND NOT JUST LIFE BEYOND THE VOL-CANO – LIFE *OUT THERE*."

Phealix followed Denise's gaze up at the sky. "So they built a ship to go exploring."

"*GREW* A SHIP, TO BE EXACT. THEY PICKED UP A FEW THINGS FROM THE SACRIFICES WHO WEREN'T … LOCAL."

Reg nodded. "Yep, that's one of the reasons we patrol Dumb Planets – to stop idiots from crashing into them."

His expression immediately after saying it stated that Phealix didn't have to point out the obvious.

"Where did they go?" Phealix asked Denise instead.

The lava shrugged once more. "I CAN'T SAY."

"Can't, or *won't?*"

"CAN'T."

"Why? I thought you and the Euwels shared everything?"

"INITIALLY, YES. BUT WHEN THEY CAME BACK, THEY HAD CHANGED. THEY'D BECOME … DISTANT. I TRIED FINDING OUT WHAT WAS WRONG, BUT THEY SHUT ME OUT COMPLETELY. THEY BUILT THE TEMPLE AND STARTED ROAMING THE LANDSCAPE FOR NEW VICTIMS TO FEED THE VOLCANO – TO GROW THEIR NUMBERS AND EXPAND THE SHIP. I HATED THE WHOLE THING."

"If you hated it so much, why didn't you stop them?" Reg said.

"I DID. AFTER SEVERAL MORE EXCURSIONS WITH THEIR SHIP, I REALISED THE EUWELS WERE ALSO HARVESTING PEOPLE FROM OTHER PLANETS TO CREATE MORE EUWELS."

"The temple," Reg ventured with a shiver. "It was more than just an incubator – it was a processing plant."

"YES, AND WITH THEIR INSATIABLE NEED FOR EXPANSION, THE EUWELS … PROCESSED *A LOT* OF PEOPLE. I JUST COULDN'T ALLOW THEM TO CONTINUE. SO, DURING THEIR LAST HIBERNATION CYCLE, I SEALED THEIR ACCESS TO THE SHIP AND ANCHORED IT TO THE VOLCANO."

"Then *we* unsealed it," Phealix said with a surge of guilt, seeing as this had happened under *her* watch. "That's also why you didn't want Reg to blow up the column – it was the anchor."

"ORIGINALLY, IT WAS THE PIPELINE FOR THE RAW MATERIALS THE EUWELS NEEDED FROM THE VOLCANO. BUT YES, IT BECAME AN ANCHOR WHEN I BLOCKED IT, AND KEPT THE EUWELS IN HIBERNATION."

"Why let us in, then? If we never entered the volcano, none of this would have happened."

"I KNOW, BUT I COULDN'T LET ANYTHING HAPPEN TO ISSY, OR YOU. I JUST WANTED TO KEEP YOU ALL SAFE. I … I'M TIRED OF PEOPLE BEING MURDERED IN MY NAME."

After a pause, Phealix nodded. "So, now what?"

"NOW, THEY WILL SPREAD," Denise said, rubbing her arms, which, like the rest of her, had turned a darker shade of orange. "IF YOU'LL EXCUSE ME, IT'S GETTING A BIT CHILLY OUT HERE. BEST OF LUCK TO YOU."

As the lava drained back into the crack, Phealix shouted, "Wait! How do we stop them?"

When she didn't get an answer, Phealix turned back to the pool of lava at the bottom of the crater. "Please, we need to know how to stop them!"

After another moment of silence, a last sigh of steam erupted from the pool.

"I'M NOT SURE YOU CAN."

CHAPTER 67

By the time they'd reached the Ja'naman village, night had already consumed the last morsel of day. Preparations were now underway to celebrate the fallen by those who hadn't fallen – at least not yet, as there was plenty of beer to be had by the unfallen to help forget how the fallen had fallen, even though they knew that no amount of beer would get the job done.[*]

A contingent of Teahupo'oan villagers had accompanied the Ja'namans back to their village, as there were important matters to discuss.

"Fine," the Priestess yielded, glaring at the Wise One seated atop his horned skull-chair on the other side of the Meeting Fire. "Ja'nama give Great Stapler back to Teahupo'o."

"And?" Issy prompted.

"*And* Ja'nama promise to no longer eat Teahupo'o strays …"

---

[*] As it turned out later, there *hadn't* been enough beer. Just remember, however, that bad planning afflicts the entire universe; not only Dumb Planets. So if your face suddenly feels tempted to project that "typical Dumb Planet" look, please advise it not to do so.

"… or *anyone else*," she added as her Cloak of Bones rattled from Issy's elbow-nudge.

The Wise One just stared at her until Roro tapped him on the shoulder. The old man sighed. "And Teahupo'o no cut head off Ja'nama … or anyone else. You sure this right, Roro? It tradition."

Off to the side, Phealix had been listening intently, unlike Reg and her two remaining Vahltans, who'd all but toppled into the fire from weariness. Thus far, she'd kept quiet, as she didn't want to meddle in the affairs of the locals … well, no more than necessary. However, seeing as meddling had already occurred, Phealix realised she might as well make the most of it.

"*Tradition* stops here!" she interjected. Getting up, she alternated her glare between the Wise One and the Priestess.

"*You* will not be cutting off any more heads," she said, pointing at the Wise One, then turned the finger to the Priestess. "And *you* – stop … eating … people. For goodness' sake, there's enough other food to go around!"

"But it tradi—"

The Priestess's protest was cut off by whimpers to the side. She swung her head to cast her coldest glare at whoever had interrupted her. The glare was lost, though, as those villagers weren't paying her any attention, keeping their focus on the sky. As the whimpering and sky-gazing spread throughout the crowd, Ongswele couldn't stop herself from looking up to see what all the fuss was about.

She did, however, stop herself from whimpering, as it was a very un-Priestess-like thing to do. But her voice quivered nonetheless as she managed to squeeze out, "What … that?"

In the distance, the stars warped as an unseen shape moved across them. The light of the first moon dimmed briefly, followed by that of the second. The warping shape then turned to approach the village, and descended in the vicinity of the village entrance, where it disappeared from view behind the huts.

Phealix grinned.

"Yours, I presume," Reg said next to her, now fully awake and on his feet along with Franki and Salli.

"Yes," Phealix replied as she strolled towards the village entrance. "You don't seem surprised."

"No," Reg said, falling in next to her. "That bag your Vahltans brought from the wreck – you found comms, didn't you?"

"Yep. Franki salvaged it from a sealed shuttle in the cargo bay, and Salli fixed it while we were scavenging for guns and ammo in the village. All we needed was power."

"My flasher."

Phealix nodded.

"I noticed someone had tampered with it," Reg said.

"If Salli had more time, you wouldn't have. You never said anything, though."

"To be honest, I didn't think we were going to make it, so it seemed kind of … pointless."

As they rounded the last hut near the village entrance, the shape came into view. With a low hum, it hung in the air like an American football with a kebab rammed into the top; a kebab comprising a mast carrying three engines, from big near the hull to small near the top. Perched on the tip of the mast was an illuminated sign depicting a Vahltan skull with two crossed bones below it. The ship's reflective surface made it hard to spot without watering the eyes of the person spotting it.

"The infamous *Jolly Dodger*," Reg said with watery eyes. "What's it doing?"

Phealix, too, wondered why two of the side hull plates had shifted aside to let the cannons drop out. But when she figured it out, she rushed to the spot the weapons had swivelled towards; a small group of warriors pointing their spears at the flying beast.

"No!" Phealix yelled, waving her arms at the ship as she pushed her way through the jittery men. "Get those things out of my face and your butts down here … now!"

The cannons retracted back into the hull, which promptly closed up again. Not long thereafter, the back of the ship lowered and settled onto the grass, forming a ramp. The light spilling from the opening revealed five armed, black-leather-clad Vahltans descending the ramp, led by a tall Vahltan wearing a black leather coat. His silver robotic arm and leg, as well as the matching silver eyepatch over his scarred eye, would have been much more intimidating had it not been for the ill-fitting wide-brimmed hat sitting atop his narrow head. She wished he'd get rid of that thing. It looked ridiculous!

"Captain," said Cap.[*] "I'm glad you're okay. We picked up your signal and came as soon as we could."

"It could have been sooner, Cap," Phealix grated, and noticed the First Hand looking her up and down, unsure about her attire. "Don't ask."

Fortunately, he didn't, so she continued, "Didn't you get the first emergency signal?"

---

[*] To alleviate any possible confusion caused by this, it's important to note that Cap is not the captain. Phealix is. "Cap" is just short for a much longer name that no one has the time or energy to explain right now, but please don't let this spoil your day.

"Er, yes, sir, but as soon as we arrived, we ran into a Militor Destroyer that gave chase the moment it spotted us. It took some time to shake them off along with the other ships they called in, but we escaped their net. Barely. Also, to be honest, sir, we weren't even sure you were alive until your second transmission. Speaking of which…"

Phealix saw him eyeing Franki and Salli before scanning the crowd for the other Vahltans.

"They didn't make it," Phealix said with a straight face.

"That's too bad," Cap said with a pained expression. However, Phealix knew this was more because he'd now have to do another recruitment run, which would greatly interfere with his *Spacebook* time.

"That's a ship too, isn't it?" said a voice approaching from behind, and Phealix had to motion the Vahltans to lower their rifles again.

"Yes, Issy. It's *my* ship."

"It's smaller than the Metal Mountain, but prettier," Issy said with watery eyes as Roro joined him.

"Thanks, Issy," Phealix said, and put a hand on the tribesman's shoulder. "I have to go, but I need you guys to promise me something. Make sure your people behave themselves, okay?"

"How we do that?" Roro frowned. "We no Chief."

"Cap, could you please arrange for that boulder over there to not be there?"

Cap spoke into his wristcomm, and waited for the *Dodger's* cannons to drop out again and swivel towards the big rock in the distance. A moment later, two large, green balls of energy flashed from the cannons, and a moment after that the boulder was indeed not there any longer. The faces of the cowering villagers affirmed that the *boom* and the resultant destruction had achieved their intended goal.

Phealix placed her hands on the shoulders of Issy and Roro and turned them to face the crowd. "From now on, *these two* are your Chief Advisors!" she said. "If you don't listen to them, the lightning will come back! Does anyone have a problem with that?"

Everyone shook their head in a way that stated they had no problem – at least not openly – against anything that could cause their body parts to move in different directions simultaneously. Satisfied, Phealix patted the two tribesmen on the shoulder before turning to Reg, who shifted uncomfortably.

"If you're thinking what I think you're thinking," she said, "don't worry; your thick head will take way too long to destroy – time I don't have. Now, if you'll excuse me, I need to be off."

"You're just going to leave me here?" the Scout said, looking torn between his relief at not being blown to bits and his dismay at not being offered a ride.

"You know, you stress too much," Phealix said, and leaned in to whisper in the human's ear. "You'll be away from here in no time. Trust me."

Flashing the Scout one last grin, Phealix ascended the ramp with her crew.

"Time to go, Cap," she said as the ramp sealed up behind them. "And get me some food, I'm starvi— Oh crap!"

"What's wrong, Captain?" Cap asked.

"Nothing. It's just … I nearly forgot something."

"What, sir?"

"A promise."

CHAPTER 68

Reg stood in place as he watched the *Jolly Dodger* take off, while most of the villagers took off to watch from someplace else, preferably a place much farther away. He couldn't understand why the ship headed towards the jungle instead of up, but he just added it to the list of things he didn't understand about pirates … or women … or, to be more specific, pirate women.

When the blurry ship vanished beyond the treeline, he turned to find Issy, Roro, Khulu and Ikkabot waiting for him.

"Are you done?" the old man said. "Because I'm hungry."

Reg's own stomach grumbled, feeling like it hadn't been fed in ages. Nodding, he followed the others back to the Ja'naman village, where the preparations for the feast resumed as if nothing had happened. Apparently, metal gods, rocky creatures and flying beasts shooting lightning weren't enough to put the locals off their food.

As hungry as Reg was, Issy had a hard time convincing him that the meat he was about to eat had come from *outside* village borders, and that the body it previously formed part of hadn't had a name and surname. Still, he ate the supposed Kuhdoo meat with some unease.

He had no problem drinking the beer, though. And even though it wasn't the best beer he'd ever had, it helped dull his senses a bit and eventually – after a few more rounds of dulling – to ease him to sleep in Issy's hut. It wasn't the best sleep he'd ever had, either, filled with dreams about a fiery-eyed Spence and flying mountains that hummed and shook. As he opened his eyes, neither the hum nor the shaking had stopped, but he was relieved to see Issy's wide-yet-normal eyes above him instead of dream-Spence's glowing eyes.

"Get up," the tribesman said, giving Reg a final shake as the hum and the vibrations died down. "I think your friends are here."

Casting his grogginess aside, Reg shot to his feet and followed Issy outside. Close to where the *Jolly Dodger* had landed earlier, a Militor dropship rested amid the grass. The rectangular, dull-brown vessel wasn't nearly as impressive as the pirate ship, which likely explained why most of the villagers looked somewhat disappointed, except for the few who were getting agitated with the grey-uniformed Caynin barking at them. They clearly weren't among those who'd received vernaculites, otherwise they would have understood what all the barking was about. Although *that* might have agitated them even further.

"What's going on here, Sergeant?" Reg said, checking the insignia on the officer's chest.

The Caynin swivelled his flabby, dog-like face in the direction of the newcomer.

"Lieutenant Kleft?" he said. "Lieutenant *Reginald* Kleft?"

Reg nodded, and waited for the sergeant to perform his fist-to-shoulder salute. "Is there a problem here?"

"Yes, sir, these little buggers won't let us pass, sir."

"These *little buggers*, Sergeant," Reg said, "are the only reason I'm still alive. They've earned my respect, so I have to insist they have yours too."

"Yes, sir, sorry sir, but we've been ordered to take you directly to Unyun, sir. Without delay, sir."

"Unyun?" Reg frowned. "Why Unyun? Don't you mean Unyun Beta? I need to report to Headquarters … immediately."

The Caynin shrugged. "I don't understand it either, sir. But I have my orders, sir, and they don't include Unyun Beta, sir."

After a pause, Reg gave a perplexed nod.

"Fine, Sergeant," he said. "Just give me a minute."

"But, sir—"

"I said *a minute*, Sergeant!"

Ignoring the lingering objection on the Caynin's face, Reg knelt before Issy. "Listen," he said. "I meant what I said just now. I never treated you with the respect you deserved. I was a fool – an A-grade asshole. And for that, I'm sorry."

Issy measured him for a moment, before nodding. "Apology accepted," he said. "Will we see you again?"

"I don't know, Issy," Reg said, before a brainwave crashed over his face. "Sergeant," he asked over his shoulder, "do you have an emergency beacon on you?"

"Yes, sir, but—"

"Give it to me," Reg said, holding out his hand expectantly.

"But, sir, we're not allowed to—"

"*Now*, Sergeant."

With a fair amount of reluctance, the Caynin finally placed the small, black device in Reg's hand.

Ignoring the grumbling behind him, Reg held the beacon to Issy. "If you ever need help, just flip this cap and press this button. Got it?"

Issy's face didn't get it, but he accepted the device with a nod.

"Sir," the sergeant said, "I'm afraid I have to *insist* we leave, now."

Knowing he wouldn't be able to push his luck any further, Reg rose with a sigh. "Till later then," he said, giving Issy's shoulder a squeeze before following the Militor soldiers into the dropship.

As the ramp started to rise, Reg turned to give Issy and his companions a salute by slamming his right fist onto his left shoulder. And, seeing as he'd forgotten about his wound, the last thing the tribesmen saw of Reg was his tear-filled eyes.

How touching, they thought. He misses us already.

CHAPTER 69

His wound had been properly treated and bandaged. He had scrubbed every inch of his body during his lengthy shower. He had dressed himself in a fresh, dark-grey parade uniform. He had submitted his report and had gone over it several times to prepare for his debriefing. He just hadn't been prepared for *who* would be debriefing him. So, for the umpteenth time, Reg shifted in his seat to adjust his uniform.

"You *really* should relax, Lieutenant," said Presidor Don Tinckles, seated on the opposite side of the large oak desk, which clashed with the rest of the furniture in the modern study. "This is not an inquisition."

Wearing a light-blue tunic with dark-blue embroidery, the ginger-furred Faylin smiled warmly, although the penetrating, dark vertical pupils splitting his green eyes remained unsettling.

Reg gripped the chair's arms to keep his hands from fidgeting.

"I know, sir," he said, "but I wasn't expecting …"

"… me?" Presidor Tinckles finished.

"Uh, yes, sir. I mean no disrespect, but … well, it's just … I thought you were more, well, into running the affairs of Unyun—"

"—than meddling in the affairs of its Militorate?" the Presidor finished again.

Reg didn't want to confirm or deny, as he wasn't sure how the highest office-bearer in the Unyun Federation would react to either, so he opted to keep his face and mouth quiet.

"Yes," Presidor Tinckles continued after a pause, "generally, I don't. But I found this matter … intriguing enough to warrant my personal attention."

"Again, with all due respect, sir, I still don't know how the matter ended up with *you* in the first place."

Presidor Tinckles waved a hand. "Oh, don't break your head over such minor details, Lieutenant Kleft. Just tell me exactly what happened."

Reg cleared his throat. "It's all in my report, sir."

"Reports are so cold, Lieutenant. I've always found the true spirit of a story to lie within the narration of the person telling it. So, please, if you'd be so kind."

Reg recognised the polite order for what it was, so he merely sighed and recounted almost everything that had transpired since his first encounter with the pirates. But just *almost* – there were some things the Federation didn't *need* to know. Things that could harm the tribes if they ever came to light. Which is why he kept those things to himself.

When he was done, the Presidor shook his head with a whistle. "Captain Phealix," he said. "She's been a pain in the butt for some time now. It's a shame you couldn't bring her in."

"Er, yes, sir. But the Euwels … what are you planning on doing—"

"Ah, yes, the Euwels. Don't worry about that, either, Lieutenant. If what you say is true—"

"It is, sir."

"—I'll get my best people to look into it right away."

"But, sir, the Militorate has plenty of people who are qualified to handle this. I, myself, will be more than happy to help in—"

"I know, Lieutenant Kleft. But, again, if what you say is indeed true, I cannot allow panic to run wild. And the Militorate is unfortunately known for springing the occasional leak in sensitive matters. So, thank you for your offer, but I'll be investigating the matter via more … discrete channels."

"The Infiltratorate?"

"Maybe."

"And me, sir?"

The Presidor measured Reg for a moment. "You've proven yourself capable of handling unknown situations pretty well, Lieutenant," the Faylin said at length. "So I think it's time for you to go out there and explore some … unfamiliar territory."

"You mean as a Rover Scout?"

"Yes."

Had this happened a week earlier, Reg's heart would have leapt instead of sinking the way it did now. He'd always wondered what it would be like to explore uncharted space; to be a maverick in the expansion of the Charted Universe. However, now, in the greater scheme of things, it felt … trivial. He needed to make a stand, regardless of the consequences.

"I'm honoured, Mr Presidor," he said, keeping his face and voice as firm as possible, "but with all due respect, the Euwels *are* out there, somewhere, and I *won't* stop until I track them down."

Presidor Tinckles sat forward. Resting his elbows on the desk with interlaced fingers, he said, "Why do you think I'm offering you this assignment, Lieutenant?"

Reg's frown must have stated that he didn't have a clue, as the Faylin continued before he could answer.

"Like you said, Lieutenant, the Euwels are out there … *somewhere*. And what better way to find them than with a well-equipped Rover Scout ship at your disposal? Not to mention the freedom to go wherever you please without all the … red tape."

Reg remained silent while the Presidor again leaned back in his chair, giving Reg the time to evaluate the benefits of the "offer", which he did.

It *does* make sense, doesn't it? he mused. The Euwels might just as well be in uncharted space as charted space, so it won't really matter *where* I start looking.

And the Presidor was right – Rover Scouts enjoyed more freedom than most other divisions of the Militorate, and having nothing or no one to tie him down was exactly what he needed.

"Er, yes, sir," he conceded. "But I'll need a crew."

Presidor Tinckles got up and strolled to the big glass window overlooking The Hub, the main centre of commerce and politics for both the constructed planet of Unyun and the Federation as a whole. No unauthorised vehicles were allowed near the Presidorate Tower, but amidst the hive of tall, bulky buildings in the distance, traffic buzzed at various altitudes; vehicles going about their business in keeping the wheels of the Federation turning – without having wheels themselves, of course.

"Yes," the Presidor said, folding his hands behind his back as he gazed at the distant activity, "I suppose you *will* need a crew, won't you? Don't fret, Lieutenant, I'll take care of it."

Getting up himself, Reg stood at attention. "Sir, I'd like to pick my own crew if you don't mind, and—"

"I'm afraid I *do* mind," Presidor Tinckles interjected without turning around. "I need to keep the circle small, Lieutenant, and if you wish to remain inside it, I trust you'll accept my terms – which, by the way, will also include you reporting directly to me."

"But, sir, Militor protocol dictates that Scouts report back to their immediate superi—"

"Not on this matter."

"The Militorate won't like that, sir."

"Again, Lieutenant, leave that to me. Now, I suggest you go get some rest, and be ready to ship out in a week or so. That will be all."

Reg opened his mouth to say something, but the Presidor waylaid him. "I said *that will be all*, Lieutenant Kleft."

Reg paused. "Yes, sir," he said, and although the city-gazing Faylin couldn't see it, he gave a salute; a more subdued salute that kept his wound in mind this time.

As their business clearly was concluded, Reg turned and marched towards the door without another word. He was thinking of quite a few, but didn't say them, as they'd likely spell the end of his career. Besides, if it meant he could keep hunting those glowy-eyed bastards, he was willing to swallow a fair amount of crap.

And there wasn't enough crap in the universe to stop him from finding Spence.

CHAPTER 70

Shortly after the study's door slid shut, another slid open to the side. It was a door no one knew of except a handful of people, including the Presidor and the figure now emerging from it.

"*A pain in the butt*, seriously?" grated the figure, towing something into the study.

The voice sounded irked, which was what Don Tinckles had expected. Still, he sighed as he turned to face Captain Phealix.

The Faylin was again dressed in black leathers, and one could hardly see the bandage around her shoulder. It was difficult not to notice her tail, though, which swished about in a clear display of irksomeness.

"I'm sorry, my dear, but you *know* I have to keep up appearances," he said, and paused to look at the cage Phealix had towed in atop an a-grav trolley. "Do you *have* to drag that thing around with you all the time?"

Phealix glanced at the cage. Staring back up at her with large round eyes was a small yet bulky grey creature with a short supply of hair.

"It's not *a thing*, Dad. It's a Night Aahp … and it *has* a name," Phealix said.

"Oh, yes, *Garth*. I still can't fathom why you'd name him after your first pet."

"Hey, Garth and I had a special bond."

"Until you drowned him."

"How many times do I have to say it? It … was … an … *accident!* I just wanted to give him a bath. How was I supposed to know his head should be above water? I was barely three, for Zolt's sake!"

"Fine, sorry I brought it up," Don said, holding his hands up placatingly. "But if I can make a suggestion – and please don't bite my head off – if you want to keep this one alive, you might want to consider changing his diet."

Phealix sighed at the energy-bar wrappers strewn about Garth's cage. "It's all he *wants* to eat, and he only wants *me* to feed him. That's why I can't leave him alone."

A whimper prompted Phealix to remove yet another bar from her pocket. She held it towards the expectant hand of Garth, who snatched, unwrapped and swallowed it within seconds.

Phealix glared at Don, and before he could say anything, she said, "I'll figure it out. Now, I hope we're not going to talk about pet food all day."

After a pause, Don shook his head and glanced at the door through which Reg had exited. "You know I don't really want *him* involved in this."

"He's already involved."

"I can order him to let it go."

"You'll have more luck ordering a Caynin to stop eating everything placed in front of him. Reg is not the type of person to let things go. He's stubborn and, in his own way, he truly cared about his friend."

"Ensign Jensis? You think he's still alive?"

Phealix took a moment before answering. "Maybe. But even *if* Spence is still breathing, I wouldn't quite say *alive*."

"Because you think his soul has been eaten or something," Don said, turning back to the window, where Phealix joined him to gaze out at The Hub.

"I know what it sounds like," she said, "but, yes, I think his life force was consumed by those things. Or maybe it's been enslaved. I don't know. But whatever's happened to Spence, Reg won't stop until he finds him."

"And if he *does* find him? I sent him on this mission to keep him out of our hair. The last thing I want is for him to find these things and do something stupid."

"I believe the human truly meant what he said. He would have gone looking for them regardless, even if it meant leaving the Militorate. At least now you can keep tabs on him … you know, in case he *does* find those creatures or does something … stupid."

Don didn't look convinced, but nodded. "And you really think there are more of these Euwels out there – aside from those you encountered on Wahyoo VIII?"

"I'd stake the *Dodger's* next big score on it. And even if there aren't, there soon will be."

"Soon? You think an attack is imminent?"

Phealix shrugged. "Who knows? It might be days … heck, it might be years! All I know is that the Euwels are planning something. Something big. And whatever it is, it will most likely affect us all."

Don turned to her. "Don't worry, I'll make sure we're ready to fight them when the time comes."

Phealix's gaze remained fixed on the world outside. "The question is," she said, "will we be ready to fight *ourselves?*"

CHAPTER 71

A week or so later, Reg dropped his go-bag in front of the Class F Rover Scout ship in its hangar on Unyun Beta, and surveyed his home for the foreseeable future.

Sporting the same light-grey paint that covered most of the other ships in the fleet, it wasn't the biggest Rover in the fleet. But it was brand-new and much roomier than the Class D patrol ship he and Spence had been cooped up in. Given, most of the extra space was packed with supplies needed for travelling through uncharted space, but the ship's designers had also added some extra room for the crew, who usually had to spend lengthy periods crammed together in what was, essentially, a box with engines. Having more elbow room went a long way in keeping Scouts sane and, in the long run, keeping down the ever-increasing costs of psychiatry and/or body bags.

The flat, broad, curved Rover also featured much sleeker lines than the patrol ship, with two powerful plus-sign-shaped engines protruding from the back. Darkened windows framed most of the cockpit, and there was no shortage of viewports throughout the rest of the ship.[*]

As its first pilot, Reg had the privilege of naming the vessel, and while Rover Scouts were allowed more leeway in the names they chose, no one understood why Reg had dubbed it *Scout's Honour*. Of course, no one knew of his promise to Spence, and no one really cared about his choices, so no one asked questions. Which suited him perfectly.

Reg stared at the ship's cockpit for a while. He'd been informed that his crew had already arrived, and although he wasn't looking forward to meeting them, he couldn't avoid it either.

Let's just get this over with, his mind grated as he picked up his bag and ascended the side-ramp to the port-side airlock.

Once the airlock had done its bit, Reg turned left into the hallway leading to the cockpit, and paused at the door. Taking a deep breath, he touched the panel, but as soon as the door slid up, he tried closing it again before anyone saw him. It was, however, too late.

"Hey, it's the monkey!" said the first of his two new crewmates.

"Don't call him that," said the second, who wasn't as fleshy as the first. "It's not PC. Remember what I told you about PC?"

---

[*] While Rovers are equipped with some of the best sensors in the fleet, exploring the unknown often requires more than technology alone, and good old-fashioned eyeballing has saved many a ship and crew from disaster. That said, eyeballing has also led many more ships and crews *into* disaster, because: A) not all eyeballs are equally dependable; and B) people's eyes often ignore one of their biggest allies: good old-fashioned common sense.

Reg's bag slid from his hand and plopped onto the deck as he stared at Khulu and Ikkabot staring at him. It took him a while to find his voice again, but when he did, he made sure he used it to full effect. "What the fhark are *you* doing here?!"

The old man, leaning on a gleaming metal walking staff, wore a green cloak that hid – Reg suspected – a grass skirt underneath.

Right arm fixed, Ikkabot had also been cleaned up to some degree, and while his head still didn't sit where it was supposed to sit, it was now housed in a brand-new metal frame attached to a brand-new, sturdy harness.

Without centuries-old grime coating them, the robot's green eyes glowed greener than before as he looked at Reg and said, "We were asked to be here."

"Yes," Khulu confirmed. "The orange man in the big hut asked us to come here. A very polite man, may I add, but still – that hut is *way* too big for him."

"No, no-no-no-no-no," Reg mumbled as he pushed past the old man and the robot to lean over the comms monitor by the pilot's seat. The contact he dialled had, of course, been stored under an alias, and was answered accordingly.

"Bogus Burgers, how may we serve you today?" an overly friendly female voice chanted on the other side.

Reg hated this non-Militor chatter. He tried to swallow his discontent, but it got stuck halfway down his throat. "This is Re— er, Mr Rodge, the new … Delivery Manager," he grated. "I need to speak to the Pres— Mr Bogus, please. It's about our new … delivery staff. I think there's been some kind of mix-up."

"Ah, yes, Mr Rodge. Sorry, sir, Mr Bogus isn't available at present. But don't worry, he's been expecting your call. He said you might be unhappy—"

"*Unhappy* doesn't even begin to descri—"

"—and that you're more than welcome to reconsider your new managerial position, should it prove too much for you to handle."

Glancing back at the Ja'naman and the robot, Reg remained silent while he evaluated whether it was *indeed* too much. However, he stopped almost as soon as he started. He had a personal mission to complete, and if he had to endure some discomfort to complete it, that's what he would do.

"No, er, thanks, that's okay," he said at length. "I, uh … please tell Mr Bogus I'm grateful for the opportunity and the … er, help."

"I'm sure he'll be *elated* to hear that, sir. Now, if there's nothing else, good luck with your delivery run."

Apparently, there *wouldn't* be anything else, because the call was ended on the other side. For a while, Reg could only stare blankly at the monitor, but eventually took a deep breath and seated himself in the pilot's chair. There was no use putting off the departure any longer; the sooner they got going, the sooner it could all end. Or so he hoped.

"Ikkabot, could you please secure Khulu?" Reg grated over his shoulder as he started preparing the ship for takeoff.

"What's a *burger?*" Khulu asked while the robot strapped him into his chair.

"Basically," Ikkabot said, "it's bread—"

"Ooh, I love bread!"

"And meat—"

"I love meat too! But I've had both before and—"

"Yes, yes, but the secret is … you take the meat," Ikkabot said, holding Khulu's hand to simulate a burger patty, "and put it between two special pieces of bread," he concluded, using his own hands above and below Khulu's patty-hand to indicate the proper positioning of the bread.

"Remarkable! Hey, why haven't you ever made *me* one of those?"

"You never asked," Ikkabot said, lowering himself into his own specially constructed charging chair next to the old man.

"And how do you expect me to ask about things I know nothing about, tin-tin?"

"Well, excuse *me* for not knowing what you don't know."

"I'll have you know that I know very little, so if it's not too much to ask, I'd appreciate it if you start filling me in on a few things."

"Like *what?*"

"You know … *things*. Must I always spell *everything* out for you, you rusty old—"

As Reg couldn't stand it any longer, the rest of the argument faded when he put on his pilot's helmet. The headgear wasn't really necessary for general piloting, but the music he could play through it suddenly seemed like the most crucial survival tool in the history of mankind. He got the feeling that, going forward, he would be wearing it quite often or – in all likelihood – permanently.

While he felt somewhat … indifferent towards the people of Earth, Reg had to give it to them – they had superb taste in music. His playlist was packed with tunes from the planet, especially some of the older rock and blues tracks. And, as he lifted the ship to exit the underground hangar, one of them filled his ears with squabble-cancelling bliss. The track, ironically, was performed by a band called *The Rolling Stones*. But Reg refused to let the stony Euwel bastards spoil one of his favourite songs, so he turned the volume up in defiance.

Although he knew every word of *Time Is On My Side*, Reg didn't sing along, because his mind was suddenly gripped by a dark thought: What if time, in fact, was *not* on his side? It might already be too late to save Spence, or to stop the Euwels. In which case he might just as well give up now and—

No, he scolded himself, stop thinking like that! There has to be hope. There has to be salvation – for Spence, for me, for all of us! Now, pull yourself together, *soldier boy!* Go do what needs to be done.

As the Rover raced away from the dwindling Unyun Beta, Reg made a pact with himself that he'd push on, no matter *whose* side time was on.

For everyone's sake, he had to.

ACKNOWLEDGEMENTS

It turns out you *can* judge a book by its cover, so my first thanks goes to Leza Menezes for turning my amateur cover design into a piece of art, and for dealing with the constant requests to shift, enlarge or shrink stuff by a millimetre.

Between the covers, I want to give a HUGE shout-out to Annika, Elmarie, Gerhard, Jacques, Jarus, Lucinda, Mark and Riaan for the time you sacrificed beta-reading Happy Meals in such a short space of time. Your feedback and suggestions were worth gold in streamlining the story and reducing the number of reader-frowns out there. I'd like to extend my appreciation to my family, friends and social-media peeps for all your support, and I apologise for my frequent absences while working on this book.

And last but not least, thanks to you – yes, *you*, the reader. Without readers, authors are just popstars singing to themselves in the shower. I hope you enjoyed Happy Meals, and if you did, please feel free to sign up to my mailing list at **www.eatonkrone.com/contact** or follow **@EatonKrone** on Twitter or **Eaton_Krone** on Instagram for upcoming releases and other random stuff.

PS: If I've overlooked anyone, sorry; I'll buy you a beer to make up for it … unless I'm broke, then you can buy me one to cheer me up.

ABOUT THE AUTHOR

After hitting pause on his planned writing career, Eaton Krone spent two decades slaving away in the fields of journalism, PR/communications and advertising – the latter devouring three quarters of his career-history pie chart along with a sizeable chunk of his sanity. He's done nearly everything copy- and language-related, from writing and editing to translation and proofreading across a wide spectrum of media. His journalism and copywriting qualifications are in a box somewhere.

Although he's pleased to continue his author journey, Eaton denies being the author of his own life, as it's riddled with way too many errors and scenes that cannot be edited or (preferably) deleted. He lives with his un-official other half in Johannesburg, South Africa. His mind lives somewhere else.